MW01148786

Creed

Michael Chavez

Quest Books
by Regal Crest

Nederland, Texas

*(A Dictionary of foreign words, phrases and terms as used herein is
furnished on the last page of this manuscript.)*

ISBN 978-1-61929-053-2

First Printing 2012

9 8 7 6 5 4 3 2 1

Cover design by Donna Palowski

Published by:

Regal Crest Enterprises, LLC
3520 Avenue H
Nederland, TX 77627

Find us on the World Wide Web at
http://www.regalcrest.biz

Printed in the United States of America

Acknowledgements

I owe a debt of gratitude to many close friends and associates for their guidance, advice, and support. Among them are my mentors and notable authors, Cindy Bellinger and Robert Mayer, and my colleague, Leissa Sharak. My thanks also go out to the gang from Mayer's Santa Fe Writers' Workshop for their encouragement and recommendations. To my friends on the mountain and in the village who read the initial drafts and gave me their insights, inspiration and support: Helen Zagadinow, Mary Search, Ellen Bell, Tori Young and Sig Olsen. Thank you Cathy LeNoir for taking a chance on CREED, and to the hardworking staff of Regal Crest for walking me though every step of the publishing maze. I want to extend my heartfelt appreciation to Natty Burns, a master editor who helped me showcase CREED. Finally, I dedicate this book to my long-term companion, David Duran, for the many years of bliss and happiness. I will always love you.

"Creed is a statement of belief, usually religious belief or faith. For most Christians the Nicene Creed, formulated in AD 325, affirms the Trinity and is taken as a fundamental test of orthodoxy. Muslims declare the shahada: "I bear witness that there is nothing worthy of worship except Allah, and I bear witness that Muhammad is the slave and messenger of Allah."
~ Extract from Wikipedia

Prologue

WALKING INTO SANTO Niño Catholic Church, Theo desperately clutched the brown paper bag he held in his hands. He hated being there—not at the church, but in Arbol Verde. His face was tight and his chest filled with worry. This fear happened every time he visited Arbol Verde, even though the northern New Mexico town and the small church hadn't changed at all since he was a child.

Walking up to a pew close to the confessional, he genuflected and took a seat to wait his turn for confession. Looking about, he recognized most of the people waiting to confess their sins to Father Marcelino Bonafacio. The local Avon lady was next, sitting at the end of one pew. She looked back at Theo and smiled. He tried to return her smile but the tip of his lip began twitching. This twitch and a guttural sound as if clearing his throat were tics that plagued him whenever he grew anxious.

Clofes Benavidez sat at the far end of the pew. He turned around and nodded to Theo. Theo felt sorry for Clofes whose son, Manuel, had become a *tecato*—a heroin addict and dealer. Manuel had been in high school when he died of an overdose in the *acequia* four years earlier. He was only sixteen. The following year Clofes' wife had died. Theo suspected life must be lonely for Clofes and his youngest son, Armando.

Theo knew the *tecato* story all too well; many in the village lived only to chase the dragon of heroin.

Tightening his grip on the brown bag, Theo scooted closer to the confessional. The scheduled time for confessions had ended fifteen minutes earlier and Theo knew Father Bonafacio had to be tired, but he also knew his mission could not be postponed. Though Theo was twenty-two years old, he had been to confession with the priest only twice before. He walked inside the small niche when it became vacant, knelt down, and waited for the priest to finish with the confessor on the opposite side. The small door slid open and the priest's voice was distinct.

"May the reassurance of the Almighty be with you. What are your sins?"

There was a moment of silence until Theo cleared his throat.

"Hey Father."

"Theo?"

"Yeah, it's me, Father."

"Why are you visiting me in here?"

"Because you told me everything that goes on in the confessional is kept secret between you, me and God."

"You have something to confess, Theo?"

"I have a confession and a favor, Father. Inside this bag I'm holding is twenty thousand dollars. Can you keep it for me and turn it over to someone?"

"Is it money from drugs, Theo?"

"Father Bonafacio, you know me better than that. It's insurance money from a friend who died."

"Why can't you keep it?"

"Because it would be stolen from me."

The priest fell silent as if mulling over this fact.

"And who will collect this money?"

"His name's Elijah Bashir and he's coming from Morocco. I don't know when he'll arrive. But when he does, I need to know."

Again, a profound silence.

"Theo, what is your confession?"

"I broke a promise to a friend."

One

A FIERCE NEW Mexico wind swept across the courtyard David Lujan shared with neighbors he barely knew and rarely saw. Staring outside his Albuquerque apartment into the moonless April night, the fifty-four year-old seasoned attorney listened to the rustling branches of the pine trees. They created an unsettling noise. The only lights outside were those bordering the courtyard walkways.

After separating from Rayèn, his wife, David's world had collapsed. His mind had become muddled. Even mundane lawyering tasks took all his effort. When the partners had suggested taking a leave of absence to pull himself together, David had refused.

They had insisted.

David stood up and followed a shadowy path that he could barely make out until he reached the front door. Opening it and fighting the blowing wind, he walked along the courtyard to his parking stall.

He missed Rayèn so much. In their many years together, they seldom slept apart, only during David's out-of-town trials or conferences. In bed he usually held her close; their fused bodies warming one another throughout the cold winter nights. During the warm summers, he slipped her nightgown off and they slept naked. After early morning lovemaking, her allure always remained with him.

Then without warning, everything changed.

When they discovered that their son, Patrick, had developed liver disease and was so ill that he lay on the threshold of death, Rayèn actually wanted to postpone further treatment and allow him to pass away peacefully. How was David to know it was a deception crafted to protect a long-held secret? And when she was finally forced to confess that secret, a huge chasm of distrust formed. The bond of faith and love gave way to unrelenting images of suspicion and deceit. Her guile was reprehensible. Forgiveness, unimaginable.

Unlocking the trunk, David removed the small metal case that was secured inside. He turned and made his way back inside the apartment. As he entered and closed the door, David flipped on a single light switch that illuminated the table lamp next to his chair. The light blinded him for a second. He placed the case on his lap and opened the cover. His hands were shaking as he removed the silver-plated 9mm pistol from the foam saddle that kept it firmly in place.

David could feel his heart draining of his life's blood. Random thoughts began to crop up. In spite of their arguments, especially when they discussed Patrick, it had still been a good marriage.

David reflected on his future; never to hold her; never to feel her moist, taut skin. Never to smell her sweet lily scent that had always lured him to her. Retiring to bed alone, getting up alone. They would never again converse in the language of silly facial expressions or hand gestures or made-up words that only they understood. Their love signals that enlivened his spirit were now distant memories. What was the purpose of going on? Tears trickled along his face, quickly turning to a low muffled cry.

As he tried to load the magazine into the butt of the weapon, it fell from his grasp. Laying the metal case on the side table, he leaned over to pick up the bullet holder. This time he loaded the pistol then turned off the light. In a few moments the hurting would end. Tears continued streaming down his face as he looked up and saw a shadow struggling in the wind. A neighbor was crossing the courtyard to an adjacent apartment.

The last noise David would ever hear would be the howling wind.

He wasn't afraid. He was ready. Raising the pistol and balancing it with both hands, he placed the tip of the muzzle in his mouth; felt the cold steel. His whole body trembled. Images began racing faster in his mind. He placed his thumbs on the trigger. All he had to do was squeeze it. Closing his eyes, David could feel the tension of the trigger as his thumbs began applying pressure. *Do it,* a small voice echoed somewhere in the deep recesses of his mind.

The telephone rang. One thumb pressed harder on the other.

The answering machine clicked on.

"Dad, it's Patrick. I need your help, please!"

Two

FATHER MARCELINO BONAFACIO had been Arbol Verde's only priest as long as Theo could remember. Homely in facial feature and in form, he was a thin man, with a high receding hairline. He actually resembled the depiction of St. Francis of Assisi whose image was painted on the wall inside the church.

A native of Spain, Father Bonafacio had wanted to pastor in his own country but the church had other plans for the bilingual priest. After serving as assistant pastor in California, he was assigned to Arbol Verde, New Mexico. Arriving as a young priest one month before Theo was born and realizing that the village was too small to support him, Father Bonafacio began pastoring in Alcorisa and Vitoria, as well, two other economically depressed villages in El Pastor County. Together, the parishioners brought in barely enough donations to support their own churches and his small stipend, but, luckily, they supplemented this stipend during the growing season with baskets of fruits and vegetables and an endless supply of the priest's favorite hot green chile peppers. Everyone either knew Father Bonafacio or knew of him. He officiated at all the Catholic baptisms, weddings and funerals and his humility and short Sunday sermons, delivered in an English and Spanish mix, caused many to really like him.

Although Theo and his older brother, Romel, were baptized at Santo Niño, neither Sixto nor Magdalena, their parents, were religious. In the predominately Catholic community, church baptism was an almost inviolate custom. And as Theo grew, he received no training in the faith until he and the priest unexpectedly became friends.

WALKING THE INDIAN Lake shoreline with his fishing pole one Saturday almost a decade ago, Theo had spotted the priest casting his rod. "Any luck, Father?"

The priest had glanced back at him and Theo, a skinny, adobe-colored boy with a shabby baseball cap, soiled T-shirt, and cutoffs several sizes too large felt embarrassed somehow. Yet the priest had given a slight nod. "A few nibbles. How bout you?"

Father Bonafacio's prominent Spanish accent was difficult to understand for some. But Theo had a keen ear and easily made out what he said.

"Not even a nibble. Mind if I fish next to you?"

"Help you self. Maybe you have more luck than me."

As Theo threw out his line and sat on the ground, the priest looked over at him. "What you name?"

Theo tried to hide his shoes which had gaping holes that exposed his toes. "Theodoro, but everybody calls me Theo."

"Theo what?" the priest asked.

"Jaquez."

"Good to meet you, Theo Jaquez. Do I know you parents?"

"Probably not. They don't go to church."

"Well, let's hope we have good luck today."

As the day wore on, the two talked about fishing and school and mutual friends in the village. The conversation was pleasant, peppered by Theo's exaggerations—that he had pulled out the largest recorded fish at Indian Lake or held all sorts of martial arts belts. His amusing banter made the day enjoyable for both of them. When the priest offered to share his lunch, the boy readily accepted. He ate faster than anyone the priest had ever seen. At the end of the day when the fish proved elusive and the two grew tired, Theo walked the priest to his car. As Theo plodded down the road, the priest pulled up alongside and offered a ride. Theo jumped in.

Meeting the priest again weeks later at Sanchez's *tienda*, the local general store that carried everything from groceries to hardware, Theo smiled. The priest carried a bucket of paint and brushes. "You're not going fishing this weekend, Father?"

"No, too busy." He looked at Theo. "Are you interested in a job? I could use help tomorrow."

Theo almost laughed at the priest's accent—"busy" somehow sounded like two letters, b and c. "Sure. I'm not doing anything," he replied.

Theo arrived at the priest's rectory early the following morning. The two started in the living room and painted their way into the adjoining dining room. Close to the noon hour the priest disappeared into the kitchen to prepare lunch. As they sat at the dining table enjoying the small feast, Theo asked, "So how old do you have to be to get into the seminary, Father?"

The priest looked down at the boy's plate, as if amazed that it was almost empty, before giving Theo an inquisitive stare. "Are you thinking of becoming a priest?"

"I dunno, Father." Theo's dark eyes grew serious. "The thing is that I need to get out of Arbol Verde."

FATHER BONAFACIO KNEW all too well the situations of many families living in the villages he pastored—they daily dealt with poverty, drugs and alcohol. The county's treatment centers helped little. Patients cycled through the program, stayed clean for a short time, and then returned to their old habits. He was sensitive to Theo's plea, but he asked the question anyway. "Why do you want to leave?"

"If I stay here I won't make it through high school. It's crazy out there...drugs and all, even outside the *tienda* I see them dealing..."

The priest interrupted. "What about you family? You parents?"

Theo looked down and grew silent for a moment. "Today's my birthday. I'm fourteen. But nobody cares about anything like that. They're only interested in..." His words drifted off. "Never mind."

At times like these Father Bonafacio hated that he was at a loss for words. What could he say to comfort the boy, or even give hope when there was so little he could do? In all probability what Theo envisaged would come true. It seemed as if God was deaf to the priest's prayers.

As those thoughts muddled through his head, Father Bonafacio saw Theo lean into him and felt the young boy's hand on his knee.

THEO WAS DESPERATE to get as far away from Arbol Verde as he could. Having learned to fend for himself as long as he could remember, Theo knew everything had a price. It was no secret about the sexual pleasures priests often sought from young boys. Theo doubted they were any different from his father's demands. Yet his proposition to the priest was gutsy. But he was willing to risk it. With his heart racing and his lip beginning to quiver, Theo cleared his throat. His stare was unflinching as his hand climbed up the priest's thigh. Suddenly, the priest jerked back and stood up. Theo's soda fell to the floor.

"What you think you doing, Theo? That's not right."

Theo leaned back in his chair. Didn't the priest understand the advance? Was he that naïve? "I'm sorry. I just thought...I mean, I heard..."

"You hear what?" the priest demanded loudly.

Embarrassed, Theo put his head down for a second.

"Theo, what you tried to do is wrong. Have you no respect for youself?"

He stood up and looked at the priest with wounded eyes. "What do you know about respect, Father? What do you know about right and wrong? Is any of that going to save me from this shithole? You think you know everything, but you don't know anything."

Their stare was intense.

"Screw you, Father." The boy began walking out.

The priest's thoughts knotted. He couldn't let the boy leave. Maybe he could still help somehow. "Stay, Theo. Let's talk about this."

Before Father Bonafacio could finish the sentence, Theo was gone.

Three

JUDE ARMSTRONG'S FRIENDSHIP with Martin Chenoweth had lasted more than than twenty years. Both journalists by trade, they worked together as free-lance writers as they traveled throughout the world. When newsworthy events happened, Jude and Marty, who lived near one another in Virginia, always managed to be there; were always among the initial wave of correspondents on the scene. Their careers thrived because they collaborated. They shared tips and even sources on occasion.

The work was challenging, demanding, and often dangerous, especially in politically sensitive areas and war zones. While researching the *Abu Sayyaf* rebel group in the Philippines, a few minutes delay in catching a taxi saved their lives. Their source and several innocent bystanders standing alongside the road were injured or died; victims of a targeted bombing.

Another time at the Serbian border near Bosnia where the massacre of innocent people was suspected, the two of them, along with a few other journalists, were captured at gunpoint by a small military unit intent on preventing them from passing. But their group broke away during a fight between the military unit and a second group trying to make their way through the blockade. They got to their destination safely.

Then there was the delayed commuter flight into New York that prevented Jude and Marty from catching a connecting flight to Korea. The doomed aircraft was shot down flying over Soviet Union air space.

The two knew better than to brood over these incidents. They'd simply look for the closest bar, acknowledge their good luck over scotch and soda, and vow to always remain intrepid.

Working so closely together, the two journalists came to know one another almost as if they were married. Marty liked everything about Jude. Though in her early-forties, Jude was still shapely and attractive with blonde hair and green eyes. Yet she rarely played the charming, pretty girl card unless the situation called for it. She was fluent in Spanish and French, smart in reporting, abrupt in manner and coarse in language. She spotted deception quickly. She had no patience for braggarts or cowards. She held her own with seasoned journalists, politicians, and polite society. And Jude could match most anyone at the bar, drink for drink.

In a Prague hotel bar late one evening after the two journalists finished covering an economic summit, their bottomless glasses of scotch emboldened Marty who was barely able to stand upright.

"Just answer me one question, Jude. Are you a lesbian?"

The drink she crooked back a second earlier came spewing out of her mouth amid side-splitting laughter. Already lit up herself, Jude replied, "Lesbian? You think I'm *lesbian*?" Before Marty could answer, she retorted, "If I'm a lesbian, than you must be gay."

Practically cross-eyed, Marty managed to say, "I'm not gay and I'm willing to prove it."

"Well I'm not either...and I can prove it, too," she challenged.

Stumbling out of the bar as it closed, the two journalists ended up in the same bed. In the morning, naked and shamefaced, neither of them spoke about it. Weeks later and entirely sober, Marty tried to confess his growing feelings for her, but Jude cut him off. She seemed dead to any sort of intimacy. Getting up the guts to propose marriage to Jude a year later as they dined in an Italian restaurant in Florence, Marty should have expected her response. A strong-willed, independent, free-thinker, Jude scoffed at the proposal. She compared it to marrying her own shadow — insipid tedium, she cruelly called it. Humiliated, Marty stopped pursuing her, but not loving her.

Jude finally grew weary of traveling and in 2002, retired, saying goodbye to Marty. She moved to San Lucas, New Mexico, a place she had visited years earlier and promised to return. A small, reclusive village hidden in the lush Sangre de Cristo Mountains twenty-one miles northeast of Santa Fe, San Lucas was quiet, secluded and beautiful.

Consuelo Soto, a Native American weaver, was Jude's closest neighbor and they quickly became friends. Almost every morning Jude visited Consuelo to sip *atole*, a blue corn drink her friend made, as she watched Consuelo weave. There were at least four different looms Consuelo worked at, dividing her time on each project. Some days Consuelo spoke about her life on the reservation, her family, her abusive, alcoholic husband, and her horrible, demanding in-laws. She didn't seem to like talking about her children. Other days she barely said good-morning. But Jude, thick-skinned, never took offense. She just sat quietly observing Consuelo weave.

Months later Jude began searching newspaper ads from Albuquerque and Santa Fe and visiting internet sites looking for a used loom of her own.

With Consuelo's help, over time Jude developed her own weaving technique and started making colorful winter scarves and shawls.

"You have to go to art fairs to sell your work," Consuelo advised.

Jude sent images of her work to winter craft fairs in Santa Fe and was thrilled at being juried in as a vendor. She purchased an outdoor tent, folding tables and chairs and a collapsible merchandise hanger, and began displaying and selling her finery on weekends.

One summer, the heat enveloped the village like an oven and the oppressive, stifling air inside sapped any desire to move too fast. With her stock of chenille and boucle yarn down to a handful of cones, Jude, who had delayed making the re-stocking trip to Albuquerque for too long, readied herself for the journey. It was then she noticed an unusual, large lump on her left breast. It alarmed her instantly. She normally avoided doctors, but instinct told her this situation needed attention. She scheduled an appointment with a doctor recommended by Consuelo.

Days after the examination, Jude checked into the hospital's outpatient clinic for a biopsy. A week later she received an urgent call for a follow up visit. She wasn't ready for the frightening news—the biopsy had uncovered malignant cancer tissue.

Referred to a surgeon, Jude went into the hospital within the week to excise the tumor. The operation became far more extensive than she'd ever imagined—the surgeon removed her entire left breast. Jude was bereft by the operation and by her loss, and Consuelo stayed close by to console her. After the surgery, the oncologist prescribed adjuvant chemotherapy. The fear that the cancer might have spread was enough to convince Jude to undertake the toxic drug regimen.

The initial weeks of taking the chemo kept Jude in bed most days. Consuelo looked after her like a nurse. Each day she brought Jude meals and made sure she ate.

The treatment continued for eight weeks. By the end of the excruciating treatment, Jude had lost too much weight and looked anorexic but her prognosis was good. During the next three months, Consuelo's herbal remedies and cooking brought Jude back around. She gained some of her weight back; she was improving.

Visiting Jude one afternoon, carrying a bowl of green chile stew, Consuelo was not expecting what she saw inside Jude's house. It looked as though someone had burglarized the house—yarn cones were strewn everywhere, chairs were overturned, and even a picture hanging on the wall was smashed and glass scattered all over the floor. Instantly alarmed, Consuelo called out to Jude. No answer. Cautiously, Consuelo walked to the kitchen. The back door was open. She glanced outside. Jude was sitting atop the rock garden staring into space.

Stepping out the door, Consuelo walked toward her. "What's going on Jude?"

Jude didn't flinch.

Consuelo sat next to her. The two women remained silent for a few moments before Jude spoke.

"The doctor called. They think the fucking cancer's spreading to my bones." There was a slight pause before Jude continued. "They want me back on chemo."

"Oh no, Jude, what are you going to do?"

"I don't know. But I know I'm not doing chemo again."

"Are you sure?" Consuelo gave Jude a hard stare.

"There's no way in hell I'll do that again."

"But, what about the cancer?"

Jude took a deep sigh and returned Consuelo's stare. "What's the worst that can happen? We all got to go sometime."

They remained quiet for several minutes until Consuelo stood up, walked back into the kitchen and returned with two bowls. Offering one to Jude, she said, "I hate to tell you but a tornado came through your living room a while ago. You're going to need this before we start putting it back together."

Jude laughed. Taking the bowl from Consuelo, they ate and spent the rest of the afternoon talking about everything and nothing, and watching the sun slowly fall behind the mountain.

Four

HOURS AFTER REFLECTING on the boy's words and haunted by his cutting gaze, Father Bonafacio drove down the dirt road until he reached the rundown house rented by the Jaquez family. He parked and made his way up the rickety wooden steps to the screened door, most of which was torn away. The porch was littered with junk—broken chairs, auto carburetors, mufflers, bumpers, broken toilets, boxes stacked ceiling high, and countless other scraps that seemed to have no useful purpose and left only a small path to the front door. The screen door, missing several hinges, was propped open with a rock. One of the four small windows on the front door was broken. The windows were covered by a cheap plastic drape.

Knocking on the door, the priest stood at the threshold and looked inside. No response. He knocked louder. Suddenly he heard footsteps. The door opened slightly. It was Theo.

He eyed the priest cautiously; the boy obviously sensed trouble. "What do you want, Father?"

The priest's face softened. "I came to take you out to eat for your birthday."

Theo studied the priest as he opened the door further and revealed himself. "Are you serious?"

"Would I be here if I wasn't?"

"Okay then, let's go." He stepped outside and closed the door.

"Don't you have to tell somebody where you going?" the priest asked.

Theo gave him a strange look. "No. They don't care where I go."

As they drove off, the priest looked over at Theo. "You like pizza?"

"Are you kidding, I love pizza."

"Okay then, let's go get pizza."

AFTER SCHOOL ONE day the following week, Theo dropped by the rectory. He found Father Bonafacio in the study where he was at work on his sermon. Theo sat down. The priest leaned back in the chair behind his desk, regarding the boy.

Glancing at the enormous bookcase filling one wall, Theo asked, "Did you read all these books, Father?"

The priest gave a slight nod. "Most of them."

The boy's clothes were a pitiful sight. He wondered how broken inside the boy must be. The priest's heart was tugging at him. "Do you like to read, Theo?"

"It's boring."

"If the book is about something you like, it can be interesting."

"So why did you become a priest in the first place?"

"Because that's the vocation the Good Lord placed in my heart."

"You mean God?"

The priest nodded.

"I don't believe in God."

"But I thought you wanted to go to the seminary?

The boy said nothing.

"Have you ever gotten to know God?"

The boy looked nervous. It was the second time he noticed the boy's upper lip twitch.

Theo stood up, walked over to the bookcase, and began inspecting the titles. He cleared his throat. "How do you mean?"

The priest opened a desk drawer and removed a small soft - cover book. He walked over to Theo. "This is a catechism of the Catholic faith. This is how you get to know God." He offered the book to the boy.

Taking the book, Theo examined the cover. "I gotta go," he said.

Holding on to the book Theo hurried out of the rectory.

Two days later the boy returned. "I started reading this catechism, but it's confusing."

"Maybe I can help you," the priest replied. "I was just starting to make dinner. Are you hungry, Theo?"

A timid smile was his answer.

"Let's go into the kitchen and we can talk while I cook."

Theo's visits became more frequent, and one day the priest stopped at the second hand store. He estimated Theo's size and bought clothes for the boy. When Theo arrived, the priest handed him the bags. Curious, Theo rustled through them but said nothing as if snubbing the gift. After dinner that evening, as Theo made his way out, he detoured for the bags and casually snatched them up.

Slowly, the two began forming a close friendship. The priest asked the boy to remove his tattered baseball cap before dinner one evening and a flow of jet-black hair dropped to his shoulders. As Father Bonafacio eyed the boy, he sensed a natural charm so endearing, it reminded him of his own youth.

THEO DIDN'T KNOW what to make of Father Bonafacio. The priest treated him kinder than anyone he had ever known and asked nothing in return. In addition to offering friendship, of a sort Theo had never known before, the priest became his mentor. While Father Bonafacio's faith was absolute, his knowledge of secular things was amazing. In their short time together Theo had learned more from the priest than anything his teachers, old lady Claussen in geography or peg-leg Garcia in history, could teach combined.

Five

IT HAD BEEN dusk when Aban Bashir met Jude's daughter Victoria. Twenty years ago, he had driven to the Virginia townhouse, parked and walked up the sidewalk as usual. Dressed in a dark suit, Aban buttoned his jacket before ringing the doorbell. The handsome Moroccan with his blue eyes had a knack for charming women. Aban was never ostentatious; his modesty, confidence, and unassuming good-looks were his alluring characteristics.

Aban had been married in his hometown of Setta before graduating from the university in Casablanca. But the arranged coupling had never been well-matched. Intent on honoring his Muslim family and Berber tradition, Aban remained married for ten years until the doctors determined Fatima, his wife, was unable to conceive. They divorced. By then Aban had accepted his first post as an assistant economics advisor to the Moroccan Embassy in Brussels, Belgium.

Aban worked hard, dedicating his knowledge, skills and talents to serving the Moroccan monarchy. It was the practice to rotate embassy staff at least every five years, and Aban welcomed each new assignment. In 1980, as payment for his diligence and loyalty, Aban received a promotion to Assistant Cultural Attaché, and an assignment to the Moroccan Embassy in the United States. The good fortune to serve in Washington, D.C. was the envy of his peers.

Several months after arriving, Aban attended a White House function. It was there he met Jude Armstrong. At that time, Jude worked as a journalist for a national newsmagazine. She was intelligent, and attractive. Captivated by her charm and poise that evening, Aban invited Jude the following day to a cultural performance of a visiting Berber dance troupe. She accepted. After that, he began seeing her with regularity. Aban enjoyed Jude's company. Despite the intimacy their relationship eventually forged, Aban always introduced Jude as merely a good friend to avoid criticism of Moslem traditions prohibiting such conduct.

The evening was warm as Aban waited at the door, then he heard footsteps. Slowly it opened. A smile came to his face as he laid eyes on Jude's daughter.

"Hi, you must be Aban?" she said as she let him in. "I'm Victoria."

"Victoria," he repeated. "Jude has told me so much about you, but never mentioned you shared your mother's loveliness."

Victoria blushed. "Thank you. Mom will be right down. Can I

get you something to drink?" she asked as they made their way into the living room.

"Are you home from school?"

"Yes, mid-term break. Mom and I plan to do some shopping and maybe spend a long weekend at the beach."

Aban was mesmerized by her beauty. It was a natural attractiveness; unblemished fair skin with no makeup that he could discern. Victoria's long blonde hair hung loosely down her back and complemented her green eyes. Her dress was bland and modest.

"I don't drink alcohol," he replied. "Maybe a glass of water."

"Okay. I'll be right back."

Aban's eyes followed her as she walked out of the room. A few minutes later Jude appeared in a stunning yellow gown accented by a light chenille ruana that smartly wrapped around her shoulders. "You're early," she said.

"You look nice," he replied.

"Thank you."

"I thought we might need the extra time to get through the traffic and ensure we don't miss the first performance."

"Where are you going tonight?" Victoria asked, walking back into the room with a bottle of water and an ice-filled glass that she handed Aban.

"To the symphony. Aban managed to get tickets to a special performance by an orchestra from Prague."

Aban poured water into the glass and took a sip. "Do you like the symphony, Victoria?" he asked.

"I've never been to one."

"I think we can remedy that on your next visit home," he said.

"I'd like that. Well, enjoy and I'll see you again," she replied as she left the room.

MONTHS LATER WHILE stopped at a traffic light on DuPont Circle in downtown Washington, D.C., Aban spotted Victoria at an outdoor restaurant. Dressed in a subtle, light colored, loose-fitting outfit that hid her attractive figure, Victoria looked lovely. At the risk of arriving late for an appointment, he was compelled to follow his impulse. Aban parked and hurried to the restaurant.

"Victoria," he said as he approached her table. "This is such a coincidence meeting up with you here."

She looked up with a puzzled expression, unable to place him.

"Aban Bashir...we met at your mother's home during your school break."

Embarrassed, she extended her hand. "Aban, of course, I'm so sorry. I have a hundred things on my mind."

He remained standing and an awkward silence followed.

"Would you like to join me?" she asked.

"Only if I'm not disturbing you."

"No, you're not. Please, sit down."

"Is school over?" he asked as he sat across from her.

"Yes, it ended last week. In fact I just came from a job interview. Something for the summer to make a little money before school starts again."

"I'm sure you were the prettiest applicant there."

Victoria blushed. "Thanks for the compliment, but they were more interested in my French translation and computer skills."

"French translation?" he repeated.

"Yes, the law firm has volumes of French material that needs to be translated. I took a short test and didn't do very well, I'm afraid. But, we'll just have to wait and see."

"I'm sure your underestimating your skill," Aban replied. "However, if they make the mistake of failing to hire you, please call me. I have a friend in mind who is searching for someone like you who is fluent in French."

"Really?"

"Yes, really."

"Wonderful, I'll keep that in mind."

"I hope you do," he replied as he gazed at her face without revealing the depth of his interest. "Well, I have an appointment so I must be off." Aban stood up and reached into his wallet for a card. "Here is my number. I'll wait to hear from you."

Six

WHEN PATRICK'S TELEPHONE message interrupted his suicide attempt, David's focus instantly shifted. The thought that his son needed help seemed to eclipse everything else. David had laid the pistol on the side table, walked to the telephone and dialed. He heard his son's voice.

"Hello, Patrick...this is dad."   He hoped his voice hadn't faltered.

Patrick was excited. "Dad, the cops are getting ready to arrest a good friend, an innocent kid I've known for a long time. They're saying he's a drug dealer and murdered someone. He didn't do it, Dad. I know him too well..."

David interrupted. "Hold on a minute, Patrick. Take a breath. Let's take this one step at a time. Now, who are you talking about?"

"His name's Theo Jaquez. He ran away from home a long time ago and the organization I volunteer for, APFT, helped him get his life back together."

"APFT," David repeated.

"Yeah, A Plan for Tomorrow. Theo's our biggest success story.

We put him in a foster home and after graduating high school, he started working. He even has plans for college."

"Where's Theo now?"

"In the hospital. Somebody broke into his apartment and beat him up pretty bad."

"Any idea why?"

"He had some insurance money they were after — fifty-thousand dollars."

"And where did that come from?"

Patrick hesitated before responding. "Dad, this gets really complicated. Can you drive down to Santa Fe and meet us tomorrow?"

"You know I'm on leave from the practice."

"Yeah, I know that, but now that you have the time, Dad, we really need your help."

There was silence for a few seconds. A sudden sense of grief and panic went through David's mind. But he couldn't deny his son's appeal.

"Okay, I'll be there," David replied as he looked out the window and noticed the wind had calmed.

As he ended the call, David's eyes wandered toward the pistol on the tabletop. Suddenly his chest grew heavy. The thought that he came so close to ending his life seemed surreal. He had lost control and it frightened him. He picked up the telephone and placed another call, this time leaving his urgent message with the answering service. Within a few minutes the telephone rang.

"David, this is Juliana. Are you all right?"

"No. Maybe. I don't know."

"Tell me what's going on?"

For the next hour David poured out the details of the suicide attempt to Juliana Ochoa, the psychologist he had walked away from two weeks earlier believing his depression was manageable. Feeling shattered, David agreed to resume therapy. When the call ended, David removed the bullet magazine from the handle, placed the pistol back in its foam saddle, turned off the lights and headed to bed

Seven

IT WAS LATE October and Jude celebrated her third year in San Lucas by participating in a craft fair on the Santa Fe plaza. The morning of the fair was cold and the sky, cloudy and dark. The outside air smelled like snow. Even though the bad weather discouraged some fair attendees, Jude was thrilled by her sales. Most of her inventory was sold. Even after paying her helper, Jude's purse was brimming with the profits. Loading up her car with the collapsible table and chairs, and what remained of her scarves and shawls, Jude started for home.

A light snow began falling just as Jude got off the interstate. As she made her way up the county road, she noticed the snow coming down heavier. When she reached the unpaved, washboard road leading up to her home, the snow began sticking to the ground. With less than two miles left to go, she drove slowly around the twists and bends. Then, while negotiating a sharp curve, Jude pressed down too hard on the brake and went into a rock that pitched her car over the embankment. The car became stuck. She tried shifting the gear into reverse and flooring the gas pedal, but the wheels only spun in the snow. Without traction, the car wouldn't jettison out. As she opened the door, the cold air hit her and she began to be afraid. By now the snow was falling heavy. Jude flipped open her cell phone. Just as she feared, no reception. The high mountains blocked the wireless signal. Suddenly, from her side mirror Jude thought she saw someone making their way up the mountain.

Seeing her car stuck over the embankment, the lone driver stopped in the middle of the road, got out and walked over to her. "Are you all right?"

She opened the door. "I'm fine. But I can't get this damn car back on the road."

"You want a lift someplace?"

He looked young; dark hair, handsome face and good manners. "I live up in San Lucas. Is that where you're going?"

"You're in luck. Come on, get in. We can come back for your car later when the snow lets up."

After considering the offer for half a second, Jude got into the stranger's warm Jeep.

"I appreciate this," she said. "My name's Jude."

Navigating cautiously up the mountain, the young man gave Jude a quick glance. "I'm Theo."

Eight

LIEUTENANT KERRY SNYDER'S tenure with the New Mexico State Police was lengthy — more than twenty-two years. It included a four-year military police stint that added to his seniority. Snyder would never have been hired, if not for his father's political influence. Elected the state land commissioner, the elder Snyder juiced his son into the state police force at a time when there was a hiring moratorium. Kerry Snyder quickly learned that in New Mexico, political influence reigned supreme. He also knew that his career could have advanced much faster but for two problems; his father losing his bid in the subsequent election, and a major lapse early in his own career.

Snyder had been an officer for fourteen months when a prison riot broke out at the New Mexico Penitentiary. Once alerted about the situation, the state police responded in force. Every available officer surrounded the penitentiary. The riot began in a main dormitory when inmates overpowered a guard. Within minutes more guards were overpowered and the inmates managed to get hold of a set of keys that opened more cell dormitories.

Cellblock D housed homosexuals and inmates in protective custody. Many of those inmates were snitches and segregated from the general population for their own protection. When the rioters reached Cellblock D, their keys didn't work. Frustrated, the rioters ran to the tool room and located a blowtorch. Returning to Cellblock D, they started cutting through the bars.

Snyder, a communications specialist at the time, was responsible for relaying information to upper level staff. When prison officials learned that the rioting inmates had Cellblock D in their sights, a message was relayed to Snyder that a backdoor could be accessed and used to free those inmates. For reasons that were never made clear, Snyder failed to communicate that message. Once the rioting inmates cut through to Cellblock D, they began random torture and killing. Many of the Cellblock D inmates were dismembered and decapitated; several were burned beyond recognition. When the riot ended, thirty-seven inmates died and over two-hundred were injured.

While state police authorities eventually got the information about the backdoor to Cellblock D in sufficient time to save those prison inmates, they chose not to act. Snyder's communication failure was inexplicably picked up by the media and he became the scapegoat for the massacre. No one came to his defense. That blotch remained in his official file and forestalled early advancement opportunities. That was until Snyder finally threatened a lawsuit over the unfair promotion of less senior female officers. Then suddenly on his next bid, Snyder received sergeant stripes. Years later, after being passed over for staff positions countless times, the frustrated officer bent the ear of a wealthy family friend known to have political influence. His promotion to lieutenant finally came through.

After attaining the staff promotion, Snyder was enjoying his status too much to retire when he first became eligible. Married but childless, Snyder volunteered his free time to coach little league baseball and serve on the Fraternal Order of Police. He occasionally appeared before the Santa Fe County Commissioners to advocate on behalf of community and police causes. Snyder was articulate and liked to schmooze with the commissioners.

Sarah Maestas was a one-term commissioner who had become Snyder's nemesis. Numerous times she had voted against funding causes he supported. Maestas had recently been harshly criticized for refusing to support a quarter-cent tax increase for police equipment and building infrastructure. The police union condemned her vote and publically declared efforts to unseat her. Suddenly, Snyder got the idea of entering politics. The prospect was exciting. There was no better opportunity to capitalize on Maestas' loss of support than the present time. After discussing it at length with his wife and co-workers, Snyder made the decision. He would leave the police force just prior to the primary election the following year, and seek Maestas' seat.

While driving to Albuquerque for a visit with the New Mexico Office of the Medical Investigator (OMI) over the Jude Armstrong matter, Snyder got an idea. His brother-in-law would make an ideal organizer to head up his election campaign. A Santa Fe native and long-time real estate broker, his wife's brother knew many of the city's movers and shakers. Snyder decided that over the weekend he would suggest the couples get together for dinner; the perfect setting to broach the request.

Arriving at OMI, Snyder was led into Chester Albright's Office. The office felt cramped. His desk and the long credenza behind it were stacked high with files. A long mahogany conference table placed in the center of the room was piled with an arsenal of books, magazines, newspapers, and assorted periodicals. Evidence boxes were scattered everywhere.

They shook hands. The director looked older than Snyder remembered; chubby, cheeky jowls, with thinning blond hair. *Apparently the job has taken its toll on him,* Snyder thought. But nobody disputed that during Albright's eleven year tenure with OMI, the department's reputation remained unimpeachable.

"Long time, no see, Kerry. Life treating you okay?"

"No complaints."

"So what's up?" Albright asked as he sat down behind his desk.

Snyder moved a pile of books from a chair and took a seat. "I'm investigating a case involving a long-term druggie who we think poisoned a victim to get at her life insurance. The victim was terminal, so there was no autopsy when she died. If the body's exhumed, what can toxicology tell us about the cause of death?"

Albright rubbed his chin with his thumb and forefinger as he contemplated the question. "It's hard to say, Kerry. Was the body embalmed?"

"I don't know that, maybe, maybe not. There wasn't a viewing and she was buried a few days after her death."

"Well, one of the potential problems involves embalming fluid. The fluid is forced through the blood vessels and into tissue, and consequently washes out most of the poison. On the other hand, if the victim wasn't embalmed, finding toxins might not be a problem.

We could also do hair analysis to find heavy metals like arsenic, lead and a few others. How long has the victim been buried?"

"She died a couple of months ago, in February."

"You said the victim was terminal?"

"Yeah, she had cancer."

"On morphine, I suspect?"

"Yeah, I think so. When hospice arrived they took all the narcotics. But I can find out easy enough. Is that a problem?"

"Well, if the victim died of an overdose of morphine that poses a big problem. The victim had probably been taking morphine for awhile to ease the pain, so it would accumulate in the body over time. We'd have to determine the exact level of morphine in the tissues and make a best guess estimate that the level was so far elevated to have caused death."

"Okay, so how do we start the exhumation process, Chester?"

"Will the relatives give you authorization?"

"No known relatives with this one."

"Then you're going to have to get the D.A. to petition the court for an exhumation order."

"I'll get on it when I get back to Santa Fe. Thanks for your help."

Nine

ONE WEEK LATER Aban received a call from Victoria. She had not been called back for the job she had interviewed for, so he made arrangements for her to meet his friend over lunch. Hamid Faraj owned an upscale Moroccan restaurant in Georgetown and, after meeting the young beauty, offered Victoria an evening hostess position. Having no better prospects for summer work, Victoria accepted the job.

Most evenings Aban appeared at the restaurant at a late hour and waited until Victoria got off work. At his invitation they often shared a glass of mint tea and pleasant conversation before walking Victoria to her car. Soon she was smitten by his charm and fatherly attention.

Having never known her real father, Victoria imagined that perhaps he was not unlike Aban. She began to enjoy all of his attention, and on the rare occasions when he failed to appear, she worried that it was over. But the following evening he would be there, once again.

She knew it was wrong to keep this secret from her mother, not letting her know about the budding relationship with Aban. Nothing inappropriate had happened between them and that mollified her feelings of guilt. Victoria tried to shut out the fantasy daydreams of Aban that went through her mind. But the idea of being with an older man — a father figure — titillated her to the point of fearing he might recognize her desire. She knew the relationship must end before anything untoward occurred. While Victoria trusted Aban, it was her own vulnerability that she questioned. But she couldn't imagine ever hurting her mother by stealing away Aban's affection.

The following week when Aban appeared, Victoria apologized for hurrying off, feigning illness initially then later fabricating different excuses why she couldn't stay for tea. But he was relentless and continued to appear at the restaurant. Late that week as Aban walked Victoria out to the parking lot, a sliver of moon barely shone overhead. As they stood by her car, Aban dared to kiss her. While she didn't see it coming, Victoria suddenly felt his lips. She knew she needed to push him away but her desire to feel him trumped that instinct. She felt him lean closer into her.

What Aban found himself doing was foreign to him. Public intimacy, especially with a single woman, was immoral. But the affection he felt for Victoria was too great.

"Please, come home with me," he whispered.

She was speechless and met his second kiss.

JUDE WAS EXCITED at the mention of her name as a nominee for a prestigious journalism award at the annual banquet to be held in August. She called Aban to invite him to the function. He was unavailable and Jude left a message. When he failed to return her call that day, Jude grew concerned, given Aban's penchant for fastidiousness. When she finally reached him two days later, his voice and attitude were different. His tone was cold and detached, almost businesslike. He was unresponsive to her giddy chat of possible peer recognition and turned down her invitation because of a prior appointment. Jude sensed something much more was going on. She was not a novice with men and relationships, and instantly knew that Aban was pulling away from her. She knew that feeling well. It was the same feeling as when Victoria's father had left her. *Why should Aban be any different,* she thought? Was it because he had always been attentive to her, never having cancelled a single date? Maybe it was his generosity or his lovemaking. She should have known it was all a pretense and never meant as a serious relationship. She was merely another stepping stone until someone else came along.

During the next weeks she grew angry, not at Aban but at herself for thinking their relationship was different. Jude vowed never again to become emotionally attached to any suitor, and her pain began to slowly disperse. One month later, when summer ended, Victoria returned to finish her last year of college.

It was early November when Jude received a call from her daughter.

"Mom, I'm taking a day off school and was wondering if we could meet for lunch?" Victoria's voice sounded strained.

"Is everything all right, honey?"

There was hesitancy in her voice. "Yes, I just wanted to talk to you about...well, I was thinking about what I would do after graduation."

"Victoria, I thought that was settled. What about your move to New York and graduate school?"

"That's what I want to talk to you about, Mom. Can we meet?"

"Yes, of course honey. Let me know when and where, and I'll be there."

For Jude, the timing couldn't be better. Since Victoria planned to move away from home and pursue graduate school, Jude was looking to change careers. Having always enjoyed traveling, Jude had revealed to a headhunter her intentions of leaving the newsmagazine. Several weeks later she received a query about her interest in an available executive journalist position with an international news organization. She responded favorably, and interviewed in New York for the position. The work involved coordinating and reporting developing news stories in Europe. It was a challenging opportunity to supervise a small cadre of journalists and photographers who she would send to remote locations. On some occasions she would accompany the team while on others she would merely coordinate their work from her office, assigning them to different places depending on where newsworthy items arose. While the company's head office was based in New York, most of her time would be working from their European office in Frankfurt, Germany. This was a dream job she thought, as she accepted the offer. Lunch with Victoria was the perfect opportunity to share the good news.

Ten

THE DECEMBER SKY was dark and cloudy portending snow and the air had a winter chill as Father Bonafacio drove home from the Alcorisa parish. The board of directors meeting had gone better than expected. After the budget planning for the three parishes, which always took too much time, the meeting had ended.

Father Bonafacio turned off the state road, crossed the *acequia* and drove into Arbol Verde. He passed the *tienda*, where a rough crowd stood around and smoked, watching him as he passed by. He proceeded a half mile before turning into the church property. He could barely make out a figure perched on his front door steps. As he maneuvered into the carport, the priest left his car and cautiously observed the stranger as he came into view. The man had a fierce, angry stare. The dirt-stained light jacket and trousers the man wore appeared as if he came off a road crew. His boots were too scuffed and mud caked to make out their original color. His matted graying hair matched his scruffy beard. The man, twice the size of the priest, tapped a long rod on his palm. It was a tire iron.

"What can I do for you?" Father Bonafacio asked, staying close to his car door.

The man ambled to the back of the car. "I'm Sixto Jaquez," he said in Spanish.

"What can I do for you Mr. Jaquez?"

"Do you like how my son gives a blowjob, asshole?"

"I beg your pardon. What are you talking about?"

"About my son, *cabron*. How do you do it? Do you pick up your robe and make him get on his knees?"

"I don't abuse anyone. If you're talking about Theo, I assure you, nothing like that has ever happened."

Sixto struck the trunk of the car with the tire iron. The priest flinched. "You're lying, *cabron*."

"I am not lying. I would never do that."

"I don't believe you. Then why does he spend so much time here? Why do you buy him all that clothes?"

"Because I'm teaching him the catechism of the Catholic faith. I get him clothes because I see he needs them."

"He doesn't need any of that bullshit."

"Everyone needs Jesus Christ."

The man's eyes, almond-shaped like Theo's but wicked, closed to a sliver. "If you're lying to me, I'm going to kill you, *cabron*. Leave him alone." Sixto stared at the priest for several more seconds, daring him to challenge the threat. Then he turned and walked away.

Father Bonafacio began shaking uncontrollably. He stood his ground until the man had walked a safe distance. Never having experienced such a hostile confrontation before, Father Bonafacio's mind was churning with thoughts of what to do next. Calling the state police was out of the question. Everybody in Arbol Verde distrusted them. Anyway, it would only aggravate the situation. The priest quickly darted into the rectory, locking the door behind him. He sat down for a second, then stood up and glanced out the window. Sixto Jaquez was nowhere in sight.

For two days the priest refused to answer the rectory door when Theo appeared. The thought of abandoning the boy hurt him deeply. He prayed and meditated about the situation. Theo wouldn't leave his mind. The next day the priest waited outside the rectory at the time Theo usually arrived, but the boy never showed up. Unable to sleep that night, the priest drove to the junior high school the following morning and asked to see Theo. Minutes later the boy walked into the school principal's office. His face was bruised; his right eye, black. Theo stared down at the floor. The priest had never seen the boy so sad; so dejected.

"How are you, Theo?"

The boy looked up at the principal then at the priest. He remained silent. His lip began quivering.

"Can we have a few moments alone?" the priest asked.

"Surely, Father." The principal walked out.

"I'm sorry, Theo. I don't know what came over me. Jesus spoke to my heart this morning and that's why I'm here. I want you to know that."

Theo continued his silence for several more moments, clearing his throat from the guttural tic that kept echoing. Then he spoke. "I'm leaving home."

Surprised, the priest asked, "When? Where are you going?"

"I need to leave home. I can't stay there anymore. I don't know where I'll go, but I need to get out."

"Tell me what happened, Theo."

"You don't want to know, Father. Even if I told you, there's nothing you can do."

"Are you sure this is the only way, Theo?"

"I'm leaving after school today, Father." His voice was resolute and Father Bonafacio sensed there was nothing that would change the boy's mind.

"I have a friend in Santa Fe. He's a volunteer who helps young people. I can call him."

"Can they help me?" the boy asked. The tip of the boys lip was shuddering like never before.

"Come to the rectory after school and I'll let you know."

By mid-afternoon Theo had arrived, carrying an old, well-worn backpack in one hand. "Can they help me, Father?"

Despite the cold weather, Theo wore only a light jacket. A second glance revealed that his clothing was layered. "I spoke to my friend. They can put you up for a few days. After that, you have to meet with a counselor. Then they decide what to do with you. Are you sure of this decision, Theo?"

Theo nodded his head.

"Let's go. I'll drive you to Santa Fe."

As they began the trip, Theo turned to the priest. "You know, I was ready to leave a few days ago."

"What changed you mind?" the priest asked.

Theo formed a slight smile. "I had a feeling you'd come."

Eleven

AS WAS HER usual practice, Jude arrived early at the restaurant. She was seated and ordered a lemon drop martini, something she rarely did at lunch. But today was different. She would boast to Victoria about being called into the company president's office and offered a substantial raise and promotion to rescind her resignation. She would speak about the perks of her new job that included unlimited business class travel and a wardrobe allowance. Jude was so keyed up and hardly able to contain all the good news until she noticed Victoria entering the restaurant and walking toward her. Her daughter looked drawn as if she hadn't slept for days. There was not a hint of a smile on her ashen face. As she approached the table, Jude stood up. "What in the world is the matter, honey?" she said as she took Victoria's hand. It felt cold. They sat down.

A tear streamed down Victoria's face as she began speaking. "Mom, I'm so sorry."

"Sorry about what, sweetheart? What's the matter, Victoria?"

At that moment she looked up to see Aban standing at their table.

"What are you doing here?" Jude asked, surprised by his presence.

He remained silent.

Jude looked at her daughter. "What is this all about?" she demanded to know, exchanging glances with both of them.

"May I sit down?" Aban asked.

"Absolutely not..."

Before she could finish, Victoria interrupted. "Mom, please."

"Please what?" she asked.

Ignoring her rebuff, Aban pulled back the chair and sat down. "Jude, your daughter and I have been seeing one another for some time now."

"What? Is this true, Victoria?"

"I didn't mean for this to happen, Mom. I'm so sorry," she said.

"Sorry?" Jude repeated.

"Jude, there's more," Aban said. "Victoria is pregnant. We're getting married, *Inshallah*"

"She's marrying you! Aban, you're old enough to be her father. How could you do this to my daughter?"

"We're in love, Jude."

"What do you know about love? Your kind doesn't believe in love. To you my daughter's nothing more than a mere possession to have."

"That's not true, Jude," he interrupted.

"Mom, we are in love," Victoria said, begging for her mother's understanding as she met her gaze.

Jude snarled at Victoria. "In love with him! Don't make the mistakes I've made with his kind, Victoria."

"We're getting married, Mom."

"You obviously haven't given this much thought. What about

graduation and your plans afterward?"

"I'm finishing school. But we've decided to get married before the baby arrives."

Jude cast her a horrified glance. "Then you do it without me. I will never consent nor participate in any marriage involving him. I hope you know you are ruining your life." Her angry voice attracted the attention of others nearby. She stood up and stared crossly at them. Without another word she walked out.

Before leaving Virginia for her new job in Frankfurt, Jude made one last effort to discourage Victoria. Their phone conversation was long and occasionally loud. It was clear to her that Victoria was infatuated with Aban and there was nothing she could say that would change her daughter's mind. Yet Jude remained unwavering in her disapproval. Jude loved her daughter and the anguish she felt at the thought of Victoria marrying a Moroccan twice her age whose religion and culture held an inferior regard toward women, was intense. But she was helpless to stop it. The following week Jude closed her house and left for her new post.

SEVERAL DAYS BEFORE Christmas, Aban and Victoria married in a simple civil ceremony in Virginia. Victoria remained living at the university and spent weekends at Aban's Virginia apartment. Both excited about the baby's arrival, they began preparing the extra bedroom in anticipation. Weeks before graduation, Victoria mailed her mother an announcement of the event and received a congratulatory card with a brief message and a check. It was obvious to Victoria that Jude was still angry about her marriage to Aban.

After graduating, Victoria moved into her husband's apartment, and one month later their child was born. The two were overjoyed at the birth of their son. Victoria picked the name, Elijah. Aban balked until finally giving in with the understanding that when the time came to move to Morocco, the boy would take on a Muslim name.

Throughout her pregnancy Victoria had experienced painful headaches, dizziness, nausea, and a sharp ache in her neck. On occasion when the headaches became too agonizing, her speech slurred. Her doctor, a young gynecologist, attributed the symptoms to a difficult first-time pregnancy. After she had Elijah, the symptoms seemed to disappear. Then early one morning as Victoria was getting out of bed, she became dizzy. This time the symptoms were fierce. The room was spinning wildly; her stomach grew nauseous. She lost her balance and held tightly to the bedpost. She screamed out to Aban who ran into the room. She tried speaking but couldn't form words. The ache in her neck was excruciating. Aban caught Victoria as she weakened and began to fall. He placed her in bed. She lost consciousness. Aban dialed the emergency number and within minutes paramedics arrived. Barely able to stabilize Victoria, they rushed her to the hospital. An elderly neighbor offered to care for Elijah as Aban sped off to be with her.

Parking, then rushing to the emergency window, Aban was escorted to a private room where the doctor broke the tragic news. "I'm sorry, Mr. Bashir, your wife had a fatal aneurism."

Unable to understand or believe the doctor's pronouncement, Aban asked, "Will she be okay?"

"Mr. Bashir, your wife passed away."

"No, you must be mistaken. My wife is only twenty-two. She's too young for that."

The doctor gave Aban an empathetic gaze. "Your wife, Victoria, passed away upon her arrival here. There was nothing we could do."

Aban lowered his head and wept.

WHEN JUDE RECEIVED Aban's telephone call, she nearly fainted from shock. How could it have happened? What had he done to her? Jude took the first flight back, and by noon the following day, she arrived in Washington. She drove directly to the hospital and insisted on speaking to the emergency doctor who treated Victoria. A few minutes later the doctor appeared.

"I'm sorry, Ms. Armstrong, but without your son-in-law's consent I'm unable to give you any information."

"But I'm her mother."

In her most sympathetic voice, the doctor replied, "Ms. Armstrong, I'm a mother as well as a doctor. I can understand your loss and appreciate your situation. But under medical disclosure rules the law does not allow me to give you information concerning your daughter's treatment unless we have Mr. Bashir's authorization."

"Get the bastard on the phone. I'll talk to him."

The doctor placed the call and received Aban's verbal consent. "What is it you want to know, Ms. Armstrong?" the doctor asked.

"Was an autopsy performed?"

"Yes, late last evening. We don't have the written report yet, but I'm told her death was a result of a cerebral aneurism."

"What's that?" she asked.

"A blood sac formed in her brain and ruptured."

"Was there any trauma to her head...to her body? Could it have happened as a result of being beaten up?"

"I'm afraid not, Ms. Armstrong. There was nothing to suggest that your daughter sustained any bruising or physical trauma."

"Are you sure? Are you absolutely sure?"

"Yes," the doctor replied.

Jude slowly stood up and walked out.

The funeral was held two days later. Victoria was buried in a Christian cemetery close to her home. The following day Aban drove to Jude's house. Taking Elijah in his arms, he rang the doorbell.

Seeing her grandson for the first time, Jude burst out in tears. Aban walked inside and offered the child to her. She held him close.

"What happens now?" she asked.

"I've requested a temporary reassignment to Rabàt, *Inshallah*."

"What about the baby?"

"Elijah will come with me."

"Would you consider leaving him with me?" she asked.

"I'm sorry, Jude. My son must be brought up Muslim."

Jude kissed the baby, handed the small bundle back to Aban, turned and walked away. She knew she would never see the child again.

JUDE COULD NOT garner the strength to travel back to Frankfurt. Her grief was too great. At a friend's suggestion, she sought out a support group that met at a local church each week. Jude found a modicum of comfort there. As her veil of anguish slowly began lifting, months later she tried returning to work only to learn that she had been replaced.

Shopping for groceries one day, Jude ran into Marty Chenoweth. It was good to see an old friend. As their conversation lingered, Marty suggested wheeling their grocery carts to the bakery department and continuing their conversation over coffee.

Jude was surprised that Marty lived so close to her townhouse. Their interests were similar; morning jogs, afternoon park strolls, and a few good strong drinks before dinner. The following morning they jogged together at the local park. It became a daily routine and their friendship blossomed. While Jude had no desire for any amorous relationships, Marty became the perfect companion. His wit and humor sometimes sent her reeling into uncontrollable laughter. Their different views on politics, business, world events, and almost every other topic kept their conversations and arguments lively over scotch and sodas. And when Marty went off on extended journalism assignments, Jude found herself longing for his companionship. Aware that Jude was fluent in French, Marty invited her to join him on an assignment in Quebec. Jude agreed. She quickly discovered that freelance work was challenging and lucrative. Before long they were traveling throughout the world and working on assignments together. For Jude, life became bearable.

ONCE ABAN RETURNED to Rabàt, he took leave from his job to make arrangements for the care of his son. Leaving Elijah with a friend, Aban traveled to Casablanca to speak with his youngest brother, Asafar and his wife, Maladh. Asafar owed a debt of gratitude to Aban for arranging his hire as an engineer with a state-owned chemical company.

Arriving at their apartment, Aban greeted Asafar in the traditional way with a kiss on both cheeks. *"Asalaam Alaykum."*

"Wa 'Alaykum Asalaam" Asafar replied as he invited his brother inside. They sat on cushions at the round, knee high table and within minutes Maladh appeared with a kettle of mint tea.

Unaware that Aban had married a Christian American or that he had a son, Asafar was sympathetic and understanding at hearing the story. "What's the child's name?" he asked.

"Elijah."

"A Christian name?"

Aban did not respond.

"How will you raise the child, considering your work situation?" Asafar asked.

"That is my purpose for visiting you today. Will you take him into your family?"

Asafar looked back at Maladh. She smiled. "Your son is my son. With your approval, we shall call him Ilyas," Asafar suggested.

Aban nodded, as he took a sip of tea. "And from this day Ilyas shall know you as his father, know your family as his family, and know me as his uncle."

At that, Maladh brought a wash basin and hand-drying towel for the brothers before setting the table with whole meal bread and the communal tagine of lamb, chickpeas and gravy. Asafar blessed the food and they began to eat.

Twelve

IN THE HOUR it took to drive to Santa Fe the following day, David's mind continued ruminating over the previous evening. His emotions felt scattered; contemplative currents of fear and anger and shame and pride flashed through his mind. His emotional state was fragile. He needed to pull himself together for the meeting with Patrick and his friend. Finally arriving, David parked and made his way into the hospital pavilion.

Patrick greeted him with a firm hug. "Dad, thanks so much for coming."

David couldn't help admiring his son for a few seconds. Despite learning Rayèn's long held secret, that Patrick was not his natural child but conceived during a pre-marital affair, nothing felt different in their relationship.

"So, where is this kid?" David asked.

"I'll take you to his room."

They walked down the corridor to the elevator.

"After you do the introductions, I think you'd better leave. No telling where this is headed, but the less you know about his case, the better."

"Sure, no problem."

Exiting the second floor elevator, they walked down the north hall corridor, passing the nurse's station, until they reached Theo's room. Theo was sitting up on the bed looking at a magazine. He watched them walk in.

"Hey Theo, this is my dad."

David extended his hand. "I'm David Lujan."

Theo's face and neck showed large areas of dark bruising and a stitch on his left brow. As Theo extended his hand, David noticed bruises on his arm.

Theo stared at David for a few seconds as if noting that Patrick bore no resemblance to his father. Standing over six feet and many pounds heavier than Patrick, David knew he must look tired. His graying hair was unkempt, his brown eyes were puffy, and his face sagged. He forced a smile. When they shook hands, Theo's was cold and clammy.

There was a brief silence, then Patrick spoke. "Okay, I'm outta here. I'll let you two talk." Patrick closed the door when he left.

"Mind if I sit down?" David asked.

"Oh no, help yourself."

David pulled the chair closer to Theo's bed. "So I understand you might be in some kind of trouble with the police?"

"I guess...that's what they're telling me."

"Where are you from?" David asked.

"You mean where I was born?"

"Yeah. Where were you born?"

"In Arbol Verde. But I've lived in Santa Fe since high school."

"You work in Santa Fe?"

"Yeah, for The Seville restaurant. I'm a chef—a cook really. There was a half-second pause before Theo asked, "Have you ever heard of the CIA?"

A strange question, David thought as his eyebrows furrowed. "The Central Intelligence Agency?"

Theo laughed. "No. The Culinary Institute of America. It's in New York. When I get the money together I'm going to culinary school. I have this idea that I want to study culinary arts there or in Spain."

"Are those your plans?"

"To go to culinary school, you mean? Absolutely. You heard of Mario Batali?"

"No, I don't think I've ever heard of him."

"He's probably the most famous Italian chef in the United

States. He won the James Beard award last year. You've heard of that, haven't you?"

David replied with raised eyebrows. "Sorry, I don't think I've heard about any of that."

"Batali lived in Spain, then after college went to London to study at Le Cordon Bleu..."

David interrupted. "Theo, tell me about you. What is it they're charging you with?"

Theo's high spirits suddenly vanished. He sighed. "Something about drug dealing and killing a friend."

"Do you do drugs?"

Theo's gaze became intense. "I don't do drugs. I never have."

"Tell me about your friend — the person they're accusing you of killing?"

"Her name was Jude Armstrong. She had cancer and died in her sleep."

"Were you with her when she died?"

A tear formed in his eye as he answered. "Yeah, I was with her."

"I understand there was some insurance money?"

Theo didn't respond.

"Did you make a claim for the money, Theo?"

His thoughts seemed far away. He remained silent.

"I can't help you unless you talk to me."

Theo's lip began quivering. "Can you defend me?" he asked.

"I'm not sure. Have the police taken a statement from you?"

Theo shook his head. "Patrick told me not to say anything until after I talked to you."

"Do you know who beat you up?

Theo was silent.

"Tell you what, Theo. Let me talk to the police and see how serious all of this is. I'll be back in a few days to talk to you again. In the meantime, if the police want to speak to you, have them call me first."

"So you are going to defend me?"

In all the years of practicing law David had developed a second sense when it came to sizing up clients. It was easy to recognize deceitful clients, especially those who outright lied. Something about their body language always gave them away — their eyes, or hands, or the little articulations in their speech. But there was nothing to indicate this kid was lying. Had he met Theo in any other situation, the kid would have impressed him. He spoke clearly, appeared honest, and had a passion in life. No visible tattoos, no piercings on his face, no strange colored hair, nothing to indicate a rebellious nature. The case intrigued David.

"I'll let you know when I come back. For the time being sit tight and get well."

Thirteen

MALADH WAS OVERJOYED at having a son in the household. From the first time she saw the child, she knew they could love him easily. Ilyas was a beautiful baby. He had the same blue eyes as Aban. His light brown hair and full angel lips, although bearing no family resemblance, gave him a sweet, innocent appearance. Their two daughters, Fatiha and Karima, welcomed their new brother and watched over him constantly. In no time Ilyas was walking and talking, and grew into a precocious child.

When Ilyas turned five Asafar talked about traveling to Setta for the circumcision ritual. Maladh suggested having the procedure done at the hospital in Casablanca where it would be more sanitary. But Asafar would not hear of it since it was the family tradition to hold the ritual at the grandparent's home and elaborate arrangements were already underway. Throughout the weeks leading up to *khitan*, the circumcision ritual, Ilyas grew excited and nervous.

"Explain again why I have to be cut down there, Ma?"

"All Muslims are circumcised," she replied for what seemed like the hundredth time.

"Will it hurt?"

"Not for very long."

"But it will hurt?"

"Ilyas, you do want to be a good Muslim?" Maladh asked

"Yes," he replied hesitantly.

"After your circumcision, you will then be able to go with your father to the Mosque every Friday and pray to God. You will learn about the Prophet Mohammed. You will learn the Qur'an and learn the pillars of Islam. You will practice to be a devout Muslim, *Inshallah*."

"What are pillars?"

Exasperated by his endless questions, Maladh replied, "Go ask your father."

ASAFAR AND MALADH received notice from the post office one day of funds being held in their name. The funds were from Aban. After receiving the first dispatch, Asafar wrote to Aban assuring that his generosity was not necessary. The income from his state job was sufficient to provide for all the family's needs. Aban responded, insisting the funds be used for tuition in a private school when Ilyas came of age.

Ilyas was enrolled in pre-school at Casablanca Academy when he turned six. Each morning Maladh would walk him to school and each afternoon, walk him home. He adjusted well, making friends easily and learning to conform to the structured program. As they walked, Ilyas' curiosity was boundless, usually jumping from one subject to another randomly.

"I played with Gabriel today and we had fun," he said one afternoon.

"Is he in your class?" Maladh asked.

"Yeah, Ma. But he never prays like me."

"Do you know if he's Muslim?"

"No." There was a slight pause, then he asked, "Why do I have to learn to read, Ma?"

"Don't you want to learn about the world?"

"Is that why you read so much?"

"I read because I want to know things."

"Things like what, Ma?"

"Do you know the first word God said to the Prophet? It was *read*."

Ilyas remained quiet for a second, contemplating what he heard, then asked, "When are we going on another picnic, Ma?"

Maladh looked down at her son and smiled, as they continued their walk home. "Soon, Ilyas, we'll have another picnic sometime soon."

Two years later, as Ilyas turned eight, Asafar began teaching his son the Qur'an. Ilyas was a good student with a talent for memorizing text. The family held a large gathering to celebrate his first recitation of *ayahs* from memory. Rewarded with coins and sweets from the relatives and friends attending, Ilyas was thrilled. Asafar's present to his son was a prayer rug with a tiny compass woven into the border, explaining that now he would always know the correct direction to face when praying. While Ilyas invariably forgot textbooks, homework and gym gear when he went off to school, Asafar made sure his son did not forget his prayer rug.

EVEN THOUGH ILYAS had many Muslim school friends, he enjoyed playing with Gabriel best of all. Gabriel was Christian and the others teased him constantly about their close friendship. He couldn't understand all the chiding and one day asked Asafar if friendship with a Christian was against Islam.

"Son, is Gabriel a good Christian?"

"I think so, Pa."

"Does he practice his faith and believe in Allah?"

"Yeah, Pa. But they go to church on Sunday."

"So, you are a righteous Muslim and Gabriel is a righteous Christian. You both believe in the same God. What obstacles could there be preventing you from being friends?"

After this conversation, Ilyas pursued the relationship with more spirit and without shame. In physical education class, they always made sure to be on the same soccer team. When they wrestled, Ilyas and Gabriel were the challengers. During swimming events, the two competed together and challenged all the others. As they grew over the years, the two became almost inseparable.

Out of school, Ilyas and Gabriel visited one another's homes and occasionally went to the movies together. Sunday afternoons were for playing soccer or cricket at the activities park with friends. One late evening, after countless rounds of chess and glasses of mint tea at a popular café, Ilyas and Gabriel left a group of friends and began walking home. Gabriel suggested the route through a nearby park. It was dark and they were enjoying one another's company so much that Gabriel led them to a grassy area where they laid on the soft ground and began admiring the bright stars. Surrounded by groves of palm trees, manicured shrubs, and the occasional whiff of the intense, spicy fragrance from the white lily garden, their spot was concealed from traffic and pedestrian walkways. They talked about family and school and sports. Then for a few minutes stillness permeated before Gabriel broke the quiet. He began describing his first sexual experience with a girl. He spoke softly as if he was reliving the event; his words were graphic and his tone, stirring.

Ilyas listened closely, wondering if it was his friend's intention to arouse him. As he looked over, Gabriel had unzipped and was stroking his member. Masturbation among Ilyas' Muslim friends was not so unusual; the challenge was always to test their virility by being the first to ejaculate. But the situation with Gabriel seemed entirely different. Provoked by Gabriel, Ilyas also unzipped and began stroking his hardened member. Gabriel glanced over, asking, "Have you ever touched another guy?"

"No." Ilyas' response was quick.

Gabriel continued stroking, then began inching closer. Ilyas froze when he felt Gabriel's hand around his penis.

"Touch mine," Gabriel suggested.

Ilyas reached down and clenched Gabriel's in his palm. Several seconds later Ilyas felt Gabriel release his grip and roll on top of him. Balancing with his arms, Gabriel's chest was high above Ilyas'. As their hardened genitals pressed together, Gabriel began thrusting his hips. The excitement was too great for Ilyas to consider the shame of his actions, and he began to return the thrusts. Gabriel slowly bent his elbows and his face moved closer. Then Ilyas felt Gabriel's kiss. Instantly an intense sensation, such as he had never experienced before, spontaneously erupted. It was an electrical charge throughout his body that continued for several long seconds.

Afterward, too weak to move a single muscle, Ilyas grew still. Gabriel rolled off. Ilyas' eyes opened in time to catch a glimpse of a star falling across the sky. An incredible euphoric sensation swathed his entire body. They lay in the stillness until minutes later Gabriel broke the silence. "We better start for home."

Ilyas stood up slowly, refusing to speak, fearing that his friend would discover his soul weeping with an incomprehensible joy.

Heading out of the park at a quick pace, they remained silent. When they reached the park entrance, their paths diverged as they made their way home. Later that night while Ilyas lay in bed, a profound sadness came over him. He knew what they had done was against *Shari'a*. For the first time he felt a strange chaos in his soul. Had the demonic djinn, those spirits that possess humans, entered his soul? Were they exerting vengeance for his immorality? Maybe even changing his nature, turning him *shaz*? Nightmares cycled in his dreams like a revolving wheel. Awaking earlier than any of the others, Ilyas sat up regretting what he had done.

The following day Gabriel greeted Ilyas as he arrived at school and they walked to class together. But in his heart and mind Ilyas knew their relationship had changed, at least as far as he perceived it. Each time the image at the park resurfaced, his soul fluttered and his penis engorged. He would go to the mosque on Friday and pray fervently to banish the djinn from his soul. With all his mental might, Ilyas pledged to suppress the internal feelings. Vowing to atone, Ilyas knew he had no choice but to sever his friendship with Gabriel. That was the only way of releasing the djinn's control. With each passing day Ilyas began to distance himself from Gabriel.

The slow detachment became obvious to Gabriel, and although he never questioned Ilyas, nor spoke to him about that night in the park, he sensed his friend's shame and remorse. At school Gabriel remained aloof and impassive. But in his solitude Gabriel was greatly saddened over the loss of his friend.

As fervently as Ilyas prayed to make his feelings about Gabriel go away, they only intensified. He grew desperate for help. But he knew of no one to seek out. He wouldn't dare seek advice from his parents or from the imam. To speak of his feelings for Gabriel was detestable; to admit to what they did was despicable. He felt his soul begin to wither.

By grade twelve the following year, Ilyas had read the entire Qur'an in as many times, but his soul had yet to recover. While he still saw Gabriel on the grounds and in the hallways at school, they rarely spoke anymore. The battle against the temptation Gabriel evoked and the tumult of the djinns' recrimination were too great to fight and only weakened his spirit.

When graduation arrived and the academy's ceremony brought all of the students together for the last time, Ilyas broke from the crowd and made his way from the gymnasium to the main building. He was unaware that Gabriel was following behind. Ilyas walked into a classroom to collect his belongings. Suddenly, he heard a voice by the door.

"Congratulations."

Startled by the voice, Ilyas turned around and stared at Gabriel.

"What will you do now," Gabriel asked.

"I've enrolled at the University of Casablanca," Ilyas replied.

"Well, good luck."

"What will you do?" Ilyas asked.

"My family's returning to the United States."

The loud voices in the hallway interrupted the moment as others entered the classroom.

"Stay well," Gabriel said as he gave a slight wave, turned and walked away.

It took all his strength to suppress the urge to call out to Gabriel. He wanted so desperately to talk to him; to be with him. He was slowly dying from the djinn in his soul. But he let Gabriel walk away, never to speak to him again. Feigning joy during the large family graduation celebration that followed, Ilyas felt lonely and lost.

Fourteen

DAVID WAS WAITING for Snyder when he arrived at the police building right after the noon hour. Dressed in a casual pullover, khakis and loafers, David looked as if he had just come off the golf course. Snyder approached David and in his usual brusque manner introduced himself.

David mentally noted Snyder's haughty attitude and ignored it. "Do you have time to talk about Theo Jaquez?"

"Are you representing him?" Snyder asked.

"Not formally."

"Informally, then?"

"You could say that. I'm considering taking his case."

"Let's go back to my office."

David followed Snyder. "So, what do you want to know?" Snyder asked as he walked around and sat at his desk.

David pulled up a chair and sat down. "Has he been charged with anything yet?"

"Nope."

"Are criminal charges imminent?"

"Yup.

"Is he going to be arrested anytime soon?"

"Maybe."

"Look, Snyder. I'm not here to play twenty questions with you. It's obvious I'm irritating the hell out of you, but I don't really care. Do you want to talk to me about Theo Jaquez's case or not?"

Snyder puckered his lips as he leaned back in his chair to

consider David's remark. David knew that sooner or later he would learn the scope of their investigation. Snyder must have known it too for he began to talk.

"The kid's in a lot of trouble. He's being investigated for fraud, homicide, and drug dealing. We have evidence he's a heavy druggie—heroin. A week before the victim died, the kid suddenly became the beneficiary of her life insurance. He was asking around about lethal drug combinations and boasted to his friends that the victim wasn't going to be around much longer. He was the only one in her house when she died, and didn't hang around too long afterward. As soon as he could, the kid applied for the insurance money, then took off to Morocco to buy drugs. When he got back, somebody found out about his stash and whacked him around pretty good."

"How do you know he uses drugs?"

"His medical record says so."

"Any idea who beat him up?"

"No, we're still sniffing around. Something will come up, though. It always does."

"What about the Morocco trip, how do you know he went there to buy drugs?"

"Figure it out for yourself, Lujan. A druggie gets a bundle of cash and immediately heads to Morocco. It ain't the kind of place to lay out on the beach, pick-up women and drink mai tai's."

"Was an autopsy done on the victim?"

"We're working on that."

"You're going to exhume the body?"

"Maybe."

"So why haven't you arrested him yet?"

"Like I said, we're still investigating. Anyway, he ain't going anywhere anytime soon. We're keeping an eye on him."

"So how soon before you arrest him?"

"We're talking with the D.A. Maybe after we exhume and test. The D.A's also talking about taking the case to the grand jury."

David stood up. "Okay, here's the deal, Snyder. Don't question the kid unless I'm around. Is that understood?"

Snyder's eyes narrowed and lips pursed. "So, is he your client...formally now?"

"Yup." David returned Snyder's cold stare as if challenging him, then walked out of his office.

Except for the medical records, it was all circumstantial evidence, David mused. They had no drugs, no witnesses to prove he coerced the victim, and no hard evidence to prove murder. No wonder they hadn't arrested Theo. For now there was nothing to be done. He would call Patrick to quell his son's concern. Steering toward the freeway, David headed back to Albuquerque. He would have just enough time to grab a sandwich before his afternoon therapy session with Juliana Ochoa.

Fifteen

MAKING FRIENDS AT the university came easy for Ilyas. Most first year students looked to one another for support in getting through their classes, and for Ilyas it was no different. Many of them gathered at a local café to talk about class work, play games and drink mint tea obsessively, which Ilyas began taking without sugar fearing his teeth would decay like so many of his friends and relatives. One evening, he joined a group traveling to an outdoor concert to hear Raissa Talbensirt, a popular Moroccan Amazigh singer. That was where Ilyas met Amalu Massoud.

Ten years older than Ilyas, Amalu had a medium build, was strong-boned, with a dark handsome face and curly black hair. His personality was charismatic, his voice confident. They spoke briefly to one another, and thereafter when they happened to meet by chance encounter, they exchanged a quick embrace, a short greeting, then went off on their way. It wasn't until Ilyas' second year at the university that their friendship began to grow.

Amalu joined Ilyas' group at the café one day. He was articulate, amusing, and devoted to Islam. Amalu spoke of his passion for the Amazigh culture—the culture of the Berbers making up a majority of the country's population. He spoke harshly of the government's refusal to promote their language, and how it was the responsibility of the Berbers to preserve their customs and way of life. He denounced the government's choice of Arabic as the official language when a majority of Moroccans spoke Berber. Amalu suggested that the government should be promoting Berber culture by teaching the language in schools and universities. Many of the students agreed.

Amalu's intense passion drew upon the group's emotions, as he suggested organizing a demonstration to call attention to the government's arrogance. Suddenly, his suggestion began to resonate among those listening to him. The group's enthusiasm intensified with several students volunteering to organize the demonstration and other's promising to participate. Ilyas remained enraptured by Amalu's magnetism.

Several weeks later, when sufficient student support for the demonstration was gathered, plans were drawn out. When the day arrived, the demonstration began on the street in front of the university and proceeded to a nearby park. Amalu got up to speak. Using a bullhorn, he urged the students to condemn the government's disrespect for Berber culture.

Moroccan police suited in riot gear monitored the crowd. The demonstration was orderly. Then, without provocation, someone threw a rock that struck a police officer. Ilyas was near the rock-thrower and observed him. The police instantly retaliated and attacked the crowd with clubs. Everyone began fleeing. Ilyas was certain he saw the rock-thrower hand signal to Amalu as they tore off in different directions. Following in Amalu's direction, Ilyas detoured down several narrow streets.

When they were a safe distance, Ilyas noticed Amalu motioning to follow. They proceeded through an alley and up a set of stairs into an apartment. Once inside the apartment, Amalu looked out the back window and said, "We're safe here." Then he proceeded to set a small pot of water on the tiny burner for mint tea.

Ilyas looked around at the small apartment. It was a single room with windows in front and back. The windows were covered with thick curtains blocking out the sunlight. In one corner hung several cabinets, high above the small counter where the burner rested. A small sink with running water was situated next to it. Close to the center of the room, cushions were scattered on the floor around a low table. A mattress was in the corner.

"Do you live here?" he asked.

"Yes, sometimes."

Ilyas sat on one of the cushions. "You know who threw the rock at the police?" Ilyas asked.

Amalu turned to him with a cold stare. "No."

As the water began boiling, Amalu placed mint leaves into the kettle, then poured the water into it. He took two small cups and the kettle to the table. "You know that the police set it up so they could attack us."

"What makes you so sure they did that?"

"Because that is the way the police are trained to control us."

"How do you know so much about all of this?" Ilyas asked.

Amalu poured the tea and slid the cup over to Ilyas. "Whosoever chooses to follow guidance, follows it for his own good; whosoever goes astray, goes astray to his own loss."

"An *ayah* from the Qur'an," Ilyas said. "I have read it many times."

Amalu began to explain the *ayah* in a way Ilyas had never heard before. He spoke as if he was a *muftis*, with scholarly knowledge about the Qur'an. Nothing more was said about the demonstration or the police attack. Ilyas remained with Amalu for several hours sipping tea and trying to learn more about the mysterious man. But Amalu would never reveal very much about himself.

The two began meeting regularly at the café for mint tea and hours of conversation. While Amalu was not a current student at the university, he had attended at one time, then abruptly dropped out. He never spoke about his work or where he derived his living expenses. He was just as stealthy about his family origin, always avoiding those subjects. But Amalu's knowledge and understanding of many things captivated Ilyas.

Amalu was often away from the city for long periods, then returned without offering any explanation of his whereabouts. Respecting his privacy, Ilyas never questioned him about these absences. Ilyas also knew it was unlikely Amalu would tell him.

One October day, when dark clouds formed overhead and the weather had turned cold, Amalu invited Ilyas to a public demonstration of university graduate students. They were gathering at a park to protest the lack of jobs. Ilyas hesitated to go, but Amalu insisted, arguing that some day he would be the beneficiary of their actions.

"You are aware that Islam requires all good Muslims to be charitable to the less fortunate and that *zakat* involves more than giving money — it requires supporting others in the pursuit of noble causes," Amalu said.

Bridled with a sense of guilt and obligation, Ilyas reluctantly went along.

The demonstrators were massed close to a walled quadrant of the park and a small podium was erected for the speakers. All was going peacefully until a speaker spoke the name of the monarch, and without warning the riot police began their attack. As they tried to flee, those demonstrators caught by police were arrested. Amalu and Ilyas were not as lucky as the first time. Crushed by the crowd, they found themselves cornered by the high wall. Their efforts at scaling the wall failed when police officers pulled them down, tied their hands, and forced them into a waiting bus.

They were driven to a Moroccan detention facility and the mass of arrested demonstrators were herded into large jail cells. Slowly the police began the process of photographing, fingerprinting, and creating a dossier on each of them. They were allowed to leave after signing a confession acknowledging their participation in fomenting a public disturbance. Ilyas reluctantly signed the prepared statement and left the government building vowing to cut off his association with Amalu.

Eight months later Ilyas was in class when a unit of Moroccan police stormed inside the room. Dressed in riot gear and carrying assault rifles, the leader came forward and in a loud, clear voice called out, "Ilyas Bashir."

Terrified at hearing his name, Ilyas remained seated.

When the officer screamed his name out again, Ilyas slowly stood up. Two officers immediately approached him, forced his arms behind his back, and dragged him to a waiting car. For the second time in his life, Ilyas was arrested.

Sixteen

MOROCCO, A MODERATE Arab nation, was first inhabited by Berber nomads more than two thousand years ago. A tolerant Muslim society, Moroccans live in relative peace alongside a minority of Christians and Jews. Its government had remained stable for many years. So when terrorists struck in Casablanca, their violence marked the worst assault in the modern day history of the kingdom.

On the night of May 16, 2003, terrorists attacked a Jewish restaurant. Blocked from getting inside, they set off explosives on the street killing and injuring bystanders and policemen. Within minutes, terrorists at a different location entered a hotel, stabbed security guards and tried to set off explosives. Before police could respond, the terrorists continued their killing spree. The carnage erupted during a third incident at another restaurant close to a Jewish cemetery. In the end, thirty-three people were killed and dozens more injured. The terrorists, members of *Salafia Jihadia*, a radical organization, set off an international alarm.

Overnight the government mounted a nationwide response to find and arrest the terrorists. Morocco's National Police, National Intelligence Service, and the Royal Gendarmerie coordinated the investigation of the bombings. It took little time before the security forces began rounding up more than four thousand suspects for questioning. Ilyas name appeared on its long list.

Led out to the waiting car, Ilyas was blindfolded and driven fifty kilometers from town to an abandoned prison. When they arrived, Ilyas was stripped of his clothing, given a prison djellaba, and thrown in a small cell. The mud-encased cell was too low to stand and barely large enough to sit. It was dank and cold. Across was a blank wall. No windows were in the cavernous dormitory so it was impossible to know when day turned to night. Only dim lighting illuminated the hallway. The moans and cries of others locked in adjoining cells were the only sounds Ilyas heard. The smell of urine and feces was strong. Ilyas was terrified.

Soon Ilyas' legs began cramping. He tried shifting positions then began massaging them to get blood circulating, but it offered little relief. Sleep was impossible, as the fear of his situation kept him anxious and worried. When two guards passed his cell, Ilyas asked for water. The guards cursed at him and walked on.

After hours in the small cell, Ilyas heard the echo of the dormitory door open again and the clacking sound of guards walking. They stopped in front of his cell, opened it and ordered him out. He crawled out and tried standing, but his legs gave way. One of the guards blindfolded him. They grabbed his arms and dragged him down the hallway, his feet scraping the rough floor. With all his might Ilyas tried to get into step, but they were moving too fast and his legs were still numb. They trod up several sets of stairs, down another hallway, then they suddenly stopped. Ilyas heard a door open. They dragged him inside and sat him on a chair. He heard footsteps walking away and the door closed.

The room was warm and stuffy. The odor of cigarette smoke was strong. His legs hurt terribly. All was quiet for a few seconds, then he heard a voice ask, "You are Ilyas Bashir?" The interrogator spoke in fluent Arabic. His voice was commanding.

"Yes. I don't understand why I'm here. I've done nothing wrong."

"Ilyas Bashir, what do you know of *Salafia Jihadia*?"

"I've never heard that name before. May I have a glass of water?" he asked, his voice breaking. Ilyas heard what sounded as if the interrogator was pulling back his chair. Then the voice was clearly in front of him repeating the question.

"What do you know of *Salafia Jihadia*?"

"I told you, I have never heard that name before."

A hard blow to his face sent Ilyas hurtling to the floor. Someone behind took hold of his hair and pulled him back up on the chair. His blindfold sagged and he was able to catch the glimpse of a tall, stocky Arab dressed in military uniform. His blindfold was readjusted. Ilyas began trembling.

Barely able to form words to speak over his fear, Ilyas repeated, "I have never heard of the *Salafia Jihadia* before. I promise you what I say is true."

"What do you know of Amalu Massoud?"

"I met him at a concert and we..." His voice trailed off. Instantly it became clear to him why he was there. It was because of his association with Amalu. Amalu was a terrorist. A second blow to his face sent him flying off the chair. As before, he was lifted and placed back.

"Tell me all you know of Amalu Massoud."

"We went to two demonstrations together. We had tea at a café occasionally. That is all I know of him."

"Maybe I can help you improve your memory."

The person behind grabbed Ilyas and shoved him off the chair. Ilyas fell to the floor. Then he felt something being placed in his hands. It had the shape of a soda bottle.

"I strongly suggest that you do not break the bottle or you will suffer a severe punishment," the interrogator said. "Remove your clothing and sit on the bottle," he ordered.

Ilyas hesitated for a second and received another blow to his face. The bottle slipped from his hands and rolled on the ground. He got to his knees and began removing the djellaba and his underclothes. Handed the bottle, once again, Ilyas placed it on the floor and squatted down.

"Are you comfortable?" the interrogator asked.

Ilyas didn't answer. Another blow sent Ilyas falling back. He could feel blood oozing out of his nose. The man behind placed the bottle back into Ilyas' hands.

"You will answer every question I ask. Do you understand?" the interrogator demanded.

"Yes."

"You may resume your position."

Ilyas set the bottle on the floor and, supported by his aching legs, attempted to balance the area behind his scrotum on the narrow conical opening. The effort was futile. The hurt, intense.

"Tell me all you know of Amalu Massoud," the voice demanded.

Ilyas began to speak, offering no meaningful information.

WHEN ILYAS PARTIALLY awoke, he was back in his cell. It took several minutes for his mind to recall where he was. A small bowl had been placed inside his cell. In the dim light it appeared to be lentils mixed with a watery substance that smelled vile. Each time Ilyas put his mouth to the bowl, he gagged. His body numb, Ilyas continued to slip in and out of consciousness. He sensed his bowels had evacuated; he no longer had control. Time was illusive and he had no concept how long he had been in the cell. He awoke to noise and looked up, barely able to make out figures in front of him. As they opened his cell, one of them ordered him out.

Ilyas crawled out. He was blindfolded and lifted, as before. He began crying uncontrollably, pleading to go home. They dragged him into a room, ordered him to remove his clothes and sprayed him with cold water. He shivered uncontrollably and cowered as the guards laughed. Thrown only a djellaba, he was dragged to another room. His clothes were stripped off and this time straps were fastened to his wrists. He was lifted just high enough to stand on the balls of his toes. The voice of the interrogator was different than the previous time; it was loud and cruel. A delay in answering the question resulted in a severe blow with a metal rod to Ilyas' limbs. The interrogation continued until Ilyas passed out.

Seventeen

ILYAS AWOKE LAYING on the floor of a large cell occupied by many others. He tried getting up but his limbs were numb. Clenching his fists, Ilyas felt as if his fingers were broken. He stayed on the floor until one of the others gently lifted his head. "You must eat, my brother, or you will die."

He felt a bowl next to his mouth and began sipping the liquid. It had a wretched taste, but Ilyas managed to hold it down. He looked up to see a face he didn't recognize then slipped back into unconsciousness.

Days later he recovered enough to sit up. The cell was filled with tens of anonymous faces. One of them with a long beard and missing front teeth approached. "*Salaam Aleikum!*," the toothless man said.

In a low whisper, Ilyas managed to respond, "*Aleikum Salaam!*"

"You have been asleep for a long time."

"How long?" Ilyas asked.

"At least two days."

There was a brief silence, then the man asked, "Did you sign the paper?"

Ilyas closed his eyes. He recalled the paper vividly. He knew immediately what the interrogator's paper contained. It was a fabricated statement of complicity in the bombing. He wasn't allowed to read it. At first he refused to sign it. He thought he was immune to further torment after the torture to his rectum, hands, legs and feet. But the cigarette burns had become incredibly painful.

"Yes. What will happen now?" he asked the toothless man.

"You will go before the court and be sentenced."

"But I didn't do anything wrong."

"My brother, look around you. Who among us would not say the same as you? Who would you believe?" He walked away.

FOR FIVE DAYS Asafar and Maladh searched for their son, but the authorities gave no information. Asafar located Aban who was stationed at the embassy in Brasilia, Brazil. Frantic with fear and concern, Asafar asked for his brother's help.

"Let me make some telephone calls and I will try to locate Ilyas," Aban told Asafar.

Days later, when Aban received confirmation that Ilyas was being held in a secret place by the authorities, he sent a message through the embassy to his brother.

Two months went by before Asafar and Maladh received any official information about their son. Ilyas was to be put on trial. Despite their pleadings, they were not allowed to see him before the trial.

On the day of the trial, Asafar and Maladh arrived at the Ministry of Justice and begged the official to speak with their son. The court official, a small, slender man with a handlebar moustache and a pronounced limp, would only allow Asafar into the room, ordering Maladh to wait outside. Asafar produced several folded dirham notes and offered them. The official made a grunting sound and led both of them into a tiny, bleak room with only a small bench. They waited for two hours until the door finally opened and a guard led in the prisoner. Asafar was about to complain that it was the wrong person until he recognized his son's dim blue eyes. But for that, Ilyas was unrecognizable. His brown hair was stringy and dirty; his face, gaunt and tight as if it had lost its suppleness. Unaccustomed to seeing their son with a bristled, scruffy beard, he looked many years older than twenty. The filthy djellaba hung down off his bony shoulders. He had a foul stench. Managing to overlook his odor, they embraced him and felt his emaciated frame. They were allowed ten minutes with their son before he was taken out to appear before the judge.

An attorney appointed by the court met with Ilyas for twenty minutes before his trial. Despite Ilyas' pleas of innocence, which mattered little in the face of his previous public disturbance conviction and the fabricated confession declaring his part in the terrorist bombing, his fate was sealed. After reading the dossier and listening to a cursory examination proclaiming his innocence, the judge sentenced Ilyas to twelve years in prison.

Eighteen

ABAN GRIEVED OVER his son's sentence. Despite his best efforts at soliciting the help of government officials, no one dared interfere in any conviction concerning the sensitive international terrorist incident.

Reassigned to Rabàt eight months after Ilyas had been sent to prison, Aban was preparing to leave government service. He had reached the age of forced retirement. He read and researched everything he could find to help his son and learned of an international human rights organization that was charging the monarchy with the imprisonment of innocent bombing suspects. He was hopeful the monarchy's response would bring about a swift prison release for his son.

Several months later, under pressure from international press reports, Aban learned the Ministry of Justice had agreed to review dossiers of all prisoners convicted in the bombing. He also suspected that at the slow pace of the court, it would take many years before Ilyas' case was reviewed. In all likelihood, his son would perish in prison.

Acquainted with certain officials from the Ministry of Justice, after several months Aban learned the names of two judges who were predisposed to providing favors for a price. Aban managed to arrange a meeting with one of the judges at a location outside the city. The meeting proved successful, except for the enormous bribe it would take to free his son—two hundred fifty thousand dirham. Aban was desperate to get his son out of prison, but where would he get the money? Ilyas had already been in prison for twenty-one months and his health was worse than ever. After giving a great deal of thought about contacting the only person who might have the resources to help, Aban decided to place the call.

"Hello, Jude," he said when he heard her answer the telephone.

There was a silence at the other end, then she spoke. "Aban...Is that you? Why are you calling me?"

"Jude, I have something very important to tell you."

"What could possibly be important enough to concern me?"

"It's about Ilyas."

"Who? Who is that?"

"Elijah. Your grandson."

"Aban, I don't even know my grandson."

"Jude, he's grown to be a very handsome, intelligent man. He was enrolled at the university before..." Aban's voice broke.

"He was enrolled? He decided to drop out?" she asked curiously.

"He was arrested and charged with terrorism — the Casablanca bombing, Jude. I assure you he had nothing whatsoever to do with it. He was not involved."

"Then why is he in prison?"

"A person he met at the university had ties to the terrorists. They accused Elijah by association. They tortured him until he signed a confession."

"So what is it that you want?"

"I need twenty-five thousand dollars to get him out of prison."

He heard Jude laugh.

"Is this a joke, Aban? Where am I supposed to get that kind of money? I'm retired now. By the way, how did you find me?"

"Our embassy, they were able to locate you."

"I should have known. Nobody can hide anymore. Aban, even if I had the money, why would I do that for somebody I don't even know?"

"Jude, he's your grandson."

"A grandson I've seen once in my life."

"Please Jude, if you can't do it for him, do it for Victoria."

"Right now I have my own problems, Aban. I can't help you."

Aban sighed. "Okay, Jude. Thank you anyway. *Salaam.*"

Before they hung up, Jude asked, "What does the boy look like?"

"He resembles Victoria more than me. His skin is light and his smile is a happy one, just like his mother. He has boundless curiosity."

"The fact of the matter, Aban, is that the doctor doesn't think I'm going to be around too much longer. So, it's unlikely I can help you. But, if something comes up, how do I reach you?"

"You're not well?"

"Let me get something to write on," she responded, choosing to disregard his question.

"Thank you, Jude."

Nineteen

RARELY HAD JUDE met anyone as polite, courteous and engaging in conversation as Theo. He admired her weaving, he asked about her designs, color selections and techniques; his probing questions ensnarled her in a conversation that covered a myriad of topics that lasted hours. Snow continued falling outside, and as darkness appeared, she invited him to stay for dinner. "I'm not much of a cook," she said. "How about salad or soup?"

"Let me make dinner," Theo asked.

"You don't trust my cooking?"

"Oh no, it's not that. But, that's what I do. I work in a restaurant and one day I'm going to go to culinary school."

Sitting and watching him, Jude was captivated by the methodical way Theo prepared the meal. While she typically threw together whatever she found in the refrigerator, Theo treated every food item gingerly. He was like an artist in the way he worked. The presentation was like something she would expect at an expensive restaurant. Never could she imagine creating anything like the dish he placed on the table — poached chicken breast with a light tarragon sauce, buttered rosemary potatoes and a small salad with vinaigrette dressing. They sat down to eat.

When they were done, Jude looked out the window. Over a foot of snow had accumulated on her courtyard table. "I think you'd better spend the night or you're likely to get stuck somewhere like me."

Theo stood up and walked over to look outside.

"Actually, I'm just house-sitting for my boss who lives a couple of miles up the hill. I guess it won't matter if I don't make it back there tonight."

Theo took the bed in the extra bedroom and in no time he was asleep. Several hours later he woke up to the sound of Jude retching violently. He got up and followed the sound to the bathroom. When he knocked, the door swung partially open. Jude cradled the toilet with her arms as she continued heaving.

He picked up a washcloth, wet it, and held it to her forehead. "Wow, that's the first time my food ever made anybody so sick," he said when she had recovered somewhat. She gave him a pathetic look.

"It ain't the food, honey. If it was, that would be the least of my worries."

Jude looked pale.

"Sorry I woke you. Why don't you go back to bed," she suggested. "I'll be all right in a minute."

"So, does this happen often?" he asked.

"Too often."

"Maybe you should see a doctor."

"That's the last thing I want to do. I have cancer. After I finished the chemo thing, I've never been the same."

Theo was silent for a few minutes. The heaving seemed to stop and he removed the towel from her forehead.

"Can I get you anything?" he asked.

"No, I'll be all right in a second."

Theo walked to the kitchen, poured a glass of water and sat down. About twenty minutes later, when all seemed quiet, he walked back to the bathroom. She was still sitting on the floor, her head lying on the toilet lid. She was asleep.

He placed his hand on her back. "Let's get you to bed." After helping Jude up and into her bed, Theo returned to his room and fell back to sleep.

The following morning the sky was clear and the sun was shining brightly. Jude was up early sipping coffee when Theo walked into the kitchen.

He smiled. "How are you feeling?"

"Okay. Get some coffee," she said. "The cups are in the cabinet above the coffeemaker."

Theo poured a cup and joined her at the table. They were silent.

After taking the last sip, Theo stood up. "You want to take a drive down the mountain to see if we can get your car free before I head out?"

"You've done enough already. I'll call a tow truck from the village."

"Are you sure?"

Jude smiled. "Yeah, there's too much snow on the ground right now. After they plow the road, it'll make it easier." There was a lull in their conversation, then Jude said, "Hope you didn't lose too much sleep last night."

"No, I'm all right." Theo grabbed his coat and left.

Later that evening Jude heard a knock at the door and went to open it. Theo stood on the doorstep carrying a small box.

"I thought you might be hungry. I made it just before I left the restaurant."

Jude smiled. She was happy to see him. "Come in."

Theo walked in and placed the box on the kitchen table.

"How much do I owe you for that?"

"A cup of coffee will take care of it."

OVER THE NEXT week Theo had stopped to visit nearly every day. Because his work schedule constantly alternated between daytime and evenings, Theo's visits occurred at irregular times. When his house-sitting job ended, Theo's visits were less frequent; usually on his days off.

Despite Theo's young age, Jude welcomed his companionship. She looked forward to his visits. Theo had the personality that engendered her confidence and trust. Revealing he was gay only helped to reassure Jude of his honesty and sincerity. With her defensive guard down, Jude spoke to him candidly about personal matters that she would never have revealed to anyone. Their conversations brought a cathartic release, particularly in view of her deteriorating health. He became a healing light to her soul.

One day as Jude sat at her loom passing the shuttle through the warp and banging the beader board, an image of her grandson, Elijah, suddenly came to mind. She imagined his smile resembling Victoria's radiant grin. She felt a longing for her grandson—a stirring emotion like never before. She got out her address book and found the international telephone number. Giving no thought to the time difference, Jude called Aban. When he answered, Jude knew she had awoken him.

"Aban, this is Jude." It took him a few seconds to respond.

"Jude, is everything okay?" he asked, obviously startled awake by the late night call.

"Yes. I forgot the time difference. What time is it there?"

"One-thirty in the morning."

"Well, I'll know better next time. I was just wondering how Elijah is doing."

"Not well. The prison is very overcrowded. They have almost no medical services, and food is scarce. He suffers from depression, constant diarrhea and rheumatism. My brother, who raised him, visits more often. He's allowed to take Ilyas food. Sometimes he can even sneak in medicine. Ilyas looks very thin and weak. I'm so concerned about him, Jude."

"I've been giving a lot of thought to the money you need for his release. Right now I don't have it, Aban. But I do have a life insurance policy..."

Aban interrupted. "Jude, after we spoke I thought about what you said. It was terribly unfair for me to ask for your help. I understand your feelings and I would feel the same way."

"No, it's not that. I was just thinking about him and grew concerned. Would you just keep me informed about how he's doing? In the meantime, I'll see what can be done...about getting money from the life insurance policy, I mean."

"Yes, I will do that. And, thank you for calling."

"You're thanking me for waking you up?" she joked.

"Yes, even at one-thirty in the morning it's good to hear your voice. *Salaam.*"

Twenty

DURING THE WEEKS leading up to Christmas, Theo rarely appeared. Jude's mood turned so sour that Consuelo abbreviated her visits. She came in the morning to share a cup of *atole*, then returned in the evening to bring a plate of food. Late Christmas Eve Jude was dozing on the couch when the sound of the door opening startled her awake. She rose up and saw Theo walk in with a grocery bag in hand.

"What are you doing here?" she asked. Her voice was brusque.

"I thought I'd hang with you tonight."

"Well, don't think you're obligated," she replied as she turned away from him and picked up her book from the coffee table.

"So why all the attitude?" he asked.

"I don't know what you mean," she replied, as she opened her book.

"Just so you know, I finally got a day off tomorrow. It's the first day I've had off in two and a half weeks. It's the holiday parties, Jude. I've been working my ass off, sometimes even doing double shifts. This is the first chance I've had to get up here."

She instantly felt ashamed. She suspected that was the case, but why hadn't he called to tell her. She closed the book and laid it on her lap as she gazed straight ahead.

Theo knew why she was angry. He had spent enough time with Jude to learn how she internalized her emotions. But he also knew how to get to her. He opened the bag. "I brought this bottle of wine from the restaurant to celebrate. You want to try a glass or should I take it home and drink alone?" he asked.

Feigning a grimace, Jude turned around to face him.

"Is that a yes?" he asked.

The grimace turned to a smile.

"Good." Theo walked into the kitchen and uncorked the bottle. Pouring a slight amount in one glass, he filled the other halfway up. Walking into the living room with both glasses, he handed the short pour to Jude, knowing too much alcohol interfered with her drugs. He scooted a chair closer to the wood stove then sat down.

"Consuelo brought some food if you're hungry," Jude said in the nicest tone she could muster.

"Nah, I just need to sit here and sip on this awhile." He placed the glass on the floor, kicked off his shoes and laid his head back on the chair. Within minutes he was asleep.

Jude picked up her book, once again, and began reading. Before an hour had passed, she stood up and went over to awaken him.

"Go to bed," she suggested. "You'll sleep better."

The following day Consuelo joined them at the dinner table as Theo laid out the Christmas feast. After exchanging small gifts, they bundled up and went for a walk in the forest. Leaving Consuelo off at her house, the two returned home and cleaned up. Then Theo put a CD into the player, and sat by the wood stove listening to the music while poring over a culinary magazine. As Jude began to weave, Theo drifted off to sleep.

Over the next year Jude's health progressively declined. Consuelo, who made sure Jude took her medications and ate regularly, came to rely on Theo to run errands. He grew accustomed to picking up Jude's prescriptions and grocery shopping. As Jude's condition grew more tenuous, Theo's visits increased in regularity. It wasn't uncommon for Jude to wake up gagging and too weak to get out of bed. Sensitive to her distress, Theo would quickly rouse from sleep and run to her bedside. During many of those late night and early morning bouts, when they knew sleep had grown elusive, they talked. Theo was fascinated by the many places Jude had visited and people she had met in her freelance career. He loved hearing her stories. She told him about Marty and the many near fatal experiences in their worldwide travels. She told him about his proposal, her refusal, and the wounded look on his face. How she wished she had treated him differently. Theo suggested writing him about her thoughts.

"Maybe," she replied. "I don't know what I'd say to him after all these years."

"Whatever's in your heart."

"Theo, haven't you noticed...my heart's colder than a freezer."

"Yeah, but it's defrosting, Jude." They laughed.

Then one evening, when the retching episodes became more severe and the pain grew more agonizing and her need for food tolerated but a few tablespoons of broth, Jude knew the end was near. Late that night when her symptoms moderated, she shared with Theo the story of Victoria, Aban and Elijah. Jude cried as never before as she gave him the account. Theo remained quiet and listened. When she finished the story, he held her as she drifted off to sleep.

Twenty-one

THE UNUSUAL NATURE of their relationship crossed Theo's mind many times. He couldn't understand how he had become so close to Jude. More than forty years his senior, she still seemed to understand him. Nothing he said shocked her. Not even when he recounted the sexual abuse he endured from his father. Jude's reality was pragmatic. "It's unproductive to allow pain from the past to interfere with life," she told him. Her many stories of calamity in her own life underscored that philosophy.

As another year came to a close, Jude's condition grew so fragile that Consuelo and Theo contacted a hospice agency. Abigale Barela, the hospice nurse, appeared one day and explained to Jude how they could help. Jude consented to receive their services, and after signing a document waiving any resuscitation efforts, the reality of her situation struck her. She grew depressed.

Jude would lie awake late into the night with Theo at her bedside. When she became too weak to carry on a conversation, he'd read to her. On one of those late evenings, Jude surprised Theo with an idea she had formulated. Her idea involved using a portion of her life insurance proceeds to free Elijah from prison. The problem, however, was getting the money to Aban without arousing the Moroccan government's suspicion. Although more than three years had passed since the Casablanca bombing, she suspected that the authorities closely monitored any unusual activity, including the transfers of large sums of money into the country. They needed to find a more clandestine method of transferring twenty-five thousand dollars to Morocco. The two began exchanging ideas.

During her lucid moments they discussed different ideas late into the night. Other times when Jude's pain became so excruciating that morphine was her only relief, she drifted into a coma-like state. She loathed the narcotic for the hallucinations they caused, and the time it took to clear her mind and regain coherence.

As they continued searching for a perfect solution, Theo got the idea of acting as the courier and delivering the money. It was a risky idea, Jude explained, because most countries imposed limits on the amount of currency travelers could import. But the enforcement was generally relaxed and affected mainly travelers suspected of drug smuggling. They talked about it in more detail, and after considering the idea for several nights, Jude finally nixed it. Traveling to a Muslim country with twenty-five thousand dollars was much too dangerous an undertaking. While Theo continued to press his idea, she remained adamant. Seeing how stirred Theo had become with his idea, Jude insisted he promise not to act on it, opting instead to have Aban travel to the United States and assume that risk. Theo reluctantly agreed to her plan, promising he would not travel with the money.

Jude's intention was to gift the remainder of her insurance proceeds to Theo for culinary school. But she also thought to leave Consuelo a token of the proceeds, as well. Finally deciding on how it should be divided, Jude needed to remind herself to discuss it with Theo. But that conversation never took place.

When Theo arrived at Jude's one cold February evening, he found her sitting up in bed. Her face had color, once again. Jude was in good spirits and joking. They were certain Jude's health was on the upswing. She would be back working on her loom in no time, Consuelo predicted.

That evening Jude managed to hold down some food. Their conversation was short. As the night wore on, she drifted in and out of sleep.

At one point Theo felt Jude take his hand and kiss it. "Thank you for being here," she whispered, as she nodded off. Theo remained next to her, covering himself with a heavy blanket to ward off the cold. He fell asleep. In the middle of his dreams he heard Jude whisper something he couldn't understand. The following morning when he awoke, Jude's face had lost its color again. She looked peaceful, he thought, as if her dreams were taking away her pain. As the fog cleared in his mind, his instincts took hold. He rose up. Something was wrong; she had stopped breathing. He touched her face. It was cold. She had no pulse. During the night Jude had died.

Theo remained next to her as tears streamed down his face. He reminisced until the first sign of dawn shone through the window. Then he went to the telephone and called Consuelo, but there was no answer. As usual, she had disconnected the telephone to get her night's rest. Theo called the hospice next. He waited. Within the hour a hospice nurse arrived, followed by a white funeral van. Sometime later a state police officer appeared. When there was nothing more for him to do, Theo gathered his belongings and left Jude's house.

Throughout the week Theo battled with the promise he made to Jude. But at the cemetery standing next to Consuelo, an overriding feeling consumed his soul concerning the obligation toward fulfilling her last wish. He knew that Jude had died regretting she would never see her grandson. It would be a fitting tribute if her grandson visited her gravesite some day. As Jude's casket was lowered in the grave, Theo made a decision. He would deliver the requested amount to Aban, leaving the remainder with Father Bonafacio to hold for Elijah. That way Elijah would be certain of receiving his full inheritance. When Elijah appeared, Theo would take him to Jude's gravesite and share stories about her. Good feelings from within confirmed Theo's decision; it was the right one.

After securing a copy of Jude's death certificate, he completed the life insurance claim forms and a passport application. Theo drove to the post office to mail them off. Six weeks later the insurance check arrived. Then his passport came. He was ready to set the plan in motion. Late one evening he retrieved the small piece of paper buried in his wallet and dialed the telephone number.

"Is this Aban Bashir?" he asked when the voice answered in a foreign language. There was a moment of silence.

"Yes. Who is calling?"

"Mr. Bashir, my name is Theo Jaquez. I was a good friend of Jude Armstrong. I don't know if you received the information but she died in February."

Another moment of silence.

"I had not heard," he replied. It was clear from his voice that Aban was shaken by the news.

"I have the money," Theo said.

"I beg your pardon?"

"The money to get your son out of prison, I have it. It's from Jude's life insurance and that was her last wish."

"Jude told you about Elijah?"

"We were very good friends. I know all about the arrangements you've made to free your son."

"I never believed this would happen," Aban said.

"I'm taking time off from work to travel there. Can we make an appointment to meet?"

"Yes, of course. Let me think for a minute." Aban then began offering suggestions for a meeting location.

The next day Theo visited the bank to cash the insurance check. It took two additional days to get the currency he had requested — five hundred bills in denominations of one-hundred dollars. Theo deposited five thousand dollars in his personal checking account for the trip and left the twenty-thousand with Father Bonafacio.

Theo stopped at a travel agency. So as not to appear too unusual, he booked a week-long visit in Casablanca, writing a check for $2,824 that covered his airfare, hotel and airport transfers. The purpose of the trip, he explained to the inquisitive travel agent, was to see his girlfriend.

Over the next several weeks Theo and Aban spoke on two more occasions to firm up the details of their meeting. The night before beginning his trip, Theo carefully divided the cash in bundles of fifty. His plan was to hide two bundles in his suitcase, one in his carry-on and the two others on his person. While he worried that the suitcase would be out of his control during the flight, he had no better plan. Sleep was uneasy that night, as he grew anxious about the journey.

Arriving at Mohammad V International Airport in Casablanca, Theo cleared immigration and went to retrieve his luggage. Standing in one of the lines that had formed at the Moroccan customs area, he looked over and nodded at Henry, the prying tourist who had befriended him on the airline and again at the restaurant in Utah during their layover. As he made his way to the front, the customs official dressed in a wrinkled, disheveled uniform and talking to another uniformed person standing next to him, waved Theo through without even a glance. Theo caught a taxi to his hotel.

On the first full day in Casablanca, Theo signed up for a tour of the city. The bus driver, a slender, youngish Moroccan with a wide toothy smile, took particular interest in Theo, constantly watching him. At one of their stops Theo noticed the driver smile at him; smiling a devious beam as his hand slid toward his genitals. Theo didn't react and walked away without looking back when the tour ended.

Having never visited a foreign country, Theo was astonished to see so much extravagance amid such poverty. Lavish homes stood next to squalid dwellings. Walking through the many souks, he came across one selling spices. Unable to resist, he went inside and was amazed at the immense variety; deep red paprika, vibrant yellow turmeric, cayenne, cumin, and saffron. For over an hour he remained speaking with the owner and contemplating what to buy. Finally, completing his purchase, Theo found his way to the beach and walked on the soft sand as far as he could go. Always aware of the purpose of his journey and leery of the strange country, Theo returned to the hotel late in the afternoon and stayed in his room the remainder of the evening. Before going to sleep, he opened the room safe one more time just to ensure the bundles of cash were secure.

Close to the appointed time the following day, Theo took a taxi to the Medina where he planned to meet up with Aban. He firmly gripped the black pouch containing the money. His heart beat fast. Arriving there, Theo nervously paced in front of the arches, his left lip slightly twitching and his guttural tic echoing. Suddenly he heard a voice speak to him. An Arab with thinning hair and sunken eyes, dressed in a djellaba, stared at him.

"Aban?" Theo asked.

Aban nodded as his sad, tired eyes continued to stare at him. "Please, let's walk this way," he said.

Theo followed Aban's quick pace. There was no conversation between them as they walked. A few minutes later Aban led him through a doorway off the main street. They walked several levels of stairs into a small room. The room had a desk and several chairs. There was an adjoining room, but all Theo could see was a window. Closing the door as he followed Aban inside, the Moroccan asked, "Did Jude die peacefully?"

"Yes," Theo replied.

"You are a very brave and righteous man to do this."

"Jude was a good friend." He offered Aban the pouch. "How soon will your son be released?"

"I'm not certain. Very soon, *Inshallah.*"

"By the way, there's a name of a Catholic priest inside the pouch that your son needs to contact when he gets out. The priest is holding something else that Jude left Elijah."

"In Morocco, my son is known as Ilyas," Aban corrected. "What is it that Jude left him, if I might know?"

"The remainder of his inheritance." There was a momentary silence, then Theo said, "Okay, well, I guess there's nothing more I need to do here."

"Do you need anything? Is there anything I can assist you with in Casablanca?"

"No, I'm all right. I've managed to find my way around."

Aban extended his hand to Theo. "Thank you, my friend. I am in your debt."

Theo shook his hand and just as he got to the door, Aban called out. "Please, wait one second."

Aban went to the next room and retrieved a box. Handing it to Theo, he said, "This is a small gift to you."

"Thank you. What is it?"

"A craft my people do well here. It's a souvenir from Morocco. I hope it will remind you of our country."

With a slight smile and nod, Theo took the box and left.

ABAN ZIPPED OPEN the pouch and saw the bundles of one-hundred dollar bills. Zipping it shut, he walked into the adjoining room and looked out the window onto the busy street below. He immediately spotted a casually dressed man across the street observing the building. The man appeared to be either European or American. As Aban saw Theo hail a taxi, it was evident that he was the source of the man's interest. When the taxi sped off, the man fixed his eyes on the building for a few seconds before walking away. Aban became frightened. Theo had been followed, but by whom? Was it Interpol? Aban suddenly began wondering whether his phone calls were being monitored. At that moment fear gripped him. He could not go through with the bribe to the judge. They were on to him. What would he do now?

Twenty-two

BACK HOME AFTER traveling in the rain forests of South America since early February, Marty Chenoweth laid his bags on the floor and walked around to make sure everything was as he had left it. The house was cold; so much different from the summer weather he left behind in the southern hemisphere a few days earlier. Away for six weeks writing for a nature newsmagazine about indigenous tribes, mining and timber incursions, and government apathy, Marty knew it would take several days to get his house back in order. He walked to the garage and adjusted the water heater temperature knob from vacation mode. He couldn't wait for a hot shower. Back inside, he strolled into the kitchen and pressed the answering machine message bar. One garbage message followed another until a strong voice with an entirely different message caught his attention. Shaken by the message, he pressed the repeat button.

"Marty Chenoweth, this is Lieutenant Kerry Snyder from the New Mexico State Police. This message is in regard to the death of

Jude Armstrong. We have paperwork appointing you executor of her estate, and I'd like to speak to you. Can you contact me as soon as possible?"

It was as if a lightning bolt had struck him. How could that be? Just one year earlier he had seen her during an overnight stay in Albuquerque on his way to the west coast. It was then that he noticed she was thin and pale. Jude was different; quiet, reflective, introspective. She told him about the cancer, but didn't belabor her condition. Their time was short because she needed to get back to San Lucas. He promised to call more often. And he kept his promise. But whenever he called, their conversations were short. Days before leaving to South America they had spoken. She sounded good. Jude gave no clue the end was so near. Marty picked up the telephone and dialed the number.

Listening to Lieutenant Snyder confirm Jude's death numbed him. Yes, he would travel to Santa Fe soon to settle her estate. After hanging up the phone, random memories of their time together began cycling through Marty's mind. He recalled the time Jude asked about appointing him as her executor. He scoffed, suspecting they would either die together in their journalistic chase or Jude would long survive him. Marty walked to the cupboard, opened a bottle of scotch and poured a generous drink. He sat down; his mind continued churning. Tears streamed down his face as he slowly relished each memory. He refilled his glass several more times before passing out.

On the flight to New Mexico, Marty looked out the aircraft's window gazing at the cloudless sky and surveying the desert below as he wondered about Jude during her last days. He retrieved a letter from his coat pocket that he had found hidden between the stacks of bills, credit card solicitations, and loan offers. It was postmarked shortly before she died. Marty had most of it put to memory, but reread it as he imagined her writing it.

Dear Marty,

I feel my strength slowly fading and my time closing in. My house is wintry cold; the whole damn mountain is cold, and we have several more months before spring arrives. I'm warm only at night, the benefit of a consoling companion. Of late I'm reminded of our many travels and the splendid experiences together, albeit precarious and at times intermittently dangerous. But our stubborn natures drove us to those backwoods and wastelands seeking the next big story and hoping to achieve journalistic immortality. How I enjoyed it, and still envy your tenacity in pursuing our feral craft. You are truly an indulgent and caring soul. Had I been more thoughtful and sensitive in my temperament, I would have recognized that sooner. But in the end, Marty, it was not to be and I have only my regrets and myself to blame.

I don't know how much time I have left, but feel the end approaching rapidly. My hope is to greet it with a steady composure (as best I can under the circumstances) in anticipation of whatever divine providence has apportioned on the other side.

Stay well and live resplendently. You deserve it.

Yours,

Jude

After landing in Albuquerque, Marty steered his rental car onto the interstate and headed toward Santa Fe. One hour later he was in the city and searching for the state police building. Finding it, Marty parked and walked inside. He approached the glass partition and asked to see Lieutenant Snyder. The officer gave him a cursory glance then dialed a number. A few seconds later a tall, slightly balding police officer with a stern gaze and a strapping build appeared.

"Are you looking for me?" he asked, as he approached.

Marty met his stare. "I'm Marty Chenoweth."

Snyder extended his hand. "Let's go down the street for coffee? We can talk there," Snyder suggested.

Marty nodded and the officer led the way out the door. The air was crisp. Snyder's pace was quick and Marty felt his heart race as his respiration adjusted to the city's seven thousand foot elevation. In a few minutes they were seated at a table as Marty began sipping water to relieve his parched throat from heavy breathing.

"How well did you know Ms. Armstrong?" Snyder asked. His tone was stiff, his eyes cold and hard.

"A long time. We were good friends."

"Any relatives? We couldn't find anybody."

Marty thought for a second. In all their time together, Jude rarely brought up her past. He had pieced together that Jude's parents died in a fire, and she was raised by a widowed aunt. After graduating high school, she moved to New York, started journalism school and met someone, but they never married. Jude had a daughter who died young. As far as he knew, there was nobody else.

"Jude never mentioned anybody still living."

As their conversation continued, Snyder's tone seemed to soften. "Her will, made out about seventeen years ago, left everything to a university in New York. We found your number in her address book. There's a bunch of her stuff, paperwork, I mean, that we brought to the station and sifted through. You can take all of it when we get back there."

"Who found her?" Marty asked.

Snyder took a sip of coffee. He was slow in responding, almost as if it were a chore. "Some kid called it in. The paramedics got there first. After one of our officers arrived, the kid left and an old Indian, a neighbor I think, showed up. A hospice nurse was there too."

"Any idea who that kid was?"

"The Indian said the kid had been coming around to help out. Theo was what they called him. That's all she knew."

"How far is San Lucas?"

"Not far...maybe twenty minutes northeast of here. I suspect you're going to want to list her house with a real estate company. My brother-in-law works for one of the best in Santa Fe. I'll give you his card. He'll help you out with anything you need. Give him a call."

"Thanks. I might do that."

Marty's non-committal reply turned Snyder's face sour again. He followed the officer back to the station and took two large envelopes filled with Jude's papers.

Twenty-three

MARTY'S THOUGHTS WERE stirring; his chest felt anxious. It happened every time he sensed a newsworthy story. But this story was personal and it was becoming disturbing.

Early the next morning, in his hotel room, Marty picked up the life insurance documents from Jude's packet of papers. The policy was issued by Standard Assurance of New York for fifty thousand dollars. A beneficiary form stapled to it named the Anderson School of Journalism, New York University as the sole recipient. It was dated March 22, 1984. Searching inside the envelope, he pulled out a folded paper. It was another beneficiary form much like the first. The form was signed and dated one week before Jude's death. Comparing her signature to the first form, Marty noticed that the handwriting was unsteady. There wasn't the free flowing penmanship as the earlier one, but uneven, jagged characters. The signature slanted downward rather than directly across the line. The sole beneficiary named on the second form was Theodoro Jaquez.

Marty found the telephone number for Standard Assurance of New York from the cover sheet and called. After a series of department transfers and conversations with several levels of authority, he finally convinced a supervisor in the claims department to tell him whether funds were disbursed on the policy.

"A check was cut to Theodoro Jaquez for the full face value," the supervisor said.

That's all Marty needed to hear as he plotted the next move. He called Winkfield Hjelle, an old friend.

Wink worked as an underwriter for Global Equity Services, an international life insurance company in the business of insuring persons with high net worth. Wink could access the Medical Information Bureau (MIB) whose vast database maintained medical files on millions of people.

"Wink, I'm investigating a case concerning possible life insurance fraud. Actually, it's personal and concerns a good friend who may turn out to be the victim. What can an MIB search tell me about the suspect?"

"Depends. If he's in the system, the MIB file will list any derogatories like diabetes, mental health problems, nicotine, drugs, like that. Give me a name and address, and I'll check it out."

After providing Wink with the information he had, Marty drove back to the police department to speak with Snyder. Directed to his office, Marty walked in.

"Have you called my brother-in-law yet?" Snyder asked, not bothering to get up from his desk

"Nope, I haven't gotten that far. I figure sometime next week," Marty replied as he took a seat.

"I told him about you, so he's expecting your call," Snyder replied with an admonishing tone. "So what can I do for you?"

"I was wondering if an autopsy was ever done on Jude."

"Nope, it wasn't necessary. She was terminal. Why are you asking?"

"I'm not sure how relevant any of this is. Maybe I'm just paranoid." Marty related the information he had gathered.

"So you think Theo may have conned your friend into signing over her life insurance money?"

"Like I said, I'm not sure."

"You think he had something to do with her death, too?" Snyder asked.

"I don't know..." Suddenly Marty's cell phone chimed. Reaching for it, he glanced at the digital window. "I've been waiting for this call. I might have more on Theo."

Marty flipped open the cell. "Hey, Wink, what's up?" Marty noticed Snyder's irritated expression at the interruption.

"I got an MIB hit on your guy."

"What did you find out?"

"About two years ago Theo Jaquez applied for life insurance from a company called 'The Seville' and was denied coverage. He's a big-time druggie. The MIB record shows an addiction to opiates – heroin. Aside from that, he's asthmatic, a smoker, and has trouble getting it up."

"Wow, anything else?"

"Nope, that's it."

"That tells me enough. Thanks, Wink." Snapping his phone shut, Marty looked over at Snyder. "My source confirms that Jaquez is a heroin druggie."

"How reliable is your source?"

"It came from Theo's medical files. So I'd say it's right on."

Snyder puckered his lips and sat back on his chair as he contemplated the matter. "I'll write up what you've told me and we'll open an investigation. If you come across anything else, I expect you'll let me know?"

Snyder's request was more like a demand. Marty decided not to quibble. "No problem," He stood up and left.

THE FOLLOWING MORNING as Marty headed into the restaurant for breakfast, the headline in the newspaper dispenser outside the door caught his attention. Dropping coins into the slot, he pulled out a copy.

Police Search for Arbol Verde Drug Abuser
Suspected of Murder and Fraud

Twenty-four

HENRY AND LAURA Karlson were seasoned travelers. Henry had retired seven years earlier and the couple relocated to Santa Fe. Having traveled to Italy and the Vatican the prior year, their destination for Easter this year was Henry's choice. He chose Morocco where they would join the Easter group tour for twelve days through historical cities in that country, then move on to Portugal.

They arrived at six in the morning at the Albuquerque airport, two hours earlier than their scheduled departure. After making their way through the security maze, the couple proceeded on to the assigned departure gate. The longer they waited, the thicker the crowd grew. Based on the throng of passengers waiting to board, the plane would be carrying a full load, Henry surmised. Since the twin tower incident, Henry, a former corporate security director, routinely studied people in his environ for anything suspicious. Surveying the crowd, a nervous young man continued to catch his eye. The man was tall and slender with a moustache and goatee styled in the manner used by young people. He had wide, narrow dark eyes, and brown skin; clearly Hispanic. He wore a blue Hilfiger sweatshirt and baggy levis. A real looker for the ladies, Henry thought. He was traveling alone and kept a sturdy grip of the small carry-on bag as he nervously paced the corridor. Henry discretely kept eyeing the young Hispanic until their boarding group was called. Henry positioned himself behind his wife as they shuffled in the crowd inching closer to the jet bridge entrance.

Once inside the plane, they found their seats in the aft section. Laura took the window seat. Henry always preferred the aisle because it was easier to stand up, stretch his legs, and get to the restroom. The flight would take them to Salt Lake City then to Paris and finally to Casablanca, Morocco. As he watched the passengers slowly filing into the aircraft, it annoyed him to see a fleshy, pucker-mouthed woman with carry-on luggage the size of a packing crate, trying to force it into the overhead compartment and creating a traffic jam. Right behind her, Henry noticed the young Hispanic again. When pucker-mouth finally managed to fit the luggage overhead and clear the aisle, the young Hispanic headed toward them and took the aisle seat across from Henry. Henry waited until everyone was finally seated before attempting a conversation. He looked over. "How's your day going?" he asked.

"Okay," was the curt reply.

He appeared anxious; uneasy.

"You heading to Salt Lake?" Henry asked in the nicest tone he could muster.

The young man's tone softened. "No, Casablanca, Morocco."

"Well, that's where we're heading. Are you joining a tour group there, too?" Henry asked.

His response was slow. "No, I'm meeting my girlfriend."

"Sounds like a plan. By the way, my name's Henry...Henry Karlson." He extended his hand.

"I'm Theo Jaquez."

Before Henry could probe deeper, a flight attendant approached Theo. The boy's face instantly drained of color, or so it seemed to Henry.

She bowed down and asked,"Would you mind terribly trading seats with another passenger who'd like to sit next to his wife here? He has a window seat in the forward section."

Theo looked over at the woman sitting next to him. She smiled at him.

He took a deep breath. "No, I don't mind." Unbuckling the seat belt, he reached down for the carry-on stowed under his feet, then stood up and moved forward.

Arriving in Casablanca the following morning, the passengers paraded to the immigration counter and then to the luggage carousel. While in line at the customs area, Henry looked over and located Theo clinging tightly to his carry-on bag and a small suitcase. Henry nodded. Theo returned the nod.

After clearing customs, Henry and Laura walked out to the main lobby where they connected with a representative holding up a Brockway Tours sign. As they were led through the airport to a waiting bus, Henry glanced back to see Theo exchanging currency.

Early the following day Henry and Laura joined their tour for a morning excursion through Casablanca. At noon the couple found a nice outdoor cafe with a view of the ocean. As they waited for their order, Laura pointed out to the beach. "Isn't that the young man you spoke to on the plane?"

"Sure is. He's meeting his girlfriend here. But my instincts tell me there's something strange about him."

"It's none of our business," Laura replied. "Remember, you're retired; you're not in security anymore."

Henry's eyes followed Theo until he was out of sight.

The next day, after returning from a morning tour of the Cathedral du Sacre Coeur and the Hassan II mosque, Laura decided to change shoes so they could stroll through downtown Casablanca. Meandering through the reception area of their hotel, Henry walked outside. Across the street was the entrance to the old Medina. The crowd was thick. As he glimpsed the parallel arches of the Medina, suddenly his eyes darted back. He thought he recognized the figure by the arches. It was Theo and this time he was clutching a dark pouch. The thought of crossing the street to greet him crossed Henry's mind until he observed someone approach Theo. It was an older man dressed in a brown djellaba. Their greeting was awkward; their exchange brief before the two hurriedly walked away toward downtown. Unable to contain his curiosity, Henry tailed them from across the street. He walked two blocks until they disappeared into a building. Henry waited. A few minutes later Theo reappeared outside the building carrying a small box. Henry observed Theo hail a taxi and speed off. As Henry walked back to the hotel, a disconcerting feeling grated in his gut. It was like the time he came across an employee copying classified company papers after hours. Unable to explain his actions, the employee was arrested and charged with the theft of confidential documents. Henry received a commendation.

Approaching his hotel, the disturbing feeling instantly changed to remorse as he glanced at Laura with her arms folded across her waist. She was not happy.

Twenty-five

FOR WEEKS ABAN monitored his every move, walking wherever he went in the city to spot who might be keeping surveillance on him. Returning home, he would immediately head to the front room of his apartment and look through the sheers out the window. But there was never anyone. He was particularly careful when speaking on the telephone, ensuring his conversations would not provoke the curiosity of the authorities who might be listening on his line. As many precautions as he took, Aban could find nothing out of the ordinary to suggest the authorities were on to him.

While still suspicious, Aban couldn't risk going through with the bribe to the judge. Not yet, anyway. Bribes were all too common in getting around the typical government's bureaucracy. But they had to be done discreetly. Otherwise, envious co-workers were likely to report the matter for their own gain or favor. Aban knew that his bribe to the judge would be regarded as a very serious matter. If discovered, the consequences for his actions would be severe. His small pension would be taken away and he would be sentenced to a long prison term. Despite that, something about the arrangement didn't seem right. How was it possible that the judge could so easily purge Ilyas prison term with the stroke of his pen? Was the Judge boasting from arrogant pride or exaggerating to extort his money?

Had he still been working for the diplomatic corps, Aban was certain his influence and the money received from Jude would open doors to those officials who he knew for certain had legitimate authority to free his son from prison. However, since he was forced to retire, all Aban had to rely on were old friendships he had nurtured during his tenure with the government. One friend he trusted implicitly was Massin El Quazini. Having met Massin the first time at the embassy in Santiago, Chile, Aban showed the agricultural officer around the city. After learning that Massin was born in a village close to Setta, Aban brought up common acquaintances, and a friendship began forming. Some diplomats within the embassy suspected Massin was an intelligence agent, but that didn't detract Aban from pursing their friendship. They continued to stay in contact and each time Aban traveled back to Rabàt, he never failed to contact Massin and catch up on family, mutual acquaintances and rumors within the government. Since retiring, however, he had not spoken to Massin. Aban called and invited his friend for tea at a local café.

Arriving early, Aban sat at an outside table. Several minutes later Massin arrived. Aban stood up and greeted his friend in the traditional way, by shaking his hand and then touching his heart. It was a sign of respect that Aban always carried out regardless of who he was greeting. After exchanging friendly conversation for several minutes about the health of their families, they began their conversation about general matters. It was good speaking to his friend again, as he missed all of the connections he had become accustomed to in the diplomatic corps. As they sipped on mint tea, Aban decided to broach the reason for the meeting.

"Massin, I have a situation that is very sensitive and I am unsure how to proceed. Maybe you, my friend, can give me some direction."

"I will do my best."

"I have never told you about this situation because I did not want to burden you. Three and one-half years ago my son was sent to prison. My son is a good Muslim. He was studying at the university in Casablanca and had the misfortune of befriending someone who was involved with those who carried out the bombings in that city. My son was not involved with the terrorist group, *Salafia Jihadia*. But only because of his acquaintance with one of their members, he was convicted as an accessory and sentenced to twelve years in prison. I say this to you sincerely and truthfully, that my son is innocent of what he is accused of doing."

"Your son is still in prison?"

Aban lowered his head as he responded. "Yes."

"How is he?"

"Not well. Slowly he is dying. My son is only twenty-four and he looks like an old man. He is slowly giving up hope every time we visit him."

"What is it that you are asking of me?"

"I have heard that His Majesty is benevolent and has pardoned many prisoners in the past. My question to you is how can I petition consideration for a pardon for my son?"

Massin was silent for a few minutes as he thought about the request. "Aban, to my knowledge there have been very few prisoners related to the Casablanca bombing released from prison. Many of those released were foreign visitors who were never directly involved, but happened to get embroiled by some accident, coincidence or stroke of bad luck. As a humanitarian gesture, His Majesty granted those prisoners a pardon. While the Ministry of Justice has attempted to quell the international criticism that many citizens were unjustly convicted, as was your son, it has done little to carry out a promise to review those cases. There is one small way I may be able to help you."

"Please, Massin, anything you can do would be a great help."

"I belong to a yacht club in Casablanca and once each month we schedule an outing. One of our members works in the office responsible for making recommendations on the grant of reduced sentences and prison pardons to His Majesty. I know this to be true because very recently he told us of over thirty-three thousand cases that had been recommended by his office and granted by His Majesty. When I meet with this member next month, I will take him aside and speak to him about your son."

"You should know that my son was born in the United States. Ilyas is unaware of his dual citizenship because he was raised by my brother's family in Casablanca since he was an infant."

"I will relay that information to my friend."

"I would be forever in your debt, Massin. Please also relay that I have sufficient resources to cover any expenses that may arise in the preparation of the petition."

"I shall do so."

Aban left the meeting with Massin elated for the glimmer of

hope. He was certain Massin had understood the inducement he was offering. If Massin's friend had any significant influence in the pardon process, the offer should interest him. After more than three years his prayers might finally be answered. The following day Aban traveled to Casablanca to visit with Asafar and Maladh.

It had been many months since Aban had seen his brother. Arriving at their home, Aban noticed that Asafar had aged considerably. His hair and beard had grayed and his face, wrinkled. His eyes appeared sunken in their sockets. Asafar rarely smiled anymore. Aban knew that each month Asafar and Maladh went to the prison for a visit, his brother's pain intensified at seeing Ilyas continuing to deteriorate. Since only two relatives were allowed one visit monthly, he accompanied Asafar only a few times a year, consigning the other visits to Maladh.

Maladh went to fill the kettle with water and prepare the mint tea. Aban sat across the table from Asafar. "I have some good news of renewed hope for freeing Ilyas from prison, *Inshallah.*"

Asafar gazed at him with interest. "What news?"

Aban told them of his meeting with Massin and his offer to solicit help from his friend.

"Will he do it?"

"I will wait to hear from Massin after they meet next month."

"You will let me know then?"

"Of course, my brother."

Twenty-six

A MAP LED Marty to a long winding dirt road up a mountain. Passing several gates and a few small pastures, he took the turnoff that steered directly to her house. He knew it was Jude's by the large Sedona pottery vats decorating her garden. He had seen them before outside her Virginia townhouse with its traditional colonial design. Jude thought they brought perfect balance to her exterior, but to him they looked out of place. They looked much better at the San Lucas house.

The exterior was plain light brown stucco similar to other houses he had passed. Her house sat on a large parcel with a well-worn fence in front. He got out, opened the gate, and drove in. An orchard of trees stood in front; the branches were just waking up from their winter hibernation. To the back he could see a rock garden that banked up a steep hill. He walked up to the porch, unlocked the door and went inside.

The house was cold. Placed opposite the large picture window that looked out on the nearby mountains was a loom. He suspected the afternoon sun warmed the room comfortably. A wood stove stood on one corner. A couch, a few overstuffed chairs and a coffee table were placed haphazardly around the room. Next to the living room was the dining area — the table filled with brightly colored yarn cones. Behind it was a tiered bookcase with more stacked yarn. He walked down a short hallway and into a bedroom — Jude's room, he suspected. The bed was made up and everything seemed to be in its place.

Walking back to the hallway and into the kitchen, Marty sat down at the small table. He opened the first envelope he'd brought and began leafing through the papers again. Copies of her death certificate were clipped together. He set it aside. Her last will and testament was brief — just four pages. He read it quickly then laid it down. Some unopened business letters from a bank, a credit card company, hospice material, doctor and hospital bills, and utility bills, all of which he piled on the table. Picking up the second envelope, he found her checkbook; it had a balance of $754.29. Sliding out the remaining documents, he began perusing them. An investment company report showed a breakdown of her monthly annuity. Next were letters from social security and her health insurance.

Suddenly Marty heard a knock at the door. He stood up and walked over to find a stocky Native American woman standing just outside.

"Hello, I'm Consuelo Soto. I live just down the street. I was good friends with Jude. I kind of keep my eye on her house to make sure everything is okay."

"Please come in. I'm Marty Chenoweth."

Consuelo gave him a quick once-over. "Jude told me about you."

"I was out of the country. I didn't hear until I got back."

"I figured something like that. Jude told me you traveled a lot. That's what I told the police."

"I talked to Jude just before I left. She sounded fine. I didn't know she was so bad off."

Consuelo nodded her head slightly. "Some days Jude was good and other days not so good. To me she also seemed like she was recovering just days before she died. But you never knew with her. She didn't like to complain. She died during the night and the following day I saw a lot of commotion here. That's when I came over and talked to the police."

"I understand someone named Theo was with her before she died?" Marty asked.

Consuelo looked away. "Yes."

"In her will, Jude appointed me to take care of her estate. So, I'd like to talk to Theo. Do you know where he lives?"

"No."

"Do you know how I can reach him?"

"No."

Marty sighed wondering why Consuelo was protecting Theo. He suspected she knew more than what she was telling him. "Jude told me how close she felt toward you. She admired your weaving, and told me you had helped her so much when she was ill."

"We saw one another almost every day. Jude was my best friend."

"After I get her papers in order, I'll be selling most of her things and putting her house on the market. Jude didn't have any relatives and...well, I think she would have wanted you to have whatever you would like. Give me a few days to get things in order and then you can come through." He turned sideways to allow her to get a clear view of the room. "As you can see, she has lots of yarn you might want."

Consuelo blushed. "Thank you." She turned and began walking out the door. Stopping briefly, she looked back, "He works at The Seville."

"The Seville," Marty repeated.

"Theo, he works at that restaurant in Santa Fe."

"Thanks."

Marty's journalistic curiosity was kicking in. What would make Jude change her life insurance beneficiary days before she died? And why would she leave it all to Theo rather than to Consuelo? The deathbed bequest didn't fit Jude's character. She never acted impetuously unless she had good reason. The thought of a swindling parasite taking advantage of a vulnerable victim stirred in his mind. He couldn't wait to hear Theo's explanation.

Twenty-seven

EACH DAY PASSED as if in slow motion. While rarely having been observant of daily prayer, Aban took out his prayer rug and beseeched divine intercession five times a day. Occasionally he would find himself staring at his telephone hoping to receive a call from Massin. Finally, the call came on a Sunday morning. Massin's tone of voice never altered enough to determine his feelings or emotions when he spoke. That was probably a learned trait required in his job, Aban surmised. So, during their brief phone conversation it was impossible to predict how the offer had been received by his friend. They arranged to meet several hours later at the same café as before.

As was his practice, Aban arrived early. When Massin got there, they greeted one another in the traditional manner, then Massin told of his conversation with Rajae, his friend from the yacht club. Massin related the facts concerning Ilyas' imprisonment to Rajae then inquired about a pardon.

Rajae had replied, "My friend, I've heard that story many, many times. Hundreds of prisoners say they are innocent of the activities they have been accused of committing. My job is to determine which among them are more innocent than the others."

"What can be done in this matter?" Massin had asked.

"The procedure must be followed. Your friend, what is his name?"

"Aban Bashir."

"And where does he live?"

"In Rabàt"

"Where is his son imprisoned?"

"Sidi Kascen."

"Inform your friend that he must secure a lawyer to file formal papers requesting a pardon for his son. I can do nothing until the proper papers are filed. Then, we will review the matter and make our recommendations. There is no deviation in the system, so I am unable to be of any help to your friend at the present time."

When Massin had finished relating his conversation, Aban asked, "Did you mention to Rajae that I am able to pay any expenses that may be imposed?"

Massin replied. "For as long as I have known Rajae, he has been a person of great integrity. He is also very intelligent and understood everything I told him very clearly. Rajae is a loyal servant of His Majesty and is both truthful and honest—small commodities as you know. I am sorry that I was unable to help you, Aban."

Aban returned home dejected by Massin's failed attempt. As he sat contemplating what to do next, Aban was tempted to return to the judge at the Ministry of Justice. But each time he thought about that option, his instincts kept telling him that it was the wrong choice. Aban was desperate of finding some way to free his son. Maybe the thing to do was to find a lawyer to file the paperwork, just as Rajae suggested. But like the promised review of the dossiers by the Ministry of Justice, every government process worked at a measured pace, which happened to be incredibly slow in Morocco.

Aban knew he needed to notify his brother about the bad news. But it pained him to see his brother suffering so much. The bad news would only grieve him more. Aban decided to wait until the following week to travel to Casablanca. Maybe by then he would have decided on whether to bribe the judge or contact a lawyer.

The following day while Aban looked through the newspaper and waited for his morning tea at the café, his eyes immediately fixed on a short article concerning Sidi Kascen prison. Many of the prisoners convicted in the Casablanca bombing were on a hunger strike, the article reported. Two had already died. But officials denied the prisoners' accounts of poor conditions, declaring all prisoners were being treated decently and humanely. The article gave no additional information. Distraught after reading the article, Aban stood up, placed a coin on the table and walked out before receiving his tea. Arriving home, Aban phoned the judge only to learn he was on leave until the following week.

Four days after his meeting with Massin, Aban received a strange phone call. The caller identified himself as Ali Kibal, a friend of Rajae. He requested that Aban meet with him late in the evening at his office. Aban agreed.

Shortly before sunset Aban arrived outside the location of Ali's office. The area was a large complex with many different types of souks. At that hour it was busy and jammed with people. He walked around several times before asking for directions to the address. After several more attempts, he finally located a long corridor that he traversed before reaching the address. He knocked. A few seconds later a man wearing a brown djellaba appeared. The man was tall and thin. He had dark features and a stern face.

"I am Ali Kibal," he said. "Welcome."

Ali invited Aban into the foyer and escorted him through a series of rooms to an office. "Please, sit down."

Aban took a seat as Ali excused himself and left the room briefly. The room was spacious and orderly; several large, intricately woven rugs lay on the tile floor. The wall to his right was lined with books. Two long tables were placed behind the ornate, dark wood desk; neatly arranged files, manuscripts and books lay on top. A computer screen sat to the right of the desk. Two high rectangular windows allowed light into the room. But since dusk had set, the overhead incandescent lighting provided only a pale glow.

Returning to the room, Ali closed the door and, rather than sitting behind his desk, moved a chair next to Aban to face him. A small table separated them.

"I understand your son is incarcerated at Sidi Kascen prison and you are attempting to gain his release?"

Aban was unsure how to respond. For all he knew, the man could be working for the police trying to trap him. "What is this all about?" Aban asked.

"Please forgive my impertinence. I am an attorney. One of my specialties is representing clients attempting to avert the government's bureaucracy."

At that moment there was a knock on the door. A middle-age woman entered carrying a tray with a kettle and two cups. She placed the tray on the table. Aban noticed the woman wore no headscarf.

"Do you take your tea sweetened?" Ali asked.

"No, I've given up sugar."

After serving the mint tea, the woman walked out, closing the door behind her.

"Let me be very frank. Rajae spoke with me about your son. He has reviewed Ilyas' dossier."

"But how is that possible?"

"Your friend provided him with the information."

"I see. And what is his conclusion?"

"We believe we can help you."

"How much will it cost me?" Aban asked.

Ali gazed at Aban thoughtfully. "I sense you've attempted enticements before?"

"In all honesty, yes. But I have not followed through with it."

"Someone from the Ministry of Justice?" Ali asked, his eyebrows raised.

Aban was impressed by Ali's understanding of the backstreet process. "Yes, as a matter of fact."

"Then you and your son are very lucky. It's no coincidence that shortly before the prisoner is allegedly cleared to be released, he is found dead in prison. And the money exchanged for the judicial pardon is never returned."

"How do you know that?" Aban asked, recalling his jaded view of the judge.

"I know many things. In my work I have access to much information."

There was a momentary silence before Ali continued. "As I was saying, your son's dossier has been thoroughly reviewed. He is a good candidate for a pardon from His Majesty. However, there is one condition that must be imposed upon your son's release."

"Condition? What kind of condition?"

"Your son was born in the United States. Accordingly, it is possible to gain his release under authority granting amnesty by His Majesty to foreign born visitors who are incarcerated in Morocco."

"But my son is a citizen of Morocco."

"I'm aware of that, but for these purposes we believe Ilyas holds citizenship in both countries. Therefore, it is possible to invoke this authority on the condition that your son leaves Morocco within forty-eight hours of his release."

Aban was momentarily stunned. "So Ilyas cannot remain here with his family?"

"I'm afraid not."

"Is this permanent?"

"I cannot say."

"Would Ilyas be provided a passport and visa?"

"Yes."

"And where would he be sent?"

"Well, that's completely up to you and to your son."

Aban paused for a few seconds before speaking; his mind deliberating what he should do. "You may not be aware that Ilyas knows nothing about being born in the United States. My wife died when he was an infant, and he was raised by my brother. My family has remained silent about that matter, ashamed that Ilyas' mother was a Christian. So Ilyas believes Asafar is his father. No one has ever told him the truth."

"Yes, I am aware of that. If maintaining the secret is your concern, as you well know, government officials in Morocco, particularly those in the prisons, never give reasons for their actions. I suspect Ilyas will be told nothing but that he must leave Morocco."

"How soon can this happen?"

"Let me first tell you before proceeding further that my work commands substantial remuneration. Just to be perfectly clear, I do not accept enticements. My work is always performed within the rules prescribed by the laws of Morocco."

"How much to get my son out of prison?"

"To gain your son's release under the conditions we discussed?"

"Yes."

"Two-hundred thousand dirham."

In less than a half-breath Aban agreed to Ali's terms.

After the meeting with Ali, Aban could not contain his joy. While it distressed him that Ilyas would not be allowed to remain in Morocco, it was possible that his son could return some day. Unable to keep the news to himself, Aban drove directly to Casablanca. He arrived less than two hours later. Asafar and Maladh were still up.

"I have some important news for you about Ilyas."

"The meeting between Massin and his friend went well?" Asafar asked.

"No, it did not go well. Or at least I was made to believe that."

"Then, what is the news?"

"I have been given assurances that Ilyas will be pardoned by His Majesty very soon."

"How soon?"

"Throne Day, the eighth anniversary of the succession of His Majesty."

For the first time he could remember, Asafar beamed a smile. "That is not so far away."

"No, it is not. But I'm sorry to tell you there is a harsh condition attached to Ilyas release?"

"What condition?"

"He cannot remain in Morocco...at least for the time being."

Asafar's smile faded, once again, to a somber frown. "But why?"

"It's a technical matter that has to do with his release. But I suspect Ilyas could move to Spain and possibly be allowed an occasional visit. After all, he will have a passport from His Majesty."

Asafar sat and tried to understand what he had heard. "Are you certain Ilyas will be released Throne Day?"

"That is what I have been told."

Asafar stood up and hugged Aban as tears streamed down his face. He would begin counting down the days to his son's release.

Twenty-eight

MONSIGNOR KEELER WAS anxiously awaiting Father Bonafacio's arrival as he re-read the newspaper article. Having recently returned from a gathering of prelates in Rome where the subject of sexual abuse was discussed, Monsignor Keeler, from the Office of the Archdiocese, knew exactly what steps needed to be taken. The matter had to be handled delicately in order to prevent further damage and protect the church's culpability and liability. Monsignor Keeler had already spoken with the attorney for the archdiocese. After this initial meeting with Father Bonafacio, their next meeting would be with the attorney to begin documenting the priest's history and the progression of the abuse. When the matter was fully documented, Father Bonafacio would be transferred to another diocese and required to undergo psychiatric treatment. If the prognosis revealed that the priest was not a chronic pedophile or unlikely to repeat the behavior, Father Bonafacio would be placed under the close scrutiny of parish authorities in a new diocese. If his condition was beyond repair, defrocking would be recommended to Rome.

Then there was the matter of the sustainability of the three El Pastor parishes. Obviously Father Bonafacio could no longer return to his pastoral duties as before, and his work would be vastly curtailed. Monsignor Keeler would temporarily assign another priest or possibly several priests from the diocese to conduct Saturday confessions and Sunday services, as well as carry out other duties to keep the parishes functioning.

Finally, Monsignor Keeler would order the priest to speak to no one, outside of church officials, about the matter. There was an established media protocol demanded by Rome, and his aim was to follow it to the letter.

When Father Bonafacio arrived, the housekeeper immediately escorted him through the foyer, down the hall and into Monsignor Keeler's office. The priest had never visited the monsignor's residence and was amazed at the exquisite furnishings. Dressed in his black cassock with red trim and sitting in his leather high back chair behind the large cherry-wood desk, Monsignor Keeler gave the priest a disgusted gaze, refusing to even rise to greet him. Father Bonafacio noted the rebuke. Monsignor Keeler put his hand out, motioning for the priest to take a seat. As Father Bonafacio sat down, Monsignor Keeler began speaking.

"I've had some experience handling these matters before, so I know what I speak of. Obviously, the relationship with this young man has been occurring for many years..."

Unaccustomed to being treated so offensively, Father Bonafacio turned red-faced. He interrupted the diocese official. "There is nothing obvious and I resent your implication. I have not had a sexual relationship with Theo Jaquez. I have never had sex with the young man. And I have never violated my vows of chastity since I became a priest. The only obvious thing here is that you have chosen to believe this fabrication in the newspaper. It is completely untrue and I challenge anyone to prove otherwise."

Surprised by the priest's adamant denial, Monsignor Keeler remained silent for a few moments studying the priest. In past experiences, most of the accused priests became contrite during the initial meetings. Then Monsignor Keeler said, "Let me assure you Father Bonafacio that we have a procedure for dealing with sexual scandals such as these. However, in order to effectuate it, we must have your cooperation. The diocese is willing to stand behind you and assist you in any way we can. But, before we can do that, you must acknowledge the transgression and agree to undertake a rehabilitation process."

Father Bonafacio's voice was growing loud and fiery. "Apparently you do not care to listen to what I have to say. If I were guilty, I would do as you ask. But I will repeat for your benefit again that I am not guilty. The allegation came from the father of the boy who is, in fact, the abuser as well as a heroin addict."

Father Bonafacio's face was filled with anger. "I appeared here this afternoon at your request, Monsignor Keeler, and it's obvious to me that you have formulated your opinion based on innuendo and fabrication before even hearing what I have to say. It's outrageous what Theo's father has done to my reputation in the community. But I challenge you to examine my work in all three parishes and find one single parishioner that will back up Sixto Jaquez. If you can do that, I will leave the priesthood immediately. There will be no need for the Church to intervene."

"Well, now, Father Bonafacio, maybe I was a bit precipitous in my assumptions." Monsignor Keeler's tone became indulgent. "It was not my intention to pass judgment before giving you an opportunity to defend yourself."

"In all the time I have known Theo Jaquez we have remained friends. Our relationship has never been sexual in any way whatsoever. In spite of his dysfunctional family, Theo is one of the most honest persons I have ever known. He visited the rectory last evening to offer assurances that the police charges in the San Lucas matter are untrue and in due time he will provide the necessary proof. After having dinner with me, Theo left the rectory."

Father Bonafacio's manner appeared earnest and sincere and

Monsignor Keeler wanted to believe what he said. But there was still the matter of the community recrimination to consider. How would the diocese handle that issue? "What are your thoughts about the emotional backlash from the parishioners and the communities you serve?"

Father Bonafacio's composure slowly returned as he contemplated the question. "It's mixed. I've received telephone calls of support and other calls, mostly anonymous, that were not pleasant."

"Do you believe you can work through all of this and resume your duties in the three parishes until things settle down and Mr. Jaquez vindicates himself of these charges?"

Father Bonafacio took a few seconds before answering. "I don't know. But I am willing to try."

Father Bonafacio's passion was tugging at Monsignor Keeler's instincts telling him that the Arbol Verde priest was unlike any of those others he had dealt with in the past. Monsignor Keeler was inclined to give him the benefit of the doubt. But if any other similar charges surfaced, he would relieve the priest immediately and invoke the pedophile procedures.

His next challenge would be far more difficult. How would he convince the archbishop to support Father Bonafacio in the midst of the scandal? Monsignor Keeler stood up, walked around his desk and approached the priest with an outstretched hand.

"I believe you and at this point I will support you, Father Bonafacio. I will discuss our meeting with the archbishop. I can't guarantee what will happen, but you've given me a great deal of new insight into this matter. Let's pray that the entire matter will be resolved quickly and everything will return to normal. In the meantime I intend to remain in close contact with you and assist you in any way I can. Thank you for this visit."

Monsignor Keeler was relieved to end the meeting. Of all his duties within the archdiocese, he detested these types of meetings the most because of his aversion to pedophile priests. But Father Bonafacio was different; he didn't fit into that mold. Monsignor Keeler only hoped that his instincts about the priest were correct.

Twenty-nine

IT WAS EARLY evening when Marty drove to The Seville Restaurant. Considering the restaurant's prime location near the Santa Fe plaza, he suspected it was upscale and pricey. The parking valet outside confirmed his suspicions as he navigated past him and parked on the street. Walking into the restaurant, he gave it a quick once-over before the maître'd appeared.

"Do you have a reservation?" the maître'd asked in a

pretentious tone.

During his long career Marty had seen that same snooty attitude too many times. "Yes, the concierge in my hotel made the reservation."

"And what hotel might that be?" he asked casting a patronizing gaze.

Although staying at a Motel 6, Marty knew about the exclusive hotel on the plaza. "The Guadalupe," he replied, matching the stare.

The maître'd's tone changed instantly. "I'm sure we can seat you tonight. Follow me, please."

The maître'd pulled out the chair and Marty sat down. The table was set with a white table cloth, linen napkins, crystal water and wine glasses, and more pieces of silverware than he would ever need. A few minutes later when the waiter appeared, Marty ordered his usual scotch and soda. When the drink arrived, Marty asked,"Is Theo around tonight?"

"Theo?" the waiter repeated.

"Yeah, Theo Jaquez. He still works here doesn't he?"

"Oh, Theo, he's one of our chefs, but he doesn't usually work at night...he works the day shift. I think he's out for the week, though. Let me ask the owner."

"Do you mind if I speak to the owner?"

"No sir, not at all. Would you like to order now?"

"I'll wait."

A minute later a stout, rosy-nosed man appeared wearing checkerboard trousers and a baker's hat. "Excuse me, you were asking about Theo?"

His accent was strong, either German or Austrian, Marty guessed.

"Yeah, I was hoping to speak to him tonight."

"He's on vacation. He doesn't get back until next week."

"Do you know how I can reach him?"

Before responding, Marty sensed the owner's hesitation and decided to sweeten his need for the information. "I'm just visiting and a mutual friend asked me to look him up. I have something for him."

The owner was sizing up Marty. Apparently convinced, he replied, "You can talk to his landlady. Theo rents an apartment on Priego Street, next to the episcopal church. It's the house to the right."

Marty finished his drink, left money on the table and walked out.

Early the following morning Marty drove to Priego Street. Locating the house, he parked. The landscape was neglected and the house, probably built in the twenties or thirties, needed a coat of new stucco and lots of work. The small detached garage, clearly built later, was probably a storehouse for old junk. He saw a young man walking his bicycle down a concrete sidewalk between the house and the garage.

Marty got out and walked to the edge of the driveway.

Probably in his twenties, the man with the bike wore a skull cap and dark glasses. He had pierced rings on his nose and lips, and large round black rings in his earlobes. The man looked scary.

"Theo Jaquez?" Marty asked.

"Nope. He lives in the second apartment in back, but he ain't around."

"You know where I can find him?"

The man snickered. "He's in Morocco."

"What's he doing there?"

"What does anybody do in Morocco, dude?"

"Any idea when he'll be back?"

"Sorry, I ain't his babysitter." Skull cap quickly checked for traffic then steered his bicycle into the street.

Marty made his way to the front door and knocked. A short, thin, almost toothless woman with an oval wrinkled face that resembled a dried plum opened the door.

"I'm looking for Theo Jaquez. Does he live here?"

She gave him an inquisitive stare. "Who are you?" She had a shrilly voice.

"My name's Marty Chenoweth and I need to speak to Theo."

"What about?"

A nosy landlady; he hated her kind. Apparently snooping on tenant's personal information came with rent collection. "It's personal. It involves an inheritance."

"Who died and left him money? His no-good parents don't have two nickels between them. How much they leave him?"

"Sorry, I can't say anymore. Do you know where I can find him?"

"He's out of town and won't be back until Friday. You can come back then."

"Thanks, I'll do that."

Just as he had turned to leave, she asked, "Is this about that lady up at San Lucas?"

Marty turned around. "What about that lady in San Lucas?"

"She wasn't going to be around much longer, Theo said. Is she the one that left him money?"

"Thanks for your help. I'll be back later in the week to see him."

"Yeah, you do that."

Thirty

ILYAS WAS UNAWARE how long he had been in prison. He

suffered greatly from sharp pain throughout his body that left him weakened; his movements were slow, symptoms of rheumatism. He would often get a fever that lasted for days. Diarrhea was a common affliction that struck too often. Ilyas spoke just above a whisper, as the chronic sore throat since the first days at Sidi Kascen had never gone away. Medical assistance for prisoners was scarce, even for those too weak to stand. Those beyond help were moved to a different section until they died.

During the day Ilyas shuffled within the grounds scavenging food from other prisoners, food brought by their visiting relatives. He counted the days until his parents or his Uncle Aban visited and brought a package. It was impossible to survive on what Sidi Kascen fed the prisoners. The watered lentil or chickpea soup, a few shriveled prunes and the rotten vegetables that prisoners fought for, along with the weakened tea that tasted salty and left Ilyas thirsty, provided little nutrition. Ilyas was a skeleton.

At night he would find a small space between prisoners and fall into an agitated sleep that only brought nightmares. Ilyas became convinced about two things — that his bad fortune was a result of evil djinn living in his soul, and that he would die at Sidi Kascen prison.

Then one day while at the toilet once again afflicted with diarrhea, he heard a guard scream out his name. He tried to answer, but his voice produced only a low noise. Someone in the yard pointed the guard in the direction of the toilets. Squatting over the opening, Ilyas looked up.

"Are you Ilyas Bashir?" the guard said.

The tone of the guard was different — not as harsh. What could he want? Family visits were many weeks away. He feebly nodded his head.

"You must come with me now."

Ilyas remained over the opening emptying his bowels. The guard waited until Ilyas finished. Standing up slowly so the pain that traveled throughout his body would not be too intense, Ilyas shuffled toward the guard. The guard took his arm and helped him out of the toilet room and across the yard. The other prisoners looked on enviously as the two made their way to the adjacent building. Transfers to the other side where prisoners were given special treatment rarely occurred.

The guard walked him into a dormitory and led him down a long row of thin mattresses evenly spaced on the floor. Others were either lying on a mattress, or sitting up reading or playing games. The guard stopped half-way down the room in front of one of the mattresses.

"This is yours," he said pointing at it. You may change into new clothes after you bathe. Let me show you where that is."

The guard led Ilyas to the end of the room and unlocked the

door. It was a small closet. Taking a prison djellaba, the guard handed it to Ilyas, then took him to the adjoining door that led into a shower room.

"I'll be back with food after midday prayer," the guard said.

Unaccustomed to asking questions since the guards never answered them anyway and sometimes beat prisoners for talking, Ilyas said nothing. He looked around at the single shower head almost as if it were a mirage. The guard left Ilyas alone. Slowly he removed his ragged, dirty clothes and shuffled to the shower. Manipulating the handles, warm water spewed out. Ilyas had forgotten that luxury. A long-ago memory of the *hammam* he regularly visited to bathe in came to mind. As he felt the modest stream of water spew over his skeleton frame, Ilyas reached up to scratch his head that itched from the vexing lice only to feel a swatch of hair in his hand. He stayed underneath the showerhead for what seemed like hours, as the warm water eased the rheumatism pain. Finishing, he put on the djellaba and shuffled back to his mattress. As he stood looking at it wondering if he could lie down and sleep, one of the men approached him.

"*Salaam Aleikum.*"

Ilyas gazed at him for a second."*Aleikum Salaam,*" Ilyas responded in his low voice.

"Why have you been transferred here, my brother?"

"I don't know."

"You must be one of the fortunate ones to be pardoned."

"Pardoned?" Ilyas repeated.

"Yes. This dormitory is only for prisoners who have wealthy relatives or relatives with high positions within the monarchy and for those prisoners that are to receive a pardon from His Majesty."

Ilyas could hardly understand what he was hearing. Why would he be pardoned? Had they made a mistake? He lay on the mattress. It felt wonderful. In less than a minute he was asleep.

Sometime later Ilyas was shaken awake. A guard was standing over him with a tray of food. There was whole meal bread, a bowl of chick peas and gravy and a small salad. He began to eat, drinking water between bites. Never in his life had he tasted anything more satisfying.

"Don't eat so much," the same man who had approached earlier said. "You must eat only a small portion until your stomach can take more food. Otherwise, you will not be able to hold it down."

It was already too late to pay attention to the man's advice. Minutes later, Ilyas became ill. The man helped him to the toilet, then back to his mattress. Ilyas slept for the remainder of the day.

The following morning the man awoke Ilyas and led him to another room where they were served bread, fruit and mint tea. This time Ilyas was more careful in the amount he ate.

"My name is Hassan El Dik," the man said.

"I am Ilyas Bashir."

"How long have you been in prison?" he asked.

Ilyas had to think about the question. "I don't know. A long time."

"Well, soon you will be free."

"Can it be true?"

"My brother, if it were not true, you would not have been brought here."

SEVERAL WEEKS LATER Asafar and Maladh arrived for a visit. In the short time since Ilyas was transferred his appearance had changed noticeably. Seeing his son smiling was gratifying; his color was returning. Ilyas had a sparkle in his blue eyes. He was beginning to walk upright and normal. He no longer complained of rheumatism and his voice was improving. The joy Asafar felt at that moment was immense.

"Why am I being pardoned?" Ilyas asked Asafar when he confirmed that that was to occur.

"Because your Uncle Aban intervened for you."

"Why has he not come to visit me?"

"We were not told until yesterday that you are allowed more visits. I am certain he will do so very soon."

WHEN ABAN LATER appeared at the prison, there was an emotional divide in his mind between overwhelming gladness that Ilyas health was slowly returning to normal and the sadness about the condition placed on his release.

"You are looking well," Aban remarked with a smile.

"Thank you, Uncle, for arranging for my pardon. I am indebted to you forever," Ilyas replied as they both strolled alongside one another inside the open courtyard. The courtyard was stark; laced with only a few palm trees and surrounded by a high wall. Most of the prisoners spent many of their daylight hours in the courtyard, reading or sitting under a palm tree playing board games. Aban tried to take a path where others would not overhear their conversation.

"I am only happy I was able to help. But there are several others you do not know that provided much more help."

"Why would they do that?"

"They cared about you."

"But how can that be when they don't even know me?"

Aban was struck that moment with the happy thought that Ilyas' precocious nature was returning. "Be glad they did not know you or your many questions as they may have changed their minds."

Ilyas laughed.

Aban wanted to reveal his relationship to his son so badly, but he worried that the boy would become angry for keeping the secret from him so long. The boy had already endured enough as it was. To burden him further with revealing the secret would be torturous. Aban also worried about the hurt it might cause his brother who had also suffered greatly. Even though it was against *Shari'a* not to reveal his true relationship to Ilyas, he saw that nothing good would come of it if he was to do so. But as to the condition placed on his son's release, Aban had no choice.

"Ilyas, I have something very important to tell you."

They stopped walking.

"What is it, Uncle?"

"It involves your pardon. In order to negotiate your pardon, I was forced to accept a condition that pains me greatly. Your pardon could not have occurred otherwise."

"What is the condition? What could be so bad to match that," Ilyas said, pointing to the wall separating the prisons.

"Ilyas, when you are released you will not be allowed to remain in Morocco."

Ilyas was quiet for a few seconds as he thought about what he had heard. "Where will I go?"

"Your father and I have spoken about this. You will be provided with a passport and visa. Spain, we think, is a good choice. It is not so far away and we hope you will be allowed to return very soon."

"I have never been away from my country. What will I do there?"

"I will give you money that will help you get started."

"You have done so much for me already, Uncle. How can I take anything more from you?"

"I have something else for you." Aban took an envelope out of his pocket. "Keep this in a safe place. One day you must travel to the United States. The envelope contains information about someone you must see."

Ilyas took the envelope. "I don't understand. Who is it?"

"A very special person you have never met, died and left you a gift. The envelope contains the name of the one holding that gift that awaits you."

Ilyas seemed more confused than ever. "Uncle, who is this special person? Is it the one who helped you secure my pardon?"

"Yes."

"What is the gift?"

"Ilyas, all of that is not so important to know today. I have already shared with you a great amount of information. Some day the rest will be explained to you."

They embraced tightly as Aban ended his visit, unaware that

they would never see one another again.

Thirty-one

ARRIVING IN THE late evening at the Albuquerque airport from his trip to Morocco, Theo retrieved his luggage and caught the remote parking bus. The April night was chilly as he paid the parking attendant and drove out. Exhausted and hungry from the long trip, Theo pulled into a drive-in and ordered take out. Once on the interstate, he managed to devour the sandwich while steering his Jeep toward Santa Fe.

As he parked on the curb Theo noticed his landlady's lights off. Lucy must be in bed, he thought. He was excited to tell her about his flying experience. First thing in the morning he would stop over for coffee and take her souvenirs — a lace tablecloth from Morocco along with a carton of her favorite cigarettes that he bought at the duty free store. Having never smoked, Theo couldn't understand why anyone would take up the habit. And Lucy had it bad, going through at least a pack a day.

Balancing his luggage, Theo walked down the driveway path, passing the first apartment — Kevin's apartment. Kevin was a barista in a coffee shop during the day and played drums at a jazz club at night. Unlocking his apartment door, Theo flipped on the light and laid everything down. Closing the door, he quickly walked to the bathroom. Suddenly he heard a knock.

"Hold on — I'll be right there," he yelled out.

Maybe Lucy wasn't asleep after all.

After zipping up, he walked over and opened the door.

"*Mi hijo*, how are you?"

It was Sixto, his father, and Romel, his older brother pushing past him into the apartment. They smelled bad; it was the stench of outdoor campfire smoke. Theo sensed trouble. "What do you want?"

Sixto walked past him to an overstuffed chair and plopped down. "We were worried about you, *mi hijo*, and wanted to make sure you were okay." They both laughed. It was the lazy snickering laugh they made when they were high.

Theo turned to his brother who closed the door. His eyes were glassy, his gait, unsteady. Romel raised his hand and brought it down in an exaggerated hand-shake gesture. Theo didn't move.

"You don't want to shake your brother's hand? What's the matter with you?" Romel asked.

"I'm tired. You both need to get out of here." Theo looked over at Sixto who was nodding.

Sixto placed his hands on the arms of the chair and stretched out his legs. "Why don't you get down here and help out your old man, like before."

"Get out now or I'm calling the cops." His voice was firm.

At that instant Romel shoved his brother from behind. Theo stumbled, but stayed up.

"You're too good to do that anymore, *hoto*?" Romel grabbed Theo by the hair and forced him in front of the chair.

With a quick turn Theo struck Romel on the chest with his elbow. Romel returned the blow with a punch in the gut forcing Theo to the floor. "You should be an expert at sucking cock, *hermanito.*"

Sixto unzipped. "*Andale, mi hijo,* for old times' sake."

Theo felt a hard kick to the ribs. He tried to rise until Romel retrieved something from his back pocket and struck Theo on the kidney. It was a large piece of metal. Grabbing Theo's hair, Romel began beating him with the weapon. Theo lay on the floor, his face bloodied.

Romel reached for the suitcase and dumped the contents on the floor. After doing the same with the box and carry-on, he walked to the bedroom and began searching through the dresser drawers and closet. Throwing off the bed covers, he turned over the mattress. Making his way into the kitchen, Romel frantically searched the pantry and cupboards. Returning, he grabbed Theo's hair, once again. "Where is it, *hoto*? Where did you hide it?"

Blood oozed from Theo's face and nose. "Hide what?" he managed to say.

"The money...the insurance money."

How did they find out? "I don't have it anymore," Theo said.

"Where is it?"

Theo remained silent.

Romel struck him in the face again. "Where is it?" Romel yelled.

Theo didn't respond.

Romel stood up and kicked his brother in the ribs, once again. "We're not leaving here until you tell me." The blows became uncontrollable. "Where is it?" he screamed. But Theo lay unconscious while Sixto drifted into a stupor.

Romel bent down and reached for his brother's wallet. Several bills and strange looking currency were buried in the flaps. He stuck it all in his pocket. Stepping over his brother, Romel raised Sixto from the chair, zipped him up and they made their way out of the apartment.

EARLY FRIDAY MORNING Marty parked in front of the Priego home, walked the driveway path to the second apartment, and knocked on the door. Just as he expected, there was no answer. He cupped his hands and looked in the window. The room was littered with clothing. Then he saw a body sprawled on the floor next to a chair. Marty forced open the door.

The noise jolted the sleeping occupant of the adjoining apartment awake.

Marty was dialing the emergency number on his cell when he looked up and saw the skull-capped bicycle kid. "What's your name?"

"Kevin."

"Okay, Kevin, what's the address here?"

"514 Priego."

After reporting the emergency, Marty tried finding a pulse.

"Oh, wow, this is some nasty shit," Kevin said as he looked over Marty's shoulder at the bloody body.

"Is this Theo Jaquez?" Marty asked.

"Yeah, that's him...or what's left of him."

"Don't touch anything until the cops get here."

"No problem, dude. He looks like a goner."

"Not yet, I don't think" Marty looked up. "Were you around last night, Kevin?"

"No, man, I had a gig. I got in late."

Within minutes the paramedics arrived, followed by two police officers. As they began questioning Marty, several plain-clothes officers arrived, then more police units. The scene began growing chaotic—curious neighbors appeared and the yellow police tape strung across the narrow pathway inadvertently blocked in the paramedic unit. By the time paramedics finished working on Theo and placing him into their vehicle, Snyder emerged and ambled over to where a police officer and Marty were standing.

"What happened?"

Marty responded. "Like I told these guys, Theo was laid out when I got here."

"Is he alive?" Snyder asked.

"Just barely," the officer said.

Thirty-two

RELEASED FROM THE hospital a few days after David's visit, Theo took a taxi to see Hans Schuldneckt, the head chef and owner of The Seville. Hans instantly walked around the cooking table to greet his young charge. With a handshake and a hug, Hans spoke loud enough for everyone in the kitchen to hear, "Look who is back?"

Born in Switzerland, Hans' experience came from working at high-end gourmet restaurants in Berlin, Munich and Paris. He had opened The Seville five years earlier and it was gaining a reputation as a first-class gourmet restaurant.

Shortly after hiring Theo, Hans recognized the boy's eager desire to learn culinary art. Theo seemed to absorb everything Hans taught him. Theo's enthusiasm seemed irrepressible. Soon he was able to handle the lunch crowd, only struggling when unexpected large parties appeared. Hans was pleased with Theo's work and oftentimes left him in charge of the kitchen during most of the day shift. Shocked after reading the newspaper story, Hans visited Theo in the hospital. Theo convinced the restaurant owner that the story was untrue and that soon the true facts would vindicate him. Choosing to believe his young charge, Hans assured Theo that his job was safe.

"Are you ready to start work, my young chef?"

"Absolutely I'm ready. By the way, now that you've worked my shift, don't you think I deserve a raise?" Theo joked.

"He wants a raise and hasn't worked for three weeks," Hans said. He looked at Theo and curled his hands in the figure of a noose. "Standing on a stepladder is the only raise you get from me," Hans replied. "Now you come to work tomorrow for the day shift?"

"I'll be here, boss."

"Okay, then we see you tomorrow."

After leaving the restaurant, Theo took a taxi home. Once there, he tried unlocking the door to his apartment, but the key no longer fit. As he knocked on Lucy's door, a few seconds later she appeared with billowing cigarette smoke coming out of her mouth. "Well, would you look at what the cat dragged in."

"Hi Lucy. I can't get my door to open."

"Come in, Theo," she said. "I changed the lock when they repaired the door. How you feeling, honey?"

"Tired."

"Well, I went into your apartment and straightened up while you were in the hospital. What a mess they made. There were clothes and stuff strewn all over the bedroom and living room. And I won't even tell you what they did in the kitchen."

"I'm really sorry about all of that."

"Don't worry, honey. They'll find who did it."

"Thanks for doing all of that, Lucy."

"Honey, just tell me one thing. Tell me what I'm reading in the newspaper isn't true?"

"Lucy, I promise none of it is true. But I can't say any more right now."

"That's what I wanted to hear. Okay, so these are your keys. Go get some rest."

THEO'S STRENGTH RETURNED quickly, but the anxiety over the police investigation was wearing thin. The police were interviewing everyone he knew. It was clear Lieutenant Kerry Snyder was behind much of it because his name was conspicuously cited in every article. It was as if the police officer had a vendetta against him.

One evening Theo decided that he needed to drive to Arbol Verde and see Father Bonafacio. He knew he had to face the priest and give assurances that all the criminal charges were untrue. It was a big misunderstanding, he would tell the priest. Theo also hoped to hear that Elijah Bashir had contacted the priest. Then he could explain the matter to the authorities and clear his name.

IN THE LATE afternoon Romel could usually be found in a corner of the parking lot by the Arbol Verde *tienda* surrounded by a small group of *tecatos*. That's where he conducted most of his business. With a casual handshake, Romel was adept at making the exchange of a small baggie for a folded bill.

Tino Sandoval, a young *tecato*, noticed Clofes Benevidez drive into the parking lot. Tino's eyes followed Clofes as he parked his truck and scoffed at them, then made his way into the *tienda*. At that moment Tino's eyes caught Theo driving passed the *tienda* in his Jeep. He tapped Romel. "Hey, *cabron*, their goes your *hoto hermanito*."

"*Deveras ese*. Are you sure it was him?"

"I know it was him, *vato*. I hear the *chotas* are after him. He did in an old lady and got her insurance money. What's he doing here, *vato*?"

"Probably going to the church to blow Father Bonafacio," Romel replied.

"Is Father Bonafacio like that, too?"

"He's a priest, isn't he, and that's what priests do, *que no*?"

"Man, they ought to do something about that shit...it's not natural," Tino said.

"Like you know a lot about what's natural, Tino. Last time you tied off, you pissed in your pants, *ese*," one of the others replied, as they broke out laughing.

Romel was quiet for a few seconds. Glancing at Tino, he said, "I need to talk to Theo. I'll see you later, *ese*."

As Romel walked away, one of them yelled out, "If Theo wants to share some of his insurance money, tell him I got a big one he can suck on."

"*Que*, I've seen it before, *vato*, and it's tiny. You must be looking through a magnifying glass?" Tino replied. The laughing grew louder.

"Why you looking at my *verga*, man. Are you a *hoto* too?" was the response that Romel barely heard as he got into his car and drove off.

Seeing Theo's Jeep parked in the church lot, Romel parked on the curb outside the property.

THEO WALKED UP to the rectory and rang the doorbell. The priest opened and invited him inside. They exchanged a friendly hug.

"How are you feeling now?" the priest asked.

"I'm okay. How are you doing, Father?"

"What can I tell you, Theo? Just praying for better days. Let's go sit down." Father Bonafacio led him into the kitchen. "You want coffee?"

"Yeah, that would be great."

The priest began brewing a pot.

"I just came by to tell you not to believe all you hear or read in the papers about me."

The priest turned around to face him. "I know you too well to believe any of that."

"By the way, I was wondering if that guy's ever come around to get his money."

"If you mean Elijah Bashir, no."

"I don't want to confuse you Father, but these days he's going by another first name. It's Ilyas Bashir"

The priest looked at Theo with a puzzled expression. "Write that down for me. There's paper and pencil by the phone."

As Theo stood up and walked to the counter, the priest asked, "So when is Elijah or Ilyas supposed to come for his money?"

"I wish I knew, Father. But, when it does happen, you'll call me?"

"Yeah, of course."

As the coffee began to brew, the priest walked over and sat down. "Is there anything you want to tell me about all of this Theo? Can I help you somehow?"

"Father, I wish I could say more. But, for now it's best to say nothing."

"I understand."

After convincing Theo to stay for dinner, at the end of the meal the priest walked his visitor to the door.

It was the beginning of a new month as the warm May weather took hold. The full moon illuminated Theo's path to the parking lot when suddenly a voice spoke to him, "*Orale*, bro."

Startled, Theo turned his head. He could clearly make out his brother's outline. The same height as Theo, Romel was lanky; his black hair, shoulder length.

When they were young, they were close; it became a way of surviving. Back then they foraged for their meals among their neighbors and relatives. Their clothes, usually several sizes too large, they stole from clothes lines or stores. They looked out for each other, sharing whatever they managed to pilfer. But then their relationship changed once Romel started using drugs.

"What do you want, Romel?"

"I need your insurance card again."

"No way. You're lucky you're not in jail for what you did to me."

Romel laughed. "So, is the priest your boyfriend?"

"You're sick, man."

"Is he holding the insurance money?"

"Leave me alone. Get out of my face."

"So the priest is holding your money, isn't he?"

Without responding, Theo unlocked the door. Romel grabbed at his arm, but Theo pulled away. Romel's grip tightened but Theo suddenly turned, hauled off and punched his brother in the face as hard as he could. Romel fell to the ground.

"*Cabron*," Romel spat out.

He stood up and searched for something in his back pocket as he tried grabbing at Theo with his free hand. Another hard blow by Theo, only this time it sprayed him with Romel's blood. Once again, Romel fell to the ground.

EARLY THE FOLLOWING morning David was awakened by the phone. Reaching over to the nightstand, he picked up the receiver, "Hello."

"Dad, its Patrick. Theo's been arrested."

David sat up in bed. "When?"

"A few hours ago. They're charging him with murder."

"So the autopsy turned up something?" David said.

"No Dad, it's not that. He's being charged with killing Romel, his brother."

Thirty-three

FINISHING WITH THE last *tecato* interview, Snyder looked out the window at the darkness then at his watch. It was eight-thirty and he was exhausted. Pleased by the witness statements corroborating his theory, Snyder placed them in his briefcase and walked out to his car. It was a three hour drive back to Albuquerque and once there, he knew he would get little sleep before heading back to the office early the following morning. His plan was to discuss the case with the captain first thing. As he backed up the car, Snyder saw Sergeant Velez leave the building and called out to him. "Do you still have some officers around the church rectory looking for the murder weapon?"

"Yeah, we had four officers out there yesterday and today. They'll be out there again tomorrow. We have them scouting way beyond the rectory, in the woods and even on the river bank."

"Good. Call me right away if you find anything."

"Will do."

As he started the long drive home, Snyder was certain that the case was coming together. He was convinced that Theo murdered Jude Armstrong for the insurance money and then traveled to Morocco to buy drugs. Now he also knew who put Theo in the hospital when he returned from Morocco. It was his brother. Snyder knew that not only because Moroccan currency was found in Romel's wallet, but a confidential report from the criminal investigation section found Romel's fingerprints all over Theo's apartment. The motive was obviously to steal Theo's drug stash. Unable to find it in the apartment, Romel confronted Theo a second time outside the rectory. But this time Theo defended himself and ended up killing his brother.

Once the murder weapon was found, the case against Theo would be solid. But Snyder knew he had more work to do on solidifying the Jude Armstrong murder. Two things were necessary; he needed evidence that morphine caused her death, and he needed to find Theo's drug stash.

There were two possibilities for getting the morphine testimony. They could send the MIB test results to the FBI lab in Washington for their assessment, or hire a private lab, just like Albright had suggested. He liked the second option because private labs usually found exactly what you wanted them to find for a price.

As to where Theo hid the drug stash, Snyder didn't have a clue. Theo was smart. Maybe he wasn't hooked on drugs after all and that's why he still had good sense. Good enough to feign an innocence that even made Snyder momentarily question his culpability. Then suddenly, like a pop-up ball coming right down on his head, it hit him. Snyder was so shaken by the notion he thought of pulling the car over to give it more attention.

"Of course, that's where it's hidden," he said aloud. "It's the perfect hiding place. Nobody would suspect."

The more thought he gave, the more convinced he became. As his mind continued racing, his thoughts shifted to the implications. If his idea was correct, the break in this case was likely to cause a scandal that would ring louder than anything he had ever experienced before. His hard work would pay off in ways he never thought possible. The exposure would be unprecedented and he'd receive all the credit. His good name would be etched into the minds of the voters. At that moment Snyder became convinced that the Theo Jaquez case was going to be key to winning the election.

CRADLING THE THEO Jaquez file, the following morning Snyder walked into the captain's office. He sat down and, after giving the captain an overview of the case, he began reciting the details. Snyder went over every bit of evidence his team of officers had collected. He slowly built up the momentum, filling in boxes like a crossword puzzle. He cleverly answered the captain's questions, embellishing those facts supporting his theory and minimizing other aspects that were void of evidence. Leaving the best for last, Snyder took a breath and waited a brief moment just to exaggerate his drug stash hypothesis. He was sure the captain would see that it all fit as tightly as a champagne cork. Then he spewed it out. He waited in silence as the captain mulled over what he had said.

"I'm not convinced, Snyder. What if we don't find the drugs? Can you imagine the scandal?"

Snyder was disappointed by the captain's reaction. "I'm absolutely positive it's there. I have a gut feeling about this. I'd stake my career on it," he replied.

"I'm going to set up a meeting with the deputy chief and the major. They can decide where we go with this," the captain told Snyder.

As Snyder was returning to his office, the desk sergeant stopped him."Somebody's waiting up front to talk to you."

"I'm really tied up now. Did they give you a name?"

"Henry Karlson and his wife."

The name meant nothing to Snyder. "Ask them to come back next week?"

"Sure. But they were in Morocco and have information about Theo Jaquez."

"Why didn't you tell me that in the first place?" Snyder hurried out front to greet them.

After interviewing and taking a statement from Henry Karlson confirming the logistics of what had to be the Morocco drug exchange, Snyder escorted them out of the building. He began preparing an outline for his presentation.

Snyder was reveling over several more developments in the case. The DNA results of the stains on Theo's shirt, worn the night of Romel's murder, were received. It was conclusive for Romel's blood and sputum. The second development was even more exciting. The murder weapon was located in underbrush by the river. It was a broken tree limb with apparent blood splattering on the jagged edges. Its location was close to the bridge on the road leading out of Arbol Verde. It was Romel's blood, MIB confirmed.

WHEN SNYDER WALKED into the conference room for the meeting, the captain was already seated at one side of the long, walnut table. His eyes glanced up at Snyder as he continued his conversation with the major, who was sitting across. Two in-house attorneys followed him inside and took a seat.

The room was large. It was typically used as a classroom for officer orientation and training. The southeast exposure of windows provided a plethora of natural light and warmed the room on chilly days. The checkerboard wallpaper with subtle beige and white contrasting tones lined the walls. Opposite the windows and high above one wall were framed photographs of the succession of state police chiefs since the department's inception in 1935. A collection of other larger photograph images taken over the years hung throughout the room.

At exactly ten o'clock the deputy chief appeared with his coffee cup in hand and took the seat at the head of the table. He began the meeting. "Okay, Snyder, what do you have for us this morning?"

Having prepared his material days in advance, Snyder began by methodically summarizing his outline of the Jude Armstrong case. He detailed the supporting evidence of each allegation against Theo, embellishing where he believed the testimony was substantial, much like he had with the captain. Then he shifted to the case involving Romel's murder. When Snyder glanced over at the deputy chief tightly pursing his lips and looking down at the table, he sensed he was including too much minutiae. Finally, offering his theory on where the drug stash was hidden, there was an immediate low muffle in the room.

The major spoke, "I'm still fuzzy about the evidence supporting the sexual thing between the priest and the suspect. What do we have on that?"

Snyder looked though his file and brought out some documents. "This is a statement from Theo's father, Sixto Jaquez. Sixto says he first learned of the sexual relationship between his son and the priest around the time his son turned fourteen. The priest drove to their house that day and took Theo out to celebrate. After that, Theo spent all his free time at the rectory. When Sixto questioned his son, Theo said he was learning catechism. But that didn't sit well with Sixto and he kept pressing his son who later admitted to having sex with the priest."

"Sex? What kind of sex?" the major asked.

"The father wasn't clear about that. But he confronted the priest who denied it. Sixto warned the priest to stay away from his son. Then, about a week later, Theo ran away."

"Did the father ever report either of these incidents to the police?" the Major asked.

"No. He thought no one would believe that the priest was abusing his son. As for not reporting his son as a runaway, Theo was a rebellious kid who never paid attention to anybody. Even if Sixto would have found him and brought him back home, Theo would have only run away again. At the time Sixto was between jobs; they were strapped for money. He figured that given enough time, Theo would make his own way back home."

"That makes no sense. Doesn't the father read the newspapers or watch TV news? Priest abuse is rampant. Does Sixto have an arrest record or drug history," asked one of the lawyers.

Snyder vacillated. "He has a domestic battery rap. But that's not unusual up there. Wife beating is pretty common in those small villages. Let's see...there's probably something on drugs and alcohol, too. Let me get back to you on that."

"Was the priest interrogated?" asked the lawyer.

"Yup," Snyder replied. "He says that when they first met, Theo put the moves on him. He got mad at the kid for trying it. After that, it never happened again."

"I bet it didn't," the major said.

The lawyers' questioning continued. "Does Theo have an arrest record?"

"No."

"Any evidence he's a drug dealer?"

"No."

"Does the priest have any history of sexual misconduct?"

"No."

Now Snyder knew why he hated lawyer' so much. They never stopped asking questions.

"Let me see if I understand the events leading to the brother's murder," one of them said. "You think Romel beat up his brother at his apartment when he couldn't find the drug stash? How did Romel find out about the drug stash in the first place?"

"We interviewed Theo's neighbor; a freak who plays in a rock band at a local club. The freak says he knew Romel through mutual friends—druggies probably. Anyway, Romel learned where his brother lived through the freak neighbor. When Romel stopped in at the club one night the freak mentioned Theo had gone off to Morocco. So when the newspaper reported that Theo had made off with Jude Armstrong's life insurance money, Romel put it all together. Why else would anybody go to Morocco if not to buy drugs?"

"That's all speculative and circumstantial," the lawyer said. "Wasn't Romel hooked on heroin?"

"Yeah," Snyder replied.

"Well, Morocco has a reputation for hashish, not heroin."

"Maybe Romel didn't know that. Regardless, Romel could deal hashish just as easy as heroin."

"How do you explain Theo getting the drugs through customs?"

"Drugs get through customs every day. Maybe they were hidden in something undetectable? Who knows," Snyder replied.

"And you have a witness that actually saw Theo exchanging

cash for drugs?"

"The witness followed Theo and the drug source to an apartment in Casablanca. Theo went inside with a pouch and came out with a box."

Snyder saw the deputy chief check his watch. Then he spoke. "So because of this sexual thing between the priest and the kid, you think the drugs are hidden somewhere in the church rectory?"

"Essentially, that's my theory," Snyder replied. "What better hiding place than a church rectory. Nobody would ever think to look there."

The deputy chief turned to the lawyers. "Can you guys get the D.A. to prepare the paperwork for a search warrant on Santo Niño Church and the rectory."

"Yeah, that's not the problem. The problem's going to be convincing a judge to sign it."

"I'm sure you guys have your favorite judges. Maybe the D.A. can call in a favor. Also, let's get the Jude Armstrong case to the D.A. quickly with a strong recommendation to send it to the grand jury."

Making his way back to his office, Snyder could hardly contain his pleasure at the decision.

Within the week a search warrant was secured. Early the following morning a group of officers assembled at the police department and Snyder led the caravan to Arbol Verde.

Thirty-four

FINISHING HIS MORNING prayers, Father Bonafacio was heading to the kitchen when he heard a loud pounding sound at the rectory door. It startled him as he approached and quickly glanced through the mesh sidelight drape. It was still dark and the priest could just make out a uniformed police officer. Opening the door, the priest saw a cadre of officers standing just below his doorstep. "Father Bonafacio, I have a search warrant authorizing us to conduct a search of the church, the rectory and the adjoining buildings," Snyder said as he handed the priest the document.

"I don't understand. Why do you want to search here? I have nothing that would interest you."

"Can you please step back Father and allow us to conduct the search."

The priest moved back and looked on in shock as Snyder began making assignments. He looked back at the priest. "Why don't you go sit down, Father. It's likely we'll be here awhile."

The priest walked into the living room and sat on the sofa.

A few minutes later there was a loud voice in the direction of the priest's bedroom. "Lieutenant, I've found something."

Snyder rushed into the bedroom. As one of the officer turned over the contents of a brown bag on the bed, four stacks of one-hundred dollar bills dropped out. A smile formed on Snyder's face.

EL PASTOR DETENTION Center typically housed less than fifty long-term inmates. Theo was assigned to a two bed cell pod, away from the short-term holding cells used for weekend arrests averaging upward of thirty detainees. Theo spent much of his time reading and exercising. That was until Matias Salas, the facility's cook, learned he worked for a high-class Santa Fe restaurant. Salas then approached Theo. "Hey bro, how bout helping me out in the kitchen?"

"Doing what?"

"Dat's a funny-ass question. Cooking, what else would you do in a kitchen?"

Theo smiled. "Sure, when?"

"Like now. Let's go, bro."

Theo's cooking talent amazed Salas. He taught Salas how to adjust gluten for different elevations, how certain herbs and spices affected one another, and how cooking temperatures affected food taste. Working from the kitchen's recipes, Theo constantly changed ingredients, combined others and always altered the cooking time. The results were remarkable. The compliments came when the inmates stopped complaining and the guards and staff began eating the kitchen meals. This was further confirmed when the commissary cart made its daily rounds and nobody was buying the overpriced noodles and cup-of-soup packages anymore.

The predominately Hispanic inmate population typically spent their time watching television, playing cards or games, or exercising. They were allowed several hours outside every day. In the cell pod areas, fights broke out rarely. Drugs occasionally made their way inside. Sexual assaults never happened. After his first two weeks, Theo traded in the baggy orange jumpsuit for one fitting more comfortably. While the daily routine at the detention center was tolerable, for Theo, he sorely missed his freedom and The Seville.

Theo knew his troubles were mounting. It was bad enough that the police were investigating him for murder, fraud, and illegal drugs. But to implicate Father Bonafacio was reprehensible. The newspaper reported that the state police had confiscated twenty thousand dollars during their raid of the Santo Niño rectory. When Father Bonafacio refused to provide any explanation, the police assumed it was drug money and confiscated it. Maintaining the sanctity of the confessional was working against Father Bonafacio.

The act of trying to fulfill Jude's dying wish was all backfiring. Theo felt helpless. He remained convinced that prematurely disclosing his motives and telling his story would find its way into the international media and alert Moroccan officials. How could he vindicate himself and the priest without placing Elijah's release at risk? If only he had had the foresight of asking Aban to stay in touch. The several times he had attempted to phone Aban after his release from the hospital, the phone went unanswered. His only choice was to remain silent until Elijah arrived to collect the remainder of his inheritance.

Theo remained confounded by Romel's death. While he had truthfully recounted to David most of the details that night, the altercation with Romel was more vicious than he had admitted. Theo knew that it was wrong to hold back those details. But he couldn't risk saying more. Not yet, anyway.

Even in his present dilemma, Theo's thoughts continually shifted to Elijah. He wondered how Jude's grandson was surviving Sidi Kascen. While they now shared a life confined, his was much more decent, more humane. He wondered what measure of strength it took to survive the terrible conditions in the Moroccan prison. Had Elijah garnered enough of it to stay alive? Had the cruel treatment hardened his mind or soul?

Since his arrest, Theo's dreams became disquieting. Sometimes Elijah manifested in his dreams. It was always the same. As they walked toward one another from opposite directions over an expanse of the hot desert sand, Theo saw Elijah's image far away. When they drew closer, Elijah's features became ghostlike. When they were only feet apart, Theo could see a longing in Elijah's eyes. With lips parched and faces burnt by the blazing heat, there was an ominous unspoken exchange. Inches before passing one another, the dream faded.

David's recent visit brought more disturbing news. The grand jury had filed an indictment on all counts in the Jude Armstrong matter. Theo's arraignment was tentatively scheduled for early the following week. The only good news was their refusal to indict Father Bonafacio on the pedophile charge, finding insufficient evidence to support the allegation.

Thirty-five

TWO DAYS BEFORE the Throne Day holiday, Ilyas was escorted from the dormitory to the prison administration office. A guard waited for him with a pen in hand.

"Can you sign your name?" he asked.

"Yes."

"Sign here," he ordered, pointing to a place on an official document. It was written in Arabic and Ilyas eyed the language carefully. The release was at the munificence of His Majesty, the King, based on Ilyas' foreign born status and in accordance with humanitarian directives, it read. Unable to understand the substance, he tried to re-read it but the guard yelled out, "You must sign now."

"Have my parents been informed that I am being released today?" he asked.

The guard feigned a loathsome expression. In a loud voice, he said, "I am sorry that we didn't have time to send word to the newspapers and spread the news to the rest of the world that Ilyas Bashir was being released from Sidi Kascen prison today."

Others overhearing the sarcasm began laughing.

Ilyas signed the form.

"You can go now," the guard said.

Imprisoned for almost four years, Ilyas' release was anticlimactic. It was not what he had imagined. Nonetheless, he was free and that was all that mattered. But how was he supposed to contact his parents? More importantly, how was he to leave the country without money or papers? Placing his hand in his pocket to ensure the envelope given to him by his uncle was secure, Ilyas walked through the thick doors, down the stone walkway and through the arched wall guarded by a small cadre of military police armed with rifles. The sudden noise and activity beyond the wall was overpowering — cars and buses traveling on the busy street, and people walking the sidewalks. He looked up at the cloudless sky. It was a warm July day; almost stifling.

He heard a voice. "Ilyas Bashir?" He turned and looked at the figure.

"Are you Ilyas Bashir?" the young man asked.

"Yes."

"We were unsure when you would be released. I have been waiting for you since yesterday. Please, this way."

"Who are you?" Ilyas asked.

"I am Ahmed. I was sent by Ali Kibal. He arranged for your pardon. Now, please, this way."

Ilyas followed him down the street to a parked car.

"Get in," Ahmed said.

"Where are we going?"

"I've been instructed to take you to the train depot."

"But what about my parents?"

"I'm sorry, I know nothing about that."

Ilyas opened the car door and got in.

Ahmed reached into the satchel he carried and took out two envelopes. Opening the first, he showed the contents to Ilyas. "Here is your passport and visa into Spain. When we get to the train depot, I will purchase your ticket to Tangiers. From there you will take a taxi to the dock and purchase a commuter ferry ticket to Tarifa."

"But I have no money to do that?"

Ahmed opened the other envelope to reveal a stack of dirham. "This is for you."

"I have no clothes but these. What am I supposed to use? Is it possible to visit my parents in Casablanca before I leave for Spain?"

"I don't know. Let's drive to a phone where I can call Ali."

Several hours later Ilyas was on a bus to Casablanca. As he sat looking out the window at the expansive crop fields along the highway, Ilyas thought of how frightening freedom was to him. Having no skills, how would he get work? How could he support himself? Where in Spain would he go? It was clear to him djinn still occupied his soul and that many more hardships lay ahead. Not until he was able to rid himself of the evil spirit would his life become tranquil.

Five hours later Ilyas arrived in the city center and caught a taxi to his home. Fatiha, his sister, opened the door. She stared at him, unable to believe her eyes. "Ilyas, is it you?"

"Yes, it is me."

They embraced as she began to cry.

"Why the tears?" he asked.

"Because you have changed so much."

"Am I so strange to you?"

She remained silent. He looked around and noticed everything was the same as when he left — the colorful tile floor, the comfortable couches abutting the two walls, the knee-high eating table and the cushions around it. Walking over to pick up a small mirror, Ilyas looked at his reflection. He hardly recognized the image staring back. His face was gaunt and his cheek bones protruding. His lips were dull and his nose, thin. Now he understood his sister's shock. "Where are Ma and Pa, he asked?

"Are they not with you?"

"No. Why would they be with me?"

"Because they left early this morning believing you would be released tomorrow — the day before Throne Day. They were going to wait outside of the prison for you."

Dejected, he sat on the couch and hung his head.

"Let me prepare some food for you."

Ilyas did not answer, but remained sitting.

Karima, the oldest sister, arrived home from shopping. She too was shocked at his sight. After their greeting she sat next to him.

"Where will you go in Spain?" she asked.

"I don't know."

"One of my friends is from Barcelona. It is a large city like Casablanca. Maybe you could go there?"

"Maybe."

"Will you come back to visit us?"

"I don't know if I'm allowed to do that."

"I wish you didn't have to go away."

He looked at her and smiled. "I wish I didn't either."

At that instant Fatiha carried to the table a tagine pot with its conical lid and a large loaf of bread. They sat at the table and when the lid was opened, the aroma of mixed vegetables, fish and gravy captivated Ilyas. For all his time in prison he had not tasted fish nor vegetables as freshly prepared as his sister had made them. He dipped the bread in the mixture and slowly savored his first bite.

By early morning when his parents had not returned, Ilyas packed the few clothes from his closet. After writing a letter to them, he left for the train depot. Arriving in Tangier, he took a bus to the ferry station. It was crowded. He weaved his way through customs and into a large room. Within the hour the ferry arrived and chaos erupted as the mass of people rushed down several sets of stairs, making their way into the bowels of the ship. Finally inside, he found a seat. Across from him was a wealthy Moroccan couple taking a vacation in Malaga. He could tell they were well-to-do by the man's shoes and by the way they spoke. The shoes were high-quality chestnut leather with a beautiful sheen. Having relatives who worked in the tannery in Fez, Ilyas could distinguish fine leather workmanship. In their short conversation, the man was very exact in everything he said. Ilyas learned that Malaga was once ruled by Arabs. The birthplace of Pablo Picasso and the heart of the historic community of Andalucia, Malaga was the largest coastal city closest to Morocco and employed many Moroccans. Ilyas also learned that work for unskilled Moroccans was very scarce.

"Like swarms of locust infesting the crop fields that is how Moroccans have invaded Malaga," the man said. "You will have much difficulty finding work there. If you want to find good work, go to Barcelona or Madrid. There are much better opportunities in those cities."

After spending one night in a Malaga hostel, Ilyas purchased a train ticket to Madrid. Arriving there, he bought a city map at the train station. Sitting down outside to study the map, he begin plotting directions in the city. Ilyas decided to make his way to the center. Once there, Ilyas walked the streets until he found a hostel. It was closed and would not reopen for several more hours. He began exploring the neighborhood. A Mosque was located only three blocks from the hostel. He would return to pray on Friday.

Making his way back to the hostel, Ilyas found the reception clerk friendly and helpful. He spoke English. Ilyas paid one week in advance and a room key deposit. Each room had four beds. At the end of each bed was a small wooden chest with several drawers. The communal restrooms had showers, but towels were rented. The clerk had recommended safeguarding belongings in one of their rental lockers or safes, but needing to conserve his money, Ilyas declined. Once he had settled in, Ilyas left to have dinner.

Unable to find a Moroccan restaurant that evening, Ilyas took dinner at a small corner eatery advertising falafel in its outdoor billboard. Sitting at the counter and waiting for his order, Ilyas sipped tea. The tea had little flavor. Several minutes later the plate of falafel was placed in front of him. It resembled the dish from home. As he bit into the chick peas and bean fried ball it was the best he had ever tasted. In no time he had finished and was tempted to order another plate. But he chose to wait until the following evening despite a craving that continued teasing his palate long into the night.

By the time he returned to the hostel, two other guests were sharing his room. After meeting and briefly speaking to them, he wrote a letter home, then fell asleep.

Early the following morning Ilyas began his search for work. Walking into most restaurants and hotels he passed along the way, Ilyas asked about any available jobs. Communication became a problem; most of the hiring staff spoke only Spanish. The application form he was asked to complete was in Spanish. Aside from his name, there was little more information he could furnish. He had no permanent address, no skills or experience, and no employment history. Determining it was futile, he gave up. By mid-day hunger pangs had begun to set in and he returned to the falafel eatery. Passing the national library in the early afternoon, Ilyas walked inside. He perused the massive collection of books and, locating the English section, spent the remainder of the day reading.

Thirty-six

MARTY WAS SIPPING coffee and reading the newspaper at his favorite café on Sunday morning. Dressed in a t-shirt, cutoffs and sandals, it was the start of a typically hot Virginia summer. After his phone conversation with Lieutenant Snyder weeks earlier, Marty had given no more thought to the Theo Jaquez matter.

He was glad that the title company agreed to mail the closing paperwork on Jude's house transferring the property to the new owner. That meant no trip back to Santa Fe. Once he signed those documents, a check for the proceeds would follow. Marty had already created a separate bank account for Jude's estate which was amply funded from the sale of all her possessions. When the title company check arrived, he would close the account, combine the money and get a certified check to the Anderson School of Journalism in New York. After that, he would notify the Probate Court that Jude's will had been satisfied and wrap up his ties with New Mexico.

As Marty continued sifting through the newspaper, suddenly a small article caught his eye. He folded the newspaper over and brought the article closer. The story involved Theo. It described an alleged sexual relationship between an Arbol Verde priest and Theo. It cited Theo's arrest for his brother's murder, Jude's murder, fraud, and drug possession, as well as a find of twenty thousand dollars in drug money hidden inside the Santo Niño rectory. Marty re-read the article several times making certain he understood it all correctly. For the remainder of the day the story continued playing in the back of his mind. Now that he believed Theo wasn't into drugs, he wondered what evidence Snyder had uncovered on the kid. How unfair to Theo after all he had done for Jude. A disconcerting feeling came over him.

Marty was convinced that Theo didn't murder Jude. He was also convinced the trip to Morocco didn't involve drugs. As he gave the life insurance matter more thought, it made no sense why Jude would reward Theo, and ignore Consuelo. After all, it had been Consuelo Jude constantly extolled during their phone conversations. Always the pragmatist, Jude acted on reason rather than emotion. And her actions were never hasty or impulsive. So what would have motivated her to leave fifty-thousand dollars to Theo? The question would not leave his mind.

Later that evening Marty retrieved a box filled with Jude's papers that Snyder had given him. He began examining each item, wondering if something might give him a clue to the life insurance mystery. Tossing aside the utility invoice envelopes, Marty gave a second glance to the phone bills. Instinctively, he opened one and began examining the register of calls. Curiously, one call was made to Rabàt, Morocco. Another invoice showed a second phone call to the same Morocco number. What possible connections did Jude have with Morocco? Could Theo's trip have been at her behest? If so, what was the purpose? Marty picked up the phone and dialed the Morocco number. When the call was picked up, the foreign language made it impossible to communicate, and Marty hung up. Growing tired, Marty turned in for the night.

As he tossed in bed, Marty raised his head slightly, opened one eye and glanced at the red digital numbers directly in his line of sight. It was two o'clock and sleep was elusive; his mind wouldn't turn off. As he lay in bed, the idea occurred to do a public records search on Jude. Maybe the Morocco connection would surface. Getting out of bed and making his way to his computer, Marty accessed the Vital Records Division for Virginia, but the database wouldn't allow him access. Early the following morning he drove to the state agency. Armed with Jude's will and the New Mexico probate court documents, Marty explained his need to research Jude's family. With a whiny voice, the chunky clerk cited the portion of state law barring access to non-relatives. Undeterred, Marty made his appeal to the deputy registrar. Taking in Marty's predicament, the administrator promptly instructed her minion to allow him access to their records.

Beginning with Jude and working his way back, in less than two hours Marty discovered information that would eventually unveil the conundrum. Victoria married Aban, a Moroccan. Several months later she gave birth to a son, Elijah. Marty was willing to bet that the Morocco telephone calls involved either Aban or her grandson, Elijah. As Marty drove home he made plans to return to New Mexico.

MONSIGNOR KEELER SLAMMED the receiver shut after Father Bonafacio's early morning call advising of the state police raid on Santo Niño. He immediately left for Arbol Verde but by the time he arrived, the state police were gone. Hearing Father Bonafacio's account of their find, Monsignor Keeler said, "You convinced me earlier that you were innocent of the sex charges. Now this! Explain to me where you got twenty thousand dollars?"

"The money is not mine. I'm only its caregiver."

"The caregiver for whom?"

"I'm not able to say."

"Father Bonafacio, when you came to my office, it was your candor and sincerity that convinced me of your innocence. But, consider the position you're placing the archdiocese in? What am I supposed to say to the archbishop?"

"The matter with this money came to me during confession of a penitent. Under the seal of the confessional I cannot disclose to you anything more."

"Does this have anything to do with Theo Jaquez?"

The priest remained quiet and didn't flinch in his intense fix on Monsignor Keeler.

"Is this drug money?"

"I assure you it is not. The money was legally obtained."

Both priests remained silent, exchanging reason and wisdom within the core of their focused eyes. To Monsignor Keeler it was like looking at a mirror image of the humble priest's heart. He sensed the priest's genuineness.

"Father Bonafacio, while I will do everything in my power to continue supporting you, my authority is limited. The archbishop is very concerned about the situation and its reflection on the church. You must understand any action taken against you by the diocese rests in his hands."

"Yes, I understand."

"As I cautioned earlier, you are to speak to no one about any of this without my consent. Is that understood?"

The priest nodded his head.

"My prayers are with you that this matter resolves quickly." With that, Monsignor Keeler left the rectory.

MARTY WANTED TO speak with Father Bonafacio. Certain that the priest knew much more than he was telling the police, Marty also suspected that the seized money was part of Jude's life insurance proceeds. Arriving in Albuquerque, Marty rented a car and drove to Arbol Verde.

Locating the church, Marty parked and rang the doorbell. No answer. He knocked, but to no avail. Marty sensed a presence behind the door.

"Father Bonafacio, I need to speak with you."

There was a momentary lapse before a response. "What do you want?"

"I'm a journalist. I need to speak to you about Theo." Marty instantly recognized his error; the priest wasn't likely to speak with anyone of his ilk.

"Please go away."

"Father, I'm not here as a reporter. I just need some information."

There was no response.

"Can you at least tell me if the money the police seized was given to you by Theo?"

Still no response.

Marty sensed the priest was still by the door. He made one last effort. "Father Bonafacio, have you ever heard of Elijah Bashir?"

At that second the door opened slightly. "Where do you know that name?"

"Father, may I have a glass of water, please?"

The priest thought for a second before allowing him inside. "Follow me."

The priest led Marty into the kitchen. Filling the glass from the sink, the priest handed it to Marty. Marty finished it and handed the glass back to the priest for more. As the priest turned to refill the glass, Marty gave a quick glance around the kitchen. Looking down on the counter by the telephone, Marty noticed a pad of paper with some writing. The name, Elijah, was crossed out and written below it was Ilyas Bashir.

The priest turned and offered Marty a second glass of water. "What do you know of Elijah Bashir?" the priest asked.

"I'm looking for him. I was hoping you might be able to help me find him."

The priest shook his head. "I'm sorry, I cannot help you."

"So, Theo has mentioned that name to you before, Father?"

"I don't know what you're talking about."

"The money the police seized, are you keeping it for Elijah Bashir?"

The priest became uncomfortable. "I cannot answer any of your questions."

Picking up the pad of paper with the writing, Marty asked, "Are Elijah and Ilyas the same person, Father?"

The priest snatched the pad away. "You must leave now," the priest demanded.

"Okay, no problem. Thanks for the water."

As Marty walked out the door, the priest asked, "Do you know if Elijah Bashir is even alive?"

"I'm hoping he is. When I find him, I'll let you know."

The priest closed the door without another word. As he looked down to the floor, Father Bonafacio noticed the visitor had slipped his business card under the door. Father Bonafacio picked it up and placed it in his pocket.

SINCE DAVID LUJAN was not returning any of his phone messages, Marty decided to call on the attorney the morning following his visit to the church.

David's law office was located in downtown Albuquerque. The attractive multi-story building was home to accounting firms, architects and law offices. Making his way inside, Marty located the building directory then took the elevator to the third floor — the law office of Serroff, Young and Lujan. Approaching the receptionist, he asked to see David.

"I'm sorry, I think he's left for an appointment already."

"Are you sure?" Marty asked.

"Give me one second; let me check." She stood up and walked away.

Less than a minute later Marty noticed someone walking toward him. The man wore a suit and tie, and carried a briefcase.

"I'm David Lujan. You wanted to see me?"

Marty introduced himself and they shook hands.

David instantly remembered the unreturned messages. "Sorry, I haven't gotten back to you, Marty. It's been hectic. In fact, I need to be somewhere that's three hours away."

"San Lorenzo? Theo Jaquez?" Marty asked.

David gave him a surprised gaze. "Yeah...and I bet you're looking for a story.

Marty interrupted. "No. Actually, I think I have a story that might interest you. It's about Theo."

"Is that right?"

"Jude Armstrong has a grandson, Elijah Bashir. He lives in Morocco with his dad, or I think that's where he's at. It's no coincidence that Theo went to Morocco right after Jude's death. I believe his trip there had something to do with her grandson."

"How do you know all this?"

"The twenty thousand the cops seized at the church, I think it's part of Jude's life insurance and belongs to Elijah."

"Where did you get your information, Marty?"

As they walked to David's car, Marty began to fill him in on what he had uncovered. Before he was finished, David asked, "If you have the time, you can ride along to Theo's arraignment with me. I'd like to hear more about your story."

Marty got into the car and they drove off.

Thirty-seven

EL PASTOR COUNTY courthouse, situated in San Lorenzo, was built in 1937 and remodeled at various times throughout the last and the present century. The two story building was designed in typically New Mexico territorial style with arched windows and a high pitched roof. Its creaky wooden floors announced anyone entering the courtroom. Hardwood paneling lined the court's walls with cornice trim below the plaster ceiling. The old dais sat high above the defense and prosecution tables and, although no longer used, had a small recessed weapon shelf to the left of the chair opening. The room had an echo if the gallery was empty. And that morning only three others besides Marty were there to observe the hearing.

David spoke with Theo briefly before Magistrate Judge Gil Esparza appeared in the courtroom. Judge Esparza, a bespectacled, slightly overweight cowboy lived on a ranch outside of San Lorenzo. First elected by El Pastor voters twenty years earlier, Judge Esparza was respected for his legal knowledge and his amusing banter. But his real fame came as founder of the San Lorenzo Rodeo Association. He called the hearing to order.

"One count of first degree murder, one count of second degree murder, conspiracy to commit fraud, possession of illegal drugs, and the sale of illegal drugs. It sounds like you've been busier than a one-armed paper hanger, Mr. Jaquez. How do you plead?" the judge asked.

"Not guilty, your Honor."

"Ms. Bernal, any statement before I set bail?"

"Your Honor, the state requests a continuation of no bail for Mr. Jaquez who we believe is a flight risk. Mr. Jaquez has the resources to flee, and we believe he will so act if he is released from custody. Mr. Jaquez recently traveled to Morocco, returning after purchasing illegal drugs..."

David interrupted. "Allegedly purchased drugs, your Honor.

We deny that allegation. The prosecution has no evidence that my client purchased drugs. Despite their best efforts, the police have been unable to locate drugs because there are none. Their case, in that regard, is purely circumstantial and we will prove it is wholly without merit. My client is neither a drug user nor a flight risk and has agreed to surrender his passport to the court until after his acquittal at trial."

Marsha responded, "While Mr. Lujan may be correct that the state has been unable to locate Mr. Jaquez's hidden cache of drugs, we have retrieved twenty thousand dollars in drug money."

David interrupted again. "Your Honor, there is no evidence that the money seized by the state police at an Arbol Verde church while conducting an arbitrary and ill-founded raid belongs to my client. In fact, this money does not belong to my client."

Judge Esparza halted the arguments. "Okay, both of you can stop polishing my buckle. I ain't here to judge the case. I'm setting bail at one hundred thousand dollars and I'll accept your client's kind offer to surrender his passport. You'll both hear from the District Court about a trial date. Now, unless either of you have anything else, let's save our breath for breathin'."

Hearing no response, Judge Esparza closed the hearing and the matter was over in less than fifteen minutes.

As they walked toward the door, Marsha turned to David. "You want to talk about a plea deal?"

He gave her a thoughtful gaze. "Nah, too early. Let me do some discovery and I'll get back to you, Marsha."

She suspected as much from David Lujan as she mentally cursed him. He was savvy and knew the system well. She also knew that in the unlikely event the case went to trial, it should be moved outside of El Pastor County. Heavy drug use was too prevalent and a sympathetic jury would make it difficult to get a conviction. But that motion should originate from the defense.

"Do you plan to file a change of venue?" she asked as if the question was routine.

"I hadn't thought about it. Would you object if I did?"

"I don't know. We'd have to give it some thought," she replied.

"I'll let you know."

AS THEY WALKED out of the courthouse, Marty looked over at David. "Why do I get the feeling she's not too high on this case, suggesting a plea deal, then asking about changing the trial site."

"You have good instincts."

"What do you mean?"

"Get in and I'll tell you."

As they drove away David began talking.

David knew El Pastor County's reputation well enough, having defended past clients involved in a host of criminal charges linked to drugs. The county, comprised of seven thousand square miles and a population of fifty thousand, encompassed the most pastoral, serene and archeologically intriguing landscape within the state. Seventy-two percent of the population was Hispanic. The county distinguished itself not for its achievements of health and social progress but for its dismal perdition. El Pastor County was made up of small towns, widely dispersed villages and American Indian pueblos. Many of its roads became impassable during the winter months. Over forty percent of county residents were without medical insurance. One quarter of the population had less than a high school diploma. Too many families lived below the poverty level. Unemployment shifted between ten and fourteen percent and jobs, mainly in service and retail industries, came with few benefits. Drug and alcohol abuse were major problems.

Heroin became rampant in the county after World War II. The drug, perpetuated within tight-knit families, became an almost inescapable cycle. Alcohol abuse was a close second. Crack cocaine and crystal meth found their niche among young people who combined them with heroin. David told the story of a father driving his two daughters, one pregnant, to a dealer's home. Waiting in the car while they had sex with the dealer, the daughters returned with their payment, two crack rocks, which they shared with dad.

"Sounds like a depressing place," Marty said.

"You think?"

"What are the chances of getting an acquittal?" Marty asked.

"This is going to be a tough case to try."

"Why so?"

"Because the D.A. has strong evidence; DNA, weapon, motive, and no other suspects. The D.A. portrays Theo as morally corrupt, cold, and heartless and the jury starts forming their initial impression. Then the D.A. inserts the Jude Armstrong portion. All that circumstantial evidence takes on a factual quality in the minds of the jurors. It's hard to turn them around after that."

"And Theo's still not talking?"

"Nope, he's not being forthcoming for whatever reason. But that's going to have to change regardless of who defends him—unless he decides to cop a plea deal."

"You're not defending him?"

"The fact is that I was away from the office for a few months and that put a strain on the partners. And there's also the expense factor; it's going to be considerable. I'd like to defend the kid, but I can't afford to take it on pro bono. I can't justify it to the partners."

Marty remained silent taking in all David said. After a few moments he spoke, "You know, I feel responsible for what happened to Theo. If I hadn't taken my suspicions to Snyder, chances are none of this would have happened."

David gave him a quick gaze. "I believe you're right."

Marty continued, "Jude Armstrong was my closest friend. When I heard all Theo did for her, payback has really been unfair to him. I've given this a lot of thought and maybe you can give me your opinion."

"About what?"

"About chasing some of these leads like tracking Victoria's husband, Aban Bashir, and their son, Elijah. I think he goes by Ilyas now."

"How do you know that?"

"Because the priest all but told me so. And I guess it makes sense because Ilyas is Arabic for Elijah."

"Sure you didn't miss your calling as a private eye?"

Marty raised a quizzical eyebrow before continuing. "On my next assignment to Europe or the Middle East I was thinking of detouring to Morocco to snoop around and see what I can find."

"Are you trying to ease your conscience?"

"That's part of it. But there's something bigger. I never knew Jude had a grandson. Theoretically, if alive he should inherit her estate."

David raised his own eyebrows. "You got a point. How often do you get out there?"

"About twice a year, but sometimes more often — it all depends on where news is happening."

"I'd be interested to know anything you find out."

"I'll keep you posted. Hopefully you'll still be on the case."

"We'll have to see about that."

Thirty-eight

ON FRIDAY ILYAS arrived at the mosque in time for midday prayer. It had been many years since he had last visited a mosque. Entering, he removed his shoes. He washed his hands, face and feet in the traditional manner, then followed the others to devotion. With his eyes focused on the ground, he prostrated as imam led them in prayer. Ilyas prayed fervently, thanking God for his freedom and his good health, and pleading mercifully to rid his soul of the evil djinn that were causing all his torment and suffering.

When he heard imam pray, "*Assalamu Alaikum Varhamatullh*", Ilyas turned to the worshipper on the right and repeated the verse, then to the left. After prayer had ended, he left the mosque.

Two weeks of searching for work and with money running low, Ilyas knew he had to preserve what little was left. One of the hostel guests suggested a food kitchen located several blocks away, and

Ilyas began taking his meal there. The food was different than anything he had ever eaten. For the first few days Ilyas would not take any of the meat offerings, fearing it would contaminate his soul. But, reasoning that his soul was already contaminated and unable to resist the tantalizing dish, he began eating it.

One day he spoke to the director with an offer to help clean up the kitchen.

The director, a short, corpulent, balding man who spoke English, replied, "I can't pay you anything. We have no money for that."

"Payment of the meal is enough," Ilyas replied. "Anyway, this is all I can offer you. I have no *zakat* to spare."

"What's that?" the director asked.

"Donations of money."

Led into the kitchen, Ilyas spent part of his afternoon washing pots and pans. Returning most days for his meal, Ilyas regularly helped clean up in the kitchen. As Ilyas was loading the dishwasher after meals one day, the director approached him. "Where do you come from?" he asked.

"Casablanca, Morocco."

"Why did you leave there?"

Choosing not to reveal too much of his past, Ilyas replied, "To find work."

"And I suspect you haven't found any?"

"Not yet."

"I have a friend who manages a large furniture warehouse and sometimes needs help unloading the big trucks. Are you interested?"

"Yes, I could do that," Ilyas replied enthusiastically.

THE WAREHOUSE WAS located seven kilometers from the hostel in an industrial part of the city. On the appointed day Ilyas arose early and began making his way by catching the only bus traveling in that direction, then walking the remaining kilometer.

When Ilyas tried introducing himself to the mop-headed, barrel-chested manager, he seemed hurried and impatient. He spoke neither English nor French and signaled for Ilyas to go away. Just then someone else arrived.

"Are you looking for day work too?" the stranger asked Ilyas in English.

"Yes, I heard there might be work unloading trucks."

Ilyas heard the two in a quick exchange, then the laborer turned to Ilyas, once again. "Let's go. There's a truck on the dock ready to unload."

As they walked to the dock, the laborer turned around, "I'm Severino Carbajal. You better learn Spanish if you're planning to work in Spain."

"Yes, I'm finding that out," Ilyas replied.

When they finished unloading the first truck, the manager ordered them to wait for a second truck. By mid-afternoon the two had finished, and after receiving their wages, went off to find a place to eat.

BORN IN A town in central Spain, Severino moved to Madrid to attend the university. Unable to find a permanent job, he became a day laborer. Both Ilyas and Severino found common interest in trying to survive in Madrid as cheaply as possible. Severino invited Ilyas to a second unloading job the following day. Ilyas reciprocated by telling him about the hostel and the food kitchen. As they finished their meal, the two left to retrieve Severino's belongings to move him to the hostel.

As their friendship grew, Severino began teaching Ilyas Spanish. The two continued working as day laborers two days each week. The wages gave them just enough to pay their hostel room and buy meals at a cheap restaurant when they missed the food kitchen. Later in the evenings they would walk to a cerveceria and talk over beer and soda.

Each Friday Ilyas attended midday mosque service. Soon he became acquainted with regular worshippers, usually exchanging complaints about the hot Madrid summers or the torrential downpours. After service one day, a worshiper stopped to chat with him.

"I see you here every Friday, do you live close by?" he asked.

Ilyas' Spanish was halting and broken. "Yes, not so far."

"My name's Mustafa. You're not from Spain?"

"No. I'm from Casablanca."

"Are you going to the university?"

"No, I no have money for that yet. I get here just two months back; look for work."

"What's your trade?" Mustafa asked.

"No trade, but almost three years at university in Morocco."

"Do you have papers? A passport?"

"Yes."

Mustafa thought for a few seconds, then suggested, "I own an electrical business. Come to see me one day and maybe I can help you find work."

"Tomorrow?" Ilyas replied.

"If that's what you'd like. Here's my card."

Illuminations, an electrical company, maintained its main business in Madrid and smaller stores in two other cities. In addition to selling lighting and general electrical products and supplies,

Illuminations also installed and repaired electrical appliances in homes and commercial buildings. More than fifty employees worked for the company.

Ilyas was waiting outside Mustafa's office the following morning when he arrived. The Moroccan impressed Mustafa with his enthusiasm and his pleasant manner. If Ilyas had the drive to learn the language in his short time in Madrid, maybe he would have that same motivation for hard work, Mustafa thought. He offered Ilyas a part-time job assisting in inventory control, and the young Moroccan happily accepted.

The work was tedious and exacting, requiring accuracy in receiving, ordering, recording, and reconciling the entire company's inventory. Ilyas worked hard and learned fast, oftentimes working through lunch and staying late. Despite the constant co-worker harassment about his broken Spanish, Ilyas laughed it off and doubled his efforts at learning the language.

Thirty-nine

AFTER DAVID RECEIVED Patrick's call about Theo's arrest, sleep never returned. Sitting and staring out his courtyard window, the thought occurred to David to call his secretary to say he would be out of the office most of the day. With support from Juliana, David had finally returned to work.

David's mind shifted to Rayèn. He wondered how she was handling their impending divorce.

In therapy, David talked a great deal about their relationship. There were many conflicts in their marriage, he told Juliana. Strict in raising Patrick and their two girls, Rayèn made sure they never missed church or Bible school. Shocked at finding gay magazines hidden in Patrick's room one day, Rayèn phoned Pastor Eric. When Patrick returned from school, they were all waiting to confront him. The following day, Patrick ran away. For five years there was no contact with him and David agonized over losing his son. When Patrick finally reappeared, he had changed a great deal. He was mature far beyond his years. Although Patrick never returned home to live, he visited often and attended all the family celebrations. And while Patrick alluded to living a gay lifestyle in Santa Fe, David vowed never to cause a rift with his son again. But then at their daughter's wedding, Patrick brought along his boyfriend, Esteban. Rayèn couldn't contain herself. Viciously attacking Esteban, branding their relationship an abomination, and demanding he end it, Rayèn's rebuke drove Patrick away, once again. David was enraged when he heard what she had done. For days he refused to speak to his wife.

Later that year, when they learned that Patrick was critically ill,

Rayèn discovered David was to be tested first to see if he was a compatible donor. Immediately, she tried to coerce Esteban into relinquishing his role as Patrick's medical surrogate, hoping she would become the surrogate and delay the transplant testing until Patrick was too far gone. Her secret would have died with her son and she would have been safe. But when an acquaintance from Rayèn's past surfaced to protect Patrick with the threat to reveal all she knew, Rayèn had little choice but to go through with the testing and the transplant operation. When David's test results returned, Rayèn finally confessed to David that Patrick was not his natural son. She had cheated on him before their marriage. While the infidelity may have been reconcilable, her scheme was unconscionable.

Talking about all of this with Juliana only reinforced in his mind that his affection for Rayèn was fading.

The coffee maker gave off a low beep interrupting his thoughts. David stood up and glanced over to the pistol case. It seemed like an eternity had passed since that desperate night he tried taking his life. Returning to therapy with Juliana had made all the difference. He picked up the case and walked into the kitchen. Opening the empty freezer, he laid it inside, then went for the coffee.

By eight o'clock David was headed for Santa Fe. An hour later he pulled into Emilia's Café and parked. Patrick hadn't yet arrived. As he walked inside and waited for the hostess, David glanced at the headlines of the local newspaper lying on the glass-topped counter next to the cash register.

Arbol Verde Suspect Arrested in Brother's Murder

The hostess approached. "Just one?" she asked, interrupting his attention.

"No, two. Where can I get a copy of this?" he asked, pointing to the paper.

"Right outside the door...there's a news rack."

"I'll be right back."

Before he could finish reading the article, Patrick arrived.

"Hey Dad."

David looked up awestruck. "Have you seen this?"

Patrick took a seat across from David. "Yeah, I read that piece of garbage this morning."

"What's this all about? Why are they bringing up the gay thing again? Is any of it true?"

"Dad, whoever wrote this story didn't bother to check their facts. Yeah, it's true that Theo's gay. But that's where it ends."

"What makes you so sure?"

"Because I know Theo and I know Father Bonafacio. If you count the times Kerry Snyder's name is mentioned in that article, that'll give you a clue who's behind it. It's a political thing, Dad. The cop's running for county commissioner here in Santa Fe. He's pumping up his image."

"What do you know about the murder?" David asked.

"I got a call from Theo early this morning after he was arrested. It was short. He said Romel came up to him and pushed him as he was leaving the rectory parking lot. Theo hit Romel and knocked him down, then drove off. Romel was alive when he left."

"What was Theo doing at the priest's house last night?"

"I don't know. He didn't have time to talk about that. What I do know is that Theo and Father Bonafacio are close friends. It was Father Bonafacio who brought Theo to A Plan for Tomorrow about eight years ago. Theo's parents are big time druggies."

"A Plan for Tomorrow. Your group? The one that helps runaways?"

"Yeah, they suspected Theo was being abused at home. They put him in a foster home and he did really well. He was one of the first clients I got to know when I joined the group. I kinda became his big brother and all through high school we hung out on weekends. He'd come over and we'd watch sports and eat pizza. Esteban and I would take him camping and fishing. After graduation he got a job at a classy restaurant and decided he wanted to be chef."

"The article talks about Theo's dad having it out with the priest. What about that?"

Patrick shook his head and snickered. "If you knew that asshole, it's more like he was pissed off Theo spent too much time with Father Bonafacio. Sixto, Theo's dad, was afraid Theo might tell the priest what was going on at home. There's nothing kindhearted about him. He's always high on heroin. They get by on welfare and food stamps."

"Did Theo tell you he was being abused?"

"Nah, he never told anybody directly. But it was obvious from his actions and what he said when he talked about living with his parents. He was afraid of them. He didn't want to charge Sixto with anything because he knew his dad would find him and kill him."

"What about Romel?"

"Another loser. He's, or he was, a *tecato* with a King Kong habit."

"What does that mean?"

"That he sold heroin to support his big time habit."

"I don't know about this case, Patrick. Here's a kid who doesn't want to come straight with me, a cop that's desperate to nail him, and a gut feeling the kid's being railroaded. This is an open murder case now. It's going to be expensive to defend him. Any ideas about that?

"A bunch of us are meeting tonight to talk about how we can raise money to help him. His foster parents, his boss, some of the volunteers, some high school friends, we're meeting at the church where our APFT group meets."

David gave a deep sigh. "Okay, let me know how things turn out at your meeting."

Forty

AFTER WEEKS IN inventory control, early one morning Mustafa approached Ilyas.

"Today you will be assigned to one of our service men and act as his helper," he said.

"Of course, whatever you want me to do," Ilyas replied.

Federico Cardenas, a young journeyman electrician, was known for his cocky attitude and edgy personality. He had gone through three different helpers over the last year—none had been able to work with him for very long. Ordered by Mustafa to take Ilyas along as his helper for the day, Federico balked.

Throughout the day Ilyas sensed Federico's impatience, but ignored it and did exactly as he was told.

At the end of the day Mustafa approached Ilyas. "How did you like the work?"

"I think I irritated Federico more than helped."

Mustafa laughed. "Don't worry, that's his nature. But he's a very good electrician. Do you want the job permanently?"

"How many days will I work?"

"The same as everyone here, five days a week."

Ilyas smiled broadly. "I'd like nothing better."

"Okay, you start tomorrow."

THE SON OF an electrician, Federico had apprenticed while still in high school. Boasting about becoming the electrical union's youngest member, he moved to Madrid shortly after graduating from school. Federico had the personality of a young, coddled boy, Ilyas discovered. He came to work cranky and bad-tempered at the beginning of each work week. Every Monday morning Ilyas learned to stay quiet until after lunch. By either Tuesday or Wednesday Federico's temper moderated. He was often arrogant and demanding and it was hard staying on Federico's good side. Ilyas constantly found himself stroking Federico's ego just to get along. He typically acquiesced with Federico's judgments and opinions, curbing his own views. But Federico did have a sense of humor, and so long as he wasn't the butt of any joke, they laughed heartily. Ilyas tried to absorb as much of Federico's skill as he could. He sensed that his endless questions sometimes irritated Federico, but over time their relationship improved greatly.

As they traveled to an appointment one day, Federico asked, "Are you still living in that hostel by the Centro?"

"Yeah. It's cheap."

"I help manage some apartments by the university. One of our tenants has left. So, I was thinking it would be ideal for you. If you want that apartment, you could move in at the end of the month."

The thought had not occurred to Ilyas to move out of the hostel. "I'm not sure. I like where I'm at for now."

"But, you could have privacy and more security for your property. And I bet the rent would be about as much as you pay at the hostel. Surely, you want that, don't you?"

"Let me think about it."

"I'll tell you what we'll do. I'll drive there after this appointment and show you the apartment. I know you're going to like it. It would rent very quickly, but I think it would be perfect for you."

Exasperated by Federico's insistence, Ilyas replied, "I'll consider it."

The apartment was located in a row of other similar dwellings. It was nicer than Ilyas could have ever imagined. It had its own bathroom and a tiny kitchen with a stove and refrigerator. The apartment was furnished with pots and pans and dishes, but they would be of little use to Ilyas who knew nothing about cooking. On one corner of the main room was a small table with two chairs. The bedroom had two single beds pushed together and a four-drawer dresser.

"We rent these apartments to university students. So the rent is not so expensive," Federico said.

"Even at that cost, I don't think I can afford it," Ilyas replied.

Federico walked away. Ilyas saw him flip open his cell phone and make a call. A few minutes later he returned. "Okay, I've managed to get the rent reduced for you."

"But, I don't have all the money for the deposit," Ilyas said.

"For God's sake, I'll lend you the deposit."

With no other excuses he could think up, Ilyas reluctantly agreed to move in.

THAT EVENING AT the cerveceria with Severino, Ilyas told him of the apartment.

"I'm thinking of moving out of the hostel, too," Severino replied.

"Why? Where are you going?"

"I lost one of the moving jobs. The other isn't enough to support me. I'm going back home."

"But what about the university?"

"Well, that will have to wait for another time."

Ilyas could not let his only friend leave Madrid. Suddenly he had a thought. "Maybe I can help you get work."

"What can you do?"

"You move in with me for the time being. The apartment has two beds. It's large enough for both of us. In the meantime I'll talk to Mustafa about giving you a job."

Since early in their friendship Severino had suspected Ilyas was different—maybe even gay. While Ilyas had never come on to him, Severino occasionally saw his friend's wandering eyes linger on handsome men passing by. Ilyas showed little interest in women and never talked about sex. But none of that mattered to Severino. The idea of living together seemed ideal, as it wouldn't be much different than their present arrangement of a shared hostel room. "You think you can put up with me?"

"Listen, my friend, I have never lived alone in all my life. I've always been surrounded by my family. In all honesty I don't know how to live alone."

"Will Federico allow me to move in?"

"Those apartments are usually rented to university students. So, I don't see why both of us can't occupy it. I'll ask him tomorrow."

"Okay, let's do it."

The two raised their glasses and toasted their agreement.

After interviewing Severino, Mustafa agreed to place him in the same part-time inventory control job that Ilyas once had. Severino performed well, and soon after memorizing the names and uses of many of the different parts, supplies, and lighting products, Mustafa transferred him to the sales department. The job suited Severino well. His friendly nature and hard-work satisfied customers and sold the company's products.

Forty-one

AFTER BREAKFAST WITH Patrick, David drove north toward the town of San Lorenzo, the county seat and the domicile of the El Pastor Detention Center. Two hours later he arrived and walked inside the building. He approached the desk officer. "I'm here to see Theo Jaquez."

The officer looked up at David. "Visitors aren't allowed until noon."

"I'm his attorney."

The officer looked surprised. "Hold on a second. I'll be right back." He stood up and walked to one of the adjoining offices. A few seconds later a familiar face walked out of the office.

"Hey, Lujan. You're here early. Is this a formal or informal visit?"

Snyder had a smug expression on his face—the type expressing self-righteous arrogance, David observed. His anger began building. "I hope you're not interviewing my client without me, Snyder, or I'll take you before the ethics board so fast you'll think you're dancing."

Snyder's expression suddenly changed. "Wait a minute. The kid never asked for an attorney."

David's voice was stern. "I specifically told you not to question him without me being present. If that's what you're doing, I want you to stop the interview now until I've talked to him."

"Let him through," Snyder instructed the desk officer. David walked around the corner through the door and Snyder began escorting him to the interview room.

"How did his brother die?" David asked.

"Theo bashed his head in."

"You have the weapon?"

Snyder stared straight ahead, refusing to look at David. "Not yet, but we'll find it."

"Just like you said you'd find out who beat up my client last time we talked?"

Snyder didn't respond. He led David into a small room. Theo was sitting in a chair nodding off to sleep.

"Are there any listening devices in this room?" David asked Snyder.

"What do you think this is, Lujan, NCIS?"

"I take that as a no. I want to talk to him alone."

Fixing his cold eyes on David, Snyder walked out of the room and closed the door.

Theo looked up and formed a slight smile. "Thanks for coming."

"Have you had any sleep?" David asked.

He shook his head. "I've been in here since they arrested me last night."

"Okay, I'm not going to ask you any questions now. I'll be back later. In the meantime if they try to question you again, tell them you want to see me. You understand?"

"Okay."

"Don't talk to anybody or sign anything unless it goes through me. I'm going to have them put you in a segregated cell so you can get some sleep."

"Does this mean you're going to defend me?"

David thought about the question for a few seconds. "For the time being I'm defending you. "

"Yeah, well, I was wondering what we had to do to file charges against my dad."

"What do you mean?"

"I want to file sex abuse charges against him. My dad's hurt so many people that I care about, I don't ever want to give him the chance of hurting Julian or Sonia, my foster parents."

David pondered Theo's request for a second. "Okay, I'll speak to the authorities and get the charges filed.

Theo nodded his head.

In a dazed, slow voice, Theo said, "When this is all over I'll make you the best braised lamb and baby potatoes you've ever tasted."

"Okay, that's a deal. Now try and get some sleep."

David walked out of the room and looked for Snyder. Snyder was sitting at a desk. Two other officers were around him. "You violated my client's rights, Snyder. Everything the kid said I want expunged or I'm filing charges against you."

Snyder stood up and walked toward David. "Look, Lujan, maybe we just got off on the wrong foot. If I had known you were representing him..."

David interrupted. "That's all bullshit and you know it. I want you to put my client in a segregated cell away from the general population. I'll be back later to talk with him after he's rested. Just to make it perfectly clear to you, I'm officially representing Theo Jaquez and I want to be present at any interview the police have with my client. Do you understand?"

"I'm getting fed up with your attitude and all your demands, Lujan."

"Yeah, well you better start getting used to it. You violate my client's rights again and I promise you'll be digging out of a hole so deep my attitude won't matter."

David walked out of the building and to his car. There was nothing about Snyder he liked and he had him pegged. An opportunist with political ambitions was the worst kind of cop. David would babysit Theo for the time being to make sure it was all done fairly. Then, if he cut himself from the case, it would be a clean break.

Forty-two

IT WAS STILL dark when Father Bonafacio rose from bed and knelt to pray. He prayed solemnly for the soul of Romel who was murdered outside the rectory. In the middle of his prayers the phone rang. There was a momentary thought of letting it go to voice message, but changed his mind. He stood up and walked over to pick it up.

"Father Bonafacio, this is Monsignor Keeler."

"How are you, Monsignor?"

Ignoring the greeting, Monsignor Keeler asked, "How long have you *really* been in a relationship with Theo Jaquez?"

"I beg you pardon?"

"Was my question not clear enough for you?"

His harsh tone, especially at that early hour, annoyed Father Bonafacio. "I've known Theo Jaquez for eight years," he replied. "As a parishioner and friend."

"Is that how long the two of you have been carrying on?"

"Carrying on what?" The priest was shocked by Monsignor Keeler's insinuation.

"Your relationship."

"I don't know exactly what you are asking me, Monsignor Keeler. All I know is that last night his brother was murdered in the rectory parking lot after Theo left from here. Is that what you are referring to in this conversation?"

"I'm trying to find a way to respond to the media responsibly. Can you appreciate my position in all of this?"

"Then maybe I'm not understanding you."

"Father Bonafacio, I take it you haven't read the Santa Fe newspaper this morning?"

"That's correct. I read the paper after my morning prayers."

"I would like see you this afternoon...in my office."

"Yes, of course."

Immediately after their conversation Father Bonafacio walked outside for the newspaper. Reading the headline, his blood rushed to his head. "Lord in heaven, what is this?"

Making his way back to the rectory the priest sat down to read the story as his head shook in disbelief.

The phone rang. It was a reporter requesting an interview. The priest declined and hung up. More calls began coming in and the priest let them roll over to voice messaging. Sitting numb, Father Bonafacio mentally reviewed his appointments for the day. With his reputation further disgraced, how could he ever shepherd the three communities?

When he heard the doorbell ring, Father Bonafacio instinctively stood up to answer it, then had second thoughts. Like the telephone, he would ignore it. The visitor was stubborn and wouldn't leave. Father Bonafacio walked to the door.

"Who is it?" he asked.

"David Lujan. I'm an attorney. I represent Theo. Can you talk to me for a moment, please?"

"No, I cannot speak with you."

"Father Bonafacio, I need to speak to you about Theo's arrest. It's very important."

There was silence for a few seconds before the priest slowly opened the door. "How is Theo?" the priest asked.

"Not great. They have him at El Pastor Detention Center. I just came from seeing him and plan to go back again later."

"Come in." Closing the door, the priest walked pensively

through the rectory to his office.

"I'm sorry to bother you at what must be a very disturbing time. However, I don't have a choice, Father. Theo's being charged with a crime he may or may not have committed."

"Theo did not kill his brother," the priest interrupted.

David had to pay close attention over the Priest's strong accent. "How can you be so sure?"

"Because I know the boy. He could never do anything like that."

"Do you know who did it?"

The priest shook his head.

"Did you hear anything outside last night after Theo left?"

"I came in here and began to prepare my Sunday sermon. About ten o'clock the police rang my doorbell. They told me Romel had been killed outside the rectory, in the parking lot. At first I didn't understand what they were saying. Then they told me his body was lying in the parking lot. Romel never came to church here. I only knew him because Theo showed me who he was. Whenever I went to the *tienda*, he was always outside with his friends. I never talked to him. The police asked me questions for about thirty minutes then they left. They stayed outside until at least two this morning. I kept looking out the window and saw there were a lot of police cars coming and going. A few of them had large spotlights they were shining in the parking lot. They were taking pictures and taking measurements. That's all I know."

"Did the police come back to speak with you anymore?"

"No. Except..." he paused briefly.

"Except what, Father?"

"Somebody from the newspaper came to the door and began asking questions. I told them to leave."

"Why?"

"Because the police said it would be better not to talk to anyone until they completed the investigation."

"And because you didn't speak to the newspaper about the sex allegation, I assume that's why they wrote that you refused to deny it?"

His elbow on the desk, the priest laid his head down on his hand.

"Father, is there any truth to the sexual allegation?"

The priest looked up at him and shook his head. "We are good friends. Everything they wrote in the newspaper is false."

"Then where did they get all the details for the story?"

"From Sixto, Theo's father."

"Just a few more questions and I'll be done. Why was Theo here last night?"

"Because he wanted to assure me the newspaper stories about the San Lucas woman were wrong and that they would soon sort it all out."

Sell your books at sellbackyourBook.com!
Go to sellbackyourBook.com and get an instant price quote. We even pay the shipping - see what your old books are worth today!

Inspected By: catalina_ciprian

00064134070

0006413

4070

c-2
S-1

"Is that the only reason?"

The priest hesitated before responding. "I cannot say any more, Mr. Lujan."

"Why not?"

"Because it involves something that was said to me in confession. I cannot break the seal of the confessional."

"Not even in these circumstances?"

"My code does not allow me to betray a penitent."

"I understand. Thank you for your help."

"What is going to happen to Theo?" the priest asked.

"I don't know, Father. It's too early to tell." As David stood up, he thought to ask, "Can you show me exactly where the body was last night?"

"Yes. Let's go out to the parking lot."

David extended his hand. "I'm sorry for what's happened to you, Father."

"Thank you. Can you do me one favor, Mr. Lujan?"

"Of course."

Please, tell Theo that I'm praying for him."

"I will do that."

Forty-three

ONE DAY FEDERICO announced, "I'm getting married. You and your friend must come to my wedding. But no one else at work must know."

"Why?" Ilyas asked, curious about the strange demand.

"Because that's just the way I want it."

Knowing Federico's unpredictable personality, Ilyas knew not to probe too much deeper. "I didn't even know you were engaged. You've never told me about your bride."

Federico laughed. "You mean my boyfriend."

Stunned, Ilyas stared at Federico.

"We finally decided to get married after living together for five years."

"Can two men marry?" Ilyas asked.

"Ilyas, this is Spain. The country has allowed gay marriage since 2005."

Ilyas remained silent.

"The reason I invited you is because I thought you and your friend..."

"You mean Severino?"

"Yes, aren't both of you a couple?"

"You think we're a gay couple?"

"You got him a job with the company; you live together, so I just assumed..."

Ilyas shook his head no.

Hiding his confusion, Federico said, "Well, anyway, you're both still invited. I hope you'll come."

Sharing Federico's invitation at the cerveceria that evening, Severino grew excited. "They're probably going to have food and drinks and music and dancing."

"I don't know, I guess."

"I want to go," Severino said.

"Didn't you understand, it's a gay wedding. Two men are getting married to one another."

"So what's the big deal? Gay men are lots of fun."

"Are they?"

"Actually, the most fun I've ever had was at a gay bar."

"You have sex with men?" Ilyas asked

Severino laughed. "Just because you go to a gay bar doesn't mean you have sex with men. I went with some gay friends to drink and laugh and dance."

"Is that what you expect will happen at the wedding?"

"I guess we'll find out."

FOR THE DAYS leading up to the wedding Ilyas remained apprehensive. In Morocco such a thing could never happen. Islam did not allow it. But while it was taught that homosexuality was unnatural, everyone knew the practice was tolerated so long as every Muslim man married and had children. To do otherwise was offensive to God. In his heart Ilyas knew he could never have feelings with any woman like those he had once experienced with Gabriel. Despite the djinn's recrimination echoing in his soul, that single experience was indelibly branded in his mind. Worried about his Muslim obligation, Ilyas preferred to stay away from the wedding. He had no desire to imbue any greater wrath from the evil djinn. But Severino was insistent that they attend. Rather than let down his friend, Ilyas went along.

It was a Friday evening when Ilyas and Severino arrived at the Toledo Hotel. Directed to the large room where the Cardenas/Serrano wedding was to be held, they were surprised by the many guests and the beautiful adornments. A red aisle runner separated the guest chairs which were perfectly arranged on both sides of the room. At the front was a large wedding arch. No less than ten oversized flower pots, each containing an assortment of colorfully arranged flowers, were elaborately tiered on each side of the arch. Two grand candle holders were positioned behind a small table to the right of the arch.

Many of the guests were mingling around a bar in the back of the room. Ilyas and Severino walked toward that area and ordered drinks. As they watched more guests arrive, the room began filling quickly.

Someone spoke to them. "*Hola!*"

Severino and Ilyas turned to see a pretty young woman smiling at them. Severino replied first. "*Hello.* It's going to be quite a party tonight."

"Most gay weddings are," she replied. "My name's Elena. I hope you don't mind, but you two are the only faces I recognize."

Unfamiliar to either of them, Ilyas and Severino exchanged puzzled gazes.

Seeing their expressions, she asked, "Don't you live in the apartments by the university?"

Suddenly Severino recognized her over the light make-up and beautiful gown she wore. "Of course, you're the apartment at the very end?"

"Yes. I've rented from Enrique since I started the university."

"Who's Enrique?" Ilyas asked.

"Federico's boyfriend. He manages apartments all over the city." There was a lull for a few seconds, then Elena asked, "So how long have you two been together?"

They laughed.

"What's so funny?"

"We live together to save money. We're not gay. But apparently we resemble a gay couple because Federico invited us believing that, too," Severino said.

"Oh, sorry."

"No offense taken," he replied.

At that moment an announcement was made for guests to be seated.

"You'll sit with us?" Severino asked Elena.

"Yes, if you don't mind."

Taking their seats, the wedding music began. Federico and Enrique appeared from opposite sides of the room dressed in matching tuxedos and white scarves. Each was accompanied by several handsome male escorts. They proceeded to the arch where the minister waited. After greeting the guests, the minister recited the traditional wedding vows, and then asked each to pledge their love, respect, and fidelity to the other. There was a nervous laugh from the guests when Federico questioned the "fidelity" word, but Enrique's swift elbow nudge got his quick response. After lighting the candles and exchanging rings, the two kissed and marched down the red carpet.

When the ceremony ended, everyone was led into the next room where tables and chairs were arranged with flowers and bows and small guest tokens at each setting. As the food was served, a trio played soft music. Soon Federico brought over his spouse to introduce to Ilyas and Severino and greet Elena. They chatted briefly, then the newlyweds moved on. When everyone was finished, a new group began playing and the tables were cleared. Federico and Enrique stood up first to dance. The parents followed. A few minutes later guests joined in, and Severino wasted no time asking Elena. Ilyas stayed sipping soda and watching every possible combination of men and women dance together.

As the evening wore on, Ilyas managed to catch up with Severino and Elena between dances. Whispering to his friend that he was leaving, Ilyas then walked over to thank Federico and congratulate the couple one more time. As he turned to leave, someone spoke, "Would you like to dance?"

Ilyas turned the other direction. A handsome Spaniard was smiling at him. "I'm sorry, I don't think so. I'm not gay."

"My old boyfriend said the same about me," the Spaniard replied.

"Huh?"

"He said I couldn't be gay either because I had no sense of color."

Ilyas grinned. "Was he correct?"

"Yes, in a way. I'm colorblind."

Ilyas laughed.

"Then would you have a drink at the bar with me," the Spaniard suggested.

"I'm Muslim. I don't drink."

"I'm a printer. I do."

His wit and straight face was funny to Ilyas.

"You know, somehow it seems like I already know you," the Spaniard said.

"Oh, what makes you think that?"

"Well, I know you don't dance, you don't drink, you're Muslim, and you're very attractive."

Ilyas blushed. "I'm not used to compliments from men."

"I'm not used to giving them. You can ask my old boyfriend."

"I'm Ilyas."

"Alejandro." There was a silent second. Then he said, "Ilyas, that's nice. So, how about that drink?"

"Yes, I'll have a soda."

Forty-four

SEVERAL HOURS AFTER Father Bonafacio had finished Sunday mass and left Alcorisa, cars began arriving from the villages of Arbol Verde and Vitoria, and congregants began filling the pews in the small church. About one hundred people squeezed into the nave which typically served no more than sixty Sunday worshipers.

Deacon Juan Garcia, who lived in Alcorisa, had been appointed by the board of directors to host the meeting. Its purpose was to discuss the scandal involving Father Bonafacio. When everyone was seated, Deacon Juan announced a telephone call he had just received that the Arbol Verde rectory had been vandalized and Luz Vigil knocked unconscious.

The congregation gasped in alarm.

A few minutes later, after getting the congregation to settle down, the Deacon began the meeting. "*Bueno*, we all know why we're here. I think we should just go over what we know as the facts instead of all the rumors being circulated. We know Sixto Jaquez of Arbol Verde accused Father Bonafacio of having sex with his son..."

Facundo Morales interrupted Deacon Juan. "My son was an altar boy and I'm wondering if Father Bonafacio turned him gay. When he moved to California after high school he got married."

"What's the problem then?" someone asked in Spanish.

"The problem is that he married a man," explained Facundo.

"Facundo, your son was always gay," someone yelled out. The crowd erupted in laughter.

"*Que estupido*, nobody can make anybody gay. You're either gay or you're not gay," someone else roared out.

"That's not true," yelled another voice.

Suddenly voices began shouting uncontrollably. Deacon Juan stopped the boisterous exchange. "We're not going to get anything done if everybody keeps yelling at one another. Let's just have one person talk at a time."

He saw Susanna Chacon raise her hand, and called on her.

"I'm wondering about all that money they found at the rectory. Where did that come from?"

"What does it matter where it came from?" someone said.

"The police planted it in the rectory," yelled out someone else.

A sudden roar of hand clapping erupted, expressing their mistrust of the *chotas*.

Again, chaos erupted and it was impossible to hear any single voice.

"This isn't getting us anywhere," Deacon Juan said after bringing the crowd back under control. "We need to decide what we're going to do."

Someone stood up in the back. "Sixto Jaquez is a *tecato*. Do we believe a *tecato* over Father Bonafacio?"

Another stood up. "Let's wait until after the trial. Then we can see how much is true and how much the *chotas* made up."

For the next hour the back and forth banter continued. Each time Deacon Juan managed to bring back order, another critical comment brought on more pandemonium.

Faustin Sanchez, who owned the Arbol Verde *tienda* and had the reputation as a strong voice in the Arbol Verde community, had asked Deacon Juan if he could say a few words. When everyone was finally quieted, the deacon called on Faustin. He stood up and walked to the front.

A native of Arbol Verde and in his mid-fifties, Faustin was a broad-shouldered, heavy figure with slicked back graying hair and a round face. It was hard to know his mood; his intense eyes, thin, stiff lips, and pouched cheeks gave no clue. Faustin was usually in good spirits, but when angered he could make the devil cower. He nervously ran his hand over the back of his head, then down his chin several times as if measuring the length of his stubble since his last shave. He looked around at all those present, then, in his heavy voice began speaking.

"I don't go to church too much, except when the *vieja* drags me here for Christmas and Easter. But the reason I'm here today is because I want to tell you about Father Bonafacio in the twenty years I've known him. Most of you remember Seneida Gonzales. She was always outside the *tienda* with all the *tecatos*. She had no shame begging for money for *chiva*. Seneida always smelled to high heaven. When Father Bonafacio came to the *tienda* one day, Seneida stopped him and asked for money. He walked up to her. I heard him ask if she was hungry; he even offered to get one of the church women to the rectory to help her take a bath and get cleaned up. She thought he was insulting her and began cussing at him. After that, every time Seneida saw Father Bonafacio at the *tienda* she always shouted filthy names at him. But he just smiled and walked past her. Then somebody found her beat up and half conscious under the bridge. The ambulance took her to the hospital. When Father Bonafacio found out, he went to see her. He stayed at the hospital with her for two days until she died. He even paid to bury her because nobody could find any family."

The crowd remained silent as Faustin continued, "When Antonio Vigil's house burned down, Father Bonafacio offered to put their whole family up at the rectory until they found someplace to stay. When they started rebuilding, Father Bonafacio was there every Saturday helping out. And the thing about it is that Antonio's family doesn't go to church here. They're not even Catholic.

"All the food we give Father Bonafacio from our orchards and gardens, he gives away to the poor. He doesn't care about their religion or even whether they go to church.

"When I read that trash in the newspaper about Sixto Jaquez accusing Father Bonafacio, I never believed any of it was true. I could never believe anything a *tecato* says over Father Bonafacio. Father Bonafacio's brought nothing but good things to Arbol Verde, Alcorisa, and Vitoria. I'm here to tell you that unless we decide to back him up over what a *tecato* says, we're going to lose him. Can we afford to let that happen?"

As Faustin finished, the sound of hand clapping began at the back of the nave. Soon every member was standing and clapping.

Someone yelled out, "We need to get some protection for Father Bonafacio until after the trial."

Someone else spoke. "Let's take turns guarding the church and the rectory. I got a trailer we can park there."

Before anyone could say more, the church door flew open and a young boy ran up to Deacon Juan. He whispered to the Deacon who repeated the message to those in the nave. "Luz is saying Sixto broke into the rectory and he is the one who knocked her out. Father Bonafacio is on his way to Sixto's house now."

"Did anybody call the *chotas* ?" someone asked.

"No, we don't want them," was the reply.

"We need to go back up Father Bonafacio," someone yelled out.

Hearing that, the crowd rushed out to their cars, and much like a funeral procession, weaved a path down the interstate to Sixto's house in Arbol Verde.

Forty-five

SINCE THE NEWSPAPER article and the raid on the rectory, only Father Bonafacio's few ardent supporters stopped by to see him. While harassing calls had mostly stopped, Saturday confessions and Sunday services were attended by less than half the membership. As he sat in his office contemplating his situation, Father Bonafacio knew the low attendance and weekly donations were not enough to keep the churches operating. He also knew that asking the archdiocese for help would only confirm the archbishop's belief that he should be replaced. But never one to run away from problems, Father Bonafacio made a private commitment to remain at Santo Niño indefinitely.

LUZ VIGIL HAD a deep affection for Father Bonafacio. In spite of her wayward reputation for giving sexual favors to lonely husbands and widowers, Luz was always treated kindly by the priest. Several years earlier when she had contracted pneumonia, Father Bonafacio visited her frequently, bringing food, hearing her confession, and offering communion. Father Bonafacio always had a smile and warm greeting when she entered the church for eight-thirty Sunday service. The priest's manner never changed. She knew he was incapable of betraying the communities he looked after. He loved the people too much, and she knew they embraced him, as well. She was certain that given more time, the people would come to their senses. Their affection for Father Bonafacio would ultimately trump the perverse allegations of the notorious *tecatos*. To show her support and keep the priest's spirits up, each Sunday before Father Bonafacio returned from twelve o'clock mass at Alcorisa, she prepared and delivered a meal to the rectory. She also usually cleaned for him.

When Father Bonafacio arrived later than usual one Sunday and saw Luz sitting outside with her arms full of food, he suggested she use the hidden key located above the back door. After that, Luz's delicious fare was usually on the table by the time the exhausted priest returned to Arbol Verde.

Making her way to the back of the rectory the day of the meeting, Luz carefully placed the food down on the patio table as she reached above for the key. Opening the door, Luz immediately knew something was wrong. Making her way slowly inside the kitchen, she was gripped with fear seeing the cabinets open and clutter scattered all over the counter and floor. She was tempted to run out, but her curiosity overtook her fear. Luz stepped across broken dishes and walked cautiously into the dining room. She heard noise in the direction of the priest's office. A nanosecond of a face she recognized came into view before she felt an object strike her head. Luz collapsed to the floor.

When she finally regained consciousness, paramedics surrounded her. She could barely make out the outlines of Father Bonafacio and the state police behind them. Father Bonafacio immediately walked forward and knelt next to her. "Luz, how are you feeling?"

Too weak to say anything, Luz merely nodded. The paramedics lifted her onto their gurney and raced off to the hospital. Father Bonafacio followed behind.

Forty-six

BORN IN MADRID, Alejandro attended the university but dropped out when funds became scarce. He began working for Enrique as an apartment rental agent until finding a permanent job with a small printing company. The remainder of the evening passed quickly as he and Ilyas became better acquainted. When the guests began thinning, Alejandro offered Ilyas a ride. Seeing Severino and Elena in an intimate embrace slow dancing, Ilyas accepted the offer.

As Alejandro brought his car to a stop in front of Ilyas apartment, he asked, "Let's go out tomorrow?"

"Thanks, but I don't think so."

"Is it because I'm gay and you're not?"

Ilyas laughed. "We have a saying in Morocco. Sharing figs can leave you with none at all."

"That's all right. I don't like figs. They give me the runs."

"I have your phone number. I'll call you."

"That's the universal answer if you don't want to see somebody again," Alejandro said.

"Then I don't mean it that way. Alejandro, you're very..." He stopped.

"Very what?"

"Very funny. I will call you. Good night."

In bed that night, Ilyas' mind continued to go over the evening with Alejandro. He had enjoyed it more than he cared to admit. Waking up the following morning, Ilyas was not surprised that Severino had not come home. It wasn't until noon that Severino appeared and plopped down on the sofa.

"Wow, what a night."

Ilyas looked up from the book he was reading. "Good or not so good?"

"Are you kidding, the best since I've been here. We're going out again tonight. I'm in love."

Ilyas laughed. "Tell me that in a month and I might believe it."

"So how did your evening go?" Severino asked.

"Okay."

"Who was the gay guy chatting you up?"

Ilyas winced. "How do you know he's gay?"

"Because of the way he was hitting on you."

"When did you have time to notice?"

"Between dances. So are you seeing him again?"

"No. I'm not gay."

"Not even a little gay? I mean, everybody's at least thought about it."

"Not everybody."

"Well, just in case you were, it's no big deal. You're still my best friend." Severino stretched out and in a few minutes he was snoring.

Closing his book, Ilyas stood up and walked outside to collect the mail. Immediately recognizing one of the envelopes, he opened it. It was from his father.

My Dear Ilyas,

It is with a grieving heart that I write to tell you that your Uncle Aban has died. Two weeks after you were released from Sidi Kascen, my beloved brother contracted a disease the doctors could not identify. After leaving the hospital, we brought him home to us and cared for him. He slowly became paralyzed and unable to speak. Yesterday night he passed on. All the family was here in preparation and imam guided us as we washed and shrouded your uncle. We carried his coffin to the cemetery early this morning.

May Allah give him an easy and pleasant journey and shower blessings on his grave.

I will write more later when my tears end and my eyes dry.

With much love,
Your father, Asafar

A crushing sadness came over Ilyas like never before. He wept. How he longed to be back home with his family. Leaving the apartment, he went walking to try and ease his pain. When he returned, Severino was gone. Ilyas couldn't bear being alone. Picking up the phone, he called Alejandro. Within the hour Alejandro arrived and suggested a visit to the Plaza de Chueca — the barrio in Madrid rife with bars, restaurants, and cafes, he explained. Ilyas agreed. Anywhere that might ease his loneliness was where he wanted to be at that moment.

The barrio was lively with an eclectic crowd meandering about. Parking, they strolled down the neighborhood and stepped into an art gallery.

"I thought you were colorblind," Ilyas said as Alejandro stood admiring a bright oil pastel sunset painted on canvas.

"I am. But I know what I like."

"This painting is so...red," Ilyas said.

"Isn't red the color of passion?"

"It's also the color of violence and bloodshed."

"I guess that's the beauty of art — everyone sees something different."

As they left the gallery and walked down the street, Alejandro turned to Ilyas. "This is known as the Castro District of Madrid."

"What is that?"

"In San Francisco, California, where gay pride first started, they claimed an area known as the Castro District for their own."

"So a lot of gay people live here?"

"Yeah, they live and work and play here."

"In Morocco we have a walled city called the Medina where Muslims also live and work and gather for celebrations. There are some Muslims who have never been outside of the Medina. All their lives have been spent there. They know nothing else but what is within those high walls."

"Do they have radios, televisions, and computers there?"

"Of course. But there's also donkey carts some merchants still use. It's like going back a hundred years."

"Will you ever go back to Morocco?"

"At present my intention is to go to the United States."

"Why? What will you do there?"

"I must pay a visit to someone."

"When will you go?" Alejandro asked.

"Soon, I hope. But first I need to secure some papers."

Alejandro led them to a trendy restaurant managed by a friend. There was a light crowd and jazzy background music. Alejandro chose a corner table with a street side view.

"They do fusion cuisine here. Do you mind if I order for us?" Alejandro asked.

"What kind of food will you order?"

"A special seafood appetizer, lamb prepared with mangos, and a surprise dessert."

Ilyas smiled. "That sounds very delicious. You know Muslims are only allowed to eat meat that has been butchered in a certain way. The animal must be killed quickly and outside the company of any other animal. The blood must be allowed to drain from the body. Prayers are said over the animal. This is called *halal* meat."

"Do you want me to ask if the lamb is *halal*?"

Ilyas grinned. "That's not necessary. Since leaving Morocco I've become a heathen."

"So does that mean you'll have a glass of wine with me?"

"No Alejandro, I'm a heathen, not a pagan."

"Is there a difference?"

"Of course. A pagan would drink wine."

When dinner was over, they strolled back to Alejandro's car. The night was warm and muggy.

"I've enjoyed your company this evening," Ilyas said.

"And I've enjoyed admiring your handsome face in spite of your lonesome blue eyes."

"Lonesome blue eyes?" Ilyas repeated.

"You were with me tonight but I sensed your thoughts were somewhere else."

"You're very observant, Alejandro."

"Maybe too much for my own good. That's how I discovered my boyfriend's indiscretions."

"And then you left him?"

"No, it was a mutual split-up."

"Do you miss him?"

"I miss sleeping alone. A bed gets cold at night."

"You are correct...about my thoughts tonight. I apologize. My father wrote with some unpleasant news. My uncle died."

Alejandro stopped and looked at Ilyas. "I'm sorry."

"It was he who arranged..." His voice drifted off.

"Arranged what?"

"Arranged for me to travel to Spain. In Morocco it is expensive and difficult to travel out of the country."

A quiet moment passed. Ilyas was smitten with Alejandro; he didn't want the evening to end. He had an intense yearning to know the Spaniard. The harder he fought the desire, the more bereft of reason he became. While the battle in his soul raged, fearing the djinn's anger would only escalate, he finally made the decision. He could hardly believe the words coming from his mouth. "Would you like my company in your bed tonight?"

Surprised by Ilyas' proposal, Alejandro was speechless.

"I'm sorry, but I don't know how it's done. Did I say the wrong thing?" Ilyas asked.

"No, no you didn't. You said exactly the right thing. I was just trying to remember if I changed the sheets this morning."

Forty-seven

JULIAN AND SONIA Castellano arrived at Christ the Redeemer Lutheran Church fifteen minutes before the scheduled six o'clock meeting. Seeing Patrick's car, Julian parked next to it. Theo's foster parents then made their way to the second floor reception hall.

Standing only five feet, Julian's thick pate of hair showed no aging, but his middle was considerable. It was in his genes he liked to say. Sonia, good-looking as ever, matched her husband's height but managed to stay slender with daily gym workouts. Her nagging at Julian to get healthy brought promising resolutions that were fleeting. His chubby hand reached out and took hold of hers as they walked into the building. Climbing the stairs to the second floor winded Julian. As they reached the top and entered the large room, Patrick turned and smiled. The smile suddenly brought back memories for Julian of when they first met Theo.

THEO WAS ONLY fourteen when Julian and Sonia took him in. The APFT organization had asked the childless couple to give Theo a temporary home until a permanent foster family was found. Initially cool to the request, their mind's quickly changed. It was a heartrending first meeting. Theo's handsome face and skinny body was draped in wrinkled clothes several sizes too large. Despite bruising around his face and eye, his smile was infectious.

"You're going to be staying with us for awhile," Julian said as he shook Theo's hand.

"Really?" His eyes lit up.

Their hearts were breaking seeing the pathetic figure in front of them. They could only imagine the abuse that had branded him.

"Yeah, really," Sonia said. "Are you hungry?"

"I don't know."

"Have you ever been to Red Lobster," Julian asked.

"What's that?"

"Well, let's go find out."

All Theo longed for was security, stability and love. He was polite and eager to do any chores they gave him. And after Julian got him interested in football, the two hardly moved from the television on Sunday afternoons, except for snacks and sodas from the kitchen. They grew close. Then one day when Julian and Sonia proposed formally adopting him, Theo turned them down without explanation.

In the back of his mind Theo feared that Sixto would find him and hurt them. His gratitude to Julian and Sonia went beyond words. They had given him the home and family he never experienced with his natural parents. And he was prepared to do anything to protect them.

It was Saturday morning as Julian and Theo were stopped at a traffic light on their way to get breakfast. Without warning, a swift crushing blow came from behind and the sound of metal breaking glass. The back passenger window shattered as shards of small slivers rocketed forward. Julian looked back. The hand of a crazed maniac reached into the car grabbing for Theo's hair.

"*Ven conmigo, cabron...hijo de puta,*" the man screamed out.

Theo's face flushed with fear. "Drive! Get out of here, now!" he screamed.

Julian floored the accelerator barely missing a car crossing the intersection. From the rear view mirror Julian saw the man run back to his car. Julian drove as fast as he dared, weaving in and out of traffic. Making a sharp turn onto a side street, Julian continued indiscriminate turns through a maze of residential streets until he was sure the man was no longer following them. He pulled over and parked.

"Are you okay?" he asked Theo.

Theo was scraping his hair with his hand and picking out shards of glass. "Yeah, I'm fine," he replied.

Julian snapped open his cell phone and began dialing.

"Don't call the cops, please." Theo's eyes were filled with fear.

"We have to report this, Theo."

"That was my dad."

Julian continued staring at Theo.

"I think my dad accidently happened to see me in the car. But if you call the cops, they'll make out a report. My dad will find out where we live and come looking for me."

Julian closed his cell and they drove home.

For the next several months they remained constantly vigilant of anything unusual. But the incident eventually faded from their minds. Sixto never again surfaced in either Julian or Sonia's lives.

PART OWNER OF a small catering company, Sonia often

recruited Theo as her weekend helper. Not only did Theo like earning the extra money, but he took to cooking like nothing before. Amazed at his natural talent, Sonia let Theo take over increasingly difficult tasks. After working a catering event at The Seville one weekend, Theo approached the owner.

"Hans, you need to hire me."

"I don't need a dishwasher," he replied.

"That's good 'cause I'm not a dishwasher. I'm a cook."

"What can you cook?"

He handed Hans the catering menu. "Take a look. I can do it all."

Hans hired Theo as a kitchen helper after school and on weekends. In no time he worked his way into the stove galley and was preparing simple dishes. Promoted to a full-time chef by the time he graduated high school, Theo was on his way to achieving his ambition.

SHORTLY AFTER JUDE died, as Julian and Sonia arrived home from work one evening, they saw that police were waiting on the curb. The officers began questioning the couple, wanting information about Theo's Morocco trip.

"He went on vacation," Julian replied. "It was a gift from a friend." Sharing what they knew about Theo's travel to the North African country, he reported to the police. "Theo intended to explore the history of spice. He studied food history," Julian explained.

The police officers snickered, then asked about their foster son's drug use.

"He doesn't do drugs," Sonia declared.

They disregarded her assertion and demanded a list of Theo's friends.

When the first newspaper article surfaced concerning the investigation against Theo, they were bewildered and confused. The charges were preposterous. But when they got the call that Theo had been beaten, they rushed to the intensive care unit. Seeing Theo's battered face and body, they knew something was dreadfully wrong. Over the next several days as Theo recovered, he assured them everything could be explained. It was a misunderstanding, he told them. He refused to say more. Julian and Sonia trusted him. But then they received Patrick's late night call about Theo's arrest for Romel's murder. Yet, despite all the charges, their faith in Theo was unshakable; their commitment to vindicate him, boundless.

NOW, SEEING PATRICK, they both returned his smile.

"Have you been to El Pastor to see Theo yet?" Julian asked.

"No. I plan to go tomorrow."

Sonia spoke. "We were there this afternoon and Theo told us your dad is representing him?"

"I'm not sure about that. Dad's talked to him a couple of times. That's all I really know."

"What's going to happen now?" she asked.

"The judge ordered Theo held without setting bail. Dad said the D.A.'s taking the Jude Armstrong case to the grand jury. After the grand jury decides what to do, Dad's filing a motion for a bail hearing. So it looks like Theo's going to stay in jail until then."

"And how much will it cost to get Theo out of jail?" she asked.

"It's hard to say. But we can talk to a bail bondsman when that happens."

"What will they do?" Julian asked.

"They usually want ten percent of the amount the judge sets along with a co-signer who can cover the full bail amount."

"What about your dad's fee?" Sonia asked.

"I'm going to talk to him about that. I'll let you know."

At that moment they turned to see Hans Schuldneckt. Within the hour other friends and co-workers would make their way to the meeting and commit their resources to Theo's defense.

Forty-eight

SOON MARTY BEGAN doubting that Theo was involved in any wrongdoing. Consuelo was the first to raise his misgivings.

As promised, before disposing of Jude's possessions Marty walked over to Consuelo's to offer her first choice. Consuelo invited him inside her home. Marty was instantly struck by the beautiful collection of tapestry of a quality he had never seen before. Flattered by his compliments, Consuelo offered him a cup of *atole*.

"I used to make it for Jude most mornings. Theo liked it too," she replied.

Consuelo appeared friendly towards him and, capitalizing on that, he asked, "How well did you know Theo?"

"I know he was good to Jude. She didn't like being alone especially when she knew her time was getting close. So, sometimes Theo would stay in her room all night and sleep on her bed. I know they talked a lot. Jude told him all her secrets."

"How do you know that?"

"Theo was real good at keeping what she said to himself. But occasionally he would slip up and say things he thought I already knew. Like the profits Jude got from selling her scarves and shawls, she donated it to charity. One time when we had to call the paramedics to take her to the hospital, she got very angry afterward. Theo told me Jude was claustrophobic and didn't like to be put in

small places like the ambulance. Theo said she was even scared of
riding in elevators because her parents had died in one during a fire.
I didn't know any of that about her. I even remember overhearing
them talk about her grandson one time."

"Jude had a grandson?"

Consuelo recanted. "Maybe not. I don't know. Jude was taking a
lot of morphine for her pain and sometimes she said things that were
crazy."

"Do you know if Theo ever took drugs?"

Consuelo burst out laughing.

"What's so funny?"

"Because I read in the paper about the police saying Theo did all
this stuff and that he took drugs. Theo wouldn't even take an aspirin
for a headache."

"Are you sure?"

"Of course. He came to Jude's house one day after work with a
bad headache. He was lying on the couch trying to get rid of it. I
wanted to give him an aspirin but he wouldn't take it. I came home
and got an herb, *yerba buena,* and made him tea with lemon and
honey. That got rid of it."

After his visit with Consuelo, Marty drove to the hospital to see
Theo, but the boy refused to speak to him without his lawyer.

Once back home in Virginia, Marty called Winkfield Hjelle
again. "Wink, is it possible that the MIB system you use could have
entered incorrect information in the file of the guy you investigated
for me earlier?"

"Highly unlikely. That just doesn't happen. The people at MIB
are extremely accurate and in the many years I've used their system I
have never run across a case where that occurred."

"Well here's my problem. The story I'm getting about this
alleged druggie is that he's as straight as they come. In other words,
my source tells me the guy doesn't do drugs at all. So I don't know
what to make of it."

"Wish I could help you out, but the report I have says otherwise.
You know that some guys mask their drug use so well, and unless
you do the lab work, you'd never know."

"Well, thanks anyway."

"No problem..."

Marty interrupted just before they hung up. "Can I ask just one
more favor?"

"What's that?"

"Theo Jaquez was recently in the hospital in Santa Fe. He got
beat up pretty bad. Could MIB review those records to confirm the
earlier report?"

"I'm not sure. If the release he signed earlier is still good, they
might be able to do that. Give me the name of the hospital and I'll

call them to see what they can do."

Thereafter, Marty gave little thought to the Theo Jaquez matter until two weeks later when he picked up a phone message and returned the call. "Hey Wink, were you able to get anything?"

"Yes, and that's the reason it took so long to get back to you."

"What do you mean?"

"MIB discovered an incongruity."

"Incongruity, what's that?"

"The initial and follow-up reports didn't match, so MIB did a detailed investigation. These guys really pride themselves on making absolutely sure their reports are totally accurate."

"So what did they find?"

"As best as they can piece together, somebody used Theo Jaquez's insurance card to receive treatment in his name."

"Is that right?"

"The strange part that's hard to understand is every physician requires new patients to provide positive identification along with their insurance card. They even photograph the patient. Unless Jaquez has a twin brother, it would be almost impossible to get around that system."

"Maybe a brother that resembles Theo!"

"Yeah, maybe. Is his brother a druggie, a smoker and an asthmatic?"

"I don't know. But does the latest report say Theo's not a druggie?"

"That's correct."

"Thanks again, Wink."

Marty thought about his next move. He needed to tell Snyder. For whatever reason Jude left Theo the insurance money, Marty was now convinced it was not dishonestly coerced. After learning about Theo's commitment to Jude, Marty believed it would be a shame to keep the fraud investigation hanging over the boy. Picking up the phone, he placed a call to Snyder. Unable to reach him, Marty left a voice message. After several days when the call was not returned, Marty placed a second call, this time leaving a message with the desk officer. A third call to Snyder the following week finally got through.

"Lieutenant Snyder, I've been trying to reach you for awhile now."

"Yeah well, I've been pretty busy here. What is it, Chenoweth?"

Marty sensed Snyder was annoyed by the call. "I got some more information on Theo Jaquez for you."

"What's that?"

"My friend who got me the medical information about Theo now says it was wrong."

"Wrong how?"

"Theo's not a druggie after all. I'm thinking that this whole thing was just one big misunderstanding."

"A misunderstanding, huh?"

Snyder's tone was filled with sarcasm.

"For whatever reason Jude gave Theo her life insurance money, I don't think it involved anything untoward..."

Snyder interrupted. "I guess you haven't heard that Theo bashed his brother's head in."

"What?"

"So regardless of what your medical guy says, we already have him on another murder charge."

"No, I wasn't aware of that."

"Well, now you know. By the way, you never called my brother-in-law on that house you were selling."

"Actually, one of the neighbors came over and made an offer. So we negotiated a deal."

"He could have still helped get the paperwork done."

"It wasn't that difficult..."

Snyder interrupted again. "I don't think we have anything else to talk about Chenoweth. So, I'd appreciate it if you didn't waste my time anymore."

Suddenly, the phone went dead.

Forty-nine

BY THE TIME the church members arrived at Sixto's house, Father Bonafacio was already inside. They parked up and down the road and assembled at the broken down fence bordering the house. Weeds and tall grass separated the fence from the house. Several old cars sat rusting on one side of the property providing shelter for feral cats and a variety of rodents. The ramshackle house had not seen a coat of paint for several decades. Over the years the wind had carried off roofing shingles and only the torn black tar paper remained. Several windows were broken and the porch appeared as if it were ready to give way anytime. If Sixto and his wife ever abandoned their home, it would likely remain uninhabited, as even the poorest among the poor passing the property shook their head wondering how anyone lived in such squalor.

"What do we do now?" one of the members asked Deacon Juan.

"Let's just wait unless we hear fighting or loud noises inside."

"Are the *chotas* coming?" someone asked.

"No, we don't want them here," the deacon replied.

After about twenty minutes the group grew restless and concern for the priest intensified. Deacon Juan and Faustin Sanchez decided to knock on the door and confront Sixto. As they began making their way through the weed patch, Father Bonafacio suddenly walked out the door and even from inside the porch everyone could see his look of surprise at the large gathering. Walking down the rickety porch steps, the priest looked at Deacon Juan and Faustin.

"What is this?" he asked.

"We heard it was Sixto that broke into the rectory and battered Luz, and we knew you came to confront him," the deacon said. "We wanted to make sure you'd be okay."

The priest smiled. "Thank you." He looked at the crowd. "Thank all of you for you concern for me. But everything is all right now."

Faustin spoke. "We decided to put a trailer at the church parking lot and take turns at night watching over everything until after the trial."

"Do you think that's necessary?" the priest asked.

Deacon Juan responded, "We're concerned about keeping you safe, Father...and about protecting the church."

The priest gave a slight bow. "I'm grateful to all of you."

As the crowd began to disperse, Deacon Juan and Faustin walked the priest to his car. "What happened in there, Father?" Faustin asked.

The priest took on a calm expression. "While Sixto and I were talking, Jesus decided to pay a visit."

Puzzled by the priest's response, the two said nothing more.

Returning from the *tienda* the following day, Father Bonafacio noticed a small camping trailer in the parking lot. It remained there unoccupied until dusk when Facundo Morales drove into the parking lot. Father Bonafacio noticed his car and walked outside. "*Que pasa*, Facundo?" he yelled out.

Facundo walked over. "We made out a schedule and tonight's my watch night."

Father Bonafacio smiled. "When you get settled, come over and have dinner with me."

"*Gracias*, Father. I'll be there in a few minutes."

After the rectory break-in, attendance at Sunday services began returning to normal. The offerings increased slightly for the first two weeks, then reverted to the regular average. Monsignor Keeler kept in close contact, always asking about the mood and the attitude of the people. Hearing that support was returning, Monsignor Keeler was skeptical. After all, in his experience with sex scandals involving priests, the upheaval usually caused schisms and tremendous congregational disorder. He decided to pay another visit to Arbol Verde.

SEEING THE TRAILER parked by the rectory, Monsignor Keeler wondered about it. Making his way into the church, he saw the altar society women cleaning the nave. He spoke to one of them who explained the reason for the trailer. Walking to the rectory,

Monsignor Keeler was met by Father Bonafacio who was standing on the porch. They exchanged greetings as Father Bonafacio led him into the kitchen for coffee and freshly baked apple *empanaditas* given earlier that morning by a parishioner. After examining the tithing records, Monsignor Keeler was convinced the situation was returning to normal. The archbishop would be happy to learn that Father Bonafacio was doing so well.

AS FATHER BONAFACIO made his way from his office to the kitchen one late morning, a shadow moved across the front door. He walked over and looked through the mesh drape on the sidelight. The Priest didn't recognize the visitor sitting on his porch step. He looked over to the trailer and noticed no cars were there. Opening the door, he asked, "Can I help you?"

Sixto turned his head slightly. "It's just me."

"Sixto, I didn't expect to see you so soon."

Sixto smirked as he looked straight ahead. "I didn't come to steal anything if that's what you're thinking. I got forty-seven dollars that belongs to you. I'm just wondering if I should give it back or cop *chiva*." As always, Sixto spoke in a mix of broken Spanish and English.

The priest leaned his back against the door threshold. "Why don't you buy food to eat with the money?"

Sixto turned around to face the priest. "A *tecato* doesn't think like that. Scoring is all we think about."

"But you had this money in your pocket for some time and haven't spent it to buy heroin."

Sixto didn't respond.

"You want coffee?" the priest asked.

Sixto stood up slowly and they made their way through the front door into the kitchen. Before sitting down, Sixto took a key from his pocket and laid it on the table. "It's not a good idea to trust a *tecato* with the rectory key."

"I don't want to replace broken windows or have anybody else get hurt," the priest responded as he walked to the cupboard for cups.

Sixto remained silent.

"You want sugar or milk with the coffee?"

"Black."

The priest placed the cup in front of Sixto whose hands trembled as he lifted it to his lips.

"The thing is I got a problem with my kidneys. The doctor said I'm going to need dialysis. So I'm thinking about going to detox."

"That would be a good idea."

"Another thing is that when we prayed the other day, it scared the shit out of me."

The priest gave Sixto a curious stare. "Why?"

"Because it got me to thinking all kinds of weird crap. You see, *tecatos* are numb to feelings. But since that day these thoughts just stay in my mind."

"Maybe Jesus is speaking to you."

"I doubt that. I stopped believing a long time ago."

"Then why did you pray with me?" the priest asked.

Sixto didn't respond.

Father Bonafacio couldn't help notice Sixto's limbs twitching.

A second later Sixto's gaze became intense. "Why the fuck did you give me that key in the first place?"

"I already told you."

"You're really fucked up, you know that?"

The priest remained quiet.

Sixto stood up and placed a wad of crumbled bills on the table. "Just stay the fuck away from me," he warned as he walked out.

Father Bonafacio didn't try to stop him.

Fifty

RETURNING TO VIRGINIA after Theo's arraignment, Marty began making internet inquiries to locate Aban and Ilyas in Morocco. All his efforts appeared futile as computer records for persons living in that country were almost nonexistent. Next he began searching for assignments in Europe, North Africa or the Middle East, but nothing was coming his way. Finally a newsmagazine offered Marty an assignment to interview Dictator Pervez Musharraf in Pakistan. Amid growing civil unrest, rumors circulated that the dictator's unstable government would fall. He accepted the offer but days before his scheduled departure, the assignment was cancelled. Then, the following month, Marty accepted an offer for a story on Palestinians fleeing from Gaza to Egypt. He eagerly accepted the assignment. It lasted several days and after filing the story, he detoured to Morocco.

It was ten o'clock on a chilly morning when Marty arrived in Rabàt. The taxi took him directly to the U.S. Embassy. He couldn't wait to see an old friend, Simon Biondi. Simon was a defense attaché at the American Embassy in Morocco. Although Simon never let on as to his real employer, Marty believed it was most likely a clandestine American agency. Old friends for years, the two met in the early seventies when Marty was only twenty-six and worked as a reporter for the International Daily Times (IDT). Assigned to cover President Nixon's Paris visit, Marty was attending a large embassy reception hosted by Ambassador Arthur Watson. His intention was to get a scoop on the Paris peace talks over the Viet Nam conflict, but no one was talking. Then he met Simon.

Like Marty, Simon was also born in Utah and graduated from Brigham Young University. Although Simon was two years older, they had much in common including growing up in strict Mormon families. Now Jack Mormons, as the evening wore on, their friendship grew closer over shots of scotch — Johnny Walker Black.

At the time Simon described his job as a lowly state department research specialist. He confirmed what Marty already knew about the Paris delegation talks. Neither H. Averill Harriman nor Cyrus Vance, the U.S. representatives, could get the North Viet Nam delegation to agree on even the most basic ground rules — a round or square negotiating table. They stayed in contact and months later Marty received a call from Simon with a scoop on a story. Researching it more fully, Marty wrote about it. Nobody was aware at the time that the Secretary of State, Henry Kissinger, was secretly negotiating with North Viet Nam. The IDT published Marty's story, and despite Washington's denunciation, the newspaper stood by it. Later, when the story was ultimately confirmed, Marty's reputation soared. As an enduring gift of gratitude to his friend, Marty was never without a bottle of Johnny Walker Black whenever or wherever they met.

Prior to traveling on any international assignment it was Marty's practice to request a list of the country's embassy personnel from the state department and peruse it for familiar contacts. Marty was overjoyed seeing Simon's name on the Morocco embassy list, and placed a phone call to him in advance of his visit. Even though it had been over twelve years since they last spoke to one another, they caught up quickly. Marty gave Simon the details of the purpose for his visit, and the diplomat offered to make some advance inquiries.

As Marty waited in the lobby of the Embassy, a slender, bald man approached in a smartly tailored sharkskin suit. Marty took a second look to confirm that it was his old friend. Their mutual surprise at how time had aged them was evident by their fixed gape. They shook hands then hugged before Marty handed over his gift. Slowly lifting the bottle from the gift bag, Simon broke into his blustering laugh reminding Marty some things never change. "Let's go up to my office," he said. "How was your trip?"

"Too long. I need to retire."

"We both need to retire," Simon replied.

Once in his office, Simon took out two glasses from his desk, opened the bottle of scotch and poured thumb size drinks. Handing one to Marty, they toasted, "To old friends," he said, as they crooked their glasses back.

They sat down, turning their chairs to face one another. "I'm sorry to hear about Jude. She was a good journalist and a good friend," Simon said.

"Yeah, and I always thought she would outlive me by years."

"I made some inquiries for you and the whole thing sounds like something out of a Le Carrè novel."

"What do you mean?" Marty asked.

"The guy you're looking for, Aban Bashir, he's dead. Rumor has it he was murdered."

"By who? Why?"

"Apparently he tried to bribe somebody from the Ministry of Justice to get his nephew out of prison. The nephew eventually got released. But rumor has it Bashir pissed somebody off carrying tales about prisoners that never made it out alive and judges that wouldn't return bribes."

"They shot him?"

"Nah, they don't do that here. It was some kind of poison, I'm told."

"But the nephew part doesn't make any sense," Marty said. "Did you happen to get the nephew's name?"

"Nope, but you can speak to this guy," Simon replied, as he handed Marty a folded paper.

Marty opened it. "Ali Kibal. Who's he?"

"He's a Moroccan attorney. He knows about the whole prison release thing. He arranged it."

After making plans to get together for dinner later that night, Marty left the embassy for his hotel room. Once settled in, he picked up the telephone and dialed the number. When the receiver picked up, Marty asked, "Ali Kibal, please?"

"You wish to speak with Mr. Kibal?" the male voice responded in English.

"Yes, please."

"May I ask whose calling?"

"My name is Marty Chenoweth. I'm American."

"And may I ask what this is in reference to?"

"Aban Bashir."

"One moment." A few seconds later a voice came on the line.

"Mr. Chenoweth, I'm Ali Kibal. What can I do for you?"

Kibal spoke English with a British accent. Probably educated in England, Marty surmised. "Mr. Kibal, I'd like to make an appointment to see you."

"What's the nature of your business, Mr. Chenoweth?"

"Aban Bashir and his son, Ilyas."

There was a pause of a few seconds, then a response. "Do you know where my office is located?"

"I have your address."

"I can meet you at six this evening."

"Thank you. I'll be there."

Fifty-one

THE POLICE CAR turned into El Pastor Health and Wellness Center in the early morning. Armed with an arrest warrant, Sergeant Velez and Officer Tafoya exited their vehicle. The sky in San Lorenzo was cloudy and snow looming. The winter chill immediately penetrated through their uniform jackets. Without a word, they made their way to the front door as Sergeant Velez pressed the button immediately below the intercom. Getting no response, he pressed it again, this time letting it ring for a bit longer. A crackling sound, then a voice came through. "Yeah, what do you want?"

"State police — we're here to serve an arrest warrant on one of your patients."

"Who's the patient?"

"Sixto Jaquez."

For the next few seconds there was no response until the officers heard the dead bolt turn and the door open. "You guys are out early; must be a nasty criminal you're after," the man said with a sardonic grin.

"Yeah, you bet," Sergeant Velez replied as they walked through the doorway.

"Name's Fedak...Jim Fedak," the man said. After exchanging perfunctory handshakes, Fedak led the two officers through a small reception area into an office.

Fedak was dressed in old jeans and a flannel shirt. Towering over six feet, the former heroin addict appeared anorexic. His face had the texture of worn, wrinkled leather and his grey eyes looked fatigued. With a slight facial smirk expressing his irritation at the police officer's imposition, he asked to see the warrant.

"Are you in charge here?" Sergeant Velez asked.

"Yup, most nights except Sundays and Mondays."

Sergeant Velez unzipped his jacket, removed the folded document from the inside pocket and handed it to Fedak

"Sexual abuser, huh? You sure you want to do this?" Fedak asked.

"That's why we're here," Sergeant Velez replied.

"Jaquez is in bad shape. I guarantee if you take him out of here now, in a few hours you'll be transporting him to the hospital."

Sergeant Velez gazed over at Officer Tafoya then asked Fedak, "Can we see him?"

"Follow me," Fedak replied as he stood up and walked out of the room. The two tagged behind. He led them down the dimly lit hallway which housed the medical section of the clinic and through two sets of doors, arriving at the residential complex. It also had the same muted lighting. It felt uncomfortably warm. The odors of stale cigarette smoke and musty sweat permeated. A steady loud moaning sound and unintelligible mumblings could be heard coming from rooms they passed. Suddenly stopping, Fedak waited for the two officers to catch up. Opening the door he backed up allowing them to have a look at Sixto. At once they both stumbled backward as an overpowering stench of feces hit their nose.

"Oh, man," Sergeant Velez sighed.

"He's got super flu," Fedak said.

"What's that," Sgt Velez asked.

"Heroin withdrawal symptoms. We look in on him about every fifteen or twenty minutes. He must have just crapped because he was clean just before you got here."

The two officers continued staring into the room. It was small with only a bed and a night stand. Rolled up in a ball, Sixto began moaning.

"How long will he be like this?" Sergeant Velez asked.

"Depends. Maybe tonight, tomorrow, next week...everybody's different."

"Can you notify us when he recovers enough to be taken out of here?"

Fedak smirked. "Yeah, I'll put a note in his chart," he said. "You got a card?"

Sixto began jerking his legs and arms; his moans got louder. The officers wanted out of there fast.

"Okay, we'll wait to hear from you," Sergeant Velez said as he handed Fedak his card and they turned to walk away."

"Hold up. I need to let you out," Fedak said. Catching up to the officers, he walked them to the front door. As they left and Fedak bolted the door shut, his mind began prioritizing the remaining tasks before shift change. Since losing two charges, Fedak had been begging for replacements. The patient load was becoming too challenging. Fedak laid Sergeant Velez's card on the reception desk and made his way back to the dormitory, forgetting his promise to note the pending arrest in Sixto's medical chart.

Fifty-two

ARRIVING AT WORK early Monday morning, David picked up Theo's file and began reading through it. While he had earlier glossed over the grand jury indictment, this time he carefully studied it. As he turned the page, the intercom beeped.

"Yes Cheryl, what is it?"

"Patrick called and wants a call back."

"Thanks."

David placed the call to his son.

"Hey Dad, just wanted know. Are you going to handle Theo's defense?"

There was a slight pause before David answered. "Look son, I'd like to be able to do that. But I have a backlog of work that needs attention. It's going to take me to the end of the year..."

Patrick interrupted. "Dad, he really needs you. If it's the money, we were able to raise seven thousand dollars in just one night. His foster parents are applying for a second mortgage and his boss promised to help out. Both Esteban and I will be contributing, as well. I know we'll be able to get lots more money for his defense."

"Patrick, aside from the expense, do you have any idea what it's going to take in terms of time?"

"I know, Dad. I hear what you're saying. But you need to understand that Theo is innocent and nobody else is going to be able to defend him like you. He needs you, Dad."

"I'll tell you what I'll do. I will try to get the trial extended. During that time I'll help you locate somebody that I trust."

"Dad, it's not the same. Please reconsider this. You don't know how much this means to me."

"I'm sorry Patrick, I just can't do it." There was an awkward pause in their conversation that gave David a few seconds to reconsider. "Okay, let me give it some thought. Maybe I can come up with something that will satisfy all of us. Let's talk again soon."

"Thanks Dad."

Fifty-three

AFTER PHONING ALI Kibal and meeting with Simon Bioni at the U.S. Embassy, Marty was exhausted so he closed the curtains and fell asleep. When he awoke, he showered and went out to find a restaurant. Returning to the hotel, he waited until the appointed time. Then, at five-thirty Marty walked outside his hotel and hailed a taxi to take him to Ali Kibal's office.

Their meeting was short—less than one hour. Ali Kibal was forthcoming after Marty explained his purpose for finding Ilyas. He provided Marty the details of Ilyas' pardon, stressing that the amnesty petition fully conformed to the laws of the Monarchy. Confirming that he was aware of Aban's death and expressing sadness upon hearing about it, Ali Kibal steered clear of saying anything more. But Marty learned all he needed to know from the Moroccan lawyer. After dinner with Simon, Marty returned to his hotel room and phoned David.

"Hey Marty, good to hear from you. Where are you?" David asked.

"Rabàt, Morocco. Got here this morning and I'll be leaving for Casablanca tomorrow."

"So you finally made it there. Got any news?"

"Yeah, I do. Theo came to Morocco to hand over some of the

insurance money to Aban. Apparently Aban intended to bribe a judge to get his son out of prison, but found another way of getting it done legally."

"Jude's grandson was in prison?"

"Yeah, but that's another story. The grandson was released on the condition that he leave Morocco permanently. I'm told he's someplace in Spain."

"So why are you heading to Casablanca?"

"When Aban brought Ilyas to Morocco, his brother and wife raised the boy. They live in Casablanca and have his address in Spain. Once I get that, I'm heading there to find him."

"Any chance of convincing Aban to travel here for the trial?"

"Nope. He's dead."

"Damn. What about Jude's grandson?" David's impatience was apparent.

"I'll try once I find him."

"What I'm suspecting is that Theo was mute about the Morocco matter fearing it would jeopardize Ilyas' release," David said.

Marty replied, "And the priest's holding the rest of Ilyas' inheritance, just like I suspected. You know, that kid's got a lot of guts risking jail time for somebody he's never met. By the way, are you staying on the case?"

"Oh yeah, I'm staying on. Some rich guy's picking up the tab for Theo's defense. Not a totally altruistic thing, but as long as he's paying for it, we're not complaining."

"That's good news."

"Thanks for all this info, Marty."

"Sure thing. Once I learn more, I'll call you."

THE FOLLOWING DAY Marty took a bus to Casablanca. Arriving by mid-morning at the central bus station, Marty took a taxi to his hotel. Leaving off his luggage, he went back to the bus station and began casually strolling around eyeing the many rent boys stationed throughout the large terminal. When a suggestive gaze caught his eye, Marty would stop, lean up against the wall, and wait for the approach. There was always the halting smile, the obvious crotch tug, then the advance. It took several encounters before he finally found one that spoke English. His name was Safi and readily agreed to Marty's proposition of translating for a generous fee. Marty hailed a taxi and they were off.

When they got to the address given to him by Ali Kibal, the two exited the taxi and walked into the building. They walked up the stairs to the second floor. Finding the door, Marty knocked. When Maladh appeared, Safi translated their reason for being there. Refusing to give them any information, Maladh suggested they return in the afternoon when Asafar was home.

At six o'clock Marty met Safi and they went back to the apartment. This time Asafar answered the door and invited them inside. They sat on cushions as Safi translated the exchange. Asafar was curious how Marty had found them. When he mentioned Ali Kibal's name, Asafar got a sour look on his face. It was apparent to Marty that Kibal was not liked by Asafar, but he decided not to pursue that subject further. A few minutes later Maladh brought mint tea and served them. As they sipped, Marty explained that Ilyas might be entitled to his grandmother's estate. He asked about the boy's whereabouts.

Asafar grew apprehensive. If he gave the visitor his son's address in Spain, Ilyas would soon learn the truth about his natural parents. But Asafar also knew it was morally wrong to deprive Ilyas of his just inheritance. After a few more minutes of conversation, Asafar told Marty of his concern about his son who had not written for several weeks. Asafar called out to Maladh who brought Ilyas' last letters. He took them from her and handed them to Marty. Marty jotted the return address on a piece of paper and placed it into his wallet. Before they left, Asafar pleaded with Marty to have Ilyas write home so they would know he was well.

Marty and Safi left the apartment and walked out to the street. Handing over several dirham notes to the rent boy, Marty thanked him.

Safi looked up at him with wistful eyes. "Would you like me for tonight?"

Marty shook his head. "No."

"I'm very good at massage," Safi replied.

"Thank you, but no." Marty extended his hand to the boy then hailed a taxi.

The following day Marty booked an Iberian flight to Madrid. Arriving after the noon hour, he checked into the hotel then had lunch. At four o'clock he took a taxi to Ilyas address. Locating the apartment, he knocked. There was no answer. As he turned to walk away, a curious young woman walking by spoke to him. Unable to understand, he replied, "I'm sorry, I don't speak Spanish."

"Who are you looking for?" she asked in English.

"Ilyas Bashir, do you know if he lives here?"

"Yes, but he is not here now."

"When will he be here?"

"He is in the United States. Maybe next week, I don't know."

"Do you know where in the United States?"

"Come later tonight and speak to his friend. He will know."

"His friend lives here?"

"Yes, he is working now. Come about seven or eight tonight."

"Thank you, I'll do that."

Shortly after seven o'clock that evening Marty returned to the apartment. He knocked and a young man opened the door. "I'm Marty Chenoweth. I'm looking for Ilyas Bashir."

The man gave him a curious stare. As he opened the door farther, Marty could see the same women he had spoken to earlier inside the apartment. "Come in. I'm Severino Carbajal." They shook hands.

Walking inside, he greeted the woman.

She stood up. "Hello. I'm Elena." Marty took a seat across from Elena, while Severino sat next to her.

"It's very important that I find Ilyas," he said.

"He left for the United States two weeks ago," Severino replied.

"Do you know where he was going?"

"To see someone in New Mexico...a priest."

"Has he contacted you since then?"

"No."

"Do you know where he was staying?"

"No, Ilyas had scheduled to be off from work and was supposed to return today."

After a brief pause Marty took out his card and wrote something in back. He handed it to Severino. "If Ilyas returns or contacts you, I'll be at this hotel for a few days. Please have him call me. He can also reach me in the United States."

Severino took the card as Marty got up to leave.

"Thanks for all your help," Marty said as he walked out the door.

Hoping that Ilyas would return to Madrid, Marty spent the next several days at the hotel. He called David to inquire of the priest if Ilyas had been there. Receiving a call the following day that Ilyas had not visited Father Bonafacio, Marty's mind continued churning as to Ilyas' whereabouts. He recalled Ali Kibal mentioning the allegations of Ilyas' involvement in the Casablanca terrorist plot. Suddenly he began making the connection. It was conceivable that immigration officials had Ilyas' name on their terrorist watch list. They may have attempted to detain him. But Ilyas could have easily overcome their hold by claiming U.S. citizenship, since he was born in Virginia. That is, unless he didn't know about his U.S. citizenship. How could he have known, growing up believing he was Moroccan.

Late in the evening Marty went back to see Severino. As he answered the door, Marty asked, "Do you know what airline Ilyas took to the United States?"

Severino looked at him with the same curious expression as the first time. "No, I don't," he replied.

"What time was Ilyas scheduled to fly out of Madrid?"

Severino thought about the question for a few seconds. "Early in the morning; I think he said he had to be at the airport several hours before the flight left. I remember he called for a taxi at about four that morning."

That meant his flight nad to leave between six and seven o'clock. "Thank you."

Marty went back to his hotel room and opened his laptop to begin searching for flights from Casablanca to Albuquerque. There were two scheduled flights. Ilyas could have gone through either Chicago or Dallas-Ft. Worth. The latter flight was the least expensive and had less flying time. Marty decided to gamble, and booked a flight scheduled to depart the following morning.

Fifty-four

FOLLOWING THAT NIGHT together, Ilyas and Alejandro began dating. The relationship wasn't totally surprising to Severino whose instincts about his friend proved true. After sharing so much time together, Severino had learned a great deal about Ilyas. Not so much by what he revealed as by what he repressed. Severino suspected Ilyas' Muslim faith was the source of his conflict. Hopefully Alejandro could help Ilyas to reconcile that conflict.

Severino and Elena also became a couple. He was spending most nights at Elena's apartment. Frequently the two couples got together for an evening out. Dancing was a new experience for Ilyas. But before long he was enjoying it. Then early one Saturday morning Severino left Elena's and walked into the apartment to find Ilyas sitting on a cushion on the floor staring at the wall. An envelope was clutched in his hand. It was the same envelope Ilyas palmed every time he grew sad for home. Despite his curiosity, Severino had never asked about it.

"Are you okay?" he asked.

"Yes, of course. I'm fine." Ilyas gave Severino a quick smile.

"No, you're not. What's going on?"

"What do you mean?"

"I mean that you're not fine and something's on your mind. I can always tell that about you."

"Why does it matter to you?"

"Because you're my best friend."

Ilyas remained silent.

"Is it Alejandro?"

Ilyas nodded. "We're no longer together."

There was silence for a few seconds then Severino said, "Let's hang out and do something today."

"I'm leaving," Ilyas said.

"Why? Where are you going?"

"To the United States."

"Are you deranged?"

"Alejandro secured for me a Spanish passport so I could travel to the United States. I could not get a visa otherwise. But he insisted on coming with me and I refused. We fought and he broke off the relationship. He is convinced I am visiting someone special there."

"Are you, Ilyas? What's this all about? You can't just leave your job. You can't leave me hanging like this. We've been through too much together. The food kitchen, the hostel, the warehouse work. We have good jobs and are finally making money. We're doing okay. So why spoil that?"

"I'm not leaving permanently. Mustafa gave me the time off."

"So you're coming back?"

"Yes."

"When are you leaving?"

"In four days."

"Where in the United States are you going?"

"Arbol Verde, New Mexico. I need to see a Catholic priest who lives there."

"My friend, you are completely deranged. What in the world are you doing?"

Ilyas laughed. "Let's go for a walk and I'll explain it to you." As they walked out the door, Ilyas folded the envelope and placed it back in his pocket.

THE NIGHT BEFORE his departure, Severino, Elena and Ilyas went out to dinner. They talked of his impending journey and the excitement of traveling so far. When they arrived back at the apartment, Severino asked, "Are you sure you have to do this?"

"Yes. It's an obligation."

"I'll see you back here in two weeks?"

Ilyas nodded. "Yes, two weeks."

"You promise?"

"I promise."

Severino hugged his friend. "Take care. I'll be waiting for you."

"And I won't disappoint you."

ILYAS' FLIGHT DEPARTED for Dallas/Fort Worth early the following morning. After a two hour layover, he would connect to Albuquerque. Having never been on an aircraft before, his heart beat fast as the plane raced down the runway and began gaining altitude. His hands grasped the armrests as his ears began popping. After several minutes, when it seemed as if the plane leveled off, his anxiety began to ease. Taking a book from his backpack, he began to read. Hours later, when the aircraft finally landed, Ilyas followed the passengers through a series of corridors to a large room where lines were being formed. Confused, Ilyas was directed to the immigration line for non-US residents. As he was called forward, in his haste Ilyas accidently handed over the Moroccan passport that he brought along to prove his identity to the priest. As he realized his mistake, Ilyas got the sudden urge to run. His chest was exploding with fear. The officer picked up the telephone, turned his head, and covered the receiver as he spoke. Within seconds two other officials appeared. "Mr. Bashir, would you please follow us?" one of them asked.

"Is something wrong?"

"We need some additional information from you," they said as he was escorted away.

Led through glass double doors, they passed a reception area, and proceeded down a hallway to a small office. An officer behind the desk looked up. His manner was polite, his face, serious.

"Please sit down," he said.

"What's this all about?" Ilyas asked as he took a seat.

"Your name is Ilyas Bashir, is that right?" the officer asked as he examined Ilyas' passport.

Too late to claim the identity in his forged Spanish passport, he replied, "Yes, it is."

"And you're from Casablanca, Morocco?"

"Yes."

"You were born in Morocco?" he asked.

"Yes."

"Mr. Bashir, your name appears on a terrorist watch list. We're going to have to detain you."

"For what reason?" Ilyas asked.

"Because of your association to the terrorist organization, *Salafia Jihadiya.*"

"But I'm not associated with them. I don't know anything about them.

"I'm sorry, but you will not be allowed to enter the United States."

"Then can I return to Spain?"

"I'm afraid not, Mr. Bashir. You'll be processed then returned to your home country."

His voice grew desperate. "But I can't go back to Morocco. I'll be arrested if I do."

"We have no discretion. The procedure is clear in these matters."

"No. Please, I have done nothing wrong. If I return to Morocco, I will be sent to prison where I'll probably die."

The official looked at the terrified traveler. "Then the only alternative I can suggest is to apply for asylum."

"What will that do?"

"Probably delay your return and get you a hearing before an

immigration judge."

Ilyas placed his hand over his pocket and felt the envelope. Regretting the trip, he sat terrified by his choices. His chest filled with fear again as horrifying images of Sidi Kascen raced through his mind. He wouldn't go back to Morocco.

Fifty-five

WISHING HE WAS less apprehensive so he could enjoy the evening, David's mind was preoccupied. When Patrick called in the early morning asking to meet for dinner, David was initially reluctant, knowing his anxiety level would be high the evening before the start of Theo's trial. But Theo's stepparents, Julian and Sonia, had pressed Patrick to arrange the meeting. They wanted to get David's views on the case.

Patrick and Esteban were already seated with Julian and Sonia by the time David arrived at the restaurant. They greeted him as he joined their table. Though he tried to give attention to the small talk that the four chattered about, it seemed as if a million thoughts were racing through his mind. Then he noticed they were staring at him.

David apologized. "I'm sorry, my mind was somewhere else."

Julian repeated his question. "How strong is their case against Theo?"

David sensed the tension in Julian's voice. It was obvious they were all worried about the trial. But what could he tell them that they didn't already know. Maybe that juries were fickle; their sympathies constantly wavering from the testimony and attitudes of witnesses, or from their steady observation of the defendant's manner, or from other courtroom drama, prejudiced by their life experiences. That occasionally judges were sympathetic. That the middle-aged prosecutor may experience an intermittent hot flash affecting her performance. David was a realist; he couldn't assuage their concern.

"The fact is that it's going to be a tough case to defend," David replied

"Do you think Theo's guilty?" Julian asked.

David responded instantly. "No, I don't. I have this strong suspicion that he's the scapegoat. Romel had lots of enemies, so anybody from the *tienda* could have followed him to the rectory that night. What happened after Theo left the rectory is a mystery. That's what makes this case so difficult to defend."

"The newspaper said that Romel's blood stains were on Theo's clothes. Is that true?" Julian asked.

David nodded his head. "Yeah, that's true."

"And they found a tree limb..." Before Julian could finish his question, David interrupted.

"I know we're all concerned about the trial. But it's not going to do us any good to go over any of these details tonight. I think we can put up a strong defense. There are too many unanswered questions that the police can't explain, and we plan to exploit all of that. If we can convince the jury that the investigation was botched; that clues leading to the real murderer have never been pursued, and that Theo was wrongly targeted as early as the Jude Armstrong investigation, I think we can get them on our side. I think we have a good shot at winning."

There was a desolate silence that followed. It was as if they sensed David's reticence to say any more. As they waited for their food, Sonia broke the glum mood.

"Now that you mentioned the *tienda*, it brought back an old memory when Grandma sent me and my sister on an errand to our *tienda*. Passing the candy aisle, I picked up two chocolate bars; one for each of us. When I got to the eggs and milk, I put the candy bars in my pocket. Armando, the owner, put the eggs and milk in a bag and marked them down in his book. Grandma always paid him at the beginning of the month when her social security check came in. As we were leaving, Armando saw the candy bars sticking out of my pocket." 'Are you going to pay for those?' he barked, pointing at them. I was so afraid he was going to tell Grandma I tried to steal candy."

"I guess we're going to have to watch you at the store from now on?" Julian said.

Everyone laughed, which momentarily took the edge off the unease. At that moment the food arrived.

Before anyone finished, David stood up and excused himself. "I'm sorry. I have too much to do before the trial tomorrow."

As they hugged him, Sonia whispered, "We're thankful for everything you've done for our son, David. We're praying for you. God bless you."

"Thanks, I can use all the prayers I can get," he replied with a warm smile before walking away.

Fifty-six

JAMES KILKENNY, A construction developer, owned JWK Investments, Inc., located in Santa Fe. For over three years Kilkenny had been negotiating a land swap with the Santa Fe County Commissioners. The offer was to exchange the county's fifty-seven acre parcel in northwest Santa Fe for JWK's parcel almost twice as large located south of the city. The county's contiguous parcel stood amid rolling pinion and ponderosa pine-laced hills with dramatic views overlooking the city. Kilkenny was fixated on acquiring that property to build a community of upscale homes. JWK had developed tentative plans to partner with two large construction companies on the project. The financial backing for the project had been promised from a New York brokerage firm specializing in large construction projects suitable for REIT retirement portfolio investments. The biggest obstacle to the land swap was the county commissioner's demand that JWK relinquish one-half of the water rights his company held. The water rights were an extremely valuable asset, and while JWK would still be able to carry out its project with its remaining water rights, it was reluctant to surrender any of them in the land swap. After countless meetings, it appeared that the county commissioners would settle for something less than their original proposal.

The county was anxious to acquire the JWK property, as the site was ideally suited for a large city/county governmental office center which conformed to newly adopted land use planning requirements for ample employee and public parking areas. Due to the high cost of land within the city, few affordable building parcels existed. The alternative was to build smaller structures or purchase existing buildings that usually required total remodels. The drawback to existing structures, aside from expensive remodel costs, was the lack of sufficient parking areas conforming to the new rules. That severely limited the county's options.

Before becoming a commissioner, Sarah Maestas was the director of the county's land use planning division. She was familiar with building codes, conditions, and restrictions, as she had drafted many of the new policies. Maestas was well-liked and respected by the other commissioners, and they came to rely heavily on her knowledge concerning Kilkenny's land-swap proposal. She had the influence to sway the vote either way. Kilkenny was meeting with Maestas to finalize the proposal.

Kilkenny and Mark Quintana, the company's chief executive officer, appeared at Maestas' office fifteen minutes before their appointed meeting time. Maestas knew they were anxious to get it started. She also knew Kilkenny was an astute and shrewd negotiator. He was known to throw in an occasional monkey wrench well after everyone thought a meeting of the minds had been reached. Their last meeting had gone on almost the entire day. She was hopeful he would raise no substantive issues during this meeting. She had copied drafts of the original proposal, the subsequent amendments, and a myriad of other items that required collaboration, agreement, and initialing. Thereafter, it would all be consolidated into a comprehensive final contractual proposal. The parcels would then be re-appraised, and inspection reports from the historical society, environmental services, the state engineers' office and countless other agencies would be secured before the final package was placed on the agenda for public discussion. After that, it would be presented to the commissioners. If all went well, Maestas expected the proposal would be voted upon within the next nine to twelve months.

She went out to greet them. "Nice to see both of you again," she said, extending her hand. "Let's go back to the conference room." They followed her into the room marveling at the stacked set of documents.

"All this for a simple land swap. Think of all the trees we could have saved, but for this mumbo jumbo," Kilkenny said pointing to the paperwork.

"This mumbo jumbo is what we're all about, Jim. Haven't you learned that by now?"

"Maybe I'm getting too old to do this anymore."

"If I know you, you'll be doing this on your deathbed."

They chuckled.

"Okay, let's get started," Maestas suggested.

For the next several hours the three became engrossed in the proposal, taking short breaks and returning to the task. They agreed on a working lunch, ordering out for sandwiches. By early afternoon it appeared it was done.

"I can't believe we're finished, but for the inspections, formalities, and that final vote," Kilkenny said.

"A favorable one I hope, considering all the time and effort we've spent on this," Maestas replied.

"Why would it be anything but that?" Kilkenny asked.

"Remember Jim, there's the primaries coming up next June. I have a hot-shot state police officer vying for my job. Since there's no Republican opposition, whoever wins that, wins the commissioner's seat."

"And he doesn't have a prayer," Kilkenny replied.

"I'm not so sure of that, Jim. There was a big backlash over the negative vote I cast against the tax increase for police infrastructure. In fact, some of the polls have him ahead of me. Recently his name's been in all the papers about a high profile murder case."

"You're talking about that kid that supposedly killed a lady for her insurance money then his brother?"

"One and the same."

"Who's defending the kid?" Kilkenny asked.

"David Lujan from Albuquerque. He's among the best but isn't cheap. Rumor has it that he's looking to dump the case."

"So what do you think will happen if the kid's convicted?"

"It will give my opponent a lot of respect and support. I'll probably be out of a job," Maestas replied.

Kilkenny shook his head. "What are the chances of getting this to a vote before the primary election?"

"Your guess is as good as mine. But I wouldn't count on it."

"Sarah, we can't let that happen. We need you to get this proposal through."

"Let's keep our fingers crossed, Jim."

Fifty-seven

DRIVING INTO DOWNTOWN Santa Fe early Sunday morning, Snyder found a parking space in a vacant lot. He got out and began leisurely walking to the radio station. Finally receiving serious media attention in his county commission bid, Snyder was in good spirits. The radio interview would be carried live and rebroadcast in the evening. Snyder's thoughts were on his talking points. Since appointing his brother-in-law as his campaign manager, they spoke on the phone almost daily. Being a real estate agent in Santa Fe for many years, his brother-in-law knew some big names with deep pockets. Snyder needed to tap those sources desperately. His opponent, Sarah Maestas, had powerful backing. Newspaper accounts reported her campaign chest was considerable. That didn't surprise him, knowing the favors commissioners could promise if reelected.

And then there was name recognition. It meant everything in seeking elective office. But Snyder felt good about his campaign. His name was getting better known. During several recent speaking engagements, the police, fire department, and teachers' unions had expressed their interest in backing him. His calendar was filling up fast with functions, speaking engagements, and meetings that would get him even more name recognition. Given the proper venues, Snyder was convinced once the public heard what he had to say and contrasted his message to Maestas' old hat diatribe, he was certain to get noticed and gain popular support.

Snyder continued to believe the Theo Jaquez case was also critically important to his election bid. What better way to elicit the public's support than to have his name linked with the investigation and arrest of a young punk who killed a defenseless, terminally ill woman for her money and then his own brother. While those crimes were unconscionable, he couldn't wait to hint at more. Snyder was hoping the trial would take place before the election, as the newspapers would surely continue crediting him for bringing the matter to justice. Once Theo was found guilty, Snyder would ride into the election on the coattails of that conviction. He could almost taste victory.

Arriving at the radio station, Snyder walked in and announced himself. Taking a seat, Snyder waited patiently pondering the message he wanted to give. It was unfortunate that the county commissioner seat didn't get as much media attention as the more visible races like mayor, lieutenant governor and governor. But once

Snyder got his foot in the political door, there was no stopping him. Fleeting images of walking up the steps of Congress dashed across his mind when an abrupt greeting plunged him back to reality.

"Kerry Snyder, you want to come this way?" the voice asked.

It was a fat, balding man with black rimmed glasses. As Snyder stood up, the man hastily introduced himself.

"I'm Rory Johnson."

His handshake was weak and his greeting, superficial. Before Snyder could respond, the man turned around and shuffled through the door down the hallway.

Rory Johnson's voice was renowned as a Santa Fe radio personality. But seeing him for the first time surprised Snyder. His portly stature with several chins, a bulbous nose and sagging jowls was not the way he had imagined his host. How anyone could take this radio personality seriously was a wonder, Snyder thought.

The radio room was small with a triangular table and overhead microphones at each station. Rory motioned for Snyder to sit at one of the stations, while he sat in front of the table with an array of electronic buttons, knobs and switches. Because of Rory's girth, he couldn't get closer than a foot from the edge of the table. Rory moved the microphone close to his mouth and began fiddling with some of the electronics.

"We're on in a few minutes, so you need to scoot up to the microphone," Rory said. "As soon as that overhead sign turns from red to green, we go live."

"Is there anything I need to know before we go live?" Snyder asked.

Rory gave him a puzzled look. "I'm guessing you know why you're here?"

"Well, I was referring to the broadcast itself."

"Oh, just speak into the mic...clearly. Okay, we have less than a minute." Rory picked up some papers and began leafing through them. The instant the overhead sign changed color, Rory began speaking in his good-natured broadcast voice. "Good morning Santa Fe. This is Rory Johnson and you're listening to Morning Docket where we bring you news, information and interviews with the movers and shakers of our fair city. Today we have with us Lieutenant Kerry Snyder, a member of the New Mexico State Police force. How are you this morning, Kerry?"

"Just fine. Thanks for asking."

"As many of you know, Kerry recently entered the race for county commission bidding against incumbent Sarah Maestas. What made you decide to enter politics in the first place, Kerry?"

"Well, politics has always interested me and having followed it for many years, I became disappointed recently in the direction certain commissioners seem to be taking us."

"What did you find so upsetting?"

"My opponent decided not to support the recently proposed tax increase to fund the police department. She would rather support a land swap deal with her good friend Jim Kilkenny, a big time real estate developer. She would give up pristine property in the enviable north side for barren acreage on the southeast side of town. I think her priorities are wrong."

"Commissioner Sarah Maestas did, in fact, oppose the tax increase for police, citing the mayor's task force report concluding the current infrastructure is sufficient to support demographic predicators indicating marginal growth; that along with unsubstantiated needs. How do you respond to that, Kerry?" Rory asked.

It was clear the fat man did his homework. "I haven't seen the task force report so I can't comment on that. But to conclude that the police department's infrastructure and equipment is adequate in the face of the threats we face in today's world is irresponsible."

"What would you regard to be the most serious threats to our city, Kerry?"

"Terrorism for one."

"Do you believe Santa Fe could be the target of terrorist activity?"

"I don't want to sound an alarm, but there are criminal elements out there that want to hurt us. What better way to gain notoriety for a cause than to terrorize a world renowned ancient city like Santa Fe. Can you imagine the fear it would generate proving that no city in America, regardless of how large or how small, is immune from terrorism."

"Are there specific threats that concern you?"

Rory's question was like hitting the lottery. The response came smooth and polished. "As you've probably read, Rory, the arrest of Theo Jaquez for the murder of Jude Armstrong to defraud her of insurance money, then the murder of his brother, Romel, has implications far beyond merely drugs."

"Are you implying there's a terrorist connection to those crimes?"

"I'm not at liberty to say too much about this matter. However, a reliable source revealed to me that Mr. Jaquez has been observed associating in Santa Fe with a Moroccan terrorist who belongs to an organization called *Salafia Jihadiya*. This terrorist organization was involved in several bombings in Casablanca, Morocco in 2003 which caused the death of many civilians, including tourists."

"Is there any reason to believe that same thing could happen in Santa Fe?"

While emphasizing his role in discovering the terrorist association, Snyder didn't want to cause a public panic. "I wish I could say more, Rory, but I don't want to jeopardize the investigation. The only other thing I would say is that by staying on top of the Theo Jaquez case, this potentially lethal association was discovered. I can assure you all the necessary steps are being taken and I'm confident our city will remain safe and protected. But, getting back to the original point, now you can see why financing equipment and infrastructure for the police department is so critically important."

"I'd like to stay on the terrorism issue just a little longer when we come back from a short message of our sponsors. Stay tuned to hear more from Lieutenant Kerry Snyder, a member of the New Mexico State Police who is challenging the county commissioner seat held by Sarah Maestas. We'll be right back."

Walking back to his car after the interview, Snyder felt exhilarated. His confidence of winning the election was gathering force like never before.

Fifty-eight

SNYDER WAS STILL asleep when the duty officer called early the following morning for an urgent meeting with the deputy chief. He immediately suited up and raced to work. Within the hour he arrived and headed for the deputy chief's office. Snyder nervously walked into the room. The gaze of the captain, major and the public information officer already seated followed him as he made his way to an empty chair. The deputy chief's eyes were fixed on Snyder.

"Can you tell me when you became a terrorism expert?" the deputy chief asked.

"I don't understand. What's this all about?" Snyder asked.

"Obviously, you haven't read this morning's paper." Throwing his copy in Snyder's direction, it landed on the floor. Snyder picked it up and read the bold print:

Theo Jaquez and Moroccan Terrorist Threaten Santa Fe

"If this was from the radio interview yesterday morning, I never said that," Snyder protested.

"You damn well said something giving that impression," the deputy chief said. His voice was loud and angry. "Do you have any idea what you've done? The mayor's phone was ringing off the hook all day yesterday. The city council called a special meeting and wants us to brief them on this alleged terrorist threat. The newspapers are clamoring for information. And the chief's mad as hell."

"My comments were only meant to raise awareness; I never said..."

The deputy chief interrupted, "You've done a great job at that, haven't you? You've got the whole damn city scared, not to mention the tourists. What in the world were you thinking suggesting Santa Fe could be a terrorist target?" The deputy chief looked down at his desk as he shook his head.

"Everything I said is true," Snyder responded.

"What kind of a fool are you, Snyder? Did you ever stop to think maybe it was two faggots getting together to do what faggots do. Explain to me how you think that threatens the city."

Snyder remained silent.

"This morning I went through the entire Theo Jaquez case file and found this letter. It's addressed to you." He raised the envelope to Snyder. "Can you tell what it is and when you got it?"

"It came in the mail a few weeks ago. Whoever wrote it claims to have murdered Theo's brother, Romel."

"So what else did you do besides punch holes and put it in the case file?"

Snyder didn't respond.

"Did you tell anybody about it?"

"I didn't think it was important enough to follow up on."

"Why not?"

"Because the language is generic—there's no details and it says nothing to prove that the author of the letter killed Romel Jaquez. The letter could have been written by anyone wanting to clear Theo Jaquez."

"Don't you think it would have been a good idea to share it with the captain, the major, myself or the district attorney?"

"I didn't think it had any evidentiary value."

"You didn't think it had any evidentiary value," the deputy chief repeated. "Okay, Snyder, here's the deal. You're out of here in less than twelve weeks. I know you're running for commissioner and you have to make speeches and attend functions. I've never gotten involved in politics and don't intend to. But I'm warning you—as long as you're a state police officer you will not speak publicly about any pending police matters. If you do, I'll fire you. You understand?"

"Yes, Sir."

"I'm also assigning the Theo Jaquez case to someone else. As of this moment you're relieved of the case. If circumstances were different I'd suspend you right now for embarrassing this department. I hope you feel lucky all you're getting is a reprimand. But do something stupid like this again and you're out of here."

"It won't happen again."

"The only other thing I want to say is that everything we talked about in here today stays in this office. If any questions come up about why you were removed from the Jaquez case, it's routine

police procedure after the case is turned over to the district attorney
for prosecution. Is all that clear to you, Snyder?"

"Yes sir."

"Good. Now get out of my office."

Humiliated and embarrassed, Snyder stood up and walked out.
Among the reprimands he had received during his career, by far this
had been the most degrading. He would remember it for a very long
time. And payback would be tremendously satisfying when he
became commissioner.

Fifty-nine

ASSISTANT DISTRICT ATTORNEY Marsha Bernal walked into
Nina Castillano's office with a bulky folder in hand. Dropping it on
the District Attorney's desk, she said, "This case is crap."

With Benjamin Franklin glasses resting on her lower nose, Nina
looked up. "You're the sniff expert. What brand of crap is this one?"

"I'm serious, Nina. Have you read the evidence against Theo
Jaquez? How am I supposed to take this case to trial?"

The district attorney sat up and began rocking in her red leather,
high-backed chair. "Okay, tell me, what's the problem?"

Marsha sat down. "The suspect, Theo Jaquez, allegedly killed
his brother. The motive was drugs; he allegedly had them and his
brother wanted them. The initial investigation reflects the suspect
has a history of drug use. But the subsequent evidence fails to back
that up. In fact, a recent toxicology report reveals no evidence of
drug use whatsoever."

"Maybe he got clean?"

"A heroin addict? Not likely."

"What else?"

"The suspect befriended then murdered a victim living up in
San Lucas. The victim had terminal cancer and he allegedly gave her
an overdose of morphine. But OMI can't confirm that the victim died
of a morphine overdose. Contrast that against a podunk lab finding
that morphine overdose was the likely cause of death."

"What podunk lab?"

Marsha looked through the file. "It's in Idaho Falls." She read
from the report. "Kamer Independent Laboratory offering skilled
analysis, consultation and expert court testimony to attorneys and
law enforcement."

"Sounds like somebody went witness shopping. Who ordered
it?"

"Lieutenant Kerry Snyder."

Nina fixed a tolerant expression on her face. "Okay, what else?"

"The suspect allegedly went to Morocco with fifty grand of life
insurance money to buy drugs. A witness who was in Morocco at the

time observed the suspect go into a building with a national and exchange a pouch he was carrying for a box. But nobody's been able to find any trace of drugs."

Marsha continued, "Snyder convinced the D.A. in Santa Fe to get a search warrant for the church in Arbol Verde on the basis of an alleged sexual relationship between the priest and the suspect; the theory being that the drug stash was hidden there. They found a bag with twenty-thousand dollars. The priest wouldn't say where the money came from, so Snyder confiscated it."

"Did they find any drugs?"

Marsha smirked as she shook her head.

Nina sighed. "What's the strongest evidence we have?"

"The brother's murder; the suspect was the only one around when it happened. There's DNA on the suspect's shirt linking the brother's spit and blood. They also have the weapon—a tree limb. But I'm not thrilled about this murder case. It has lots of holes."

"When's the arraignment?"

"Tomorrow."

"Okay, let's come up with a deal for them. What would you suggest?" Nina asked.

"Let me give it some thought," Marsha replied as she stood up and walked out.

An experienced assistant district attorney, Marsha thought the case smelled worse than reeking garbage. She had no appetite to take this one to trial.

Sixty

SEVERAL DAYS AFTER Romel's murder, Snyder drove to Arbol Verde to personally interview witnesses. The police station interview room was small. Painted a drab green, the only furniture were two folding chairs and a long, narrow metal table. Entering the room, Snyder's chest was pumped out, his face rigid and his hands curled in fists as if he was ready to brawl. He stared at the man sitting on the chair and his steel grey eyes were chilling. The officer's look was pure bile and the man sensed Snyder's disgust. The man looked away quickly and rubbed his hands nervously under the table.

"How old are you, Tino?" he asked.

"Twenty-eight."

"How long you been a *tecato*?"

"I don't remember. A long time."

"You know every time I see guys like you sleepwalking on my streets I have to spit on the dirt. I wonder why you're even alive. You contribute nothing to society but trouble. Look at you? You're filthy, you smell like raw sewage, you're repulsive. You look forty-eight, you know that?"

Tino kept his head down and just listened.

Snyder remained silent for a few moments just to heighten the pressure he knew Tino was feeling. Then he asked, "How well did you know Romel?"

"We hung out."

"Did you two take care of business together?"

"Sometimes."

"What do you know about his murder?"

"Just what I heard around, that Theo killed him."

"Why do you think Theo killed him?"

"I don't know."

"Come on Tino, don't play dumb with me. Why did Theo kill his brother?"

"I don't know. All I know is that we saw Theo drive down the street in front of the *tienda* and somebody said he was going to see the priest at Santa Niño."

"Did you know Theo was queer?"

"Everybody knew that."

"So what was he doing going to see the priest?"

"Romel said he was going to give the priest a blowjob."

"So if Theo was going to see the priest for sex, what did Romel want with him?"

"I don't know."

"Who supplied Romel with heroin?"

"I don't know. He would never tell me."

"Was he dealing that night?"

"Yeah, but he didn't have much. He was pissed off because he ran out of shit."

"So he didn't even have any for himself?"

"Yeah, that too."

"Okay, so let me get this straight. He ran out of heroin and got mad because he had sold all his baggies and couldn't get high. So he went to see his brother. Is that right?"

"Yeah, I guess."

"You think he would have gone to see his brother to get a blowjob?"

"No, Romel didn't get into that stuff."

"So, I'm asking you again, why did he go see his brother?"

"I told you, I don't know."

"Did you know that Theo knocked off an old lady to collect her insurance money?"

"Yeah, I heard that."

"And did you know that Theo had come back from Morocco with his own drug stash?"

"Romel told me Theo had gone to some foreign country but didn't know where."

"How did Romel know that?"

"Because he showed us money his brother had given him. They were bills from a foreign country."

"So, if Romel knew that his brother had a stash, doesn't it sound reasonable that he would have asked Theo to help him out? Maybe he wanted to steal Theo's stash."

"I don't know about that. Maybe."

"Well, doesn't it make sense that Romel was going to be hurting if he didn't get his fix, so he needed to get it someplace?"

"I guess."

"And something went wrong and Theo ended up killing his brother?"

"Yeah, I guess."

"So you think it's possible that Romel wanted Theo's drug stash?"

"Yeah, I guess."

"And they got into a fight and Theo ended up killing him?"

Tino remained silent.

Snyder blew up. "Look at me you piece of garbage. I'm asking you again. Did Romel go see his brother to steal his drug stash?"

"Yes."

"And that's what you believe?"

"Yes."

"And you think they got into a fight because Theo wouldn't give it to Romel?"

"Yes."

His voice moderated again. "Okay, that's all I wanted to know. I'm going to write out an affidavit of what you told me and I want you to sign it." Snyder got up and walked out of the room.

Sergeant Velez was at his desk when Snyder approached. "How many more *tecatos* did you pick up at the *tienda*?" Snyder asked.

"Four. They're in the holding cell," Sergeant Velez replied.

"Okay, I'll get Tino's statement ready and as soon as he signs it, get him out of here. I want to finish up with the rest of them before they start getting sick on me."

"By the way, you got a call from Chester Albright," Sergeant Velez said.

Snyder got excited. "When did he call?"

"About an hour ago."

"I'll be in the back office."

Pulling out the chair from the desk, Snyder sat down, picked up the phone and dialed. "Hey boss, you got something for me?"

"Nothing that's going to make you jump up and down," Albright replied.

"What did you find?"

"The only toxic substance in the body was morphine. There was a significant amount. But, it's almost impossible to say death was attributable to a morphine overdose. Even if we could determine the amount she was taking and make an educated guess as to the accumulation in the body, we might possibly find that the level was so far elevated it caused her death. But that would be a stretch and only one opinion that can be easily refuted. So, after considering all of this, I can't say conclusively that morphine was the cause of death."

"Could you at least say there was a likelihood she died of a morphine overdose?"

"Snyder, what didn't you hear? Absolutely not, I'd be guessing because there is no conclusive tests to prove that happened."

"Chester, this is a cold-blooded murderer that bashed in his brother's head. This is the same guy that coerced the victim to sign over her insurance money, then used it to travel to Morocco and buy drugs. This is a really bad actor, Chester. Help me out here?"

"If you want somebody to say she died of a morphine overdose, hire professionals that sell testimony in court. I'm not risking the integrity of this office by testifying to something that may or may not have happened."

"No problem, Chester. We'll just have to find some other way to get this done."

"Do what you have to do."

Snyder slammed the phone down.

Sixty-one

ONCE ILYAS CHOSE to apply for asylum in the United States, the immigration agent took his statement and handed him documents to review and sign. "You'll be held at a detention facility indefinitely until your case goes before a judge," the official advised. "Do you understand?"

Ilyas shook his head and began reading the statement slowly, making corrections and inserting more details. Afterward he was moved to another room with several others, and given a meal. Within the hour two guards appeared and escorted them to a bus. They were driven to the Dallas Federal Detention Facility.

When they arrived, all their possessions were confiscated. They were fingerprinted and processed, then issued uniforms and taken to the men's section. The facility was sterile with walls painted the color of dormant grass and bare concrete floors. The two-story building had a guard station in the center of each floor. Tables and chairs were placed around the guard station and televisions were affixed to walls at both ends. Each cell had two beds, a wash basin and toilet screened by a short wall panel. Ilyas was placed in a cell alone. While Ilyas hated incarceration, the facility was a resort compared to Sidi Kascen.

Several hours later their cells were electronically opened and the detainees were escorted to the dining hall. After the meal, they were allowed to mingle outside their cells and watch television, read, or play games. By eight-thirty they were ordered back into their cells until breakfast the following morning.

After the second day an Ecuadorian detainee was placed with Ilyas. Two days later the Ecuadorian was transferred out and replaced with a Colombian. Ilyas stayed mostly to himself, speaking with others only when necessary.

On the fourth day Ilyas was taken to a small room and interrogated by two agents of the U.S. Department of Homeland Security. The meeting lasted for several hours as Ilyas recited his story and tried to convince them that he harbored no terrorist sympathies or affiliations.

After almost two weeks at the facility, a guard handed Ilyas a letter; his hearing would be held in three days. He could hardly contain his anxiety. At night his dreams were filled with the same horrific nightmares he experienced at Sidi Kascen. In his mind Ilyas sketched out what he would say to the judge. He would deny involvement with any terrorist organization. He would describe the condition of Sidi Kascen and the consequences if he returned to Morocco. He would tell of living in Spain, holding a job and having an apartment. He would plead to be allowed to return there rather than Morocco. He had to make the judge understand that returning to Morocco would seal his fate to prison where he was certain to die.

On the appointed day Ilyas and several other detainees were taken to a van. The drive was less than twenty minutes. Guards surrounded them as they exited the vehicle and walked through an underground tunnel, up the elevator to a main corridor. From there the detainees were escorted into a courtroom. They were all seated together. Guards stood by the exits. Attorneys began filing into the courtroom. Finally the judge appeared.

As each case was called by the clerk, those detainees represented by attorneys proceeded to the front, met their representative and sat at the table facing the dais. After conferring briefly, the attorney made the presentation, then the judge asked questions and ruled on the case. Everything seemed too formal and ominous, Ilyas thought.

When his case was called, Ilyas slowly stood up, walked to the front table and took a seat.

The judge began addressing the court reporter with a preliminary statement about Ilyas' detention by INS officials at the Dallas-Ft. Worth airport, the expedited hearing requested by the Secretary for the Department of Homeland Security based upon Ilyas' name appearing on the terrorist watch list, and his affiliation with a terrorist group *Salafia Jihadia...*

Ilyas interrupted. "But I am not a member of that group," he said, attempting to correct the judge.

"You are out of order. You will remain silent until I have finished my statement," the judge ordered. "Do you understand?" His voice was firm.

"I am sorry," Ilyas replied.

The judge continued for several more minutes. When finished, he looked down at Ilyas. "I assume you are acting *pro se,* on your own without counsel. Do you wish to make a presentation?"

Ilyas began just as he had outlined in his mind in the days leading up to the hearing. His voice was contrite but strong. His presentation, bound by the limitations of his English vocabulary, was coherent. He spoke about his arrest in Morocco and the forced confession. Then he spoke about his prison sentence. When he described conditions at Sidi Kascen, the judge listened attentively. He spoke about the pardon and about his new life in Spain. Ilyas knew his presentation was longer than any of the others, but it appeared that the Judge was giving full attention to his plea. Ilyas ended by telling the judge he had no objection being denied entry into the United States, but begged to return to Spain rather than Morocco. Knowing it was a sign of subservience that the judge might understand, Ilyas bowed his head when he had finished. A brief period passed before the judge responded.

"Mr. Bashir, while I empathize with your plight and acknowledge that your situation is compelling, my ruling is governed by laws established to protect the security of the United States. The law does not allow a grant of asylum in situations such as yours; cruel prison conditions do not establish a substantive basis for favorable consideration of your petition. Additionally, I have little discretion with terrorist watch list detainees and am obliged to rule based upon the policies set forth by the United States Department of Homeland Security. Despite your denial of terrorist affiliation, and I note an absence of probative evidence in support of that assertion, the fact that your name is allied with it becomes dispositive in this matter. Thus, I have no choice but to order that you shall be returned to Morocco, the country of your birth, at the earliest possible date."

Tears trickled down Ilyas' face at hearing the judge's ruling. His body deadened; he was unable to move. Guards appeared, took his arm, stood him up and escorted him back to his seat. The rest of what took place in the courtroom was a blur to Ilyas. He lay in bed that night haunted by the ruling. How soon would he be extradited? Could he dispute the ruling? Ilyas began contemplating his next move.

The day following the hearing passed uneventfully. Restless in his sleep, Ilyas began having thoughts of suicide. He thought of ripping the sheet, tying one end to the overhead ventilation grate and hanging himself. But that was impossible without rousing his cellmate. Learning from detainees that laundry detergent was a potent poison, Ilyas wondered where he might find it. The morning light began to shine through the overhead window too soon for him. As the cells opened and the detainees filed to the dining hall, Ilyas' eyes darted in every direction like never before in search of other options to escape or take his life. Just as he placed his breakfast tray on the dining table, two guards appeared.

"Mr. Bashir, you need to come with us," one of them said.

Panic struck him. Ilyas was escorted back to his cell. His confiscated possessions were lying on his bed. He was ordered to change clothes as they remained by his side, then he was escorted to a waiting van. They drove off and forty-five minutes later, the driver exited the interstate and followed the highway signs to the departure ramp of the airport terminal. Once there, Ilyas was led through airport security and down several corridors, to his departure gate. As they waited, someone appeared and spoke to the guards.

"I'm with the U.S. Marshal's Office. I'm here to escort a detainee back to Morocco."

A brief exchange took place between the guards and marshal. A few minutes later the marshal walked over to Ilyas.

"Mr. Bashir, I'm Officer Renfro. I'll be your escort on the aircraft."

Ilyas didn't respond.

Renfro sat next to Ilyas until the gate attendant made a general boarding announcement. Renfro and Ilyas were allowed to board before any of the other passengers. Finding their assigned seats, Renfro motioned for Ilyas to place his bags in the overhead compartment and take the window seat.

"What time do we arrive in Casablanca?" Ilyas asked.

Renfro got a bemused look on his face. "I didn't know you spoke English." He looked at the paperwork. "It looks like we get in about seven forty-five tomorrow morning."

Ilyas glanced out the window as his mind roiled with fear and his chest filled with foreboding.

Seconds later, as Ilyas looked around the cabin, it appeared that every seat was filled. A barely audible announcement came over the intercom advising of their scheduled route, the cruising altitude, and the weather report. Just then Ilyas noticed a flight attendant walking down the aisle with a gaze fixed on them. Approaching Renfro, the flight attendant bent down and whispered a message.

"Are you sure?" Renfro asked.

"Those were my instructions," was the response.

Renfro looked over at Ilyas and without explanation said, "Let's go."

He stood up, backed up and waited for Ilyas to make his way

out of the seat. "You better get your carry-on. We may not be traveling to Morocco today," he said.

Ilyas pulled open the overhead bin and collected his two pieces. Renfro followed him down the aisle to the aircraft door. It wasn't clear to Ilyas what was happening, but any delay in returning to Morocco was good, he kept thinking. Two men in suits were waiting for them as they walked out the aircraft door onto the jet bridge platform.

"Is this Ilyas Bashir?" one of them asked Renfro.

"This is him."

"Mr. Bashir, would you please come with us."

"What's this about?" he asked.

"You're being released from custody."

The words didn't register. "I'm what?" he asked.

"There's a gentleman waiting to see you in our office. I believe he can explain all of this to you."

As he followed the trio down the corridor, Ilyas looked out the concourse window to see the Morocco-bound aircraft pushing back. His mind and heart racing with wonder and surprise, he couldn't believe what he thought he had heard. Ten minutes later they reached the airport offices. Walking through double glass doors and down a narrow hallway, they stopped in front of one of them. A slender, older man with a winning smile immediately stood up. "You're Ilyas Bashir?" he asked.

"Yes."

The man extended his hand. "My name's Marty Chenoweth. You're a very difficult person to find."

Ilyas remained silent.

Renfro spoke, "So I guess you won't need me anymore?"

"No, we won't," one of the men replied, as he shifted his gaze to Ilyas. "You're also free to leave anytime you'd like, Mr. Bashir."

Wanting to get away as quickly as possible, Ilyas looked at Marty.

"Let's go get something to eat and I'll explain everything to you," Marty said.

The two walked out of the office and went searching for a quiet airport restaurant.

Sixty-two

RETURNING TO HIS office after lunch, David picked up his message slips. He noticed one from Mark Quintana of Santa Fe. The name had a familiarity that he couldn't quite place. He set it aside with the intention of returning the call later. But before getting to it, Mark Quintana called again.

"David, you probably don't remember me; I'm Jeannie

Quintana's brother."

The image instantly struck him. David recalled when his family still lived in Santa Fe and he was dating Jeannie, a young, beautiful high school sophomore. Mark was a scrawny kid with an awesome baseball swing. Given a decent pitch, Mark could knock the ball out of the little league field almost every time. It was hard to believe his thin arms carried so much punch. Many summer evenings he and Jeannie spent hours at the park watching her brother play, then would go off for a hamburger with friends before ending the evening on a trail off Rodeo Road, making out. "Yeah, of course I remember you. I always wondered if you ever made it into pro baseball."

"No, I didn't. But at least it paid for my college."

"Good deal. How's Jeannie? I haven't seen her in probably thirty years."

"She's married, three kids, one in college. They're living in Denver."

"Wow, time just keeps slipping by," David replied. "So what can I do for you, Mark?"

"The reason I'm calling is to ask for a favor. I work for a land developer in Santa Fe—JWK Investments."

"Doesn't ring a bell," David replied.

"The company's been here for a long time. You'll probably recognize some of the properties we've developed—*Tierra del Fuego* or *Villa Estancia*?"

"Yeah, of course, their pretty high-end developments."

"The company's owned by James Kilkenny."

"Humm, still don't recognize the name. So what's the favor?"

"He'd like to meet with you."

"That's not a problem. My secretary can set him up with an appointment."

"Well, that's just it, David. He'd like to meet away from your office."

"What about?"

"Theo Jaquez."

"I don't understand. What about Theo Jaquez?"

"I can't say anything more. But my boss suggested noon tomorrow at Roosevelt Park."

"Are you coming along?"

"Nope. It'll be just you and him."

"I don't know if I want to do that, Mark."

"I understand. Believe me, right now I'm feeling like Don Corleone's underling doing this. But I assure you, David, this whole thing's on the up and up."

"I need to think about this."

"No problem. Is it okay if I call you first thing tomorrow for your answer?" Mark asked.

"Yeah."

"Great. Talk to you then."

Throughout the day the strange meeting request kept cycling through David's mind. Before turning in that night, David decided against the Roosevelt Park meeting. If Kilkenny wanted to see him bad enough, he could make an appointment just like everyone else. But when Mark's call came first thing the following morning, David's curiosity overtook his trepidation. He agreed.

David pulled into the park and remained in his car wondering what was supposed to happen next. He looked around and noticed the casual pace of the people lingering about; couples sitting on the grass taking their lunch, parents with their children in the playground, a young man and his dog playing Frisbee.

He got out and walked onto the grass. Locating an available bench, David sat down. The September day was warm even as the shade from the large oak tree shadowed the park bench. A few seconds later he looked toward the area opposite where he had walked across and noticed a figure heading in his direction. The man wore a casual light blue sport shirt and tan trousers. He was tall with tousled, white hair and easily blended in with the noon-time park crowd. Approaching, he extended his hand. "Hello David, I'm James Kilkenny."

David looked up. The man's face was tanned. He was probably in his mid-sixties and looked fit. They shook hands.

"I'm not used to clandestine meetings," David replied.

Kilkenny's expression remained cordial. "Do you mind if I sit down?"

"Help yourself."

Kilkenny glanced around the park. "Nice day, isn't it?"

David gave him a curious gaze. "Yeah, but I don't think we're here to talk about the weather...or are we?"

Kilkenny smiled. "No, we're not. I'm sure you're curious why I asked to meet you outside your office."

"That crossed my mind."

"I'm aware that you're representing Theo Jaquez in a murder case. I'm also aware of your reputation as a defense attorney."

"Okay. What of it?"

"I have a strong interest in ensuring Theo Jaquez is acquitted."

"Well that makes two of us."

"Then maybe you'll answer one question. Do you believe he's innocent?"

"Kilkenny, I don't know you, or much about you. And I sure as hell don't think it's any of your business what I believe about my client."

"Would it change your mind if I told you that I'm prepared to finance Theo Jaquez's defense provided that you remain his counsel."

"Why would you want to do that?" David asked.

"As I said earlier, because it means a great deal to me that Theo Jaquez gets acquitted."

"Do you know him?"

Kilkenny maintained the same grandfatherly type smile as he spoke. "No, I've never met him."

"What makes you so certain he can get acquitted?"

"I'm not certain of that at all. That's why I asked you the question. I've researched your credentials and reputation. I've made some inquiries about the case and happen to know much of the evidence is weak. I'm willing to gamble that if anyone can get him off, it will be you. But before I decide to make the investment, I need to hear your answer to my earlier question."

David thought for a few seconds before responding. Weighing the question against Kilkenny's offer seemed reasonable. "Most of the charges are bogus. The only real charge is his brother's murder and my gut feeling is that the kid didn't do it. There are a lot of holes in their case; they short-cut the investigation. Now it's your turn."

"What's that?"

"Why would you finance Theo's defense?"

"My reasons are entirely business related and my company has the economic resources to gamble on a favorable outcome at the trial. An acquittal would benefit my company a great deal."

"I'm sensing there's a political aspect to all of this."

Kilkenny's bushy eyebrows furrowed. "Now I see why you're so highly regarded." There was a brief pause, then Kilkenny asked, "Do we have a deal?"

"Let me give it some thought."

Kilkenny took out a business card from his wallet and handed it to David. "If you decide to accept my offer, bill your services to this address."

Kilkenny stood up and extended his hand. "It's unlikely we'll need to meet again. I hope you'll accept my offer." At that, he turned and strolled away in the direction that he came.

Sixty-three

FATHER BONAFACIO MADE his way from the rectory to the church on a sunny Saturday afternoon. Walking to the confessional, he gave a slight smile and nod to those waiting. As he glanced at the many people sitting in the pews, he was grateful for their faith in him. He entered the small niche, and sat down, kissed his stole and recited a short prayer. Starting with the left niche, he opened the small window and began listening to the litany of sins from the congregant.

Every Saturday afternoon, without fail, Luz Vigil and Estella Tafoya were among the church members waiting for confession. Having set aside the afternoon just for that purpose, the two women were in no hurry. They waited patiently across the aisle, observing each friend, acquaintance or neighbor scooting one place over in the pews closest to the confessional niches. Luz and Estella were usually among the last to move to the confessional pews. With their rosaries in hand, the two women discreetly took note of the time each confessor remained in the niche and the duration of their penance. Combined, it showed the gravity of their misbehavior and made for good neighborhood gossip.

During the idle moments, each time the church doors opened, curious eyes turned to see who came in. One of those times Luz heard unusual muffled banter as most heads turned. Her hand rose over her mouth to quiet the gasp when she saw Sixto walk down the aisle of the nave. His button-down shirt and trousers were wrinkled but clean. His gray hair was disheveled but his face shaven. His expression was stoic, but he seemed to be made nervous by the many faces staring. Signs of his time in detox were evident; his face had color, his eyes were clear and focused and his gait steady. He took a seat in the confessional pews to wait his turn. Some more muffled conversation before one of the young men in the confessional pew stood up and walked out the door. The young man returned to his place within several minutes. Suddenly, several of the volunteers who manned the church trailer at night appeared. They sat in the pews closest to the back of the church waiting and observing as Sixto inched closer to the confessional niche.

MORE THAN A week in rehab, Sixto recovered enough to learn from Fedak about his impending arrest. He stealthily slipped away. Over the next day he hitchhiked to Arbol Verde, and once home, went to bed. He slept restlessly for only a few hours, arising before dawn, showering and changing clothes. Locating the keys to Romel's car, since his own had broken down months earlier, Sixto made his way out the door and drove away.

Sixto had been warned about "the chucks," the voracious hunger following heroin withdrawal. He had it bad. For the first time he could remember, his mind wanted something other than *chiva*. Visiting the home of a close cousin, he was welcomed inside and fed until he was full. Managing to borrow twenty dollars, Sixto drove off and eventually ended up at the trailhead of El Rito Mountain. He parked and sat contemplating his next move. Several hours later, Sixto got back on the road and drove to Santo Niño church.

When his turn came at the confessional, Sixto stood up and

entered the niche. The men in the back came forward and took positions as close as they could get to the confessional in case there was trouble. More people had gathered in the back of the church, curious at what was about to happen. There was dead silence in the church as everyone waited. A few minutes later Sixto came out of the niche and began making his way down the aisle. He looked over at Luz and stopped briefly, then continued out the door.

In the two seconds they exchanged eye contact, a glimpse of Sixto's soul was revealed to Luz. While not a single word was exchanged, she thought she sensed remorse.

Sixto got into the car and drove away. Pulling up to the side of the *tienda,* he called over a familiar face. They spoke briefly, then there was a veiled exchange in their handshake before Sixto drove off to Indian Lake. That was where his body was discovered one day later, his arm still tied off.

Theo was at work preparing for the Sunday brunch crowd when the mid-morning call came through. Removing the cell phone from his pocket, he looked at the incoming number. Selective in the calls he took during working hours, on this one Theo walked to the back sink and flipped it open. "Hey Patrick, what's up?"

"I got some bad news for you?"

"What?"

"Your dad, they found him at Indian Lake. He OD'ed."

There was a brief silence. "Oh, okay."

"Are you going to be all right?"

"Oh yeah, for sure. But I really need to get back to work. Thanks for the call."

Snapping his phone shut, Theo gave no more thought to the news.

Sixty-four

JUDGE JELLISON, FIRST elected twelve years earlier, lived in Santa Fe where he normally held court. An overflow of cases in El Pastor County caused a shuffling of the excess, and in the rotation he was assigned the Theo Jaquez murder case. A thin, balding man who wore thick glasses, Judge Jellison was an avid trench art collector and a scholar of WWI history. Fairness and impartiality along with keen legal ability defined the judge.

Beginning with the various motions before him, Judge Jellison questioned the parties, heard the arguments, then ruled on the merits of each one. Jury selection began next.

The thirty potential jurors came from communities, towns and villages located within El Pastor County. The task was to agree on a panel of twelve jurors and two alternates. Discussing his thoughts with Stephanie, David's inclination was to select older, assertive females who could identify closely with Jude Armstrong and young Hispanic men who could empathize with Theo's actions in defending himself against his brother. Stephanie agreed and suggested they also include jurors who knew or had experience with heroin abusers. Contrasting the lifestyles of the two brothers might have a favorable influence in their deliberations, Stephanie offered.

The first potential juror was a middle-aged Anglo male. A devout member of a pentecostal church, his conservative leaning was evident. David rejected him. A young, unmarried Catholic woman who worked as a grocery cashier during the day and attended community college at night was next. She was familiar with heroin abuse, having lived with an addicted boyfriend at one time. Both sides agreed on her. As they questioned each potential juror on the list, both sides carefully evaluated the prospect before agreeing. By the time Judge Jellison called a recess for lunch, the two sides had agreed on eight jurors. Resuming court one hour later, the final four jurors and two alternates were selected. The trial was ready to begin.

Marsha presented her opening statement declaring that they would prove beyond a reasonable doubt that Theo murdered his brother in reprisal for a beating he had sustained several weeks earlier. Her statement was long and detailed; it included much of the evidence they would present. She spoke in vivid expressions clearly aimed at rousing the jurors. Then she brought out a photo of Romel's mutilated face and showed it to the jury. The abhorrent image was shocking. Marsha declared Romel's murder was the result of uncontrollable sibling rage. Asking the question in the language of the predominantly Hispanic jury, *"quen mata a su hermano?"* , Marsha urged the jurors to listen carefully to the facts and use their best reasoning. She was certain they would find clear intent, means, and capacity to convict Theo of killing Romel.

When she finished, David stood up and walked slowly to the jury box. He gazed at each juror, hoping they would see the sincerity in his eyes and translate it to his words. He began by citing the circumstantial nature of the prosecution's evidence. He spoke about his client being prejudged from the very beginning because of media hyperbole. He told them about the grand jury's indictment against Theo in a related matter, and how it was later withdrawn when the matter was re-investigated and the true facts became known. The investigation in the murder of Romel, he declared, was rife with the same bungled investigation, prejudgments, and specious conclusions. David urged the jurors to see the case for what it really was—a rush to find a murderer that resulted in charges being brought against an innocent victim. He urged the jurors to evaluate the case not on presumptions or probabilities but on the facts. His client was not capable of killing his brother, David declared. As they came to know his client, they would also come to that same conclusion. Citing a blatant miscarriage of justice, David pleaded with the jury to free Theo of the charge and let him resume his life. At the conclusion of David's statement, the judge adjourned for the day.

When the trial resumed the following morning, Marty was the first witness called by the prosecution. Testifying that he first learned of Theo Jaquez when he arrived in Santa Fe to settle the estate of Jude Armstrong, the young man aroused his suspicion. He spoke about reporting his misgivings to Snyder who initiated the formal investigation. The attorney's questions then directed Marty to the occasion he visited Theo's apartment and found him unconscious on the floor lying in a pool of blood. After describing that scene in detail, the assistant D.A. passed the witness.

So far no surprises, David thought. He was relieved that the story was exactly as he understood it to be.

During cross examination David delved into Marty's relationship with Snyder. His objective was to show that Snyder had targeted Theo from the very beginning, and despite exculpatory evidence, was intent on charging Theo.

Marsha objected. "Your Honor, the line of inquiry that Mr. Lujan is attempting to pursue goes beyond the scope of this charge and is irrelevant. That matter is not germane to the instant charge."

David responded, "Your Honor, the assistant D.A. opened that line of inquiry in having this witness recount his acquaintance with my client and Officer Snyder. That gives me the right to continue the inquiry."

The judge overruled the objection and allowed David to continue.

For the next ninety minutes David had Marty recount the Jude Armstrong matter. Marty discussed his own investigation and spoke about Consuelo Soto's account of Theo's friendship with Jude. He revealed the Medical Information Bureau's incongruity and the difficulty in reaching Snyder. Characterizing Snyder as arrogant, aloof and uninterested when told of the incongruity, Marty then discussed his discovery concerning Theo's Morocco visit. He ended his testimony by citing Snyder's threat. Despite frequent objections from the prosecutor, most of which were overruled, David was pleased that Marty's testimony reflected not only the prejudicial nature of Snyder's investigation, but also gave the jury a clue to Theo's character and personality.

Pamela Jacobs, the Santa Fe Daily News reporter, testified next, stating that during a conversation with Snyder over another matter, he revealed to her certain details concerning the Jude Armstrong murder and fraud investigation the police had initiated against Theo. Her story on that investigation was published the following day. A copy was offered into evidence and Jacobs read aloud the portion relating to the fifty thousand dollar life insurance policy Theo had obtained.

After lunch when the trial resumed, Theo's neighbor, Kevin, was called to the stand. Kevin's appearance sorely lacked courtroom decorum. With pierced rings on his nose and lips, black rings fixed in his earlobes, tattoos up and down both arms, torn Levi trousers and a well-worn Bart Simpson T-shirt, Kevin objected to taking the oath on the Bible proclaiming his agnostic views. The judge ordered the witness to affirm that his testimony would be truthful. Startled by the judge's stern voice, Kevin instantly complied.

Testifying that he played in a rock band at a local bar, Kevin spoke of his long acquaintance with Romel and how he appeared at the bar one late night shortly after the Santa Fe Daily News article appeared. Romel asked about Theo's whereabouts. Hearing that Theo had traveled to Morocco and wouldn't be returning until the end of the week, Romel left the bar.

David's cross examination of Kevin was brief and was targeted at identifying Romel as a heroin user and dealer. His efforts were successful.

The prosecution called the hospital's emergency room doctor, then two nurses who all testified on the extent of Theo's injuries arising from the beating he sustained after returning from Morocco. David waived cross-examination of those witnesses.

Tino Sandoval, who was Romel's closest friend, testified next. Tino appeared to be in a stupor; his walk stiff, his face drawn and his eyes glassy. Tino responded to each question in a flat monotone void of affect. Declaring his own heroin addiction, Tino testified that he had hung around outside the *tienda* with Romel early in the evening on the day he was murdered. Upon seeing Theo's car pass the *tienda*, Romel left, stating he had business with his brother. When asked whether Tino knew the nature of that business, he replied that he did not. But he quickly recanted when Marsha challenged Tino's affidavit given to Snyder.

Marsha passed the witness and David successfully elicited testimony that Romel was a known heroin dealer with a score of enemies that disliked him immensely. Tino's memory became mixed-up in recalling names or specific threats against Romel. Soon Tino began losing focus and his responses became jumbled. David gave up.

The hour was late and Judge Jellison adjourned for the day.

SERVED WITH A subpoena to testify as an adverse witness for the defense, Kerry Snyder was scheduled to appear in San Lorenzo the third day of the trial. He sneered at the subpoena, convinced his words would never be recorded in any trial. Considering the state's evidence against Theo and the presumably favorable plea deal he was certain the parties had negotiated, Snyder believed that the only possible obstacle was convincing the judge to accept it.

Snyder received periodic updates from Sergeant Velez who was in the courtroom. In their last phone conversation, Snyder learned a jury was being selected. He wondered why they were going through all the posturing and began growing nervous. Early the following day when Snyder tried calling Sergeant Velez, the call went to voice message. Several hours later Velez returned the call. "They started the trial, Kerry."

"Is this a joke?" he asked

"It's no joke. We're on a break...they have Marty Chenoweth on the stand."

Snyder could feel his blood drain. *How could this be happening?*

"I'll call you back," he said to Sergeant Velez as he dropped the phone and collapsed in his chair.

Sixty-five

"TELL ME AGAIN, how did I become a citizen of the United States?" Ilyas asked Marty.

Marty knew he had to explain the details slowly and allow Ilyas enough time to absorb every bit of it. Otherwise it was likely he would become unnerved and flee back to Spain. It was important to gain his confidence and convince him to testify for Theo. He was the linchpin in clearing Theo of the Jude Armstrong charges. Marty opened his shoulder bag and took out the file he had created.

"Your mother is Victoria Bashir. Her nationality was American when your father, Aban, married her." He offered the marriage certificate to Ilyas. "She died when you were just a few months old."

"No, that can't be true. My mother and father are Moroccan. Aban was my uncle."

Marty gave Ilyas a few minutes to reflect on what he had said. Then he handed Ilyas a copy of his birth certificate. "This is yours."

Taking it, Ilyas examined the document. The memory of reading the prison release document labeling him foreign born, came to mind. "This birth certificate is for Elijah Bashir."

Without correcting him, Marty continued with the story. "I was very good friends with your grandmother, Jude Armstrong. Did Aban ever tell you about her?"

"No."

"Did you know that she provided Aban with the money to arrange for your pardon from prison?"

Ilyas remained silent.

"Your grandmother died last year," Marty said.

Still, Ilyas said nothing.

"Have you heard the name, Father Marcelino Bonafacio?"

Instinctively touching his pocket to feel the envelope, the name instantly jolted Ilyas' attention. The thought of the countless times Ilyas had speculated about his connection to that name came to mind. At that instant he knew all that Marty said was true.

"How is the priest involved?" Ilyas asked.

Marty was getting way ahead of himself. "That's who you were intending to visit?"

Ilyas nodded his head.

"Can I ask how you got that name?"

"My Uncle Aban gave me an envelope the last time I saw him." He went on to tell Marty Aban's parting words.

Marty looked down to see that Ilyas had barely touched his sandwich. "Aren't you hungry?"

Ilyas shook his head. "This is all so difficult to understand. Why would my parents and my uncle keep the truth from me?"

"Why don't we go outside and get some air. We can talk more while we walk around."

Marty took one of Ilyas' bags and they proceeded out the airport doors. For several hours they strolled the perimeter as Marty provided the details of Theo's involvement and tried to answer Ilyas' countless questions. As dusk approached on the February evening, and the air grew chillier, they went back inside the airport. When it appeared that Marty had gained Ilyas' confidence, he asked, "Would you agree to testify at Theo's court hearing?"

"Does Theo still remain in prison?"

"Not anymore. He's allowed to go free until the trial."

"If I don't do this, what will happen?"

"Well, it will be difficult to prove Theo's actions to the jury."

"What is a jury?"

"In this country anyone convicted of a serious crime has the right to be tried by their peers. In other words, citizens are selected to sit and hear the evidence of a case, and then they confer with one another to decide whether the accused is guilty or innocent."

"Then what purpose is the judge?"

"To keep order in the courtroom and rule on what evidence may or may not be presented."

"The judge doesn't decide if someone is guilty?"

"No, he does not."

"Does the judge decide how long someone stays in prison?"

"Yes, that's another function of the judge."

Marty could almost feel the tumult going through Ilyas' mind.

"I don't know about doing what you ask, Marty. I'm terrified about being sent back to Morocco if I stay here."

"That won't happen. You are a citizen of the United States."

"Even now as we speak, Marty, it is very hard for me to

understand all that you have told me. I'm so filled with nervousness. Do you understand what I am saying? You have no idea what it is like at Sidi Kascen."

"I can only imagine your anguish. But there is an innocent young man that risked everything to free you from prison. Now he is faced with the same injustice that you experienced."

Ilyas remained silent for a few moments, then said, "I was raised a good Muslim and I submit to the will of Allah. We are guided by *shari'a* that teaches to prefer others over oneself. If I was tempted to violate my religion, it is now because of how confused I feel inside. After almost being sent back to Sidi Kascen, the only thing I want to do is get on the next airplane to Madrid."

Ilyas paused to take a deep breath. "But I will return with you to speak with Theo's attorney. And I will also return from Spain and testify at the trial, *Inshallah.*"

Sixty-six

THEO SAW ILYAS sitting in David's conference room as he walked in. His eyes instantly fixed on the Moroccan. There was a familiarity he couldn't place. Or maybe it just seemed that way. Walking over and extending his hand, he greeted Ilyas. "Hey, I'm Theo."

Ilyas stood up and shook it firmly.

"Where's David?" Theo asked.

"He left to take a telephone call."

Theo sat down across the table. Their eyes darted back and forth with irresistible curiosity. "How's it going for you?" he asked.

"It's okay.

There was a slight pause before Ilyas asked, "How are you handling all of this?"

"Just taking it one day at a time. By the way, thanks for being here."

"Surely."

Theo tried looking away but Ilyas' eyes were like a magnet, and the magnetic pull was forceful. He sensed his lip begin quivering as he cleared his throat. Ilyas was more masculine than he had imagined. Several days of beard growth added to his attractive appeal. His blue eyes were incredibly striking. Strands of brown hair hung down his forehead almost touching his eyes. At that moment it was hard to imagine the pain and torment this man had endured in prison. Seeing him for the first time, Theo noticed there was no clue of any of that. The image of Jude's wily smile came to mind as Theo noticed the slight resemblance.

"Have you ever seen a picture of your grandmother?" Theo asked.

The question took Ilyas by surprise. By Islamic custom his grandparents would never be photographed. Then he remembered. "Are you speaking of Jude?"

"Oh, I forgot. You just learned about her recently."

"I understand you were good friends with her."

Theo smiled. "Yeah, we got to be close friends."

"I'm very curious about her."

"I can help there. You want to hook up later?" Theo asked.

"Huh? What is that?"

"You want to get together tonight for dinner? You like mechoui and couscous?"

Ilyas thought for a second. "You can make mechoui?"

"Yeah, I've made it before. But since I live in Santa Fe, which is an hour away, I was thinking we could go to a Moroccan restaurant here in Albuquerque."

Ilyas smiled. "Of course, I would like that very much."

"Okay, let's do it. I'll pick you up about five?"

Ilyas nodded.

"So when do you go back to Spain?"

"Tomorrow afternoon."

At that moment the door opened and David walked in. "I guess both of you have already met?"

Theo responded, "Yeah, we did"

"I just finished talking with the assistant D.A. She's got an offer for you," David said, gazing at Theo.

"Oh, what kind of offer?"

David looked over at Ilyas. "I think we're done here. The trial starts in about three months. I have all your contact information. I'll put a rush on your U.S. passport and make sure you get your ticket and travel money well before we need you here. Do you have any more questions for me?"

"No, David. I think you've answered everything."

"You know you can call me any time night or day if you run into any problems."

"Yes, I know that."

David stood up and extended his hand. "Okay then, I'll look forward to seeing you sometime in May before the trial."

Ilyas reached for his hand as he stood up. "Thank you for all your kindness, David." Then Ilyas looked over at Theo. "Good bye."

"See you soon," Theo said.

Ilyas left the room.

When Ilyas was gone, David cautioned, "Don't get too close to him before the trial."

"What do you mean?"

"The D.A. could contaminate the jury's mind by convincing them both of you concocted the Morocco story. Since we don't have

Aban here to corroborate your meeting with him, the best we can do is attempt to reconstruct it with circumstantial evidence through Ilyas."

Theo nodded his head. "So what did the assistant D.A. offer?"

"Manslaughter. Ten years, but you could be out between four and six years."

"And you told her what?"

David smirked. "What do you think I told her?"

Theo lowered his head and smiled, reassured by David's faith in his innocence. "I was visiting with my parents this morning before coming here."

"How are they doing?" David asked.

"I feel pretty awful putting them through all of this. You know, they took out a loan on their house to get enough bail money for my release. They even paid my rent during the time I was in jail. Julian and Sonia have done so much for me."

"At times like these it's tough for everybody, Theo."

Theo nodded.

"Let's talk about something else, Theo. I need you to be straight with me. Now that we know the Jude Armstrong story, you have to tell me everything that happened the night Romel was killed."

Theo mulled over where to begin the story. This time he held nothing back. Reciting every detail, he told David of Sixto and Romel's visit to his apartment when he returned from Morocco and how his brother viciously beat him. Then he turned his story to the night at the rectory and talked of how Romel had gotten up after the first blow and reached into his back pocket to retrieve a weapon. But before Romel could get at it, Theo threw a second harder blow—a blow so forceful it splattered Romel's blood and spit on his shirt before his brother hit the ground a second time. Jumping into his Jeep, he sped out of the rectory parking lot. Even in the partial darkness Theo was almost certain of seeing the mirror reflecting Romel getting up.

Sixty-seven

THE DAY WAS chilly as Marsha Bernal parked outside the Albuquerque restaurant. It wasn't often the assistant district attorney met over lunch with a defendant's attorney, but the Theo Jaquez case warranted the exception. Since Theo's arraignment Marsha and David had spoken several times to discuss a plea bargain and a change of venue motion—offers she raised and he rejected. Today Marsha had arranged to meet David for lunch at a neutral location. It would provide a relaxing atmosphere for what she intended to discuss.

It was still early as she approached the hostess and, quickly surveying the restaurant, asked for the corner table that seemed to offer privacy. Once seated, she kept one eye on the entrance and the other on her wristwatch, knowing that David's punctuality would clue her in to his interest in their meeting. An early arrival meant he was eager, late meant he was posturing. Exactly two minutes after their appointed meeting time she saw him walk through the doors. He immediately spotted her, said a few words to the hostess and walked over as she stood up.

"Marsha, I bet you needed to get out of San Lorenzo and get your fix of the big city," David said as he extended his hand.

She smiled. "Yeah, but after a few hours of this traffic and congestion, I can't wait to get back." They sat down and she took a sip of water. She started, "Thanks for agreeing to meet, David."

"No problem. You're on my turf now, so I don't feel so threatened."

"What do you mean?"

"This restaurant, it's one of my favorites."

"I'm glad you like it. Actually, somebody suggested it to me."

"Well, you won't be disappointed." He took the linen napkin and placed it on his lap, then looked up at Marsha again. "I suspect you want to talk about the Theo Jaquez case?"

Marsha opened her briefcase, took out an envelope and handed it to him.

"What's this?" he asked.

"It's a copy of an anonymous letter we received. The writer claims to have murdered Romel Jaquez."

He opened the envelope and quickly read the two short paragraphs, then looked at the postmark. "This letter was covered under my discovery petition. How come I didn't get it with the rest of the material you sent over?"

"Because I just learned about it. The state police sent it to me."

"And I'll bet you Lieutenant Kerry Snyder tried to hide it?"

Marsha took on a look of surprise. "What makes you say that?"

"Because that's the way he likes to do things."

"If it makes you feel any better, he's been taken off the Theo Jaquez case," Marsha said.

"After the terrorist fiasco in Santa Fe, I'm not surprised. They should have taken him off a long time ago."

"That's what I wanted to talk to you about. Everybody's on edge over that situation." She took another sip of water, then gave him a sober look. "Who's Ilyas Bashir?"

David began to chuckle.

"What's so funny?"

"That your people wouldn't have discovered who he was before this. Ilyas Bashir, also known as Elijah Bashir, is Jude

Armstrong's grandson. After Theo delivered twenty-five grand to Morocco to get him out of prison, Ilyas came to collect the rest of his twenty thousand dollar life insurance inheritance the priest is holding."

"Jude Armstrong's grandson," Marsha repeated. It took a second to sink in. "The police report said she had no living relatives."

"Yeah well, your file would have a lot more juicy stuff like that if Snyder hadn't cut off his connection with Marty Chenoweth."

"How's Chenoweth involved?"

"Sorry, Marsha, you're going to have to find that out on your own."

"I know this is privileged information, David. But would you be willing to tell me what was in the box Theo exchanged for money in Morocco."

"Are you serious?"

"Of course I'm serious."

"A Moroccan teapot."

Marsha closed her eyes and rolled back her head just as the waiter approached.

HEARING MARSHA'S ACCOUNT of the conversation with David, District Attorney Nina Castillano scheduled an urgent meeting with the deputy chief and the Captain. The officers arrived at the San Lorenzo County Courthouse early the following morning and Marsha recounted what she had learned. They initially rebuffed David's account. But as they carefully reviewed the sequence of events and the witness statements, and considered the fact that Jude Armstrong's murder was dubious, there was no cache of drugs, and Theo had no history of drug abuse, the account became more plausible. If David's account was true, the grand jury needed to be served with these substantive facts and reconsider their outstanding indictment. The deputy chief remarked how the newspaper would have a field day embarrassing the Department if they ever learned the true identity of the alleged terrorist.

"Before making a final decision on any of this we need to interview Marty Chenoweth," the deputy chief declared.

"Will he cooperate?" Marsha asked.

There was a slight pause before he responded. "If anyone can get Chenoweth to cooperate it will be Lieutenant Petit who's taking over the Jaquez investigation."

"What's so special about him?" Nina asked.

"Not him...her. Lieutenant Allison Petit is one of our finest staff officers," he replied.

Sixty-eight

ALLISON PETIT WAS hired as the first female state police officer in New Mexico. Despite the continual harassment during boot camp and for several years after earning her badge, Allison refused to resign. Proving herself when she sighted and killed a rapist holding a teenage victim and a police officer hostage, Allison finally got the respect of her peers. After that, she was initiated into the exclusive state police fraternity.

A high achiever, Allison always exceeded the demands of the job. When special assignments arose, she was first to volunteer. As a result, promotion to sergeant came quickly. Earning a degree in criminal justice while attending night school, Allison was pegged as a potential staff candidate. And when a position finally opened up, despite intense competition Allison won the accolades and votes of the examining panel and became the youngest lieutenant in the history of the New Mexico State Police force.

After being assigned the Theo Jaquez case, Allison began putting the evidence to memory as she read each witness statement. An interview practice that Allison insisted upon was to document witness statements accurately as related without understating, overstating, exaggerating or embellishing the account. Too many times she had seen officers slightly modify a statement by inserting their own words rather than the words of the witness, and in so doing giving the account a different spin. As she reviewed the Theo Jaquez case file, one particular witness statement caught her attention. It was Snyder's interview of Sixto Jaquez. He wrote:

> "The witness states Father Bonafacio appeared at their home on his son's fourteenth birthday and took him out for dinner. Sometime thereafter, the witness asserts that his son indicated he was in a sexual relationship with the priest. The witness then drove to the Santo Niño rectory to confront the priest who denied such a relationship existed. The witness requested that the priest stop seeing his son..."

She was astonished at the mediocrity of the statement. The assertion that the priest and Theo were having sex was conclusionary with no actual basis of support. Had she been in charge, the officer would have been chastised and ordered to re-interview the witness. Perusing several other statements taken by Snyder, Allison was not impressed. While never before doubting Snyder's professionalism, Allison couldn't help wonder why the shoddy investigation. Much of it lacked critical probity.

Briefed by the captain on the meeting with the district attorney in San Lorenzo, Allison placed several calls to Marty's home in

Virginia. They went unanswered. Learning that he was a freelance writer, Allison did a computer search and located newspapers and magazines featuring Marty's work. She telephoned several and finally got his cell number. Placing the call, he answered at once.

"Marty Chenoweth?" Allison asked.

"Who is this?"

"I'm Allison Petit with the New Mexico State Police. I'd like to meet with you and talk about Theo Jaquez."

"What happened to Kerry Snyder?"

"He's been assigned to another project."

"Well, I'm glad to hear that. What do you want to know?"

"Can we meet face-to-face someplace?"

"Right now I'm in Ontario, Canada. I won't be back in Virginia for another ten days."

"Can I meet you in your Virginia home then?" she asked.

"Fine with me."

Early in the morning of the appointed day, Allison appeared at Marty's home. Sitting at the dining room table, she began the interview that went on until the early afternoon. When it was finally over, Marty invited her out to dinner. She weighed duty against desire, with the former prevailing.

"Maybe another time," she said, gathering her things together. "Thanks for being so candid.

"Not a problem...glad I was able to help."

On the plane headed home Allison couldn't understand how the Jude Armstrong investigation could have become so botched. From the onset the case seemed based on supposition and unconfirmed allegations. Despite exculpatory evidence, Theo remained in the crosshairs of Snyder's investigation. Allison was fairly convinced none of it had merit. At that moment her respect for Snyder began fading. Allison decided to distance herself from Snyder. He was bad news.

SNYDER WAS STILL seething from the deputy chief's reprimand. Having marked off another day on his short-time calendar, forty-three more remained before retirement. Although taken off of the Theo Jaquez case, Snyder remained very interested. At every opportunity he questioned Allison about the case, and was surprised to learn she was meeting with Marty. What could be so important that she would fly to Virginia for the meeting?

The day after Allison returned, Snyder stopped by her office to ask about the interview. But this time she was cold; her responses were vague and evasive. Something about her had changed and he sensed Marty Chenoweth was behind it. Snyder became determined to find out all Marty had told her.

At eight o'clock that evening Snyder drove to the state police building, parked, and walked up the stairs. He always preferred the stairs to the elevator. As he made his way into the central office, the duty officer greeted him. "Isn't it late for you to be coming around here, Kerry?"

"Hey, when duty calls. But don't worry because soon you won't be seeing me around here anymore."

"Yeah, well, just remember us poor stiffs busting our butts while you're on the beach sipping cold margaritas."

"I'll be sure to send you a postcard. Where's the janitor? I need to get into an office."

"I don't know. I'll beep him. Where you gonna be?"

"Allison's office. I left a file for her to review and need it back."

Walking into Allison's office, Snyder found the case file lying on the center of her desk, and picked it up. He walked to his own office and began reading Marty's statement. The more he read, the more inflamed he became. Flushed with anger, Snyder stormed out of the building. As he raced home, his body tensed with rage. How dare Chenoweth label him arrogant and pompous. Chenoweth's statements about him were all lies. Why was Chenoweth trying to smear his reputation?

Snyder wouldn't let him get away with it. Once home, Snyder marched to the back bedroom he used for an office. Opening his personal phone book, he dialed the number.

MARTY WAS WORKING late into the night. His concentration was totally focused on his most recent project. When the telephone rang, he looked at the caller ID window and noticed the New Mexico area code. Instinctively pressing the record button, he picked up the telephone. "Hello!"

"You piece of shit. What do you think you're doing trying to ruin my reputation?"

"Snyder. What do you want?"

"Did you think I wasn't going to see all the garbage you said about me?"

"Actually, that didn't even cross my mind," Marty replied.

"It should have."

"Why?"

"Chenoweth, you started this whole thing and I went along with you. Now you're backing off of it and trying to take me down. That's not going to happen."

"You know what, Snyder? In the whole scheme of things, you were the least important part of the Theo Jaquez case. Anyway, you asked me not to bother you any more, remember?"

"That's a lie. You promised to let me know anything you found out."

"I tried, and you wouldn't listen. You wouldn't even return my calls."

"What makes you think you're so almighty important? You expect me to drop everything just to get back to you?"

"I would have appreciated a return call after a few days," Marty replied.

"You're a lying sack of shit. I hope you're not planning on returning to New Mexico."

"Is that a threat, Snyder?"

"Chenoweth, if I hear you're anywhere within range of my jurisdiction, I doubt you'll make it back home in one piece."

"Well, I'll keep that in mind. You have anything more on your mind?" Marty asked. The receiver went dead. Replacing the phone, Marty pressed the stop button, clicked open the window and ejected the mini-cassette.

RETURNING FROM LUNCH two days after his conversation with Marty, Snyder was walking into the police building when he saw David Lujan sitting in the visitor area. He approached the attorney. "You waiting for someone?"

David didn't bother standing up. "Yeah," he responded as he stared up at Snyder.

"Anything I can do?"

David shook his head slowly, never taking his eyes off the officer. "No."

Turning around, Snyder mumbled something under his breath as he walked away.

IT WAS FOUR o'clock in the afternoon when Snyder looked up to see two officers in his doorway. "Yeah, what do you want?"

"Kerry, we need to get your badge and your weapon."

"What the hell are you talking about?"

One of the officers holding an envelope walked over and handed it to Snyder. "You're being placed on administrative suspension pending an investigation."

Thirteen days before the Theo Jaquez trial was scheduled to begin and twenty-two days before reaching his retirement date, Lieutenant Kerry Snyder was fired.

Sixty-nine

WHEN THEIR MEETING ended, and as Theo left the building, he thought of canceling the dinner date over David's concern. But it seemed so innocent. Theo couldn't conceive how dinner at a public restaurant could be used against him by the prosecution. But more than that, Theo was fascinated by Ilyas' story and wanted to hear about it firsthand. He decided to go ahead with the plan.

At exactly five o'clock he rounded the corner and headed in the direction of the hotel. As he drove under the portico, Ilyas walked outside.

"Been waiting long?" he asked as Ilyas got into the car.

"Actually, I spent the afternoon walking around the city and managed to get lost. I finally found my way back just in time."

"It's a little early for dinner. I was thinking of parking and walking around Albuquerque's Old Town. Is that okay with you?"

"I'm your guest, so whatever you'd like to do."

Theo glanced over admiring Ilyas' clear blue eyes again, and smiled. "Do you miss Morocco?" he asked.

"I miss my family. In Morocco I was always surrounded by my family or friends. There is very little privacy because we live so close to one another. When you're accustomed to that, it becomes very difficult to be alone."

There was a momentary silence before Ilyas asked, "Are you frightened about going to court?"

"In all honesty what frightens me more is that if I'm sent to prison it will delay my plans to attend culinary school."

"You want to become a cook?"

"Absolutely." Theo's smile lit up. "When I was growing up, nobody in my family cooked. It wasn't until I moved in with my foster family that I learned about cooking and food history."

"Food history?"

"Yeah, by reading about the history of food, you learn to understand and appreciate how it's all connected. For example, where do you think we learned to use spices like cinnamon, ginger, saffron, cumin and caraway?"

Ilyas chuckled. "I don't know, but I think you're going to tell me."

"Arabs gave us those spices. In Morocco one of your famous dishes besides couscous is bastilla. The name comes from the Spanish pastilla, which means pastry."

"You impress me. You must be a very good cook."

"Yeah, well, I can hold my own in the kitchen."

"Now I'm wishing I could have tasted something you prepared."

Theo looked at his watch. It was almost five-thirty. "I don't know how hungry you are, but if you feel adventurous, we can drive to my apartment in Santa Fe and I'll fix you a meal to remember."

"Did you ever cook for my grandmother?" Ilyas asked.

"I cooked for Jude all the time. She was easy to please."

"Very good then."

Theo got a confused look. "Very good then, what?" he asked.

"I would like to taste your cooking."

Theo looked over and smiled. "Very good then, let's get out of here and get on the road."

AS THEO DROVE down the freeway their conversation flowed smoothly. Topics seemed to crop up without much effort. Ilyas displayed an insatiable curiosity on just about everything. Were Americans religious? Did they go to church or pray often? What sports did they like? Was it criminal to criticize the president? While Theo tried keeping the dialogue light and neutral, it occasionally shifted to more predictable conversation.

Ilyas was curious about Jude. He wanted to know as many details of her life and character and personality that Theo would share. He listened attentively as Theo told the story of how they first met and began their relationship.

Arriving in Santa Fe, they stopped for a few groceries. As they shopped inside the store, Theo got a strange feeling as if they were being watched. Once home, Theo parked on the street and they each grabbed a grocery bag. Struggling with the door lock, Theo finally got it open and walked inside. Ilyas followed to the kitchen and laid the bag on the table. As Theo began putting the food away, Ilyas walked around the apartment. "You live here alone?"

"Yeah."

"This is a big apartment for just one person."

"By American standards this is called an efficiency unit."

"What's that?"

"A small apartment."

"In Morocco a family would live in an apartment this size." Ilyas walked back into the kitchen. "Do you have a picture of my grandmother?"

"Go to the bedroom and look on top of the dresser."

Ilyas turned around and as he walked through the bedroom door, the photograph was the first thing to catch his eye. The image was of Theo and Jude smiling at one another with a loom as the backdrop. He picked it up and examined it closer. Unlike his brown hair, his grandmother had light, long hair, prying eyes, and a nice smile. He took the framed photograph into the kitchen. "She does not look old enough to be a grandmother," Ilyas said.

"I bet she was a knockout when she was young."

"What's that?"

"A beautiful woman."

"Yes, I think so." After examining it for a few moments, he returned it to the dresser. Back in the kitchen, he asked, "Why aren't you married?"

The question took Theo by surprise. "Because I'm going to culinary school first."

"Then you'll get married?"

Should he reveal the truth or lie, Theo thought. Ignorant as to how Ilyas might take the truth, he had a split second to decide. "I won't get married...I'm gay." Theo expected a curious assault of questions. But there was no discernable reaction.

"What are you going to make?"

Maybe he hadn't understood the response, Theo thought. Maybe he didn't understand that gay meant homosexual. Either way, he had no intention of broaching the subject again.

"Bastilla."

Ilyas' face flushed with delight. "Can I help?"

"Yeah, get some eggs out of the refrigerator and put them to boil."

Ilyas looked at him curiously. "How do I do that?"

"Ah, don't worry about it. Grab a soda from the fridge and have a seat while I get this all together."

Seventy

AS HE SAT watching Theo prepare the meal, Ilyas talked about growing up in Morocco. He told of large family picnics celebrating holidays. He talked about Ramadan, and the Islamic requirement to fast for the entire month, taking neither food nor water from ninety minutes before sunrise to sunset. He spoke of the most special night during Ramadan called *Lailat al-Qadr* when prayers reach God with greater strength. Then the day after the last day of Ramadan, *Eid ul-Fitr*, the festival of fast breaking where Muslims wear new clothes and relatives visit with gifts, and everyone feasts on special dishes. Theo was fascinated hearing Ilyas tell stories of his culture and religion. He laughed when Ilyas told about strict Islamic rules requiring hospitality, kindness and generosity, even for distant relatives overstaying their visit by weeks and who leave only when the food pantry becomes empty. Something about Ilyas' glowing face resonated in Theo's soul.

When the food was ready and the two sat at the table, Ilyas bowed his head discreetly, whispering a prayer. At the first bite his face lit up with the same glow as before. "You are truly a food master. This is so wonderful."

Theo blushed. "Thanks. The secret to good bastilla is saffron."

"That is the spice of the Arabs?" Ilyas asked, remembering what Theo had said earlier.

"That is probably the most expensive spice there is. The saffron I use comes from Spain."

"I will send you some saffron when I return."

"I'll keep you to that promise."

After the meal they continued their conversation as they cleaned up the kitchen. The hour was getting late when Theo suggested, "Maybe we better get on the road to get you back to Albuquerque."

Ilyas winced. "I can sleep here tonight if you would rather drive me there tomorrow."

Relieved by the suggestion, Theo said, "Yeah, sure. That would help me out. I'll sleep on the couch and you can sleep..."

Ilyas interrupted. "Why can't we both sleep on the bed? It is large enough."

Theo's tight grin had little connection to the back flips his mind began executing at the proposal. "Yeah, why not."

By ten-thirty Theo began yawning and they decided to turn in. Once in the bedroom, Theo pulled back the bedspread as Ilyas undressed leaving on his underwear. Pulling off a blanket, Ilyas wrapped himself in it and lay down. Theo finished undressing and, disappointed sleeping next to a mummy, got under the sheet, covered up with the other blanket, turned off the bedside lamp, and quickly fell into a deep slumber.

As the first ray of light sieved through the sheers in his bedroom window, Theo slightly winched open one eye noticing Ilyas was not in bed. Suddenly both eyes opened wide as he rose up. There on the floor covered in the blanket with his feet bent to his chest, back to the wall, and head down, Ilyas sat motionless.

"Are you all right?" His voice startled Ilyas who lifted his head.
"Yes."
"What are you doing?"
"Thinking."
"Thinking about what?"
"Why did you risk the trip to Morocco?"

Trying to clear the fog from his mind while rubbing his eyes, Theo asked, "I don't understand your question. Are you asking why I decided to be the courier?"
"Yes."
"Because it was Jude's last wish. Because she wanted you out of prison."

"Would you have still gone if you had known the consequences; that you would have become the prisoner?"

Theo thought for a second about his answer. He fluffed his pillow, sat back on the headboard, and began his story. "After leaving my home in Arbol Verde and coming to Santa Fe, I was placed with a foster family that took me in. About the time I graduated high school I met someone that changed my life. His name's Patrick. He's David's son. Patrick became almost like an older brother. One day we went fishing and he told me about a philosophy he had learned from someone very close. It's a Spanish *creencia* called the *Camino Sagrado*. He said that when we're born God gives everyone two gifts, a purpose and a path. We were all put here for a reason and our job is to find out why we're here and pursue our purpose. We do that by navigating the road called the *Camino Sagrado*. Patrick said that when we're young we learn everything we need to navigate the road. Our parents and family and church and friends teach us the difference between good and bad, right and wrong, truth and falsehood, love and hate. And then one day we start our journey. The journey is guided by road signs and guideposts. All along the way we're surrounded by miracles, blessings, coincidences, accidents, misfortunes, good and bad luck — these are all road signs guiding us along if our eyes are open wide enough to recognize them. On our journey we meet others and help them where we can and maybe even discover a special person to love and to share the journey. Patrick explained that you know you're on the *Camino Sagrado* if you feel joy and peace and calm in your soul. That's what's called *aclaracion* or clarity. And just before your life ends, when you get back to the place you first started your journey, you'll get a feeling like you have never experienced before. It's called *aclaracion completa* or complete clarity, where you experience ultimate peace — no worries, no doubts, no fears. From that second to your last breath you'll know that your soul is getting ready to leave and you'll welcome the journey that awaits."

Ilyas was intently listening to everything Theo said.

Theo continued.

"I try to live my life by that philosophy. I didn't travel to Morocco ignorant that there wouldn't be any backlash. Because one thing I've learned is that there's no certainty in anything you do. I went there because the road signs led me there. I never wanted to be beaten up by my brother, or go to jail, or be accused of murder, or go to trial. But the reality is that it all happened. And in spite of that, I can still look at myself in the mirror and feel *aclaracion*. So that tells me I'm on the *Camino Sagrado*. To answer your question, I couldn't have done anything differently. To do so would have breached the purpose God has in store for me."

Ilyas was speechless, trying to take in everything Theo said. Then he asked, "How do I repay you?"

Theo thought for a second. "By remembering the saffron you promised."

Ilyas smiled.

AFTER THEO PREPARED breakfast and as they sat down to eat, Ilyas turned to him. "You know, my reason for visiting the United States in the first place was to fulfill a promise." He took out the envelope and handed it to Theo. "Do you know how to get in touch with this priest?"

Theo instantly recognized the envelope. He knew it was pointless for Ilyas to meet with Father Bonafacio as the remainder of the inheritance money was in police custody. Moreover, it was unclear when or if the money would be returned. Rather than explaining the embarrassing police allegations leading to the raid on the church property, Theo decided to discourage Ilyas from visiting the priest. Without opening the envelope, Theo replied, "I gave that to your father when I delivered the money. The priest lives in Arbol Verde, a village north of Santa Fe which is about two hours away. The direction is opposite of Albuquerque and I'm afraid you'll miss your flight if we go there this morning."

"Do you know why I'm supposed to see him?" Ilyas asked.

"Yes." For a few seconds Theo had to thrash his mind for an explanation. "It's a matter dealing with your grandmother's estate."

"Oh. Marty explained all of that to me," Ilyas replied.

Puzzled by what Marty may have said, Theo decided to say nothing more.

After breakfast Theo drove Ilyas back to his hotel in Albuquerque and waited while he showered and changed, then made off to the airport. Stopping at the passenger departure curb, Theo got out of the car to bid Ilyas good-bye. As they shook hands, Theo noticed Ilyas' peculiar gaze. Laying down his small luggage pieces, Ilyas turned and hugged Theo while whispering something in Arabic. As Theo returned to his car and drove off, tears streamed down his cheeks. The Moroccan with the insatiable curiosity and winsome face had stolen his heart.

Seventy-one

SNYDER RACED DOWN the road in the late afternoon headed for the Santa Fe Airport. Dressed in civilian clothes, he liked feeling the power of his fuel-injected, turbo-charged, dual-carb sports car. As to the number of times he had been stopped for speeding, Snyder had lost count. Once they saw his badge, the conversation usually shifted to the size of the engine and the beauty of his pride and joy.

Earlier in the day Snyder had taken a call from Isaac Lacy. Lacy was an undercover officer assigned to the Drug Enforcement Task Force (DETF). After the raid at Santo Niño when no drugs were discovered, Snyder received authorization to seek assistance from DETF for shadow surveillance. Lacy and two underlings were assigned to the case.

The team began tailing Theo in August, one day after his release from El Pastor Detention Center. A short time later the shadowing became intermittent when Theo's activities became too banal. He left for work, returned home for several hours before heading off to the gym, then returned home afterward for the remainder of the evening. When they failed to find any suspicious activity by late September, all surveillance abated. But while Lacy shopped at a grocery store one recent evening, he happened to spot Theo and a companion. As he steered his shopping cart closer to the two, Lacy's suspicions became aroused by the companion's foreign accent, his clothing style and his olive skin tone. He overheard their conversation about Morocco. He grew suspicious and decided to tail them. Several days later he called Snyder to share his information.

Snyder spotted Lacy's car immediately as he arrived at the small airport. Parking next to it, he got out and joined the undercover officer. "I thought you guys had stopped shadowing the fag," Snyder asked.

"We did, until I saw him last week."

"Oh...what's that about?"

Lacy reached over and opened the glove box. Taking out a small envelope, he handed it to Snyder. "Take a look at these."

Snyder opened the envelope and began leafing through the photographs. "Who's the boyfriend?"

"His name's Ilyas Bashir. He's originally from Morocco, but now lives in Spain."

"So what's he doing here?"

"He's not here anymore. He went back to Spain. But he's on the terrorist watch list. He's connected with a fanatical group that bombed Morocco back in 2003."

"How long were the two together?"

"I don't know that. After I spotted them, Theo drove to his apartment where they stayed the night, then he drove Bashir to the Albuquerque airport, stopping only to pick up his luggage from a hotel."

"So what were they doing all that time?"

"Your guess is as good as mine."

"Is the terrorist a fag, too?"

"I'd be surprised. Back in their country ragheads are stoned to death for doing stuff like that."

"Can I take these?" Snyder asked.

"Be my guest. I have the disc if you need any more copies."

As Snyder continued studying the images, Lacy said, "You might want to get with your people, talk about this situation, and suggest calling in the big guns. When it comes to investigating terrorists, the feds are the experts. Their spooks are pros at handling these cases. Besides, they have the money and equipment to shadow, wiretap, trace money, hack computers...like that."

"Thanks for the suggestions." As Snyder opened the door, he turned to Lacy. "By the way, I'm leaving the force. You've probably heard I'm going into politics."

"Yeah, I heard something about that."

"I hope I can count on your support," he said.

"No problem. Good luck."

Seventy-two

SEVERINO AND ELENA greeted Ilyas' return with the exhilaration of a long lost relative. They insisted on celebrating all night until the early morning. Happy to see Ilyas back at work, Mustafa shook his hand and, after hearing about his immigration problem, advised against visiting the United States ever again. Ilyas had every intention of returning to testify at Theo's trial, but decided to leave that conversation for another day.

Federico refused to believe the story Ilyas had concocted about his immigration difficulties, convinced his helper was quarantined to ensure he carried no foreign gay diseases into the United States.

While Ilyas' life returned to normal, the internal tumult was still thrashing. The secret his parents and his uncle had kept from him violated *shari'a*. Now that the truth was known, Ilyas felt betrayed. While he loved them no less, he needed time to come to grips with his feelings.

As Ilyas sat alone in the apartment, paper and pen in front of him, hurtful feelings were rummaging through his mind. He couldn't find the words to begin the letter to his parents. How could he write that he loved and missed them, but also that he felt violated at learning their secret? It was all so bewildering. Finally taking the pen in hand, Ilyas brought the paper closer and began writing. But his letter began differently by expressing feelings of strength and warmth and encouragement that he had only recently discovered. The letter began: Dear Theo...

The following week Ilyas received a reply to his letter. His heart racing, he opened the envelope, unfolded it and began reading. Theo wrote about his delight in receiving Ilyas letter. He discussed his job and the impending trial. Theo went on to express the loneliness he felt driving back to Santa Fe. The words evoked a shared sentiment. It was the same loneliness that had blanketed Ilyas' heart as well. He read the letter several times trying to find other feelings buried between the words and sentences. He wrote back that very afternoon, revealing that he too was gay.

One of Theo's letters suggested exchanging electronic mail. Having rarely used a computer but for inventory control when he first began working at Illuminations, Ilyas asked Severino to teach him. They visited an internet cafe and in no time Ilyas learned to access the web and send out electronic mail. Thereafter, most days after work Ilyas could hardly wait to stop by the internet café to read Theo's message, and return the e-mail.

In one of Theo's messages, almost as an afterthought, he mentioned his father's death. To Ilyas, it came across in a cold indifference. Curiously, Ilyas e-mailed back asking about Theo's apathy toward his father. In his typical way of explaining life through the prism of cooking, Theo replied, "Making a loaf of bread is not so difficult. While it only requires yeast and flour, salt and water, to rise you need time and patience, attention and a good environment. Neither of my parents ever baked bread, not for lack of ingredients."

Before Ilyas went to sleep that night, the meaning of Theo's response cycled in his mind. He rose early the following morning and this time the words came easier in composing a letter to his parents.

Several weeks later, in their daily message exchange, Theo shared the good news that the grand jury had withdrawn the indictment on all the charges against him related to Jude's death. All that remained now was the charge involving his brother's murder. While Ilyas was happy about the development, he worried whether his testimony was still needed. Posing the question to Theo, Ilyas received a reply that David didn't think so. Ilyas could sense Theo's disappointment amid his own. Somehow Ilyas knew he had to find the money and the time off to be there to support Theo at the trial. He thought of the inheritance that Marty had spoken about. As the trial date closed in, one afternoon Ilyas placed a phone call to the United States.

"Hello, Marty!"

"Ilyas, this is a surprise. Is everything all right?"

"Well, when we spoke several months ago you mentioned that I might inherit some of my grandmother's estate. Is that still true?"

"I'm not sure. As I told you when we first met, your grandmother left all of her estate to a university in New York. Since then I've contacted a probate attorney to have her will altered so that you would become the sole beneficiary. The attorney filed papers with the court, and that's where it stands."

Saddened by that information, he replied, "Okay, thank you Marty."

"When I hear anything more, I'll let you know."

Marty could sense the disappointment in Ilyas voice, and just as they were about to hang up, he asked, "By the way, did you ever get to visit with Father Bonafacio?"

"No, I didn't have time to do that."

"You do know that he's holding the remainder of your grandmother's life insurance money for you?"

Confused, Ilyas replied, "Isn't that what we just spoke about?"

"No, Jude's life insurance is separate from her estate. I believe Father Bonafacio is holding about twenty thousand dollars."

Ilyas couldn't believe what he was hearing. "How can I reach him?"

"Let me get to my cell phone directory and I'll give you his number."

Having never met or spoken with the priest, Ilyas thought of exactly what he would say before placing the call. After introducing himself, Ilyas politely inquired about the money. When the priest confirmed he had it, Ilyas requested a small amount be wired to him. It would be enough to pay for the trip.

Before starting work one morning, Ilyas went into Mustafa's office. Busy at his desk, Mustafa looked up, "If you're coming in here to ask about a reassignment from Federico, you're wasting your breath."

Ilyas chuckled. "I would never ask for a reassignment. We get along fine."

"That's good. So then you're here to ask for a raise in your wages."

"No Mustafa. I'm fine with my wages. But I need some time off."

"No." Mustafa resumed what he was doing.

"Please, listen to me Mustafa," Ilyas pleaded.

"Several months ago you took off almost three weeks. That's more than anyone of your tenure is eligible to receive."

"I have an obligation that I'm committed to carrying out."

"And what is this obligation that's more important than your job?"

"At great risk, a friend carried out a promise that ended up saving my life. Now he needs my help."

"Would you be traveling to the United States?"

"Yes."

"Then no. What if the same thing happens to you as before?"

"That problem is all resolved. It cannot happen again. All I need is one week."

"My answer is final."

Recalling something said to him many years earlier, Ilyas invoked the wisdom of that truism. "Mustafa, we are both good Muslims. The Qur'an requires that we give *zakat* to the poor. In some cases *zakat* involves more than giving money. Sometimes we are asked to give something more precious than money, especially if it is for the sake of righting injustice because in the end we will all benefit from that. I have such an obligation."

Mustafa contemplated what Ilyas had said. "One week; how can I be sure you will be back in one week?" he said as he looked up at Ilyas.

"I promise I will be back."

Mustafa could see the seriousness of the request. "Okay, you get one week off work only if you find a substitute to work with Federico."

"But Mustafa..."

"That's my decision. Now leave because I have work to do."

As he walked out of Mustafa's office, Ilyas went in search of Severino.

Seventy-three

"SO YOU BELIEVE raising the terrorism issue was the reason you were fired?" Pamela Jacobs, a reporter for the Santa Fe Daily News, asked Snyder during her interview at a downtown cafe.

He knew Pamela well, having provided her with many exclusive scoops over the years. "After I mentioned the terrorism issue to Rory Johnson, the deputy chief ordered me never to talk about that again or I would be fired. Then he reassigned the Theo Jaquez case to someone else"

"Why do you think he did that?"

"Could it be because there's a lot more to what I revealed than the department wants to let on?"

"Like what?"

"Before my radio interview the public was complacent, never imagining Santa Fe could become a terrorist target. What I said wasn't meant to cause panic, but only to raise community consciousness. If there was no support for that theory, I would have never raised it. But I backed up what I said by citing the fact that the Moroccan associating with Theo Jaquez was a member of a terrorist cell that bombed and killed innocent civilians in Casablanca, Morocco. In addition, we know that Theo Jaquez traveled to Morocco carrying a lot of money he fraudulently obtained after killing Jude Armstrong with an overdose of morphine. We have witnesses that saw a mysterious meeting between Theo and another Moroccan. I can tell you now that I have photographs of meetings here in New Mexico between Theo Jaquez and the terrorist. I challenge you to ask the department to dispute these facts? They can't do that because these facts are well documented. Should I have remained silent about all of this? Take a look at Oklahoma City and New York City and tell me if I was wrong."

"How recent are the photographs?"

"They were taken within the last few months in Santa Fe and Albuquerque."

"How do you explain the Jude Armstrong charges that were dropped?"

"I happen to know a meeting took place between the assistant D.A. and Theo Jaquez's attorney, David Lujan. As we both know, Lujan is very prominent with a lot of influence and savvy. Shortly after that meeting the D.A. went back to the grand jury and got them to withdraw the Jude Armstrong murder charges, the fraud conspiracy charges and the drug charges. They had to do that for two reasons; first, one of the principal witnesses suspiciously recanted critical testimony against Theo. A lot of what remained was merely circumstantial evidence. And second, they've agreed to a plea deal. Since I was the most visible officer in the case, wouldn't the implication to the public be that somehow I bungled the investigation and that was the reason for my firing? That's a perfect subterfuge rather than to say I was fired for alerting our community about the terrorist connection. "

"That's a very elaborate plot you suggest. Do you still believe Santa Fe is a terrorist target?"

"I'll tell you this. When I'm elected commissioner, I will do everything in my power to ensure Santa Fe does not become a terrorist site."

"What do you think your chances of winning are?"

"I'm convinced that Theo Jaquez is guilty of murder. But because of the plea deal, the public will never know the full story. When Theo Jaquez is led away to prison, I believe the public will recognize my role in keeping our city safe from murderers and terrorists, and side with my vision on the important issues over those of my opponent. I'm optimistic of winning over the public's confidence, along with their vote."

Seventy-four

LEAVING MADRID ON the same flight as the previous time, Ilyas arrived at the Dallas-Ft. Worth airport in the early afternoon. He traversed the long corridors alongside the other passengers until they reached the immigration hall. Recalling his last visit, Ilyas was filled with worry as he approached the officer's booth. The officer gave Ilyas a quick glance, opened the passport, stamped it and waved him through. Ilyas walked to the Albuquerque connecting gate and waited for the plane's departure. Finally arriving, he caught a shuttle to Santa Fe, then a taxi to Theo's apartment.

AS THEO DROVE home from work, anxiety set in as he thought of the start of his trial in San Lorenzo the following day. The reality of his situation was taking hold. Theo parked his Jeep on the street when the notion suddenly struck him that if convicted, he would not be returning to work anytime soon. He would lose his apartment and Jeep. Theo got a nervous jolt in his chest. He continued walking down the sidewalk to his apartment and tried not to think about any more of that. Suddenly he saw a figure stooped at his doorstep.

Ilyas stood up.

As Theo approached, Ilyas offered a small packet he had in his hand. "I brought you this. It's saffron."

Ilyas' blue eyes were glistening; his face brandished a child-like smile. Theo took the bag and instinctively put his arms around Ilyas, then kissed him. He felt Ilyas' arms reciprocating. Then a voice came from behind.

"Whoa man, you guys need to take that stuff inside."

Theo glanced over. "Hey, Kevin."

"Hey man, I guess I'll be seeing you at the trial tomorrow."

"Yeah, I guess."

"Okay then. Carry on, dudes," he said as he walked his bicycle to the street.

Once they were inside the apartment Theo took control. Closing the door, Theo walked behind Ilyas and slowly began unbuttoning his shirt. Kissing his neck gently, Theo managed to remove it then pulled off his own. Slowly turning Ilyas around and softly feeling his chest, Theo could see Ilyas was enjoying the moment. Taking his hand, Theo led Ilyas into the bedroom. As Theo sat on the edge of the bed untying his shoes, Ilyas remained standing momentarily, then slipped out of his loafers, unbuckled his trousers and let them drop. After removing his own trousers, Theo rolled on top as they tenderly kissed. Within moments they were naked, then Theo felt Ilyas deep inside him. All of his senses were captured in the love he felt for the Moroccan at that moment. It made him forget everything else. If only it would last forever.

WHEN THEIR LOVEMAKING was over, Theo fell soundly to sleep. Ilyas lay next to him, admiring Theo's dark hair and handsome face. Thoughts of making love to Gabriel in the park many years earlier came to mind. He had been wrong all along about the djinn. They were not a curse at all, but a blessing. They were a guidepost Theo had spoken about. He knew that to be true because of the intense joy and peace he felt at that moment. *Aclaracion*, Theo called it. Ilyas made a promise. Hence, he vowed to listen and follow that inner voice.

Seventy-five

LIGHT THIN CLOUDS outlined the sky on the morning David arrived in San Lorenzo for the start of Theo's trial. Searching for parking in front of El Pastor County Courthouse, David noticed every space taken. He drove around the block and found an empty spot along the street. Collecting his briefcase from the backseat, David walked toward the building. As he looked over, a crowd was waiting to get inside for Theo's trial.

He walked down the street to a nearby café to meet Theo and

Patrick. Sitting in the far corner with both of them was Ilyas. David smiled as he approached. "Good to see you. I didn't know you were coming," he said extending his hand to the Moroccan.

In a low, almost inaudible voice, Ilyas replied, "I thought maybe I should give the people a look at a terrorist." They chuckled.

David looked at Theo. "Let's take a walk."

Glancing at the two others, David said. "We'll be back in a few moments."

Leaving the café, they headed down a narrow side street outside the view of anyone from the courthouse. David asked, "What's going on between you and Ilyas?"

"We're together."

"When did that happen?"

"Shortly after I met him at your office. We stayed in contact by letters and e-mail when he went back. Yesterday he was waiting at my apartment when I got home."

"I should have guessed from all the crazy terrorist stories Snyder was fabricating. Who's sharing your room?"

"It was supposed to be Patrick, but he moved to another room. So it's just Ilyas and me."

"I want Patrick back in your room and Ilyas in Patrick's room. These small towns don't take too well to gay people, much less gay couples. If word gets out that the two of you are together, that's going to be on the jury's mind when they begin deliberating."

"Okay, I understand."

"It crossed my mind when I saw Ilyas this morning about putting him on the stand as a character witness. He could really cast you in a good light as Jude's loyal friend. But there's the downside about the publicity over the terrorism thing. Even overcoming that, if they discover you guys are partners that could hurt more than help. I need to give this some more thought."

Theo remained silent.

"Did you get any sleep last night?" David asked.

"Some."

"How are you feeling this morning?"

"Scared."

David patted Theo's back to reassure him.

"By the way, I got another call from the D.A.'s office sweetening the plea deal—manslaughter, two to seven. You could be out in eighteen months."

Theo stopped and looked at David. "What do you think I should do?"

"I think you should start thinking about that braised lamb and baby potatoes you promised."

Theo smiled. "Okay, I can do that."

"So are you all right with the sleeping arrangement?"

"Oh yeah. I'll explain it to Ilyas."

"Good. Let's get to the courthouse."

David, Theo and Patrick walked across the street to the courthouse together and Ilyas trailed behind. Since his identity had not yet been widely known, the thought was to keep it that way as long as possible. As they approached and made their way up the steps, Theo recognized many of the people from Arbol Verde waiting to get inside. Father Bonafacio and Luz Vigil were at the top of the steps. Henry Tafoya who owned the Conoco station in Arbol Verde was talking to Clofes Benavidez. When Theo walked by, Clofes turned to him, saying, *"Theo, no te preocupes. Todo va estar bien."* Clofes had a sincere, almost pained look on his face.

"Gracias," Theo replied.

Theo glanced over to his left. His mother stood there, almost hidden behind a pillar. Magdalena was short with an emaciated frame. She wore a grey blouse and blue pants that fit loosely. Her graying hair hung straight down and her dark eyes seemed to have a creamy coating over them. She looked much older than her forty-three years. Leandro Trujillo, a long-time *tecato*, stood next to her.

It wasn't a surprise to anyone that Leandro had moved in days after Sixto died. Leandro and Sixto were friends, having worked together years earlier. When they first met, Leandro, five years Sixto's junior, still lived at his parent's home. When Leandro occasionally got kicked out following a drunken brawl with his alcoholic father, he showed up at the Jaquez house, sometimes staying for weeks. Arriving home early one day, Sixto found Leandro and Magdalena naked in bed soundly asleep. Quietly, Sixto picked through Leandro's trousers finding a few bills. He took it all as compensation for Magdalena, using the money for *chiva*. Afterward, no mention was made of the indiscretion or the theft.

Leandro continued showing up, oftentimes bringing baggies of *chiva*. For Sixto the ritual was always the same. The distinct sulfur smell always excited him as he anxiously anticipated heating the spoon. Tying off and filling his veins with a rush so intense that made his head explode, Sixto slowly nodded off as Leandro and Magdalena slipped into the bedroom for sex. Sixto knew all about that but didn't care as he had become almost impotent. Only long bouts of oral stimulation satisfied him. Magdalena was inept at doing that. It was then that he began using Theo. Later, as Magdalena's indiscretions grew beyond Leandro, Sixto encouraged it, demanding her visitors either bring money or *chiva*. Enraged if they failed to come through, Sixto began forcing Magdalena to prostitute among a wider circle in exchange for the poison.

Theo had witnessed and suffered through too many of those episodes. Magdalena had become a stranger to him and any hint of familial love or affection vanished long ago. He grew indifferent toward all his family. It preserved his sanity. After leaving home, Theo rarely thought of them for all the pain it brought back. He gave a slight, almost indistinguishable nod then quickly looked away as they continued into the courthouse.

As they slowly made their way through the security gauntlet and into the courtroom, Theo met up with Julian and Sonia. He hugged them tightly as they greeted one another.

"Be strong, Theo. We love you and we believe in you," Julian said. Sonia turned away briefly, trying to hide her tears.

"Thanks. I love you both, too."

David spotted Marty who was subpoenaed by the prosecution. He nodded and Marty returned the nod. They would speak later outside the courthouse. Stephanie Holloman, David's associate, had arrived early and was already seated. He greeted her then took a seat. Opening his briefcase, David began arranging files on the table. Within a few minutes Judge Harley Jellison appeared on the dais, sat down and called the hearing to order.

Seventy-six

STATE POLICE OFFICER John Armendarez was assigned to the Criminal Investigations Section or CIS. The CIS was tasked with investigating incidents dealing with aggravated assaults, battery and murder. Armendarez was the prosecution's next witness when the trial resumed.

"Mr. Armendarez, were you called to investigate a matter in Santa Fe involving Theo Jaquez at his apartment?"

"Yes I was."

"What was the nature of the call?"

"CIS received a call from the Santa Fe Police Department inquiring whether we wanted to process a crime scene involving a violent assault within the city limits."

"Why would they ask you to conduct an investigation rather than use their own resources?"

"Because we had an open investigation on Theo Jaquez. It's my understanding that Lieutenant Kerry Snyder arrived at Mr. Jaquez's apartment early in the morning after the assault. He informed those officers about our investigation, and that's when they notified us."

"How long after receiving the call did you respond?"

"Within thirty minutes."

"What did you find?"

"By the time we arrived, Mr. Jaquez had already been transported to the hospital. We secured the crime scene and began our routine procedure of gathering evidence."

"What significant evidence, if any, were you able to gather at the crime scene?"

"Primarily fingerprints and a partial shoe print. The print was fixed in the victim's blood."

"Were you able to make a fingerprint match?"

"Yes we were. The fingerprints found in the bedroom, the living room and kitchen where items had been disturbed were matched to Romel Jaquez."

"And what about the footprint?"

"We had some difficulty with that. The partial print was made from a cheap athletic shoe that we traced to several department stores. We conducted a search of the home where Romel Jaquez resided and after examining his footwear, we were not able to find a match."

"Did that end your investigation of that article?"

"No, it didn't. Sometime later we conducted a second search on the same home and discovered the footwear that we believe matched the print."

"Who owned that footwear?"

"We believe it belonged to Sixto Jaquez inasmuch as he was wearing the shoes."

"And who is Sixto Jaquez?"

"He's the father of Romel and Theo."

"Were either Sixto or Romel questioned or arrested?"

"By the time we had completed our investigation Romel Jaquez had been killed. Sixto Jaquez was questioned and denied owning the footwear, telling us he had taken the shoes from his son's closet. He also denied participating in Theo's assault. We had no direct evidence linking the father to the assault, so we had no basis to arrest him."

"Now I'm going to direct your attention to the murder of Romel Jaquez. In relation to Theo Jaquez's beating, when was Romel killed?"

"If you're asking the time period between Theo's beating and Romel's murder, it all occurred within a three week period."

"And were you called to investigate Romel's murder?"

"Yes. I was part of a team that conducted the investigation."

"What time did you receive the call?"

"At eight twenty-seven in the evening."

"And who notified you?"

"A state police officer responding to the call. Apparently a pedestrian was taking a short cut through the church parking lot and stumbled on the body."

"What time did you arrive on the scene?"

"Approximately ten o'clock that evening."

"What did you do when you arrived at the church parking lot?"

"We immediately secured the area and began our routine procedures of examining the body, collecting and documenting the evidence, photographing the scene, and interviewing witnesses."

"Can you describe what you saw when you arrived?"

"A bloodied body was lying face up; the feet bent underneath and arms outstretched. The victim's face had been pummeled forcefully with a protruding blunt object. The facial cavity had collapsed so it was impossible to identify the victim. The chest and abdomen had similar strikes."

"Did you later identify the victim?"

"The victim was Romel Jaquez. We found identification on his body that night. Later we compared fingerprints, dental records and blood type to confirm it was Mr. Jaquez."

"Did you locate the murder weapon?"

"We located it but not that night."

"When and where was it located?"

"Several days later underneath some brush by the bridge leading out of Arbol Verde."

"And what was the murder weapon?"

"A thick tree limb with protruding branch stems extending two to five inches along its circumference."

Marsha introduced the tree limb and, after having it identified, marked it as an exhibit.

"How do you know this was the weapon used to kill the victim?"

"Several of the protrusions were stained with what we believed to be blood. DNA analysis later revealed it matched the victim's blood."

"Based on the position of the body and the evidence you gathered, what is your best hypothesis of how the victim was struck?"

"We believe that the victim may have turned his face to the attacker and was struck with the first forceful blow, knocking him to the ground. It penetrated his right eye. Once the victim was on the ground the attacker commenced to strike several more times at his face. The victim instinctively raised his hands in a defensive position and diverted the blows to his chest and abdomen. As the blows continued, the victim lost consciousness. The evidence appears to indicate that the attacker remained striking the victim long after he died."

"How were you able to formulate this hypothesis?"

"From a number of different sources; initially it was from my observation of the extent of the injuries and the position of the victim's body. Afterward, I met with the chief of the Office of the Medical Investigator in Albuquerque, Chester Albright, who performed the autopsy, along with two of his forensic experts. In our discussion we concluded that was the most plausible explanation given the nature, extent and severity of the trauma the victim's body sustained."

"Were there any witnesses at the scene?"

"No."

"Do you believe robbery was the motive?"

"No. Romel's wallet was intact. His money was still there."

"Were you able to determine who attacked and killed Romel Jaquez?"

"Yes, we were."

"Can you tell us how you came to make that finding?"

"We spoke with the priest who was in the rectory at the time of the murder. The parking lot where we found the body is quite a distance from the rectory. While he was not able to give any information as to the assault, he provided us with a possible suspect who had visited at a time proximate to the murder. That was Theo Jaquez. We sent a unit of officers to Mr. Jaquez's residence that night to question him. The officers noticed what appeared to be blood stains on the shirt he wore and immediately placed him under arrest. His clothes were taken into evidence and DNA analysis was later performed. The results revealed that both blood and saliva on the shirt matched that of Romel Jaquez."

"Thank you. I have nothing further."

Before the witness was passed, Judge Jellison called a recess.

Seventy-seven

RETURNING FROM LUNCH, David's first witness was Father Bonafacio. The priest spoke about how his relationship with Theo evolved. He described the scared young boy that courageously ran away from a drug-plagued, sexually abusive home and became a responsible young man intent on pursuing a career in culinary arts.

Marsha did not cross-examine the priest.

David called Julian then Sonia who each testified of having unofficially adopted Theo. They talked of his honesty, good nature and dogged culinary pursuit. They each spoke of the joy he brought to their household. David then called Hans Schuldneckt, owner of The Seville Restaurant. Schuldneckt testified about Theo's maturity and passion for hard work.

A short recess was called, and when trial resumed, David acted on instinct and called Ilyas to the witness stand. As David's examination began, Marsha continually interrupted, objecting to the relevancy of Ilyas' testimony. Overruling most of Marsha's recurring objections, Judge Jellison allowed much of the testimony into the record.

Ilyas described his life in Morocco, the circumstances leading to his incarceration, and the conditions at Sidi Kascen prison. His story gripped the jurors and everyone in the gallery. He spoke about the horrible treatment in prison and his chronic medical afflictions. He related the last conversation with Aban concerning the person who financed his pardon from prison. Only later did he learn it was his grandmother, Jude Armstrong. He told the jury of Theo's brave undertaking in acting as courier; an act that ultimately brought about his release from Sidi Kascen and saved his life. Without forewarning, Ilyas began citing a verse as natural as if he was crafting it from his own words.

> *"O mankind! We created you from a male and a female and made you into nations and tribes that you may know and honor each other. Indeed the most honorable of you in the sight of God is the most righteous."*

"What was that?" David asked.
"It's a verse from the Qua'ran."
"What does it mean?"
"That regardless of our creed, in the end we're judged by our compassion for one another."
Marcia stood up instantly and objected to the admission of the verse. Once again, Judge Jellison overruled her.
David was pleased with Ilyas' testimony and passed the witness. Marcia's cross examination was brief and unimpressive.
Rather than call Snyder to the witness stand and disrupt the empathetic mood Ilyas had created, David announced to the judge that his next witness would be a lengthy examination. At that, Judge Jellison adjourned for the day.
That evening as David sat in his hotel room going over the pages of notes he had compiled for Snyder's examination, something kept bothering him. It was like a piece of a puzzle that was missing and he couldn't put his finger on it. David finally turned in for the night and sleep came unusually quick. In the darkness of the early morning as he lay in bed, random images filtered through his mind. Suddenly a quirky notion arose that gave him an idea. As David gave it more thought, something within him began stirring. He jumped out of bed and began pacing the room.
As the morning light broke, acting on instinct David called Marty, Father Bonafacio, Stephanie and Patrick to his room. He told them about his idea. Their reaction was hopeful and encouraging. Immediately afterward, Marty and Father Bonafacio drove off to Arbol Verde. Agreeing to say nothing about the early morning meeting to anyone, the three others headed to the restaurant to meet with Theo and Ilyas for breakfast before the trial resumed.

AGAINST DAVID'S ADVICE, Theo had spent the night with Ilyas. It was unfair to forbid them from being together in the circumstance Theo found himself. At breakfast Theo was sullen and quiet. Over the course of the trial he had begun turning inward. Theo knew that Ilyas understood the emotion better than most and he appreciated his lover's empathy. As hard as he tried Theo wanted to believe that he was still journeying the *Camino Sagrado*; still feeling *aclaracion*. But as he stared into the mirror that morning, for the first time he felt numb. Did this portend a verdict and attending fate that would separate him from the two things he wanted more than anything; culinary school and Ilyas?

NOTICING THAT THEO'S breakfast plate was hardly touched, David was seeing his client's emotional decline. There were only two witnesses left and Theo was one of them. David estimated that his examination of Snyder would last most of the morning then after lunch Theo would take the witness stand. In the deadened condition he saw his client, David was becoming increasingly anxious. Once again, he suggested they go outside and take a walk before trial resumed. As they left the restaurant there was a brief silence between them, except for Theo's occasional guttural tic.

Then David spoke. "What I'm about to say to you must always stay just between us."

Theo looked at him curiously, but remained quiet.

David continued. "When Patrick phoned me late one evening I was seconds away from ending my life. The only thing that prevented me was his message for help. Somehow I managed to hold off on my intention for that moment. When I returned his call, it was a plea to help you. He told me about your situation and begged me to drive into Santa Fe and visit with you. I wouldn't be here today if it hadn't been for that phone call. It came precisely at the second that saved my life. Fate has a way of weaving disruptions like that through our lives and sometimes they get us back on track."

Theo replied, "Patrick calls them guideposts directing us through life."

"So he's told you about the *Camino Sagrado*?" David asked.

"Yeah."

"I don't know if I believe in that philosophy, but I do believe that life's disruptions are a way of making us stronger. That call got me back to doing what I do best. And the situation that took me to that dark space is slowly correcting itself. So, just like Patrick, I'm putting a call in to you right now to pull yourself together, Theo. I really need you to be yourself on the witness stand in court this afternoon. Do you understand what I'm saying?"

Theo nodded his head.

David stopped and gave him a sober look. "Do you really understand what I'm saying?"

Theo's staid expression slowly formed a wily smile. "Let me ask you a question?"

"Okay."

"Do you want chocolate mousse or wine-poached pears with the braised lamb?"

Relieved, David slapped Theo on the back as they headed to get the others.

Gathering outside the restaurant, they walked back to the courthouse. Theo looked up to see Clofes Benavidez standing on the steps, once again. Clofes and Sixto had gone to school together, and Theo suspected he must be about forty-six. With his bloated face and red, ruddy nose, Clofes looked much older than his age. Even though many of the curious church visitors had returned home after hearing the details concerning Father Bonafacio's involvment, Clofes hadn't missed any single part of the trial. Theo grew curious about his unusual interest. Passing him, Clofes reached out to shake Theo's hand and repeated the same message as the first day. *"Theo, no te preocupes. Todo va estar bien.*

"Gracias, Clofes," Theo replied as they proceeded inside.

Seventy-eight

"HOW LONG WERE you a state police officer, Mr. Snyder?" David asked after calling the witness to testify when trial resumed. They had already gone through the introductions and David began the substantive questioning.

"About twenty-three years."

"Are you still an officer?"

"No."

"Why?"

"Objection, your honor. This has no relevance..."

David interrupted. "Your Honor, the question is extremely relevant to show that this witness has a history of prejudicial conduct toward certain individuals including my client. This witness led the investigation against my client. I aim to show that he was predisposed to abusing his authority during the time he acted as an officer of the law."

The judge overruled the objection and asked David to continue.

David walked over to the witness stand. "Why are you no longer a state police officer, Mr. Snyder?"

"I was discharged."

"You were fired," David interrupted. "Why were you fired?"

"It was politically motivated."

"Is that so?" David walked back to the defense table and picked up some papers. "Mr. Snyder, back in 1985, were you one of the officers called to the New Mexico State Penitentiary to try and restore order after a riot erupted?"

"Yes I was."

"What exactly was your assignment?"

"I was a communications specialist. I related the events that were reported to me, to higher authority — to my supervisors."

"Do you recall who occupied Cellblock D?"

"Prisoners in protective custody."

"Can you explain what protective custody is?"

"Snitches, homosexuals, pedophiles, prisoners that wouldn't survive in general population."

"Were you aware of the potential harm that would come to the prisoners in Cellblock D if the rioting inmates reached them?"

"No more than any other cellblock."

"I see. Well, at some point did you receive information about a secret access door that could free those Cellblock D inmates before the rioters reached them?"

"Well, at the time..."

"Yes or no, Mr. Snyder. Did you receive information about a secret access door for Cellblock D?"

"Yes."

"And did you communicate that message to your superiors?"

"Higher officials received that message through another source."

"Your honor, would you instruct this witness to answer my question?"

Judge Jellison gazed at the witness. "Mr. Snyder, I'm directing you to answer the defense counsel's question?"

"What was the question?" Snyder asked spitefully.

"Did you communicate the message about the cellblock access door to your superiors?"

"No."

"Why not?"

"There was a mix-up in communications."

"I see. Can you tell me what resulted after the rioting inmates reached Cellblock D?"

"A few of the inmates in protective custody died."

"A few died," David repeated. He glanced at the newspapers in his hand and after having Snyder identify it, he introduced it as an exhibit.

David continued, "It says in this newspaper copy recounting the incident that those in protective custody were tortured and burned alive. Is it your recollection, Mr. Snyder, that prisoners in Cellblock D were tortured and burned alive?"

"If that's what it says."

"So there was a mix-up and you failed to communicate that message to your superiors. Were you reprimanded for that mix-up?"

"Yes."

"During the time you served with the New Mexico State Police how many written reprimands did you receive?"

"I don't remember."

"Two?"

"I don't know."

"Five?"

"I told you, I don't know."

"Would it surprise you to learn that there are a total of nine letters of reprimand in your personnel file detailing a myriad of department infractions?"

"If you say so."

"Let's talk about more recent matters, particularly those concerning my client. Can you tell us if you were ever informed by Marty Chenoweth that Theo Jaquez was a heavy drug user?"

"Yes."

"When?"

"When he first came to my office to discuss his suspicions."

"Did Mr. Chenoweth subsequently contact you to try to correct that understanding by asserting his sources were wrong and Theo Jaquez was not a drug abuser?"

"Yes."

"Did you do anything with that information?"

"I don't understand your question?"

"Did you place that information in his file?"

"No. I didn't think it was necessary."

"Did you notify your superior or anyone else about that information?"

"No."

"So you kept it to yourself because you didn't think it was important for anyone else to know. Did all this occur at a time when you were investigating Theo Jaquez for drug dealing?"

"It may have been, I don't remember."

"Then maybe you remember this." David turned and retrieved the letter he had received from Marcia. "Can you tell me whose name is on the envelope?"

"My name."

"You were the recipient of this letter?"

"I was."

"What does the letter say?"

"The author claims to have murdered Romel Jaquez."

"What did you do when you received and read this letter?"

"I filed it in the investigation file."

"Did you share it with anyone?"

"No."

"Did you bother investigating the claim?"

"There was nothing to investigate. There's no name and it was generic. I just thought some whacko sent it to try and clear Theo Jaquez."

"But you didn't bother showing the letter to your superiors for their opinion?"

"That's correct."

"Would you say you have a tendency to withhold exculpatory information from your superiors?"

"That's a lie."

"Is it, Mr. Snyder?"

For the remainder of the morning David continued a relentless inquiry into Snyder's investigation of Theo and Father Bonafacio. The witness's explanations and answers were short, inarticulate and discernibly hostile. Snyder's face gave a new shade to the color red, as the jury took note of his obvious deceit. When David passed the witness to Marcia, her attempt at restoring Snyder's credibility rang hollow. The damage was too crushing to repair.

When Snyder's testimony came to a close, Judge Jellison adjourned for lunch

Seventy-nine

DAVID AND STEPHANIE walked outside to get fresh air and confer.

It was no longer necessary for Ilyas to remain circumspect, as his identity had already been disclosed with Marty's earlier testimony. Theo walked over to Ilyas who was waiting for him outside the courtroom. "It doesn't sound good, does it?"

"Just be glad your trial is in the United States and not Morocco."

"I want to be with you so badly," Theo said.

Ilyas smiled. "And I with you, *Inshallah*."

"What will you do if I go to prison?"

"I'll follow my soul."

"Where?"

"Wherever I find *aclaracion*." He smiled.

The two remained silently standing next to one another and returned to the courtroom when the trial resumed.

David began cross examination by attempting to elicit an alternative hypothesis from Armendarez. He queried the officer about the possibility that someone else murdered Romel after Theo drove out of the parking lot that night. While Armendarez didn't entirely rule out the theory, he regarded it as highly improbable. The only persons who knew of Romel's whereabouts had remained at the *tienda*. Most likely if Romel had observed a suspicious car following his vehicle on the drive to the rectory, he would have either confronted the driver or watched from his car before walking to the rectory parking lot to confront Theo.

David questioned the officer's hypothesis asking how it was possible that Theo would have walked into the woods, found a tree limb, then returned to surprise his brother with a blow to the face. Armendarez replied that a more likely scenario was that when Romel approached Theo, he had the tree limb in his hand. At some point it fell to the ground and Theo retrieved it. It was dark and Romel looked down at the ground searching for the limb. When he suddenly looked toward his brother, that's when he was struck in the face.

"That makes no sense," David retorted. "Romel had a weapon in his back pocket that he could have used rather than the tree limb. Why wouldn't he have used that weapon?"

Armendarez offered no explanation.

David asked for an explanation why Theo's trousers or shoes had no blood stains. Armendarez had no explanation.

"That remains a mystery," he said.

When David questioned why no blood was found in Theo's Jeep from the tree limb he allegedly tossed out upon leaving Arbol Verde, Armendarez offered no explanation.

"Were there any other suspects or persons of interest that you investigated?" David asked.

"No."

David handed Armendarez the copy of the letter he had received from Marcia during their restaurant meeting. "Have you ever seen this letter?"

"Yes, but it provided nothing to convince us the author of this letter was the attacker."

"So you investigated no other suspects besides my client, even though you had this letter from someone claiming to be Romel's murderer?"

"That's correct."

"Are there clues you could have ascertained from this letter in pursuing other suspects?"

"I suppose there could have been."

"But you decided not to do that?"

"It's my understanding that was a departmental decision. I was not present at that meeting."

David's instinct told him Armendarez wasn't totally convinced Theo killed his brother. "I have one final question, Officer Almendarez. With all of your skill, experiences, and training in the CIS unit, are you entirely certain Theo Jaquez murdered his brother?"

Almendarez's mind mulled over the question. The few seconds delay in answering was telling of his uncertainty. "Granted there are some concerns we've been unable to explain, but, based on the totality of the circumstances, I believe so."

As Armendarez left the witness stand, Marsha announced the prosecution's presentation was concluded and Judge Jellison adjourned for lunch.

DAVID, STEPHANIE, THEO, Patrick and Ilyas walked down the street and found a less crowded restaurant. The conversation was light and topical. David sensed the group was too disheartened by Almendarez's testimony to talk about the proceedings. Despite the many unexplained details that remained, Almendarez had been too convincing. David knew he had to continue to remind the jury that those details should form the basis of reasonable doubt and lead to acquittal. He knew he also had to bolster Marty's testimony concerning Theo's nature and character. While it should have impressed the jury to hear of Theo's friendship and loyalty to Jude Armstrong, David knew that more was needed. It had to be of the quality that would cast serious doubt on the jury's minds as to Theo's capacity to murder. He intended to pursue that strategy aggressively.

Eighty

EVEN THOUGH MOST of David's witnesses had characterized Theo in flattering terms, the fact remained that Theo was the only likely suspect in Romel's murder. David was counting on Theo's sincerity in his testimony to convince the jurors he wasn't capable of killing his brother. If that genuineness failed to come through, it was very likely Theo would be convicted. This time it was David who only picked at his food as his mind stirred in anxious hope. As they headed back to the courthouse, Patrick stayed behind to take a phone call. Just as they reached the courthouse door, Patrick called out to David. He waited for his son who came up and whispered in his ear.

"Marty and Father Bonafacio think it's Clofes Benavidez," Patrick said.

David looked at Theo. "Who's that guy that's always talking to you on the steps here in the mornings?"

"You mean Clofes Benavidez?"

"Yeah, what do you know about him?"

"He lives in Arbol Verde. He's a driver for a propane company. Why?"

"Let me talk to Stephanie for a few minutes alone. We'll be inside in a second."

Theo, Ilyas and Patrick proceeded into the courtroom. A few minutes later David and Stephanie entered and took their places.

Theo was braced to be called to the witness stand. His heart was beating rapidly and his lip twitching uncontrollably. When Judge Jellison stepped up to the dais and reopened the hearing, David stood up.

"Your Honor, I call Clofes Benavidez to the stand."

Suddenly there was a surprised outburst in the courtroom. Puzzled by what he thought he heard, Theo looked up at David as if he had made a mistake. The judge quickly gaveled the gallery back to order.

As surprised as anyone, Marcia looked over at David. During the entire investigation that name had never surfaced. She grew unnerved, wondering what testimony he could possibly offer the defense. She asked to approach the judge's dais. As both attorneys went forward, Marsha complained that Clofes Benavidez's name was not on the witness list provided to the prosecution. Thus, he should be prevented from testifying. David defended his action by attesting that it was only within the hour he had learned of substantive evidence involving Clofes Benavidez. Judge Jellison cautioned David that he would allow the testimony provided it directly related to the outstanding charge, and reserved the right to limit or even stop the examination if it strayed from that condition. The attorneys returned to their respective tables.

"Is Mr. Clofes Benavidez in the courtroom?" the judge asked.

The tall, heavy-set visitor stood up from the back of the gallery.

"Are you Clofes Benavidez?" the judge asked.

Nodding his head, Clofes answered, "Yes."

"Mr. Benavidez would you come forward and take the stand."

Slowly Clofes made his way down the aisle and through the low swinging doors; his stride reflected more strength of mind than fear. He wore heavy Dickie work pants and a long-sleeved twill shirt. His belt, fastened too tight, squeezed out his belly. He was a rugged figure whose large hand cloaked the Bible, as he took the oath. As Clofes sat down, his eyes caught David's, conveying that he was prepared for the inquiry.

In all his years of practicing law, David had never called any of his own witnesses to testify without knowing what they would say. The principles of basic trial technique ran through his mind; never ask a question unless you know the answer. David cast trial technique aside and decided to take the risk. His actions would either be judged as utterly idiotic or exceptionally clever. He began the examination. "Mr. Benavidez, where do you reside?"

"Huh?"

"Where do you live, Mr. Benavidez?"

"In Arbol Verde."

"How long have you lived there?"

"All my life. I was born in Arbol Verde."

"Mr. Benavidez, do you know the young man sitting at that table?" David pointed at Theo.

"Yeah. That's Theo Jaquez."

"And do you know his family?"

"Yeah."

David walked back to the defense table and retrieved the letter, then handed it to Clofes. "Mr. Benavidez, would you open the letter I just handed you and read it to the jury?"

Clofes slowly removed the letter from the envelope, unfolded it and began:

Dear Officer Snyder,
    I read in the newspaper that you arrested Theo Jaquez because you think he killed his brother. He didn't do it. I killed Romel Jaquez. You need to let Theo go and look for me.

Suddenly a tear formed in Clofes' eye. He pulled on his shirt sleeve to wipe it, then he lowered his head to massage his eyes with his fingers. Or was he wiping away more tears? A few seconds later, Clofes resumed reading the letter.

I'm sorry to cause all this trouble for Theo. He's a good person and I have nothing against him. Please, let him go. I am the person you're looking for.

When he had finished, Clofes handed the letter back. David asked, "Do you know who wrote this letter, Mr. Benavidez?"

Clofes looked at Theo and slowly nodded his head.

Judge Jellison interrupted. "Mr. Benavidez, you need to respond to the questions. Your answers are being recorded."

"Yes," was the almost indiscernible response.

"Did you write this letter?"

"Yes."

As anxiety gripped his gut, David asked the question. "Mr. Benavidez, did you kill Romel Jaquez?"

It was clear Clofes was holding back an emotional anchor as he responded. "Yes."

This time the gallery erupted in a louder outburst. Judge Jellison hammered his gavel ordering the gallery to remain silent and threatening to clear the courtroom. In a few seconds order was restored.

"Why did you kill Romel Jaquez?" David asked.

"Because he killed my family. Because he took everything away from me," Clofes said in a clear voice.

There was a brief silence as Clofes looked down to the floor trying to muster the courage to continue. Tears became a rivulet. He began.

"My son Manuel, he was a good boy. He obeyed me and was good at school. But then one day I went to the garage and saw him sitting on a box. I saw what he had done. The needle and spoon were on the floor. His eyes were like he was drunk. I slapped him but he just fell down to the floor and didn't get up. I found out it was Romel that gave him *chiva* and showed him how to put it in his veins. A few months later the state police called me at work that they found my son in an *acequia*. Manuel had overdosed and died. After that everything changed. My wife got sick. She worried that Armando, my other son, would become a *tecato*. When I came home from work one day she was lying on the couch. I thought she was asleep. But she had died. They said it was a stroke or heart attack or something like that. But I know she died from worry."

Clofes took a few deep breaths before continuing.

"I had to throw Armando, my son, out of my house. He was stealing from my wallet...when I went to the post office for money orders to pay the bills it was almost all gone. I knew that Armando was on *chiva*, just like Manuel. I drove to the *tienda* to get groceries one afternoon and I saw Armando talking to Romel. I saw them shake hands like they do to exchange the *chiva*. Inside the *tienda* I was trembling because I was so mad. I saw Romel get in his car. I went to my truck and followed him."

Clofes continued. "Romel parked under a tree close to the church. I passed him, then turned around, turned off the headlights and parked. I got out and watched him. I saw Romel get out of the car. I stayed far behind when he walked into the Santo Niño parking lot. I stayed hidden behind some trees. Romel was sitting on the bumper of Theo's Jeep, and when Theo came out of the rectory, I saw them fighting. Theo knocked Romel down, and when he got up Romel tried to push Theo. But Theo punched him again and Romel fell hard on the pavement. Theo got into his Jeep and drove away. I looked down where I was standing and picked up the tree branch. Romel was getting up. He didn't see me until I got close to him. When he turned around, that's when I swung the branch at him as hard as I could. He fell down and I stayed hitting him. When he tried to speak, I smashed the branch down on his face."

David was at a loss for words. Clofes testimony was dramatic and unexpected. He could think of nothing more to ask the broken man sitting on the witness stand. David passed the witness.

Marcia stood up and approached Clofes. "Mr. Benavidez, what is your religion?"

"Catholic."

"Do you go to church."

"Yes."

"To confession?"

"Yes."

"Did you confess this sin to your priest?"

David sprang out of his seat. "Objection."

Before Judge Jellison could hear the basis or rule on the objection Clofes had answered the question.

"No."

"Mr. Benavidez," the judge shouted out. "You are not to respond to a question if there is a standing objection. Do you understand?"

"Yes."

"I'm striking the answer and sustaining the objection."

Marcia continued. "Mr. Benavidez, I heard your story. You have my sympathy on the loss of your family. But, how can this jury believe that you really murdered Romel. How do we know this isn't just a subterfuge; that you made all this up to clear Theo Jaquez of these charges?"

Clofes stared at her for a few seconds than slowly stood up. Reaching into his pocket, he drew out his hand and slapped down on the railing what he had retrieved.

"I took this from Romel. It was around his neck. It's a medal of a dragon from hell and reminds me where the *tecato* is now."

Instructing the bailiff to place Clofes Benavidez in custody, Judge Jellison called a recess and a meeting in his chamber with the two attorneys. When the parties returned to the courtroom and the judge reopened the trial, the assistant D.A. made a motion to dismiss the charges against Theo. Granting the motion, the judge thanked the jury and dismissed them. He then closed the hearing.

Theo turned around to Ilyas with tears in his eyes. He then turned to David and hugged him. "How did you know?"

"I didn't. I took a chance."

"I don't understand," Theo said.

"I remembered a story your foster mom told about how *tiendas* operate. This morning Father Bonafacio confirmed the Arbol Verde *tienda* lets some customers sign a receipt book for their groceries and pay later. Marty and Father Bonafacio drove to the Arbol Verde *tienda* with a copy of the letter and compared the handwriting to the receipt book signatures."

"Thank you, David. I don't know how I'll ever repay you for this."

"I think poached pears sound pretty good."

Eighty-one

DAVID OPENED THE freezer door in his apartment and saw the case containing his pistol. Most everything in the apartment was either in boxes or in storage. How to dispose of the 9 mm pistol kept plaguing his mind throughout the move. It seemed so long ago that he was sitting in front of the patio window on the verge of ending his life. He didn't want to think about that haunting night ever again.

The gun case in the freezer was frosted over and, wiping the ice crystals in the sink, David carried the case out the door as he closed it for the last time. He decided to swing by the police station and drop it off on his way to the airport.

His thoughts shifted to the remarkable gathering after Theo's trial.

ARRIVING BACK IN Albuquerque after the trial, David fell soundly to sleep. His slumber continued until late the following morning when the telephone awakened him. It was Theo with an invitation to a dinner celebration at The Seville that evening.

A few minutes late getting to The Seville, David was escorted by the maître'd down a hallway to a party room used for special occasions. From a distance he saw Marty, Father Bonafacio, Julian, Sonia, Patrick and Esteban gathered, with drinks in hand, exchanging conversation. Just before entering the room he noticed Theo's neighbor, Kevin, admiring Consuelo Soto's necklace. A stocky woman with handsome Native American features, Consuelo was dressed in a white blouse that accented the beautiful turquoise squash blossom around her neck and an array of silver and turquoise bracelets around the sleeves of her wrists. Kevin was dressed in a black T-shirt and torn Levi jeans and adorned with rings on his septum, lips and ears. Tonight Kevin's hair was spiked like the crown around the Statue of Liberty. The incongruity between Consuelo and Kevin would have made a priceless photo, David thought. Theo and Hans Schuldneckt appeared through a back entryway and joined Ilyas just as David walked into the room. Everyone turned to face David and began applauding his courtroom victory. Embarrassed by all the attention, David raised his hands chest high as if to end the clapping, smiled and shook his head as he surveyed the gathering, then walked over to hug Theo. A few minutes later his co-counsel at the trial, Stephanie Holloman and her husband arrived. Following close behind was Theo's landlady, Lucy Johnston.

While the appetizers of lobster pockets were delicious, the braised lamb and baby potatoes were unlike anything David had ever tasted. When Theo brought out the wine-poached pears, all were in awe as they savored the dessert. Sitting around the table talking and laughing and exchanging stories, everyone was in high spirits. It was already common knowledge from the newspaper account that Kerry Snyder had withdrawn his nomination for county commissioner. Rumors circulated that Snyder and his wife planned to leave Santa Fe.

It had been a perfect evening and David knew it would be a very long time before he would ever meet up with Theo and Ilyas again.

TURNING FIFTY-FIVE SEVERAL months after that gathering, David began having fleeting thoughts of leaving the partnership and embarking on something entirely new. Much like his marriage, practicing law was beginning to lose its luster. Secure that his investments and the proceeds from divesting his portion of the partnership were sufficient to provide a comfortable living, David occasionally pondered what novel endeavor he could pursue. During long workdays of particularly tedious lawyering tasks, the ephemeral daydreams began coming to him more and more frequently.

Then one day David received a phone call from Marty. The freelance journalist was finally retiring and embarking on a sailing adventure around the world. David recalled a time while sharing a bottle of scotch with Marty just before Theo's trial. The journalist, who was skilled at sailing, had revealed that dream. While David's water craft expertise amounted to a single lake sailing experience, after about a dozen elbow-bending exercises on Johnny Walker Black he was sold on the idea. But now the reality of Marty's phone invitation to join his year-long odyssey took a more sober assessment. Just as quickly as the invitation was extended, it was declined.

Afterward, the idea of going off on an extended ocean sailing journey to exotic countries began slowly ruminating in David's mind. Some days he vacillated about whether he should call Marty back and discuss the plan in more detail, while other days he was resolute in the decision that it was a foolish undertaking. When David arrived home after tiring workdays, the sailing idea began playing in his mind more often. Picking up the phone late one evening, David called his friend, Juliana Ochoa. David hadn't spoken to the psychologist in months, and after a brief exchange, invited her to lunch the following day.

Juliana had a knack for placing feelings in their proper perspective. When David told her of Marty's sailing invitation and how preposterous the idea was, she surprised him by taking an opposite view. Juliana said she knew David well enough to discern that his battle was over his desire for change pitted against the fear of leaving the law practice. She envisioned David standing on the airplane threshold, parachute ready and anxious to freefall. But experience had taught her never to push, she explained. He had to jump. As she tried to offer support, she became David's sounding board. By the time lunch was over, Juliana confessed that she was certain David was set to take the leap.

Returning to his office, David placed a call to Marty. "Hey, buddy, is your sailing invitation still good?" he asked.

"You bet."

"Then sign me up," David replied.

"No problem, I was waiting for you to change your mind. What took you so long?" Marty asked.

"I had to repair my compass."

Marty laughed.

David continued working for four months, ensuring his case files were smoothly transitioned to his successor. As his practice came to a close, David felt not one tinge of regret. He spoke with Marty weekly, formulating plans, charting routes, plotting ports of call, and discussing the hundreds of issues confronting their journey. He immersed himself in reading everything he could find on sailing, course plotting, mapping, and ocean navigation. He found more time to spend with his two daughters, sometimes having lunch or dinner together or taking in a movie. It took careful planning to meet since the oldest was married and both were wrapped up in their careers.

One day David decided to invite Rayèn to lunch and share the news. She was stunned and surprised by his decisions. "Are you going through a middle age crises?" she asked.

"Nope, just navigating the youth of my older years," he replied.

She didn't understand. But that didn't matter. In their short visit two things were crystal clear. The spark in their relationship had totally extinguished, and he could hardly contain the excitement of beginning the journey.

On his final day at the law office, David left early and, after completing a list of errands, drove to Santa Fe to join Patrick and Esteban for dinner at The Seville. Once seated and having ordered, they went over the plan agreed upon. David would leave his car at the airport parking lot for the two to retrieve over the weekend. For the next year they would have the use of the car. Handing over a large envelope, David detailed the contents; his will, life insurance papers, bank and investment information, itinerary with ports of call, and a myriad pieces of other information. As David recited instructions on bank deposits of divestment proceeds from the law firm, the waiter suddenly appeared.

"Mr. Lujan, the gentleman at the table to your left has asked to take care of your bill tonight."

As David glanced over, he recognized James Kilkenny seated with two others in business suits. Similar to when he met Kilkenny at Roosevelt Park in Albuquerque, the property developer was casually dressed in a polo shirt.

"I'll be right back," he said as he stood up and walked over to Kilkenny's table.

Seeing him approach, Kilkenny stood up and extended his hand.

After exchanging greetings and introducing his two guests, Kilkenny said, "Since I never took the opportunity to congratulate you on that infamous trial, I hope you'll let me pick up your bill tonight."

"That's kind of you," David replied.

"Indeed, that's the least I can do."

Kilkenny's eyes communicated much more than his words.

"I'm glad it all worked out," David said, as they shook hands again and he returned to Patrick and Esteban.

As the evening ended David hugged Esteban then his son. Of all his family David knew he would miss Patrick the most.

"You'll send us postcards from the places you visit, Dad?" Patrick asked.

"You know I will."

"I love you, Dad," Patrick uttered with a tear in his eye.

"I love you too, son."

Epilogue

THEO AND ILYAS entered the quaint restaurant in the Chueca district of Madrid. It was late in the evening. There was soft background music and only two other couples. Within the hour the restaurant would fill with customers. Theo insisted on ordering for both of them. It was unfortunate his partner didn't drink wine — what an enhancement wine brought to a good meal. He recalled how Jude enjoyed an occasional glass. His thoughts momentarily shifted to her gravesite visit they made just before leaving New Mexico. It was there that Ilyas invited Theo to move to Spain. It took little convincing and within two weeks all of Theo's worldly possessions, which included a small library of food history and cooking books, were carefully packed and shipped. After a tearful farewell and with a heavy heart, Theo left to join his lover and pursue his vocation.

Finishing their meal, they walked out of the restaurant and began the one mile trek to their apartment. Theo couldn't stop talking about culinary school and at every opportunity Ilyas interrupted with his incessant questions. After all it was the remainder of Jude's life insurance proceeds that was funding Theo's education.

"Have you given any thought to Severino and Elena's wedding cake?" Ilyas asked.

"Of course, and it will be special. But I want it to be a surprise to them."

Theo hardly noticed when Ilyas reached for his hand and enfolded it in his own as they continued down the street. Two young lovers holding hands walking down a busy street without the slightest mocking stare from anyone. Indeed, no one seemed to notice or care. To Ilyas the gesture was symbolic of the reverence he gave to their relationship. For a second Theo stopped talking and beamed a tender smile at Ilyas — a gesture intended to acknowledge his mutual affection. Ilyas's soul was filled with joy and peace and calm. It was *alcaracion,* Theo insisted. And together they were journeying the *Camino Sagrado.*

Dictionary of Words, Phrases and Terms

Acequia - Irrigation channel or ditch
Aclaracion - clarity
Aclaracion Completa - complete clarity
Amigo - friend
Asalaam Alaykum - May peace be upon you
Assalamu Alaikum Varhamatull - Peace and the mercy of God be upon you
Atole - drink made from blue corn flour
Cabron - (vulgar) you bastard
Camino Sagrado - blessed road
Chiva - heroin
Chotas - police
Creencia - a belief
Deveras ese - Is that so, man
Empanaditas - turnovers
Ese - hey man
Hermanito - little brother
Hoto - (slang) gay man, homosexual
Inshallah - God willing
Mi hijo - my son
No te preocupes. Todo va estar bien - Don't worry, everything's going to be all right.
Orale - come on
Pues que es la problema? - Well, what's the problem
Que estupido - That is stupid
Que no - Isn't that so
Que nos importa - What does it matter
Salaam - Peace
Shari'a - Religious law in Islam
shaz - queer
Tecato - heroin user
Tienda - shop, store
Tu hijo siempre era gay. - Your son was always gay
Vato - dude, guy, homeboy
Ven co migo, carbon...hijo de puta. - (vulgar) come with me, bastard...son-of-a-bitch.
Vergas - (vulgar) penis
Wa 'Alaykum Asalaam - And peace be upon you also
Zakat - charity

Other titles you might also enjoy:

Secrets in the Attic
by Damian Serbu

In *Secrets In the Attic*, Jaret Bachmann travels with his family to his beloved grandfather's funeral with a heavy heart and, more troubling, premonitions of something evil lurking at the Bachmann ancestral home. But no one believes that he sees ghosts, and no one else saw his grandfather's ghost warning him to stay home except his dog, Darth. Grappling with his sexuality, a ghost that wants him out of the way, and the loss of his grandfather, Jaret must protect his family and come to terms with powers hidden deep within himself.

ISBN 978-1-935053-33-0
Available in both print and eBook formats

Struck
by Keith Pyeatt

A POWER AWAKENS, A DESTINY BEGINS

When lightning strikes Barry Andrews as he hikes among petroglyphs in Albuquerque, it's more than an accident of nature. It's a calling. The surge of energy awakens abilities he's carried since birth. Earth's fate is now tied to Barry's, and Barry's destiny is linked to the past.

A thousand years ago, the ancestors of the Pueblo Indians built an advanced civilization in Chaco Canyon. Seeking to tame their harsh environment, they used the precise alignment of their pueblos to tap into powers they ultimately couldn't control, and their meddling almost ended life on Earth. The Anasazi abandoned Chaco Canyon to prevent future generations from repeating their mistake. But the pueblo ruins still hold power, and the desire to control it remains strong. One man, driven by greed, ignores Anasazi warnings and exploits the ancient secrets of Chaco. Now Barry must join forces with a Native American elder, accept his role as warrior, and save the earth.

ISBN 978-1-935053-17-0
Available in both print and eBook formats

OTHER QUEST PUBLICATIONS

About the Author

Born in New Mexico, Michael Chavez is a discerning adventurer, who resides high in the Sangre de Cristo Mountains where he crafts his work. He can be reached by email at Mikezev@aol.com.

VISIT US ONLINE AT
www.regalcrest.biz

At the Regal Crest Website You'll Find

- The latest news about forthcoming titles and new releases

- Our complete backlist of romance, mystery, thriller and adventure titles

- Information about your favorite authors

- Current bestsellers

- Media tearsheets to print and take with you when you shop

- Which books are also available as eBooks.

Regal Crest print titles are available from all progressive booksellers including numerous sources online. Our distributors are Bella Distribution and Ingram.

CPSIA information can be obtained at www.ICGtesting.com
Printed in the USA
LVOW061057161012

303021LV00001B/1/P